ELLENA'S SECRET

Ladies of Munro, Book 2

Elizabeth Donne

ARE YOU SIGNED UP FOR DRAGONBLADE'S BLOG?

You'll get the latest news and information on exclusive giveaways, exclusive excerpts, coming releases, sales, free books, cover reveals and more.

Check out our complete list of authors, too!

No spam, no junk. That's a promise!

Sign Up Here

www.dragonbladepublishing.com

Dearest Reader;

Thank you for your support of a small press. At Dragonblade Publishing, we strive to bring you the highest quality Historical Romance from some of the best authors in the business. Without your support, there is no 'us', so we sincerely hope you adore these stories and find some new favorite authors along the way.

Happy Reading!

CEO, Dragonblade Publishing

Additional Dragonblade books by Author Elizabeth Donne

Ladies of Munro Series
Sophia's Letter (Book 1)
Ellena's Secret (Book 2)
Verity's Choice (Book 3)

Dedicated to my mother,
who has shared in the entirety of my journey.

CHAPTER ONE

Tuesday, September 20th, 1814

"WHAT ON *EARTH* are you wearing?" Ellena's father demanded as she entered the room. "I thought I told you to get rid of your old wardrobe."

Ellena paused on her way to the breakfast table, her mood falling at once. *Oh, dear.* She had hoped their last meal together could be pleasant. Or at least civil.

"It's my walking dress," stated Ellena, her eyes focused on the steaming pot of tea that waited for her just a few steps away. "The rest of my gowns have been given to Miss Kinsey. You did give permission for her to have them."

Henry Trenton sniffed in disapproval, his thin lips pressed tightly together. "That attire is no longer suitable for you. That is why I let the groundskeeper's daughter have them. But you are about to become a viscountess. I would have thought you knew better." He prodded the air with the butter knife to punctuate his sentences. "You will go and change at once. How can you enter noble society in such drab garb? I will not have you shame me, Daughter. I have invested much in this match."

Ellena tightened her jaw. It was always a battle with her father. Everything she did mortified him. She felt, once again, the stifling sensation of his will exerted over hers. Her nails dug into her palms.

She hated the thought of her pending nuptials. Her father

would have understood if they weren't so very different. For him, it had been a resounding success, snagging the most powerful man in Munro as his son-in-law. But Ellena had not yet even laid eyes on her betrothed.

Her father had told her very little about him. Her inquiries had been largely dismissed. To Henry Trenton, the contract was signed, and no further details were at issue. She would meet her betrothed soon enough. And they would be married for better or worse. In her father's simplified universe, it mattered little whether the bride was pleased with the groom, as long as *he* was well pleased with *her*.

Ellena balked at her own powerlessness. Today, she might finally be free of her father's suffocating presence, but in just two weeks, it would be her husband who ruled her. She strained inwardly against the bit that seemed to be ever between her teeth.

"I wish to have one last walk," Ellena explained to her frowning father. She made an effort to keep her voice steady, though her hands had begun to sweat. "I think it good to stretch my legs awhile before being confined to the carriage for half the day." She did not mention Jillian. Her parents did not approve of her friendship with the groundskeeper's daughter.

Henry Trenton leaned forward in his chair. "This will not do, Ellena. There will be no time for such nonsense. Go and dress yourself properly."

Ellena's heart raced. She had had a lifetime of this. Nineteen years of being told how a lady should behave. *No climbing trees. Stay out of the sun to spare your skin. Delicately-stitched shoes are not for running.* The only reprieve from a life so strictly dictated was the time she had spent with Jillian Kinsey. She needed that last walk with her, to hear her sensible voice alternate with unrestrained laughter. If she was going to get through the next two weeks, she needed to draw strength from her dearest friend one last time.

She took a breath to steel herself.

"Father, the carriage will not be ready for at least an hour. It would be a small thing to manage a short walk. Especially if I do not waste time changing my attire after. This garment is far more comfortable to travel in. Besides, it will only be coated with dust with so many miles of road ahead. Why ruin an expensive dress? Cousin James and his dear Charlotte do not need to be impressed by me. Once I am with them at Thorn Bush Hall, I will have a servant draw me a bath, from which I may rise, reborn, like a phoenix."

She smiled a tiny smile at such an image, saw her father's face, and sobered quickly. Her attempt at persuasion had had no effect on him. She had not told him what he needed to hear. Now she lowered her eyes, her voice, too, dropping to quiet acquiescence. "Father, be assured, when I meet the viscount, I will be all I should be."

Before her father could respond, Ellena crossed the floor and collected a warm crumpet from the platter on the sideboard. Once seated, she poured a cup of tea and busied herself spreading butter and marmalade, avoiding her father's glare. Whatever he now said, he could not physically force her to comply. And any displeasure he expressed would be lost to history once she had departed his house.

But Mr. Trenton was silent. Her lack of obedience would be rather a shock to him. She had often annoyed him by resisting his orders, but in the end she had always relented to his ultimate authority over her. Despite the occasional spark of rebellion, she had never mutinied outright before. *Still*, Ellena thought with some satisfaction, *I have also never submitted utterly.*

"There you are!" Her mother's voice as she entered the breakfast room had an edge of exasperation to it. It often did. "Honestly, I spend half my days running after you, Ellena. Why are you not dressed?"

"I *am* dressed, Mother. I will change into the finer frock you chose for me once I am with James and Charlotte."

Mrs. Trenton cast a quick glance at her husband. His surly

silence spoke volumes. And yet Ellena was still in her walking dress. Her mother would hardly pursue an argument her husband had already lost.

"Henry, are you quite convinced I should not make the journey with our daughter? She has so little good sense. Heaven knows what she will get up to when I am not there to keep an eye on her."

Mr. Trenton tapped his forefinger on the tablecloth.

"We have spoken about this at length, Margaret. You know my mind is made up. It is but a half day's journey. She will not be staying at an inn and therefore needs no one to attend to her. Alfred is chaperone enough. James and Charlotte will take care of her in Munro."

Mrs. Trenton's shoulders slumped. "I was hoping to spend this next week or two with her. Help her settle into things a little. She won't even have her lady's maid. You've always made us share mine. The one Charlotte will temporarily provide will be a complete stranger to our daughter."

Ellena tried to ignore her mother's quiet pleading. It would be to no avail. Her father would not wish to be parted from his wife. She kept all the annoyances of daily life from him. And his needs were always paramount.

"Charlotte will do the job just as well," he said.

Mrs. Trenton flinched at these words. Ellena watched as the inevitable unfolded. Her mother splayed her fingers in frustration, then released control. Her face became flaccid, devoid of expression. She bowed her head and gave her staple reply. "Of course, you are right."

Ellena had seen it too many times. It was the fate she most dreaded for herself.

But here, in this awful moment, she could still claim the minutest of power.

Pushing back her chair, she rose and murmured, "Please excuse me; I will be taking that walk now."

Her father barely acknowledged her. If she was going to be

willful, she knew he would not show acceptance of it. Her mother was too numb to speak.

Ellena hurried down the corridor and slipped through a side door into the garden, following a path toward the cluster of workers' cottages at the edge of the grounds. A blonde girl of her own age sat on a low stone wall, watching three young boys at play. She looked up as Ellena approached and jumped from her perch with a liveliness that matched that of her brothers. She reached out her hands, grasping Ellena's with a sudden warmth. The boys danced gleefully about them, adding to the lightness of mood.

"Hey ho, hey ho, here's the new lady of Munro!" they sang with more enthusiasm than harmony.

"All right, you horrible little urchins." Jillian grinned. "You may each have a spoonful of sugar if you leave us be. You will have me all to yourselves soon enough."

This was a wonderful bribe, and the three boys disappeared into the cottage to claim their prize.

"Well!" Jillian stood back to have a good look at Ellena. "Not quite what I expected future nobility to look like, but I guess you'll do." Her eyes crinkled with mirth. "Actually, you look more like Nancy Fallon, that adventurous orphan from those books you used to read to me."

"Don't tease. You sound like Father," Ellena complained. "There is finery enough, but it is all packed with my trousseau. Though if Father had his way, I would be primped and preened in silk and jewels. Mother has been fussing all morning, making certain I am well prepared to play the role they have brokered for me. I believe Father is quite ready to push me into the carriage himself." She turned away, her face a frown. "I wish I were half as keen to be on my way."

Jillian put her arm around Ellena's shoulders. "I am sure all will be well," she said softly. "Your parents have some odd notions of happiness, but they would never choose someone who would make you miserable."

"He is horribly rich. They assume I will be happy."

"Well, as long as his riches are horrible, and not he!"

Ellena shrugged. "Mother says Lord Howell is highly respected by his servants—a far more meaningful accolade than the toadying approval of society at large. That is something, at least."

"True," agreed Jillian. "And he has met your father toe to toe in their negotiations. So, we know the great Henry Trenton does not frighten him."

"Ha, that shall be his greatest quality!" Ellena laughed wryly. "I have never known a man more feared in business than my father. There is nothing more important to him than to acquire money and not be parted from it. To that end, he will do whatever it takes. The bespoke furniture he sells is pure artistry, but that alone has not been the reason he has built such wealth. There are other merchants who offer similar stock. Father, however, never backs down when brokering a deal. Even the representative of the prince regent was unable to match Father's wits."

"When do you finally meet the mysterious Lord George Howell?" questioned Jilly, who had never had much patience with such dull topics as finance.

"I shall be deposited at my cousin James's house in Munro this afternoon. I am sure a meeting will be arranged with his lordship for tomorrow. Since my parents will be coming up for the wedding, Father wants it all to be over within a fortnight. He is expecting a new shipment then and cannot be occupied with *frivolities*."

Ellena rolled her eyes and her friend giggled. It was such a relief to speak freely and share her feelings openly. In Ellena's small, confined world, Jillian helped her breathe.

She liked to think that they needed each other equally—she, because she had no siblings with whom to bond, and Jillian because she wanted sanctuary from too many. The Kinsey boys were not rude or wild, but even the mildest of boys would tease their sister good-naturedly. Having bantered until her endurance was too sorely tested, Jillian would slip along the path to the great house and retrieve her friend from the tiresome rigors of being always a lady. They would walk solemnly while in sight of Mrs. Trenton's window, then skip away to the meadow to plait flowers in their hair and pretend at being nymphs, bound only to the grass and hills and not the whims of men.

How much of the joy that Jilly had always brought her would fade when she entered the viscount's household? Even the wedding promised little to look forward to. The absence of Jilly at what should be a celebratory occasion was hard to bear.

"I wish you could come," Ellena told her friend, "but Father will never allow it. I don't see why it should matter that you are the groundskeeper's daughter. You are my dearest friend! I can't bear the thought of such a lavish, public wedding where I don't know a soul except my parents and my cousin. If Father weren't so stingy, I would at least have a lady's maid of my own to support me. Instead, it is James who will share in my brief courtship and special ceremony. It should be you! After all, he and I have never really been close." She shivered a little. "There is something of Father in him. And the things he says..." Ellena scowled. "He can be such a dolt sometimes!"

"At least you will have Charlotte. I seem to remember she has a sweeter nature."

"That is a blessing, yes, but I would far rather it be you."

"Now, now," Jillian soothed, "I still believe you will be happy. Come, let us laugh a little before we are parted."

Ellena smiled weakly. "I shall endeavor to be brave, but I confess I am filled with apprehension. Mother would be surprised at my faltering after all the years spent preparing me for this very outcome. But with you, I know I can be honest. I am, in fact, far from ready to enter into marriage with a perfect stranger. How can I ever be ready for such a task?"

It was a question for which Jillian could have no answer. They were spared an awkward silence by the approach of Ellena's mother.

"Your father is waiting at the coach," announced Mrs. Trenton, ignoring Jillian. "Your trousseau chest has been strapped onto the back and your cloak is on the seat. I do not believe there is anything else."

So efficient, her mother. Ellena thought to declare that she might like her mother's arms wrapped tightly around her, or even to see a tear in her eye. Instead, she bit her lip and squeezed Jillian's hand. It was time to go, and she would have to revert to her training for a gentleman's wife to see her through. She gave Jilly a quick embrace. "I shall write to you every day, without fail," she whispered. Turning from her friend, she dipped her head and bobbed a curtsey to her mother.

Mrs. Trenton said nothing. Her face was drawn and sad. Her mouth was a thinly pressed line, holding back against the escape of her unspoken thoughts.

On an impulse she would normally have resisted, Ellena stepped forward and put her arms cautiously around her mother. There was an initial stiffening, and then a sort of collapsing inward, as if a barrier within her mother had dissolved. Mrs. Trenton's arms crept gingerly about her daughter's shoulders and her cheek rested against Ellena's hair. She breathed in sharply, but the release had a wobble to it.

Then, as though recalling some briefly forgotten rule, Mrs. Trenton straightened up and pulled away, holding Ellena by the shoulders at arm's length. Her eyes were strained with unshed tears and she patted Ellena's shoulder in the absence of words. She turned suddenly and headed toward the coach, where Mr. Trenton stood waiting.

Ellena was compelled to follow. When she reached the carriage, she nodded to her father, who offered his hand for her to step up. She entered the shadows of the coach compartment and settled into the deep, leather-cushioned seat.

Mr. Trenton did not linger. His purpose here was done. Ellena was on her way, and he had business to attend to. Her mother would, as always, follow in his wake.

Ellena watched through the window as her mother hesitated, looking a little lost. Her husband called to her, but she did not respond at once. Instead, her eyes locked with Ellena's. Her hand came to her lips, and the tips of her fingers pressed against them as she swallowed hard. She blinked, a tear escaping her efforts at restraint. She wiped it away roughly. Henry Trenton called again, and this time, she turned and followed him obediently into the house.

Ellena heard the clicking sound of the coachman's tongue, and the wheels jolted forward down the drive. There was no point in waving. She was quite alone.

Though it would have been encouraging to have her parents stay and watch over her departure, she did not dwell on their absence. What would be the point? She had learned that no expectations meant no regrets.

She did wonder, though, at her mother's sudden show of sentiment. Ellena remembered, albeit very distantly, a time when she had been little and cuddled and adored. But always the long shadow of her father had fallen over the scene. *"Do not spoil the child so, Margaret,"* had been his constant refrain. And Mrs. Trenton, ever dutiful, had complied.

More and more, little Ellena had been left with her nurse. And Mrs. Trenton had become, like her husband, detached and cool. Only—it occurred to Ellena now with some distress—this had perhaps been an act of self-preservation and not the absence of affection.

Would this be her fate also? Would Lord Howell expect her to be always echoing his choices, never following her own instincts? The thought of losing herself in this way made her shudder.

As the coach climbed the little hill behind the house, a sudden movement caught Ellena's attention. She peeked through the space between the dark velvet curtains and saw Jillian waving furiously. She was out of breath from racing up the slope to keep up with the horses and must have been worried that Ellena would not see her, for she broke into a brilliant smile when her friend's face appeared within the window.

Ellena waved back with enthusiasm. Dear Jilly! Bless her! They continued waving and calling out good wishes until the coach rounded a corner and Jillian disappeared from sight. Ellena threw herself back into her seat as she was jostled by the coach's lumbering motion. Her last view of her home had been as a backdrop capturing the moment of Jillian's energetic farewell. It was an image she clung to as the carriage drew her closer to her destiny.

LORD HOWELL KICKED off his wet boots with vigor. He sank into the chair, groaning with satisfaction as he allowed the tension of the day to sink into the upholstery. His damp, stockinged feet steamed in front of the fire.

The morning had been difficult. But the lion's share of his unease stemmed from the pending meeting with his betrothed. What had he been thinking! He had been too hasty. He should at least have met the girl once, confirmed that she was everything he expected.

But someone else would have snapped her up. She was beautiful, unworldly, and trained to know the role expected of her. At least, that was the talk. And if women knew one thing, it was how to ferret out information about each other. The fact that the ladies of the *ton* felt threatened by her—when she was but a merchant's daughter in a country town—told him that she must be made of superior stuff.

And how the women had talked! Even though Miss Trenton had never visited Munro herself, the parlors and ballrooms had been abuzz with news of her. All it would have taken was for someone's distant aunt to have met her, quite coincidentally, while convalescing in the quiet, little district. Or a gentleman may have been fortunate enough to be introduced to her at a local soiree, and wrote to his sister of this remarkable gem hidden in the countryside. One letter—that was all that was needed. Then the flurry of scribbling would have begun. And the chatter. Oh, that infernal chatter!

If he did not carry the responsibility of providing an heir for his title and estate, he would far rather have remained a bachelor. The women in his acquaintance did not inspire him. And he was certain they felt the same about him. Yet they would flutter their eyelashes and tilt their fans and preen for his attention, all the while summing him up and finding him lacking. He knew the look.

The heat of the fire and the irritation of his thoughts made his coat an uncomfortable and unnecessary burden. He stood briefly to ease it off. A crinkling sound made him pause. Ah, the letter. His valet had handed it to him this morning, but he had been in a hurry and shoved it into his pocket. He groaned at the thought of its contents. He didn't have time for Vivienne and her nonsense.

He pulled the offending article from his coat and sat down again with a resigned thump. Best to get it over and done with. He tore open the seal and unfolded the page to discover her small, scrawling script.

Dear Brother,

The earl and I have received notice of your pending nuptials. Should I thank you for the invitation? Truly, it is a most questionable affair. Who is Miss Ellena Trenton that she should inherit our mother's title? From what I understand, her father's money is earned through trade. Really, it is bad enough that you engage in similar demeaning practices. But I had hoped your chosen bride would elevate your choices and remove such a blight from our family's reputation.

Lord Howell closed his eyes and rubbed the furrows that he knew were forming on his forehead. Vivienne hadn't changed at all. If anything, her new position as wife to the Earl of Chesterley only gave her permission to behave more intolerably. For who could stand up to her and her special brand of meanness? He had invited her to the wedding as a formality. It was expected. But he would just as soon have invited his kitchen staff. They were good, honest folk, and he could respect them.

He forced his attention back to the letter. But it was just more of the same. *Blah blah…he was a failure…blah blah blah…*

At least he would receive no such correspondence from Georgina, the elder of his two sisters. Their mother would never allow it. Ever since she had made her home with Georgina, communication from that quarter had grown more civilized. Besides, Vivienne had always been the real instigator.

His mother's letter had already arrived a few days prior. It contained the usual reserved tones, but she was happy he had made a decision at last. She was satisfied that the girl's reputation—and that of her family—was sound. If his bride behaved herself, brought a handsome dowry, and bore him a son, there was nothing further to concern her.

Lord Howell picked at a speck of mud on his trousers. Nothing in life was perfect. He had chosen as best he could. There was no point in hoping for more. Love? He had not been taught he deserved it. But if Miss Trenton was uncomplicated, and a little kind, he believed he could be content.

CHAPTER TWO

THE JOURNEY BY coach was a tad disorienting. Ellena had a very vague sense of where she was, having never been farther from Trenton Grange than to visit their nearest neighbors or, on occasion, stop by the village center.

After two hours, they had changed horses and she had taken the opportunity to stretch her legs a little. As per her father's instructions, Alfred the coachman stayed close to his mistress. Mr. Trenton did not want her to attract any unsavory attention.

Now they were on the second half of their long trek, and Ellena's body rebelled. Her back ached and her legs were irritable with sitting. But there would be no reprieve until they reached the great northern city of Munro. The only amusement was to watch the route unfold through the window.

The landscape had shifted from gentle undulating hills—mostly under cultivation—to fields littered with scrubby bush and rocks until they, in turn, had given way to sparse woodland. Even now, her environment was changing again. The shadows thickened in the deeper forest, which crowded around the path cut over time by myriad hooves and wheels.

She could see a river running alongside the road but could not discern the sound of its waters, as the weather had changed too, and rain was pelting down on the roof of the carriage. Poor Alfred sat huddled atop the driver's seat in his thick cloak and broad-rim hat. At least here the trees protected them from the worst of the deluge.

The absence of the sun further hampered her efforts at guessing the lateness of the hour and added to the dreariness of the passing time. Her lack of companion did not help matters.

Despite her father's desire to acquire wealth and status, he remained frugal. Or perhaps he believed that money saved was money earned. Be that as it may, it had meant that Ellena and her mother had shared a lady's maid. And she had remained with her mistress when Ellena had left. Her cousin and his wife would serve as chaperones in Munro. But this journey between residences she would suffer alone.

She had eaten the biscuits and sandwiches Cook had packed for her, though these had done little to ease her appetite. The only consolation was knowing she would reach Thorn Bush Hall in time for tea.

The hunger pangs became intermingled with nervous apprehension at the thought of finally meeting her betrothed. There was little to distract her, as the rain obscured much of her view, and her wandering thoughts were mostly treacherous.

What sort of man secured his betrothal to a stranger? *She* had little choice, but Lord George Howell was at the center of Munro's cosmopolitan society and surely interacted with a multitude of worthy young ladies suitable for marriage. Having both money and position, the viscount could afford to choose any bride who suited his taste. Why, then, would he select a woman upon whom he had never cast eyes?

Perhaps it was his pride—knowing he could have any woman—that had led him to pick a choice fruit. After all, hadn't her mother gone to great lengths to ensure she was unblemished in both beauty and reputation?

It had seemed an impossible task at first. Ellena's brown tresses contained a distressing hint of red, and the gaze of her hazelnut eyes was too bold—at least, those were her mother's words.

What if Lord Howell merely wanted a bride he could show

off? The thought made her stomach churn. She had had enough of that. When she had been younger, her father had sometimes allowed her to be present when they'd had company. But it had only been as a symbol of his wealth—a pretty doll wrapped in garments of imported cloth. How she wished she could have been more daughter than commodity!

Maybe Lord Howell sought her for her solitary, restricted upbringing—a wife unused to the corruption of society. Did he want to mold her according to his own designs?

Or could there be some murky secret that sullied the Howell reputation and kept the Munro families from allowing their daughters to be considered by him? Her father would be horrified if this should be the case. The triumph of winning the interest of Lord Howell would quickly turn to sour defeat and embarrassment. Her father did not like to lose. Having a viscountess for a daughter, only to be sullied by his association with her new name, would be a shame he would not bear well.

A sudden, sharp crack, like lightning, jerked her free of all thought. Ellena's heart clenched and her eyes flew skyward. Were they in danger of being struck?

The horses, startled by the loud clap, reared in unison. Alfred cried out as their hooves crashed down on the muddy path. The carriage lurched, fear driving the animals forward at an increasingly alarming rate. Alfred grunted as he fought for control, but it made no difference. The scenery flashed past at great speed with Ellena clutching at the sides of the coach. She stared as a figure on horseback, his pistol aloft and ready to fire again, tore past her window. A black cloth across his mouth and nose disguised his features. Ellena felt the blood drain from her face.

Highwaymen!

Paralyzed with shock, Ellena had no means of escape and could merely retreat into the corner of the carriage as it was hauled along by the terrified horses. They rounded a bend with the full impetus of their momentum. The entire coach jolted as it bounced hard over an unseen obstacle, its heavy structure creaking ominously as it slowly careened and toppled, its side slamming down against the mud and leaves that matted the forest floor. Ellena was thrown against the door frame, the impact sending a sharp spear of pain through her shoulder. The wooden compartment shuddered as it dragged along the ground, the harness straps snapping under the strain. Without the wild energy of the horses, now separated from its weight, the carriage finally became anchored in the vegetation at the river's edge.

Jagged stems of shrubbery stabbed at Ellena through the shattered window. Her dress was torn. Her hip was bruised as she had fallen, but she could still move. Nothing was broken. Rain infiltrated the cabin through the opposite window, now facing heavenward. She pulled her cloak tightly around her, then cautiously put out her hand to raise herself onto her knees.

She fell back in alarm. Her hand had gone right through the space of the window beneath her! Where she had expected the touch of soggy earth, she had found a rush of air! The roof of the carriage hung precariously over the river's edge.

Above the boiling current and the rain rose the noise of several men shouting. It would be mere moments before the bandits came for the trunks strapped onto the back and discovered her, alone. She had no guarantee that they would merely strip her of her possessions and nothing else.

Where was Alfred? Was he wounded? She gulped. *Dead?* Surely, he had not deserted her! Then again, what could one man do when outnumbered? No, he could not help her. And she could do nothing for him without risking her own life.

She dared not hesitate.

Ripping the soggy velvet curtaining from the window frame, she wrapped her hand as best she could and hastily pulled the remaining shards of glass from their housing.

The sounds of voices drew nearer. Ellena panicked and fairly threw herself out of the confines of the wreckage, her bodice scraping against the splintered wood of the window as she fell.

Her bruised body hit the churning surface of the river and

was pulled into its seething mass. Terror rose in her throat, and the cold made her gasp. Her limbs flailed. Her sturdy walking shoes filled with water, dragging her down. Ellena's feet kicked at the rocky bed, forcing her head above the frothing waters as they carried her downstream at great speed.

Her cloak wrapped about her, its sodden weight threatening to submerge her. Ellena struggled to untie the neck ribbon. She fought against its stranglehold with numb fingers. The heavy cloak floated free, to be snagged at once by the shrubs at the river's edge. Just in time, Ellena twisted away from a boulder in her path.

The cold began to gnaw at her very bones. She had to put as great a distance as possible between herself and her would-be attackers, but the freezing waters drained her energy. Soon she would be too weak to pull herself up the slippery mud of the riverbank.

She pushed on, her stamina waning until, at last, the river slowed. The embankment eased its gradient, softening with lush vegetation. Ellena reached for the side and hauled herself onto the cushioned, grassy slope.

She fought to catch her breath. It came in gulps. Shivering uncontrollably, she rubbed her arms, but her frozen fingers made little difference to them. Ellena looked around in desperation, with no real hope of finding a dry place to rest. She was too terrified to venture any distance, not knowing which direction the attackers may have taken.

She could barely see through the unrelenting curtain of rain. Ahead of her, running parallel to the water's course, she could make out the route along which they had traveled earlier. It followed the river faithfully, with a backdrop of thick forest. She turned away. It was best to steer clear of the road for now.

On the other side of the river was dense shrubbery that stretched away beyond the water to blend with the forest. Perhaps it could offer some sort of barrier from the rain. It would at least prevent her from being sighted from the road. But it meant crossing to the opposite bank.

Ellena shuddered at the thought of re-entering the icy water. Mustering up the necessary willpower, she rose to her knees. On the edge of her hearing came the sound of drumming hoof beats. It came from the direction of the abandoned carriage and far more likely belonged to the mount of a bandit than a rescuer.

She hurled herself onto the ground, her nose making her uncomfortably aware of the soggy, rotten vegetation beneath her. The approaching sound thundered loudly above the drone of the rain. The rhythmic beat suggested only one horse. It passed without stopping or slowing, giving Ellena the courage to risk an upward glance. The horse was riderless, and one of their own.

She had to fight the urge to follow it. Surely, it would make its way back home? It may even settle after a few miles. She could find it and…

No, it was too risky. The men who had attacked the carriage might very well have the same thoughts and follow the animal's trail to re-capture it as part of their prize. The sooner she was out of sight, the better.

She turned back to the river with renewed determination. Gingerly, she lowered herself into its freezing waters. The riverbed was smooth and silty here, creating a calmer current through which she could push herself with minimal difficulty.

But the slope on the opposite side was steeper and scoured from rock. She searched its surface for a grip. Her hands grabbed and slipped repeatedly. Fatigue ate away at her strength. Ellena felt the renewed edge of panic and took a deep, calming breath. She scouted the length of the bank, left and right.

Twenty yards farther downstream, a tree bent low over the water's edge. Ellena let the pull of the water carry her until she could reach the overhanging boughs. She grabbed a sturdy branch with both hands, braced her feet against the stony sides of the watercourse, and heaved. Her fingers ached with cold, her wet gloves doing nothing to stave off the painful sensation. Ellena strained with exhaustion against the weight of her soaked dress.

Gritting her teeth, she swung her hips to the side, landing abruptly on the hard ground. She sat for a full minute, recovering herself, until her shaking limbs drove her into action once again. Without much hope, she looked about for the promise of shelter.

The rain and late-afternoon gloom—in addition to the mottled forest shadows—made it hard to discern much. The dimmed sun seemed to glimmer in the dampness of the distant thicket. For a moment, Ellena thought her eyes were deceiving her. *Could it be?* Yes, it was…a light!

She took a few wobbly steps forward, hardly daring to breathe. Not thirty yards away was the ivy-clad structure of a small stone dwelling, complete with a cozy fire glowing inside. She recognized its humble form as the typical cottage of a woodsman or trapper. Whoever they might be, they were home.

Ellena hesitated. Who currently sat by the cottage's warm hearth? Desperate men, or an honest laborer? Perhaps he might even have a wife and children. She needed to be sure. She crept up to the window and knelt beneath it. Then she slowly raised her head until she was at eye level to the ledge.

The inside of the small building consisted of one large room. The furniture was sparse, and there was no touch of a woman's presence. A single bed, a small table, and two unexpectedly comfortable-looking chairs were the only furnishings. There was no stove or basin, as if the structure served only as a shelter and not a residence. Of course, for Ellena's purposes, that would do well enough.

The lure of the fire mesmerized her—until it dawned on her that there was no one seated by it. For an awful moment, Ellena thought she had been spotted and imagined herself being stalked in the failing light. Just as she was slowly turning to survey the edges of the clearing, she noticed movement from within the building. The front door had opened, and a single figure entered the dwelling from the rain.

He was a tall man, his shoulders broad. And—Ellena realized with a flush of embarrassment—he was dressed only in his boots, linen breeches, and shirtsleeves. He walked straight to the fire and warmed himself in front of it. The cold gnawed at Ellena through her dripping dress. Her skin was numb and her joints stiff. In the end, it was not so much a decision as an impulse for survival that jerked her up to her feet and prodded her around the corner to the front door.

A horse was tethered under the overlapping branches of a cluster of low trees. There was no cart for wood or furs. And the horse was a fine steed, well-bred and groomed. So much for her theory of woodcutters and trappers. Whoever the stranger was, his employer had supplied him with an excellent mount.

Unless it had been stolen, of course.

Well, Ellena, you are lost, alone, and about to catch your death of cold. The evening is upon you and you are hungry. You are better off risking your life with one man and a warm fire than hiding in the damp forest from armed brigands.

She took stock of herself. It was not a pretty sight. Her auburn hair hung in straggling strands. Her dress was muddy and torn, the simple floral print unrecognizable under the smears of dirt. Thank heaven she had worn a simple garment, and not one of her best gowns. The stranger must not guess at her family's wealth. With any luck, she would enlist the man's help without giving him reason to consider her a possible pawn for barter. Ellena considered her options. She dared not pose as a servant girl. Her educated tones and unspoiled looks—even though currently rather unkempt—would give away her privileged upbringing. No, she needed an altogether different alias. And she knew, in a moment of clarity, exactly what it would be.

Having gathered her wits and ordered her thoughts, she took a steadying breath. And knocked at the door.

CHAPTER THREE

THERE WAS A pause. Footfalls approached. Another pause. Ellena waited. What on Earth kept the man? As he opened the door, she had her answer. He had stopped to put on his trousers—and cock his pistol, which was now aimed at her forehead.

Before she had time to fully register her fear, his expression had changed from distrust to disbelief, his hooded eyes widening, his mouth falling open slightly. He looked about. She was obviously alone. His horse grazed peacefully. There was clearly no imminent threat. He relaxed a little and lowered his weapon.

By now, Ellena was shivering violently and the man at last seemed to notice. Whatever else he was, he was not heartless. He promptly emptied the doorway of his frame and motioned her inside.

After the stranger replaced the pistol on the table, Ellena found her tongue.

"Th-Th-Thank you, sir," she stammered through chattering teeth. "F-F-Forgive my b-barging in upon you. I am afraid I am rather lost and c-catching my death of c-c-cold."

The man gestured her toward the fire. When at last he spoke, it was with eyes focused determinedly away from her—a young woman whose soaked clothing clung to the curves of her body.

"You can hang your wet things over a chair and wrap yourself in this." He presented her with a blanket. "Let me know when you are done." With that, he opened the door again and stepped outside.

As soon as the door closed behind him, Ellena stripped off her wet garments, including her drenched chemise. She quickly threw the thick, woolen blanket around her trembling frame. There was no choice but to push aside her prudish reflexes. She could not afford the luxury of modesty. Besides, this man, if not a gentleman by birth, was clearly one in manners. Nevertheless, when she opened the door for her host to re-enter, she clung tightly to the blanket, pulling fistfuls of its warm cloth close to her chest.

It was all quite an unnecessary precaution. The man, now rather wet himself from standing outside in the rain, motioned her again toward the fire and pulled up a chair for her to be seated. She ensconced herself in its plush upholstery, the heat from the fireplace massaging her aching limbs. Her companion remained standing awkwardly. Ellena felt ashamed that her garments were drying over the only other chair and that he must stand in his damp clothes because of her.

"Thank you again," she said earnestly. "I am afraid your kindness has rather inconvenienced you."

"It is nothing." He did not look at her, but rather stood to the side of the fire so as to dry himself without blocking her from its warmth. He seemed even more ill at ease than she was. Miraculously, she had stumbled upon a shy soul, surprised in his undergarments by a bedraggled maiden on his doorstep, a maiden who now sat—naked, but for a blanket—only a few feet from him. Ellena almost laughed out loud. To think but minutes ago, she had felt so frightened and lost.

A measure of courage returned to her in the presence of this tongue-tied benefactor. He must surely be expecting some sort of explanation for her arrival at his doorstep. Time to spin her tale. She began with the necessary introduction.

She introduced herself with a lie. "My name is Nancy Fallon." She doubted this gentleman would have ever heard the name.

The alias would have been known to Jillian, though. Sometimes they would pretend to be the character from the books Ellena had so often read to her friend. Then they were orphans gone adventuring, far out of sight from Ellena's watchful parents. Nancy Fallon was an easy enough name to remember and rather aptly suited to her situation.

"Dominic," he mumbled. Nothing else. No surname. No further detail. He seemed mesmerized by the floor. Ellena did not have the heart to inquire further, and he did not appear to notice his answer was incomplete. And so it remained. She would have to call him "Dominic," as if they were childhood friends—more than friends, even, for a lady to call a gentleman by his given name. Well, so be it. After all, had he not acted with a nobleness deserving of friendship?

"Dominic…" She tested the sound on her tongue. "I am most grateful to make your acquaintance."

She stuck out a hand from the depths of her blanket and offered it to him. Dominic stared at her naked arm. He swallowed hard and shook her ungloved hand gently, as if it were fragile. Then he quickly released it. His gaze lighted upon the table, which displayed not only his loaded pistol, but also his supper. His face lit up with relief.

"May I offer you something to eat?" He moved quickly toward the table as though her answer had already been given.

"If you can spare anything." She tried not to sound too eager. In truth, she was famished. She watched him cut a generous slice of bread, followed by cold meat and cheese. He brought it to her on a rough wooden plate, then resumed his position by the fire.

Ellena ate with as much decorum as her hunger could allow, then lowered the plate onto the floor. She leaned back in her chair. She was warm and dry, her hunger appeased, and her person apparently safe. Now she needed to enlist Dominic's help still further. It was time to put forth the rest of the lie.

"I suppose you are wondering how I came to be at your door in such strange circumstances," she began.

"Um…yes," he admitted, his gaze still hovering upon the space at his feet. "but I did not wish to broach the topic until you were comfortable."

"Thank you. I assure you your hospitality has been the finest I have ever encountered. I cannot imagine greater generosity possible, even from a nobleman."

Dominic looked curiously at her. Perhaps he thought she was mocking him. She quickly continued.

"Of course, I have never had the honor of meeting anyone of such fine society, as my father has provided a very sheltered life. In fact, it was in pursuit of his wishes that I was traveling by coach to Munro to take sacred vows. I understand some women find great peace in a life of seclusion." There. It was said. And it was near enough to the truth that she need not perjure herself. She did not know much about being a nun—she wasn't even Catholic—but she hoped she sounded convincing.

"You are joining the sisterhood?" His mouth fell open and he stared at her openly for the first time. Without his usual reserve, he asked, quite plainly, "*Why?*"

"I am merely doing what my father bids me."

"Is he a very religious man that he commits his daughter to a cloistered life?"

"Certainly, he has clear ideals for me. He does what he thinks is best."

"There is no sound match to be made instead?"

"My father has made up his mind."

"Would he not consider a position for you as companion or governess? Forgive me, but you sound like someone who has received at least some measure of education."

Ellena was happy for her new acquaintance to draw his own conclusions. She continued to lead him along a path that meandered increasingly from the truth. The less her story resembled the facts, the better her chances of remaining anonymous. If she was to fulfill the marriage contract with the prominent Lord Howell, then Ellena Trenton could never exist in this compromised situation.

"My parents insisted that I receive a proper education," she explained, happy to offer a kernel of truth. "They did not consider it a sacrifice."

Dominic nodded. "A noble attitude, to be sure. You are amply qualified to teach the girls at the convent, then." He said this more to himself, as if, at last, it all made sense.

"Yes, my life will be filled with blessings." Ellena tried to keep the hint of doubt from her voice. It was best not to dwell too long on her unknown future. "However," she continued, "my journey was not as fortunate. We were attacked by brigands. I fled but was separated from my few belongings and my chaperone."

"What?!" Dominic's eyebrows drew together in a frown. He balled a fist and pressed it to his lips. "I shall have to report this to the authorities. We have not had such an incident in years."

Suddenly, his head whipped up and he looked directly at her for the first time.

"Were you hurt?" he inquired, concern etched upon his face.

"Not by the armed men," Ellena assured him, "but in my encounter with the river, when I nearly drowned trying to escape. No lasting harm, though. Merely scrapes and bruises. Nothing more."

"That is a relief." His look and tone were so sincere, Ellena's cheeks grew warm. No man had ever gazed at her with such honest interest. It did not help her self-conscious state that the gentleman who gazed at her thus was undeniably handsome. Until now, she had been focused solely on her safety and finding a solution to reach Munro. But now Dominic's eyes drew her attention, their brown, gold-flecked irises pooled with worry beneath the dark tendril of his almost-black forelock. His jaw was strong, but not overbearing. And his shoulders... Well, solid muscle was all too visible through his white shirt, rendered rather transparent by the earlier rain. He seemed oblivious to both his own good looks and their effect on her. Instead, his features remained etched with concern, his broad forehead wrinkled, his full lips pouting until he spoke again.

"Nevertheless," he continued, "these criminals must be brought to justice. Our public roads should be a safe place for our citizens. I shall speak to the council about it post-haste."

He was quite animated in his declaration. The passion of his response surprised Ellena. It was in such sharp contrast with his earlier behavior. Public safety was clearly an issue of great importance to him, if his raised tones and intensity were any indication.

The random clues Ellena had been collecting now fell into place. Dominic's educated speech, his accountability to town council, and the use of such an oddly furnished abode—all pointed to his possible role as county sheriff. He might well need a small dwelling in which to overnight as he traveled the region for which he was responsible.

"Which town do you call home then?" Ellena pondered aloud.

"Munro," replied her host. "Odd coincidence, is it not? My hometown is soon to be yours also. Now that I think on it, I have passed the convent several times and thought it well-situated. I seem to remember the chapel is near the river. You may find it a pleasing environment for quiet study and contemplation."

Ellena screwed up her nose in distaste. She hoped the Howell Estate House would not be similarly located near rushing waters. "I do not believe I would welcome such proximity to a river after today's ordeal."

Dominic's face fell. "Forgive me. I had not meant to remind you of your harrowing experience."

"Oh, a river will not be a reminder only of ill," she assured him. "After all, it carried me safely to your kind protection, did it not?" She offered a smile to further convince him that his words had done no harm.

Dominic relaxed visibly. After a few moments, he cleared his throat.

"It occurs to me I may be of service to you, Miss…er…Fallon, was it?"

"Please, call me 'Nancy.' Since I am to call you by your given name, I shall not withhold the same privilege." She indicated the blanket that was all that stood between them in this isolated shelter. "Our circumstances are far from regular. Convention must necessarily be adjusted to accommodate the strangeness of our situation. Using our Christian names seems the least of our improprieties."

He stared at her blankly. Had he forgotten his incomplete introduction? Would he now insist on formalities? Ellena hoped not. It was a delicious little pleasure to speak so intimately with this sweet and handsome stranger.

"Miss Nancy, I…"

"No, no, not 'Miss Nancy'—just 'Nancy.' Goodness, you make me sound like an old schoolmistress!"

"Er… Nancy…"

"Yes?"

"It… Well, it occurs to me I may be useful in helping you reach your new home in Munro."

Don't panic, Ellena! He doesn't know where that home is!

"I would be much obliged," she replied with forced calm.

"It is actually most fortuitous that you should find me here this evening."

"I should say so indeed!"

"What I mean is, I was supposed to return to Munro this very afternoon, but the heavy rains compelled me to shelter in this rather spartan dwelling. If the morrow provides good weather, may I offer you a ride into town? I'm afraid we'll have to share my horse, but the city is little more than an hour from here."

"If you could take me as far as the convent gate, I would be most grateful," Ellena answered, relief flooding her veins.

Although Dominic's offer was exactly what she wanted to hear, Ellena's practical thoughts were momentarily dislodged by more corporeal ones. Dominic was a very *manly* man. It was impossible not to notice. She would be sharing a horse with someone who was thoroughly appealing, sitting a heartbeat away from his broad back and powerful shoulders, her eyes falling constantly upon his dark locks.

She drew a breath, a shiver of delight racing through her core. It would be fine indeed if Lord Howell were as gentle as Dominic. And perhaps, if his forelock curled in the same way…and if his mouth were as sensual…

Her thoughts pulled up short. She had never thought of a man in such terms before. But it was true: Dominic's face had character—a complicated blend of kindness, intelligence, and yes, sensuality.

Ellena coughed lightly and made an effort to stop staring. She did not want to add to his self-consciousness. Instead, she thanked him for his offer, relieved to have secured her passage to Munro.

"If my father were here," she told Dominic, "he would be grateful that so gallant a gentleman has taken pity on me." She knew it sounded girlish, but she meant every word of it. "I accept your offer without reservation."

"Good, then it is settled. I shall deliver you to the convent, where the nuns will take good care of you."

Ellena hoped that the nuns would, indeed, take pity on her. She would have to spin a convincing story to replace the truth of her adventures, but she had plenty of time to think it through. She trusted that they would at least allow her to send a message to her cousin. None of which Dominic needed to know.

"As for the loss of your belongings," he continued, "I imagine it will be of little consequence when you take a vow of poverty. At least you will be able to put this unhappy experience behind you."

Ellena was thinking that the experience had not been entirely an unhappy one. She allowed herself a moment's reverie and completely missed what Dominic said next. He looked at her expectantly, and she jolted from her thoughts with an apology.

"I'm sorry—I think I misheard you."

Dominic blushed a deep crimson. "I was merely suggesting

we turn in for the night." His eyes flicked nervously from her to the narrow bed and back.

Ellena blanched. What was he thinking?

As if sensing her doubts, Dominic hastily explained. "If the arrangement pleases you, may I offer you the simple cot? I shall seat myself before the fire with my back to you. It is the best modesty I can offer in this confined space."

Ellena exhaled her fears. She had doubted his intentions, but he remained honorable. In fact, he was willing to sacrifice his own comfort for her, a stranger. She was about to protest that she would manage quite well in the chair and need not rob him of his own bed. But he misread her concerned expression and added, "Of course, there is the question of sleeping attire." His earlier awkwardness returned. "I, um, could offer you my clean shirt. I always carry one in my saddlebag in case my business obliges me to overnight somewhere. The garment would be quite…roomy and cover you sufficiently to avoid any…er…indiscretion."

Dominic was in a near-sweat with the effort of navigating the delicate topic. He retrieved a handkerchief from his trouser pocket and dabbed his brow.

Ellena had no easy rejoinder. She had felt cocooned in the large blanket. The idea of sleeping in a flimsy nightshirt in the same room as this man—any man—was troubling. At least the item of clothing was laundered and not taken off his back. *That would be an intimacy far greater than the use of his given name.* She struggled to harmonize her strict upbringing with the necessity of this situation. Within two weeks—she reminded herself—she would be sharing a bed with her husband. She would need to discard all naïve notions and be a wife by day *and* night. But Dominic was not that man. To lie in his shirt, in his bed—and him only a few feet away…

"All right," she whispered.

They repeated their original procedure. Dominic waited outside. At least the rain had now stopped and the trees dripped only sporadically. Ellena pulled the crisp, starched shirt over her head, drawing its generous length down to her knees. She signaled with a knock at the door, then threw herself onto the bed and pulled the covers up to her chin. When Dominic returned, his eyes were focused on the fire. He took over her seat and blanket. As he pulled the folds over his shoulders, Ellena saw him dip his head towards the covering, his nose briefly resting against the material that still carried the smell of her body.

"Goodnight, Dominic," Ellena called from the bed with a small voice.

"Goodnight...Nancy," came the quiet reply. Then all she heard was the crackling of the fire.

Ellena peeped from her covers to see the muscular form of Dominic wedged into the chair. She was convinced that he could never rest properly while seated upright thus, and she berated herself that he should suffer for her sake. However, not many minutes later, a peaceful snoring confirmed that he was, in fact, quite comfortable.

Ellena lay awake for some time, partly because she had not fully made peace with wearing Dominic's shirt. It lay upon her skin like the hand of a stranger, though she tried to push such images from her mind. The honest truth was—the matter of the shirt excluded—Ellena felt more at home with this sweet man than she had ever done at Trenton Grange—barring, of course, the times spent with Jillian.

But she had a deeper secret to confess: she was jealous of Nancy Fallon, of her freedom from duty, of her friendship with Dominic. Tomorrow, she had to reclaim her identity as Ellena Trenton. Yet despite all the promised privilege of a life as Viscountess Howell, she would give it all up for another day as Nancy.

Chapter Four

ELLENA AWOKE BEFORE the morning sun could seep through the woodland canopy. The fire had gone out and the air had the characteristic edge of an after-rain chill. She crept out of bed, collected her dress and shift, and pulled them over her head before Dominic stirred. She wished she could thank her host by offering him a good breakfast. Under the circumstances, the best she could do was prepare a plate from the remains of dinner. She put it to one side, ready to serve, then set about making herself a little more presentable.

With her fingers, she tried as best she could to comb the tangles from her hair, which had lost most of its curl. She rolled and re-pinned it at the back in an attempt at a little dignity. Her dress was still quite filthy and torn in several places. She wished she had a needle and thread to repair the worst of it.

She was bewailing the absence of her sewing basket when a sound from the chair alerted her that Dominic was awake. He stretched and yawned, then took stock of his surroundings. For a moment, he froze, staring at the blanket, then the fire that had long since turned to ash. All at once, he whipped around, his body relaxing once his eyes had fallen upon his guest.

Ellena stood up to greet him. "Good morning," she said, as she moved toward the table to collect his breakfast. "Won't you keep your seat? It is my turn to serve you. I hope your rest was not too much compromised in that chair."

"I slept well enough," he murmured in answer.

Dominic accepted her breakfast offering with muttered thanks, but he did not yet eat. Instead, Ellena felt his eyes upon her as she returned to the table and cut a slice of bread for herself. The nape of her neck grew warm under his scrutiny. As she brought her plate to the empty chair, Dominic hastily returned his attention to his own meal.

Ellena nibbled a little at her food, but she was anxious to be on her way. By now, her cousin would have sent news to her father, alerting him that she had not arrived as expected the previous evening. They would be looking for her in due course and must not find her in this predicament. If it were discovered that she had spent the night unchaperoned with a man, the shame would be unbearable, and her reputation would never recover.

Fortunately, her companion found no reason to delay their departure. They left the cabin as the sun's early rays were just pushing through the leaves. There was little preparation needed, other than fitting the saddle and repacking the saddlebags.

Once ready, Dominic lifted Ellena effortlessly onto the back of the horse, his warm hands circling her waist. She could feel his arms tense beneath her fingers as she leaned on him, his raw power contrasting with his mumbled apology at having to handle her so roughly. With his foot now in the stirrup, he brought his other leg up, then stopped. He could not swing up onto the animal's back without his foot striking Ellena. He dropped back down and looked around.

"I am afraid there is no easy way for me to mount up without risking unseating you," he said, scratching his head. Then his frown cleared. "The bridge is not far. I will walk beside you until we reach it. Then I can climb up on the railing and manage the maneuver more easily."

With that, he took the reins and began to walk along the narrow path that followed the river's course. Soon, they spied, across the water, the spot where the carriage had overturned.

There was no sign of horses or driver. Had Alfred escaped? Or had his body been carried away by the current?

As the awful idea gripped Ellena's heart, tightening it in a fist of fear, they turned to cross the river. A little way farther upstream was a small bridge. She had not spotted it the day before. It must have been at this point on their journey that they had been set upon by the bandits. Her escape had carried her downstream, away from the crossing.

Dominic drew his pistol and stepped forward cautiously to inspect the wreckage. The carriage had been ransacked. None of her belongings could be salvaged. Ellena could do nothing but resume her journey to Munro empty-handed. At least there was no sign of blood. Alfred might still be alive.

Dominic put his pistol in his saddlebag, led his mount to the side of the bridge, and drew the reins back over the animal's head. Tensing his shoulders, he pulled himself up onto the high, wooden railing. He spoke softly, and his horse nickered, standing strong and still. From his elevated position, Dominic leaned forward, placed one foot in the stirrup and shifted onto the seat, dragging his other leg over the saddle until it slung in the opposite stirrup.

As he coaxed his horse into a gentle walk, Ellena's side-saddle perch felt increasingly precarious. But what to hold on to? Or whom? She considered the man in front of her, whose proximity was both reassuring and disconcerting.

"Would it be an impertinence," she asked hesitantly, "if I were to steady myself upon your frame?"

"Oh." Dominic swallowed hard. "I believe, in this circum-stance, your safety is more important than the rules of propriety." He cleared his throat. "Please do as you feel necessary."

Ellena slipped her arm around Dominic's chest. In doing so, her torso leaned forward and pressed against his back. She felt him stiffen with apprehension and then breathe out an almost imperceptible sigh. Ellena allowed herself to ease her weight more fully forward, until she rested against Dominic, sensing the movement of the horse shifting into his hips. The tension between them vibrated almost tangibly, but neither she nor Dominic spoke of it, choosing instead to cast their thoughts elsewhere, until they had settled their bodies into the natural rhythm of the horse's gait.

As the minutes passed, Dominic continued to say not a word. Ellena assumed he was mentally preparing his report to the council, with suggestions on how to improve safety upon the roads. He seemed to take his responsibilities seriously, and she admired his commitment.

Of course, Ellena thought drily, her own father was also deeply committed to his work, but the effects were not as inspiring. Her betrothed, Lord Howell, was bound to share her father's views, being a man of business himself. *Really, it is like marrying Father.* The idea made her groan inwardly.

As if on cue, a welcome distraction appeared, ready to sweep her mind clear of its tortuous thoughts. The trees were thinning, and a burst of color greeted the two travelers as they emerged from the gloom of the forest. On either side of the road spread fields of late-summer wildflowers, pouring in waves over roots and stones, splashing up against the slope of the nearby ridge and frothing around the trunks of isolated trees. The scent from the profusion of gillyflowers was so sweet as to be quite heady. Ellena's mood was instantly improved and she spent the next several minutes in the happy contemplation of the countryside's abundance.

"Is it much farther?" ventured Ellena, wishing this journey did not have to end. The freedom from care, the brilliance of the sunny morning, and the warm expanse of Dominic's back upon her cheek, all worked together to capture a moment of perfection. She wanted to hold on to it forever.

"We should see Munro in the distance very soon now," he replied. "At the top of the next rise, we will find the city spread before us. Of course, we will not reach the city proper. The convent is situated at the edge as we enter. You will not be able to get a full sense of the grandness of the architecture, the parks and fountains, the excellent museums. But I imagine you will find joy enough in the well-tended gardens of the cloister."

Dominic appeared to have a great fondness for this corner of his shire. To her, Munro was new, even daunting, but to her companion, it clearly held cherished memories.

"Have you lived there long?" Ellena asked. "You seem to know it well."

"All my life. And yes, I know every corner of it. Partly because it is my duty, but mostly, because it has such personality, one wants to make its closer acquaintance."

"And do its citizens have such charming personalities also?"

"Yes and no. They really are no different to any other town or city. There is greed among the best of us and grace within the worst of us."

"That is nicely said," Ellena remarked.

As the surroundings became increasingly familiar to him, Dominic began to speak more easily, and the eloquence which had remained hitherto obscured came to the fore. Ellena was certain that he was a man of some consequence, for his turn of phrase was elegant and spoke of more than a rudimentary education. She wondered if it was likely he knew Lord Howell, perhaps had even met him in the exercise of his duties. It was tempting to inquire after Dominic's opinion of the viscount, but the specific mention of the Howell name would arouse suspicion. After all, why should she, a stranger to Munro, ask after its leading citizen? Instead, she approached the matter from an angle, in the hope that Dominic might reveal even the smallest of relevant details in his answer.

"Are the gentry very fine, then?" she asked. "My hometown can offer nothing grand or opulent to entice such visitors. I therefore know nothing of their nature or habits. And..." She suppressed the discomfort she felt at sustaining her lie. "Since my world will shrink even further at the convent, I expect I will learn even less about lords and ladies. What is your opinion of them?"

Dominic's answer was unflattering indeed.

"I do not think you miss much in having spent no time with that class of society. Snobbery is a common element among the very wealthy. They take their position a little too seriously, I think. After all, they are no better in character, only in status. Remove their expensive wardrobe and lavish homes, which they have only gained by birth or marriage, and one is often left with very little worth considering at all."

Ellena was in full agreement with his opinions. In recent months, she had had the unlucky privilege of being paraded amongst the "finest" of society—such as could be persuaded to venture to their quiet neighborhood—as part of her father's plans to marry her well. She had found these so-called elite to be mostly dull of wit and narrow in thinking, having needed to adjust neither dullness nor narrowness in the presence of those they deemed inferior. They were ruined by their self-importance, circling the same tired topics, slapping each other on the back in agreement, seldom developing such sophisticated skills as tact or grace. Ladies tittered and gossiped and flirted. And the men assumed themselves irresistible, oozing power, money, and a flawed attempt at charm.

There were the rare few who could carry a conversation past the superficialities into a realm of meaningful discussion. However, such intolerably serious behavior was soon dealt with by the hostess, who would draw the unfortunate subject of her disapproval into a hearty game of bridge. Ellena would then find herself joined by some gentleman whom she had, until then, managed to avoid. Needless to say, entering into society had left her with a deeper appreciation for the quiet life at Trenton Grange.

"...and so, you see, Nancy, I had not meant to imply our entire city was decadent."

Ellena realized guiltily that Dominic had been talking to himself.

"I have had the mixed fortune," he continued, "of seeing its best and its worst. And despite its shortcomings, I am still proud to lay claim to it as my home."

"I wish I could see it as you do," Ellena lamented. "I am afraid it does not promise as much for me."

There was a pause.

"Forgive the impertinence of my question," Dominic replied, "but are you not happy with your father's plans for your future? I only ask because you do not speak of it with any enthusiasm."

"I do not mind your frankness. And your observation is sound. I enter a life not of my choosing. But I am an obedient daughter. Besides, there are worse fates that may befall young ladies."

Dominic was quiet for a while. Then he asked, "Would your father not rather have you marry an honest man who expects but little dowry? Surely, he would not fear for your reputation if it were a sound match?"

Ellena did not know what to say. How was she to explain her father's thinking to a man like Dominic?

"Of course," Dominic added quickly, "if your father has made his decision, he will have had good reason, and you are right to obey. I did not mean to insinuate otherwise. I hope you will pardon my question. Please forget that I asked."

"There is no offense to pardon," Ellena assured him. "You spoke as someone who, no doubt, would consider such a match innocent enough. But there are men aplenty who view marriage as an arena of trade. If the transaction is not profitable, it does not take place."

Dominic was silent at these words. Then he said softly, "I am all too familiar with the system of which you speak. My marriage is also one resulting from such an arrangement. I admit it can be an uncomfortable affair. But it is often the best solution for those not easily blessed in love."

So! He was married. And it was not a love match. Ellena's heart went out to this man who had so much to offer as a husband yet seemed unconvinced of his own worth. She pictured him as a suitor among the ladies, desperately trying to merge with the background, faltering when he spoke, enduring the exchange of knowing looks behind extended fans. She wondered what his wife was like, and whether she had come to appreciate his qualities during the course of their time together.

Ellena hoped *her* betrothed would be as gentle and mild-mannered as Dominic. If only the viscount would talk to her as openly and listen to her with the same earnestness. How she wished she could at least pursue a friendship with dear, kind Dominic.

Certainly, he was not the most naturally charming of men, but it seemed to her a lesser fault than cruelty or infidelity, practices with which her husband-to-be might well be familiar. All she really knew of the viscount of Munro was that his wealth had bought him a young bride. Was that enough upon which to build a shared life? She shuddered as she imagined a relationship as cold and strained as that which her father offered his wife. Ellena knew that she, like her mother, would be thankful to be well cared for, protected by money and status. But what of the niceties between man and woman? Would she and Lord Howell speak to each other with ease? Or would she be more possession than partner? And if her husband did not show her a measure of tenderness, how would she bear his touch?

Ellena wished her mother had given her greater insight into marriage and men. Without it, her imagination tended to fill in the gaps with alternating bouts of excessive romantic drama and cold, unadulterated fear.

Truly, the thought of her betrothed made her quite anxious. She would have but a few days to get to know him before she would be forever wed to him. She was terrified of what he expected from her as a wife. She had heard of young girls whose dowries sold them as little more than slaves to old men. At least she knew there was not a significant difference in age with her betrothed. Her mother had assured her he was but a few years older than herself, well-educated, and an accomplished man of business, which, though a rarity among the titled class, had made his family hugely rich. Having trained Ellena from childhood to expect a marriage arrangement of more convenience to her father than herself, Mrs. Trenton had said little that might give Ellena hope to love this stranger. *"Pleasant enough, I suppose"* was hardly an encouraging vaguery.

Ellena emerged from her roaming thoughts and became aware once more of Dominic's close warmth. She imagined nestling her face into the folds of his coat, as if to hide from the fears of her unknown future in the friendly recesses of the finely tailored cloth.

A church spire was the first hint of Munro to present itself as they topped the rise. Its austere symbolism restored the burden of propriety to the two riders on their shared horse. Ellena straightened her back, pulling away from Dominic, holding on with just the flat of her hand. Dominic squared his shoulders.

The path descended slowly, winding toward its destination. They proceeded in silence. Ellena felt weighed down by thoughts of farewell, not only to Dominic, but to the ease of existence that had accompanied the time spent with him.

They approached Munro's walled abbey just as the bells rang out the hour. Its melodious chiming did little to lift Ellena from her cheerless thoughts. The horse continued forward. A soft breeze stirred the scent of musty autumn leaves. The final gong sounded, but time did not stop. The horse carried Ellena relentlessly forward.

As they passed under the arched entrance to the private drive, she closed her eyes and, after a deep breath, whispered goodbye to Nancy.

CHAPTER FIVE

ELLENA HAD TO do a fair degree of persuading for Dominic to leave her at the entrance to the drive. He wanted to escort her all the way into the convent building, as though some further misfortune might befall her on this last stretch of her journey.

"But, Dominic," she reasoned as they stood upon the graveled roadway, "just look at me." She indicated her torn and dirty dress. Dominic's eyes obeyed, lingering perhaps longer than Ellena felt necessary to establish her disheveled state. Her cheeks warmed, and her fingers crept to her neckline as if to shield it from his gaze.

"It is not appropriate," she added, and his eyes lowered at once to her feet, "for a young woman to be chaperoned by a stranger. Least of all a man."

He nodded. "Of course. You are right."

"You," she hastened to add, "have been the epitome of a gentleman in every sense. I could not have been in better hands. However, it is the look of it, you understand."

Dominic straightened his broad shoulders. "You need not explain further. I should not have pressed you on the matter. I wished merely to see you safe to the last. But you are wiser than I. I had, for the moment, forgotten our situation."

Ellena smiled. "It is thanks to your chivalry that we have experienced the minimum of awkwardness, despite the circumstances. For that, I can never thank you enough."

She looked at her hands, which fidgeted. "I..." Her hands held her attention. "I wish..." She pushed her palms to her sides and looked up into Dominic's face. "I wish we could be friends. But I believe it is best that our parting is final." Her heart pinched at the words.

Dominic drew a sharp breath and released it slowly. "Yes, I suppose that is for the best."

He looked past her, up the long drive. "You will be all right? I mean, here, with the sisters?"

Ellena did not want to end their time together with a lie. "Whatever happens," she said, "I will try to make the best of it."

"They are blessed to have you," came the soft reply. Then, quite abruptly, Dominic turned and mounted his horse. He touched his forelock—that wonderful, sensual curl—and maneuvered his steed past the gates.

Ellena watched him go. Her heart hitched when he looked back and waved. She returned the gesture and was rewarded with a rueful smile from the parting figure. Then she marched resolutely up the drive. She dared not give him any further thought, lest he anchor himself in her heart.

She managed to find the Mother Superior by enlisting the help of a young student rushing along the outer corridor. Soon, Ellena was standing in the neat, formal study of the woman she had been seeking. The senior nun, like her study, was neat to perfection, but her eyes were kind and her manner patient. Ellena kept her story short to avoid too many questions. She left out all names except her own, relaying the true facts up to the point where she'd been carried off by the river. Here she felt compelled to tell a blatant lie and hoped that her true innocence in the events would balance the dishonesty that was now necessary.

"I waited until I was certain the bandits would have left," she explained. "Then I made my way back to the deserted carriage and sheltered inside for the night. In the morning, I followed the road onward to Munro. I was very fortunate, indeed, for, along the way, I met a farmer and his wife who were taking their cartload of produce to the midweek market at Munro. They kindly brought me here."

Her lie complete, Ellena was one again able to look the abbess in the eye. However, her posture remained humble, as she was about to throw herself upon the woman's mercy.

"Is it possible for me to remain here tonight?" she wanted to know. "I have a cousin in Munro, but I think it best I write to my father instead. He needs to know that I am safe, but also that my trousseau has been lost. He will likely have very exact notions as to how I should proceed. Would this be in order? I do not wish to be a burden upon your hospitality."

The abbess nodded. "The hand of God has sheltered you thus far, my child. Regardless of your hardship, He has spared you any real misfortune, save the loss of your worldly belongings. And I can say from my own experience that this is no great loss at all. Now, far be it from me to withhold assistance where God has clearly shown it necessary. You shall have a hot bath, a stout meal, and a clean dress from our store of donations. When you are ready, your letter shall be sent to the stagecoach inn. I trust that is sufficient?"

Ellena assured her it was. Within the privacy of the simple room offered to her, Ellena received the promised bath and meal, which her tired body gratefully received. With renewed energy, she set about drafting a letter to her father. Her first question was to ask after Alfred. It gnawed at her, not knowing what had become of him, and she wanted reassurance of his safety more than anything else.

Her urgent inquiry made, she offered reassurance of her own well-being, though she did this more for her mother and Jilly. Her father was a man of action. Ellena repeated the story she had manufactured for the abbess but placed far more emphasis on her excitement at soon seeing her cousin James and Charlotte. By pointing to the future and the imminent conclusion of her father's plans, she hoped he would not linger on questions about the night she'd been missing.

The letter was passed on to the stagecoach leaving just after the noonday bell and would reach Trenton Grange by the late evening. She would have to wait patiently for a reply until the following day.

Ellena wandered around the grounds to distract herself from her thoughts. She absolutely must not think about Dominic. But she did not want to think about anything else.

If only Jilly were here. That would be exactly what she needed to work through her muddled feelings. With Jilly, she could speak freely and without fear of judgment.

Ellena walked more briskly, keen to shake off her agitation. When she had tired of circling buildings that were not open to outsiders, she went in search of the riverside chapel Dominic had recommended.

It was empty. She sat for a while on a pew near the back, drinking in the silence that demanded nothing from her. It was unlikely she would ever enjoy such seclusion at Lord Howell's estate. There would be an army of servants who, though busy with any number of tasks, would nevertheless observe her movements night and day. She felt the familiar resentment rise in her chest. Her life would always be somehow constrained.

As she sat, grimly contemplating her future, she conjured the image of a quiet existence in a woodland cottage. It seemed very enticing. Just herself and a gentle man with a dark, curling forelock. And those sensual lips.

AT NOON THE following day, a horse and rider drew up at the convent gates. The wearied man stumbled a little as he dismounted. He must have traveled at a furious pace, because his horse was steaming. After allowing himself a minute to catch his breath, he moved to untie a large parcel from behind the saddle and withdrew a smaller item from within the saddlebag.

Ellena stepped down to the courtyard to offer the horseman some cool water. Only then did she realize it was their coachman, Alfred.

He tipped his weathered hat to her, his face wreathed in smiles.

"Miss Trenton! I am mighty pleased to see you safe and well. What a scare we all had, not knowing if you was alive or dead…or worse."

Ellena's relief was equal to his own. "Oh, Alfred, I was just as afraid for you! Tell me, how *did* you escape?"

Ellena led Alfred up the steps and gestured him to a seat at the edge of the garden, where she joined him. He carefully placed the package next to him but held on to the small pouch. His hat was gripped with equal ferocity within his curled fingers.

"Well, miss, wiv' those bandits coming upon us so sudden-like, and the horses bolting and all, I'm sorry to say I didn't think very cleverly. I just tried to calm the poor creatures, and not aught else. When the carriage overturned, I fell out the driver's seat and rolled onto the ground. Next thing I knew, there was three men on horseback circlin' round, all wiv' pistols. I was frozen to the spot. They had a look of death in their eyes, they did. Anyways, one of them gets off his horse and comes over and says, 'What's your cargo?' and I gets all fired up thinking to keep them from you and I says, 'None of yer bleedin' business.' And he gives me a mighty blow to the head with the butt of his pistol. I'm afraid I wasn't much use to anyone then."

His narration ground to a halt and he squirmed a little, unable to look Ellena in the eye.

"It's all right, Alfred, all is well now. You did your best. You were outnumbered. They were armed. What more could you have done?"

His shoulders sagged with relief.

Ellena smiled in encouragement. "I'm curious, though. How did you get back to Trenton Grange?"

"The blow mostly just stunned me. I got me a hard noggin, the wife always says. I could hear voices and saw blurry figures running about. I lay on the ground, too dizzy to get up. They was tryin' ter take the horses, when one of the beauts rears up and strikes the bast... Um, sorry miss... I mean, the man... He strikes at one of the men wiv' his hooves. The fellow lost his footing and his grip on the reins and the horse was gone in a flash. Now *that* set the scoundrels into a right fit of arguing. One of them was dead keen to go after the animal, but they didn't trust each other, see? He figured they might not wait around for him before they split wiv' the spoils. So, they quit wiv' what they got, dragging out a cart hidden a ways off to carry their ill-gotten gains."

"Did they just leave you there?"

"I guess they figured I was dead. Besides, they got what they came for, the bast... Er, the rogues. Well, eventually, me head stopped spinning and I could stand without looking like I'd had too many rounds, if you catch my meaning."

Ellena suppressed a smile at Alfred's colorful narration and nodded for him to continue.

"So, of course, I first checks the coach to see if yerself is harmed. When I found no one, I didn't know what to think. It was a dark hour, to be sure, and I don't mean the time of day, neither. I started walking back toward home. I thought maybe yerself would also follow this path if the young miss weren't utterly lost. I hoped and prayed that stray horse would make its way back to its stable. Then the lads at the posting house would know something was wrong and send help. Imagine my surprise when I found the animal grazing about two miles down the road, wiv'out so much as a care in the world!"

"How fortuitous!"

"Yeah, and lucky too!" Alfred nodded. "Well, I got them reins and drove that horse at full gallop to the posting house. I changed horses as quick as I could and put that new beast to work too. It was no small surprise to the master when I finally came tearing into the yard! I've never seen the color drain from the master's face like that before. To be sure, he was greatly affected by the news of your disappearance. The master sent out a search party at first light. When they found your cloak at the river's edge, they didn't know what to make of it. They searched all day and returned only after dark, afraid to face the mistress with no news. We was all mightily relieved when your letter arrived shortly after. I had been allowed to rest that day, so I asked the master if I might have permission to deliver your parcel. Sort of to make up for the other lot what was lost. And to see you was well with me own eyes."

By now Alfred was beaming with the excitement of a happy ending. He reached for the package beside him and passed it to Ellena.

"The master had to get two of your dresses back from Miss Kinsey. Of course, she was happy to send these back your way. Now *she* was in a right state when she heard you was missing. She cried when the news came that you was safe at last. I think she would have brought these dresses to you herself, if such a thing had been seemly, but I did promise to send you her very best wishes. Your father also gave me this." Alfred presented the fist-shaped leather pouch.

"The master says you're to give this money to young Mr. James Trenton. He is to get you more clothes and whatnot, and a wedding dress to replace the other one. Then his lordship the viscount can see to the rest after the wedding." His face lit up. "I can't believe it's only a few days away! You must be excited, miss! We're all sure you'll be the prettiest bride Munro has ever seen."

Ellena felt the weight of the coins in the drawstring bag. They would meet her needs precisely, with no room for excesses. Her garments would need to match the standards expected by her parents, but they would be tasteful, not lavish.

She drew from her dress pocket a letter written in preparation for this moment.

"Thank you for your kindness and loyalty, Alfred. You must rest awhile before your hard journey back to Trenton Grange. I will see to it that you have some refreshment before you go. And your horse needs tending. When you are both sufficiently recovered, I have a small favor to ask of you. Will you please deliver this letter to the door of my cousin at Thorn Bush Hall? You need not wait for a reply."

"Certainly, miss. It would be an honor to be useful to you. I welcome anything I can do to make up for letting you down before."

"Come now, enough of that. There is no blame and no atonement necessary. You have always done your best and that is enough. Do me this one small service and then make your way safely home. That is all I require."

"Thank you, Miss Trenton. God bless you. And many good wishes from us all for your coming nuptials."

"Thank you, Alfred."

Ellena rose, her arms encircling the parcel of clothing that Alfred had handed her. She was sorry to be parted from the coachman, who represented the familiarity of home. Staying with her boorish cousin James offered little to look forward to. And as for meeting Lord Howell... Well, the less she thought about it, the better.

She managed a smile and made her goodbyes to Alfred, promising to send his refreshments along shortly. After another "Thank you" and "God bless you," Alfred released Ellena from conversation, and she made her way at once to the abbess to inform her of the latest developments.

LORD HOWELL STOMPED into his study. Of all things—highwaymen! On one of their main routes, too. Really! Whatever next? It was a most unwelcome bit of news. He already had enough to deal with. *And* his betrothed was late in arriving in Munro.

In a way, this last complication was a good thing, seeing as his plans were now behind schedule. It just meant there was even less time to get to know the stranger who would be his bride. Perhaps he should not have booked the wedding service for next Friday already. But Henry Trenton had been adamant that he was only coming up to Munro for that weekend. His daughter's wedding seemed to be nothing more than an inconvenience to him.

That man was truly the most dispassionate human being Lord Howell had ever encountered. Barring his own father, of course. It had made for a pitiful childhood. He should know. Although it may have been different for a daughter. Miss Trenton would not have carried the same burden of duty that he had. And she had no siblings to torment her. Still, a father as cold as hers…

He had expected to have to persuade Trenton of his good intentions, especially since he had carried out all negotiations via correspondence only. But the merchant had only been interested in numbers. He was an absolute savage when it came to numbers. It had been almost a challenge to deal with him.

There had been not one request to soften the experience for young Ellena. No stipulation to accommodate a companion in one of Munro House's many guest rooms. No insistence that she should at least meet her betrothed before the engagement contract was signed. No demand that her future husband do right by her, or else. Just…nothing.

He swallowed down the guilt. That was what he had wanted—a young woman who would accommodate his own insecurities. But he had believed more would be asked of him in return. Instead, she was being delivered like a package. And via the hands of her odious cousin James Trenton. Poor girl.

Lord Howell supposed he should be grateful to the man for suggesting his cousin as a promising match. No doubt he hoped to benefit from the connection, as Miss Trenton's father would, being in the same family business. As such, the dinner Mr. and Mrs. James Trenton had attended had been time well spent. In every other way, it had been a loathsome way to spend three hours. The viscount had left as soon as it had been polite to do so. He had made it clear to his friends that any future soiree that the Trentons might attend should not include him. He simply did not have the patience for such a selfish, sniveling weasel, even if his wife was an angel. In the end, it had been Mrs. Trenton's assurance that her husband was not exaggerating that had convinced him to look into the possibility of a union with Miss Ellena Trenton. A more beautiful or intelligent wife he could not hope to find, Mrs. Trenton had said.

And he had purchased her like a piece of rare furniture from the Trenton catalogue.

He sank into the nearest chair and buried his face in his palms. What could he offer her as compensation? Dresses? Jewels? He winced. If these were the sorts of things to placate her, he might as well have married one of those harpies in his social circle. Charm and romance were out of the question. He was no good at it. At least he had finally outgrown his childhood stutter. But he was not a man of words. Not around women.

What would Miss Ellena Trenton make of him? With his wealth and title, she would surely expect him to be oozing confidence. And he did—when it came to business. His father had drummed it into him, taught him to take no prisoners. But it was not so with the ladies.

His chubby, stammering childhood self had been an easy target for his older sisters. There had been so many opportunities when Mother had been busy elsewhere in the house. They would cast a critical eye over him and practice their vindictiveness on him. He'd been too little to understand it had been born of boredom and jealousy. They were intelligent, with nothing to do but strut and giggle and find husbands.

He'd become wary of their presence. Even when he was older and had shed his physical awkwardness, he avoided them. And when the time came to enter society and find a wife, he recognized the same pettiness in the ladies of the *ton*. Layers of silk and carefully coiled hair could not disguise the judgment in their eyes. He could picture them tittering behind their fans. *Why does he not speak? He thinks himself too good for us. His mother was a foreigner—what do you expect?*

He felt his jaw tighten whenever he was introduced, his stutter threatening to return. He had nothing to say, and no way to say it. So he worked long hours instead, which made his mother worry—about him, and the future of the Howell estate.

Well, he had solved that problem at least. Or merely created a new one. Somehow, he and the soon-to-be viscountess would have to produce an heir. And if the experience was going to be a happy one, he would have to find a way to overcome his own fears before he could comfort his bride in hers.

First, she had to get here. He had expected news of her arrival yesterday already. Surely, her father would not have reneged on his contract?

A flush of relief rushed from him. If Henry Trenton had changed his mind, he would be free of this cumbersome arrangement, and free of blame. Perhaps there was time to investigate other avenues—more reasonable ones. Maybe it was not too late to choose someone for himself who felt right, from the very start.

He felt a flush of disappointment. There had been someone. Someone who had felt right almost from the moment he had met her. A rare creature who had looked at him without judgement. To the contrary, she had looked at him the way a woman did when… Well… He almost blushed just thinking about it. She had looked at him with desire. Not for his home or title. For *him*. But he had let her go. He had had no choice.

There was a polite knock at the door. Lord Howell sighed and stood wearily.

"Enter."

The grey-haired butler did just that. "Sir, your two o' clock appointment is here."

Lord Howell nodded. Branson knew not to announce men

like Simmons by name. It was time to see to business once more.

As for Miss Trenton, if he had heard nothing of her arrival by tomorrow, he would write to her father. Perhaps he would not be dealing with the intricacies of marriage just yet.

CHAPTER SIX

ELLENA BID GOODBYE to the sisters, having given a small donation from her funds in gratitude for their hospitality. She assured herself that her cousin James, who had come in person to fetch her with the carriage, would not know the pouch was a little lighter.

Soon, she was on her way to James's home across town, answering his steady stream of questions, and growing increasingly agitated at her cousin's insensibility. He really had not changed at all.

"And you were all alone in the coach the whole night?" James's interrogation continued. "How appalling! And the highwaymen did not return?"

"No," replied Ellena, "I was most grateful that they did not."

"And to happen upon the old farmer on that road…" James shook his head in amazement. "You are positively blessed, Ellena. A charmed life, you know, that's what it is. You lead an absolutely charmed life."

"A 'charmed' life, you say?" She repeated his words incredulously. "I suppose if you exclude the actual attack by three armed men, one might think so."

James remained unperturbed. "Yes, well, one's blessings appear magnified in the presence of suffering, do they not? To be sure, when Charlotte lost her favorite necklace, I replaced it with one of similar design, but with less costly gems. She was so grateful, I believe she now loves this new piece even more than the one she lost."

The lack of response made him peer into the dim light of the carriage. "I say, I'm not boring you already, am I?"

"Hmm? Oh... Er, no... Of course not. Forgive my lack of concentration. I did not sleep much last night."

James nodded sagely, his red curls catching a glint of sun with each dip of his head. "I imagine it would be difficult to rest well in a convent, what with all that prayer and fasting going on." He wrinkled his narrow nose at the thought. "Then again, such practices have their merits, I suppose. Better to be a nun who is pleased with her lot in life than one of the city's poor. That sort are always needy and never satisfied. Perhaps their lack of piety is what holds them back in life."

"My dear cousin!" Ellena exclaimed in shock. "I believe the poor are so near to starving that one may consider them to be in a permanent state of divine contemplation!"

James Trenton was about to open his mouth in retort, his pale, freckled skin growing pink with indignation, when they turned up into the drive to Thorn Bush Hall. Ellena was grateful that their arrival at his home was imminent. The thought of one more minute confined alone with her cousin set her teeth on edge.

Though fashionably situated in the best part of town, the property had a pleasing touch of the country about it. The drive was long and meandered through tall trees, opening up as it approached the house. At the edge of the lawn, low box hedges framed well-tended evergreen shrubs and herb gardens. There were few flowers, being early autumn, but Ellena could imagine the palette of color that would delight in the bloom of spring.

"Ah, here we are," James announced with satisfaction as the horses pulled up to the steps of the house. "May I say it is a pleasure offering you the protection of our home—and ourselves as chaperones—while you make your acquaintance with Lord

Howell."

"Thank you, James," Ellena replied, relieved that their conversation had returned to simple civilities. "I hope not to be a burden on your household. Oh, which reminds me… Father sent this." She held out the little money bag with its attractive contents. "He asks that you use these funds to procure a small but suitable wardrobe for me to use during the brief remainder of the engagement. And I'm afraid my wedding gown was also in the stolen trousseau. We will need to have a new dress made posthaste. Personally, I would be satisfied to wear any of my existing dresses, but Father insists we should show off our new position with something more opulent."

James beamed more at the pouch than at Ellena. "I shall accompany you on a shopping expedition first thing tomorrow. Charlotte will be delighted. She has been quite preoccupied with preparing the nursery for the baby. It will do her good to spend some time in town instead of being bound to the house."

"That sounds perfect. And do you know a reputable dressmaker? I should not waste time if I am to have a gown ready within a week."

"I shall make inquiries on your behalf."

A footman opened the carriage door and stood stiffly as James and Ellena descended from within. Charlotte must have rushed out at the sound of wheels on gravel and was waiting on the steps to receive them. Beside her stood a sweet young boy, about two years old. At the sight of Ellena emerging from the compartment, he hid his curly, blond head in the folds of his mother's skirt. Its front panel lay taut across her large belly, as she was six months with child. Her own blonde locks bounced cheerfully as Charlotte took his little hand and led him forward with the beaming pride of a young mother.

"Clarence, dear, come and greet your Aunt Ellena. Isn't she pretty?"

The boy did not seem to care for his new aunt's looks. He disappeared behind his mother and would not acknowledge

Ellena.

"How refreshing, Charlotte," Ellena said, laughing, "a young man not lured by beauty alone! You must be commended for raising him well. If you continue in this way, he will assuredly choose wisely when he is grown."

"Hmph," James grumbled, "our son will choose even more wisely if he listens to his father and finds a wealthy widow with no children."

"*James!*" came his wife's retort. "You are quite insufferable sometimes. What will your cousin think of you?"

"She will no doubt think me a clever man to encourage a profitable courtship. After all, is her father not a master in all manner of investments?"

Ellena clutched her hands to her breast sorrowfully. "Alas, I am no widow, since you deem them such a fine prospect in marriage. Perhaps if I were, you might find an even better match than Lord Howell for me."

"No, indeed," Charlotte interjected with a tone of great earnestness. "There are few men as worthy as the viscount. He has greatly honored the family by choosing you. But you shall see for yourself soon enough. Won't she, James?"

"Mm, yes. I shall send word of your arrival. He will want to arrange a meeting with you at the earliest opportunity. It will likely be over dinner tomorrow night. That will give you the chance to show off the fruits of your shopping efforts."

Charlotte clapped her hands in childlike glee.

"Oh, what excitement! Ellena, do come inside and let me show you to your room. It is a little small, but it has the most wonderful view over the back garden. James can torture us further with his comments at supper." She frowned at her husband over her guest's shoulder, but he appeared quite unaffected by it.

Young Clarence was deposited in the care of his nurse while Charlotte led Ellena through their home. She spoke with much zeal but surprisingly little knowledge about the pianoforte, the tapestries, the art and antiques that James collected in much the same way Ellena's father did. She paused in a side room so that Ellena could admire the set of porcelain statuettes that were Charlotte's own collection.

"James buys these to spoil me," she said shyly.

Ellena could tell, at a glance, that they were not the fine quality such figurines could be. Her practiced eye knew that each shepherdess with crook or maiden with flower bouquet had been purchased without investment in mind—not the typical behavior of a Trenton.

"Aren't they lovely?" Charlotte sighed happily.

"I can see they bring you joy," Ellena admitted. "Did James choose them for you?"

"Oh, no! I usually spot something I like in someone's home, and then my thoughtful husband sources them for me. He does not always manage to find the exact replica, but I love them all the same."

Ellena imagined James had no intention of wasting money on such knick-knacks. He would have found whatever item was similar enough at the lowest possible cost. As such, Charlotte's collection was sweet in its ceramic simplicity but of no real value other than sentiment.

"I keep them here, out of the way of the household bustle," Charlotte explained. "I would not have them damaged by the brush of a careless elbow."

Ellena was certain James wholeheartedly approved of their secluded position.

"Of course, I do not expect him to lavish all his gifts on *me*," she continued. "I would far rather have a toy for little Clarence. Seeing our son happy makes me happy too. Why would I need more than that?"

Ellena smiled and nodded, reminded once again that Charlotte was love and innocence bound tightly as one.

How strange that James—in every way the model of a Trenton—should choose a wife who was so different to him. In

Ellena's home, her parents worked together as a silent, efficient machine, each cog clicking into place, turning the wheels of their well-placed efforts forward toward greater success. In contrast, Charlotte exuded a deep warmth that Ellena did not feel James entirely deserved. Indeed, her value was inestimable—she had borne him a son. For James, purchasing the occasional trinket for his wife's pleasure would be a small price when securing his future.

The guided tour through Thorn Bush Hall came to a close at the end of a dark passage—Ellena's room. The location brought to mind the gothic novels of which her mother had so sternly disapproved. Charlotte opened the door and Ellena entered with a flutter of romantic drama, like a heroine about to be locked in a tower. She wondered if Lord Howell was the type of gentleman who would ride up on a white charger to rescue her.

The room *was* small, as Charlotte had warned, and they had passed several larger unoccupied ones en route to her own. But before Ellena could entertain any petty thoughts, Charlotte explained her choice.

"This is one of my favorite rooms." Charlotte beamed. "The others along the corridor are rather damp, I'm afraid. They get little sun on this side of the house. *This* room is on the corner and enjoys the full advantage of its south-facing position. Also, the birds build their nests in the tree just there, next to the rose garden, so you will have birdsong and the perfume of roses to fill your senses."

Ellena immediately crossed the room to the window and drank in the heat of the afternoon sun on her face. Tendrils of ivy curled past the window, which had a bay seat. Charlotte was right—the room was charming. And—she noticed with a surge of pleasure—they had managed to squeeze in a writing table.

She pressed Charlotte's hand warmly. "It is everything I need and more, Charlotte. Thank you. I think I shall write a quick letter to be delivered by the last coach, if you don't mind. With all the turmoil of the last few days, I am sure Mother would want reassurance that all is well. And I am eager to tell her of my delightful accommodation. It truly is a corner of heaven."

"You really like it? I hoped you would. You will find the writing desk well-stocked with paper and ink." Charlotte stood a moment, considering the room anew. "You are certain you do not need help settling in? I could send you my lady's maid. It is a pity you do not have an abigail of your own, but I understand you will be well attended once you are mistress at Munro House."

"You are very kind to think of it," Ellena told Charlotte politely, "but, as you see, I have almost nothing to unpack."

Charlotte's eyes lost a little of their sparkle. "Oh," she said. "Well, then, I suppose there is nothing more I can do." She looked sadly at the door.

Ellena thought quickly. "A pot of tea would be welcome."

Charlotte's smile returned. "I will have one sent up immediately. Would you like a sandwich with that?"

"No, no, I am not hungry at present. But I am certain to be famished by dinner. I can't wait to see what your cook has prepared. I am sure it will be delicious."

Her cousin-in-law's smile deepened. "See you at dinner, then," Charlotte said before leaving Ellena to her writing.

Ellena set straight to the task at hand. She penned a short letter to her parents, assuring them that all now proceeded with anticipated smoothness. She told them what they needed to hear and felt little inclination to expand upon this with further details. She sealed and addressed the letter, then began a second with greater enthusiasm.

Dear Jilly,

I write to you in a borrowed dress that once was mine. I am sorry to have taken back that which was so freely given. Thank you for, in turn, offering it so freely to me. Rest assured, I shall return it to you, and add another gown besides, once I have the allowance owed a viscountess.

It is strange how quickly circumstances change. In two

days, I have played the role of departing daughter, helpless maiden, rescued damsel, devout postulate, and recovered cousin. And I have not yet tackled the prescribed role of future bride! My mother's careful instruction did not cover such giddy topics as chaos and adventure. But I am fortunate to be safely in Munro at last and shall not dwell on all that has preceded my arrival at my cousin's home.

No, indeed, for there is enough to bewail right here! Honestly, if James should exchange his head with that of a donkey, none could tell the difference, for his mouth produces little more than a constant braying. He's a Trenton through and through when it comes to matters of finance, but he lacks the quiet dignity of my father. The things he says! I fear I shall need to exercise great restraint not to roll my eyes periodically.

But I am, perhaps, too dramatic.

Charlotte, in contrast, is all warmth and kindness. Motherhood has given her something meaningful to fuss over and she is a very devoted parent. James must be thrilled that she would rather have a new rattle for little Clarence than a dearer item for herself. I suppose things will change if their next child is a girl. Charlotte is sure to spoil her with pretty things and "give James a headache," as Father loves to say.

I do so miss talking to you, and already, I am two days late with my first letter! I promise to allow no more distractions to prevent our daily correspondence. Mere highway robbery shall not be sufficient cause for delay in future.

Please forgive that this letter is so brief. Dinner is in an hour and I must close my eyes awhile if I am to endure James and his odd opinions.

You, on the other hand, may offer no such excuse. I expect an immediate reply with no detail spared. What is your newest escape from your brothers? Does Cook still make her excellent biscuits now that I am not there to pester her for them? It feels as if I have been away an eternity already. Perhaps when I am settled in my permanent accommodation, I will feel less spare. Meanwhile, a letter from you will supply me with great happiness and much-needed comfort.

Do give my best to your parents and rambunctious siblings. Tell them I shall send them a present as bribe to take pity on their sister. But it shall have to wait until I have an allowance from my new husband. Hopefully, I shall have news of him in my next letter.

Till then, I am, as always, your devoted friend,
Ellena

CHAPTER SEVEN

DINNER WAS SURPRISINGLY pleasant, as James excused himself early to attend to some paperwork. Ellena guessed that he found women's chatter to be as tedious as she did *his* dull insights.

The ladies retired to the drawing room for coffee. In the absence of James, Ellena was tempted to ask Charlotte about Lord Howell. She knew that James and Charlotte had met the viscount at dinner with a mutual acquaintance. They might not all be fast friends, but Charlotte would have a measure of insight into the man's character, and certainly would, at the very least, be able to describe his physical features.

But her potential informant was called away to the nursery to read little Clarence his bedtime story and kiss him goodnight. By the time Charlotte had returned, Ellena's eyelids were drooping.

"Oh, I have been a terrible hostess!" Charlotte declared in a statement so patently false that Ellena was obliged to correct her.

"Nothing could be further from the truth, dear Cousin. My adventures are merely catching up with me."

"Then you should rest. I can keep my own company well enough."

"I thought we might talk a little more."

"I think not. Look how you are yawning! Straight to bed with you now. We will have the whole morning together for shopping and gossip. I intend to point out all the sights en route and hopefully spot a few ladies worthy of mention, to boot. You will need to have your wits about you." Charlotte's eyes sparkled with anticipation.

Ellena stifled another yawn. "If you are certain…"

"Yes, of course I am. Off you go."

Charlotte's mothering was a welcome balm after so much chaos and confusion. The bed, too, was remarkably comfortable. Especially since the last two nights had been spent in the rough simplicity of a cabin and a convent.

Ellena awoke refreshed and excited at the prospect of obtaining new clothes and a closer perspective on Munro. She needed to move forward and start embracing her life here. The sooner she made this city her home, the less homesick she would feel.

It was strange, though, to imagine any adventure that did not include Jillian, or any sorrow that would not have been greatly reduced, having been confided to her childhood companion. A pang of insecurity twisted in her heart. Did Jillian likewise feel the loss of her friend? Or did everyone at Trenton Grange go about their business as usual, even though Ellena no longer had a part in it? What was Cook making for dinner? Had the gardener pruned the rosebushes yet? Was the new foal settling in?

Lost in thought, Ellena waited rather more patiently than James did while Charlotte gave final instructions to the nurse. She had been reluctant to leave her son behind, but he would not be amused in a ladies' boutique. James clearly envied little Clarence his freedom. The morning would not pass as quickly for him.

Fortunately, Ellena had a quick, discerning eye and the three of them were not long in the pursuit of ladies' garments. Ellena chose five dresses that flattered her figure and completed the image of worthy prize.

"You may discard the ball gown from your selection," James instructed. "There will be no occasion to wear it prior to the wedding. And if you set aside another dress, we can add some simple jewels to complete the presentation."

"You will need a bonnet," Charlotte added, immersed in the

joys of shopping, "and some ribbon. Oh, and gloves!"

Ellena followed her cousin and his wife to the jeweler, the milliner, and finally, the haberdashery. Her feet were aching from traipsing across the hard Munro cobbles. She longed to kick off her shoes and find a grassy meadow like the one to which she and Jilly would often escape. Instead, there were rows and rows of gloves waiting for her inspection.

She reached for a white pair, long enough to stretch all the way past the elbow. They were exactly what she needed for her first meeting with the viscount. Her dinner dress was short-sleeved and would reveal the unattractive scratches from her recent escape in the woods. It was best to disguise such imperfections.

With gloves in hand, the shopping was finally done.

"Are we leaving already?" asked a crestfallen Charlotte. "Our little expedition cannot end so soon! James, we must stop for tea. Ellena has seen nothing of Munro besides a handful of retail establishments." A twinkle appeared in her eye. "If we choose one of the more fashionable tea rooms, we may observe Munro's finest inhabitants on display. Ellena should have a taste of the sort of society with whom she will be mixing."

James did not protest, and Ellena was happy to rest her tired feet. Soon, they were enjoying a plate of scones and cream while Charlotte provided juicy titbits of information on each couple that paraded past them.

"Ooh!" Charlotte cried, her enthusiasm not in the least abated, despite the constant stream of commentaries that had preceded this latest sighting. "That is Lady Penrose and her daughter, Frances. Their family hosts the most wonderful parties. But I am sure you will put them to shame once you are mistress at Munro House. Just think, it will be they who are impressed to see *you* in the not-too-distant future."

Ellena only listened with one ear, her attention distracted by her cousin. James was restless at the table. His thoughts seemed preoccupied with the much emptier bag tied at his belt. When he fingered it once more in agitation, Ellena could stand it no longer.

"James, you are sure there are sufficient funds left for my wedding dress? We have not overextended ourselves this morning?"

"Don't be silly, dear," Charlotte interjected. "You only bought three dresses. And your necklace was obtained at a song! Really, I have never before seen anyone bargain as well as my own clever James. You certainly have the sharp skills of a Trenton. I envy you that. I'm afraid my little head is not meant for business, is it, James?"

Ellena ignored Charlotte's comments and looked fixedly at her cousin. "You would tell me if there were a problem, wouldn't you? I'm sure I could return the jewels and regain a fair portion of the price if you believe it to be necessary."

James did not answer her immediately. He seemed to be wrestling with his thoughts. An icy hand gripped Ellena's heart. Surely, her father had not been so frugal at this critical point? To wear fine clothes but no jewels in the evening would be to appear the pauper princess. Lord Howell would surely lower his opinion of her family and herself at their first meeting. It would not only affect her father's standing in the powerful man's eyes, but also likely weaken her position in the household. A beggarly wife could not hold her husband's respect.

James seemed to reach a decision. "There is no cause for concern, Cousin. I was merely thinking of which dressmaker would give the best service we can afford. If we choose wisely, she will include some embroidery in the bargain."

Ellena sagged with relief. "I do not need anything as fancy as all that. We will keep to simple elegance. If the flow is soft and unfettered, it will lend a quiet sophistication."

"We shall see." James stood up. "Charlotte, do not cut your outing short. I shall leave the carriage for you and Ellena. If you will excuse me, I have a matter to which I must attend."

"What of the wedding dress?" Charlotte asked. "We must make quick work of ordering it."

"I shall have an answer for you this afternoon," James replied. He planted a kiss on his wife's forehead, then turned and walked briskly from the table towards the exit.

"But, James…" Charlotte protested to his retreating back. When he did not respond, her body sagged and her smile disappeared.

Ellena's uneasiness returned. James had no pressing appointment—he had put the morning aside for them. Why was he suddenly off in a rush?

"I apologize for James," Charlotte said softly. "That was most unlike him."

"Where do you think he has gone?" Ellena asked.

"I haven't the slightest notion." Charlotte toyed with the spoon from her saucer. Then, quite suddenly, she lifted her head and placed the spoon firmly back in its place. "More cake. That is what we shall have. James shall be sorry he missed the opportunity. Let him see to the matters of men. They are strange things, after all, are they not? But I, for one, am not in the habit of letting a perfectly good morning go to waste because of their foibles."

Putting her words into action, Charlotte waved at a waiter and relaxed into her chair. Soon she was chatting merrily again.

But Ellena could not concentrate. Something was afoot and she was certain it had to do with her. She made polite conversation but had to be constantly prompted by her companion into answering.

Eventually, Charlotte took pity on her.

"Oh, my dear, here I prattle on, but your thoughts must certainly be on dinner tonight. After all, you will be wanting to make a strong first impression. We shall go home at once. I will send you my maid. She has a flair for arranging my hair. She will know just how you should wear yours to best flatter your fine features. I may even have a pretty shawl to add to your ensemble. The autumn evenings lately carry a nip in the air."

Ellena was relieved to be returning to Thorn Bush Hall, where she did not have to endure any more small talk. She even played a little with Clarence, who had begun to warm to his aunt. She tried not to let her doubts gnaw at her. Charlotte's maid curled her hair. Ellena had to admit, it needed a little attention. But she could not push the worry from her mind.

It was only when James returned home some hours later—red-faced and with a whiff of brandy about him—that Ellena realized she had not worried enough.

CHAPTER EIGHT

L ORD HOWELL WAS in a foul mood. The servants avoided him as he skulked in his study.

His dinner with the Trentons this evening could not be canceled, but he rebelled against it inwardly. His long-awaited bride was not as high on his list of priorities as she had been a week ago. To be honest, he now regretted the contract with Mr. Henry Trenton for the hand of his daughter. But he could not insult the girl or her family by postponing their dinner appointment. After all, they were not to blame for his current agitation. It did nothing to improve his mood, however, when James Trenton—the very man he was supposed to meet with later—was suddenly announced by a flustered servant. The viscount attempted to stifle his irritation and stood to greet his visitor.

"Good day, Mr. Trenton. I was not expecting you until this evening."

His visitor tipped his head in acknowledgement. "Ah, yes, I apologize for calling upon you so abruptly. Indeed, we all very much look forward to dining with you tonight—Ellena most of all." He cleared his throat, coughing lightly into his fist. "However, I have come to speak to you on a delicate matter, one that I should like to discuss without the ladies present."

George Howell felt his ire rise again. He had enough on his plate. The last thing he wanted was to deal with any difficulties associated with James Trenton. He struggled to suppress his irritation. After a longer silence than he would have liked, he managed to say, "Oh? I have not been made aware of any complications. I understand Miss Trenton arrived safely yesterday and is enjoying your hospitality until the ceremony next Friday."

"Certainly, certainly. She is quite content and keenly awaits her introduction to you." Trenton paused, his bowed shoulders and lowered eyes switching to a sad shaking of the head. Neither his servility nor his supposed concern appeared genuine to Lord Howell. This did not surprise him. James Trenton and his wiles were well known to him.

"Of course," Trenton continued, the expression of pretended distress now settled on his features, "my cousin would be too proud to tell you what difficult circumstances she has endured on her eventful journey here."

"What do you mean?"

"Her coach was held up by armed men."

"What!" The viscount exploded. "Another robbery! On the same route!" He began to pace the floor, his thoughts turned inward, James Trenton momentarily forgotten. "It seems we need a regular patrol to re-establish the law on our roads. We cannot have our stagecoaches held up every other day. It simply will not do!"

A sudden thought struck him. He stopped his furious pacing and pointed his attention sharply at his guest. "Was anyone hurt? Did they harm her?"

"No, my lord, but they did make off with her trousseau chest—which brings me to the reason for my visit."

Lord Howell narrowed his eyes. He could smell a weaseling deal brewing. Trenton's pale face was flushed with greedy expectation. But the man was in over his head. He just didn't know it yet.

"I was wondering, Lord Howell, whether you have decided yet what to bestow upon our Ellena as her wedding gift?"

The viscount eyed his guest suspiciously. "There is a family piece—a tiara—that I had in mind. But what has this to do with you?"

"Well, it occurs to me that your bride is without a fitting dress for the occasion, hers having been in the stolen chest. Her father has replaced several of her gowns, but it might be a sign of goodwill if you would consider covering the expense of her bridal raiment. Perhaps as a wedding gift instead of the jewels? I am sure you understand, the bride of Munro's foremost citizen cannot be frugal with her attire for such a public celebration."

Lord Howell stood, unmoving, temporarily rooted by the other man's audacity.

"The bride's clothes prior to our marriage are her own affair," he replied stiffly. "They are not deductible from her dowry."

"Ah, yes, but without a suitable gown—one that reflects her position as the new viscountess—might one not, perhaps, expect a delay in the proceedings?"

The veiled threat drove straight to the heart of Lord Howell's simmering irritation, causing it to boil over into indignant rage.

"I believe there might be cause for more than just delay," he hissed. "I think I might well consider canceling the whole affair. I have no guarantee that the girl was not ravished by the bandits." He drove an accusing finger toward the horrified James. "How do I know she is still fit to be my bride? Perhaps she will not need a wedding dress, after all!"

Trenton staggered back under the fury of his words. "I can assure you…"

"Can you, indeed? What proof can you offer that her virtue is unblemished?"

"I… There were… You must believe…"

"I *must* do nothing of the sort! Do you think I shall risk my family's name on some arbitrary girl whose reputation may be tarnished?"

James Trenton shrunk visibly. He wrung his hands. "There must be some way to convince you of her innocence. Please forget my earlier suggestion. It was not thought through. I beg you to accept our pledge of commitment. My cousin is all she should be. We would not dream of insulting your honor with such trickery."

"Would you not? We shall see. You can tell Henry Trenton this: I shall know soon enough if my bride was no maiden. If he hopes to make a fool of me, he will discover he is dealing with a formidable enemy."

"Please..." Trenton's face was white as a ghost. "You must..." His eyes searched the room, as if to find the right words. "I mean..." He threw his hands forward pleadingly. "My uncle is a man of honor like yourself. His word is oath."

"Unlike yours, perhaps?"

"I did not lie to you!"

"No." Lord Howell pinned his opponent with a withering glare. "Just a little insinuation and self-service, perhaps? I wonder what Miss Trenton's father would think of your efforts on his daughter's behalf."

"*Please*, he does not know of our meeting. He holds you only in the highest regard. I have committed an error of judgment. I see that now. I beg you not to let it interfere with your plans to wed my cousin."

"Very well. But I wish to hear no more such *suggestions* from any of your family. Is that understood?"

"Perfectly." Trenton's ashen face flooded with relief. "You are most generous to ignore my *faux pas*. Er... May I ask you not to mention this awkward incident to Ellena or her father?"

"Mr. Trenton, you may be sure of one thing: I will be wasting no further thought on it. Now, if you will excuse me."

"Of course, of course." His visitor nodded vigorously. "Thank you." He managed a watery smile. "Er...till tonight, then?"

"Goodbye, Mr. Trenton. Do see yourself out."

The man bowed hurriedly before he fled.

Lord Howell stared at the space Trenton had vacated. He had never liked the man. Spineless little toad! How *dare* that sniveling weasel enter his home and risk enmity between the families mere hours before the introduction to his betrothed? Well, James Trenton would not be making *that* mistake twice.

As the viscount's emotions gradually subsided, a flare of guilt touched his conscience. He had implied a very distasteful slight upon Miss Trenton's person. He had only said it to put her cousin in his place. Really, he did not doubt for a moment that his betrothed was…*untouched.* He blushed at the mere thought. He was very thankful there had been no witnesses to his outburst. James Trenton would say nothing—of that much, he was certain. No, he could safely put his hasty wording in the past, where it belonged.

Driven by the dregs of guilt that persisted, Lord Howell tried to shake off his earlier negativity toward the evening that lay ahead. It really wouldn't be fair to give his bride-to-be anything but the best Munro House had to offer. And that included the mood of its master.

He wondered what the young lady expected from their first meeting. He knew she was of sound character and had beauty to match. But what if, deep down inside, she was just like all the other women of Munro's so-called *fine society*? What if, having won the privilege of his money and position, she treated him with ingratitude and disdain?

He had specifically chosen a young woman with a sheltered upbringing, hoping fervently that she would be undemanding and easy to please. The ladies of his acquaintance were not so. But what if Miss Trenton, suddenly exposed to the worldly abundance of a viscountess's life, became spoiled and silly? Or worse— he shuddered—perhaps she would emulate the ways of her new peers. Despite his unmatched position in Munro, he had endured more than his share of vicious gossip. His title did not protect him from such cruel speech. Oh, they would not say it to his face— well, his sisters would. But Lord Howell was all too familiar with derisive looks that were not hidden well enough.

He rubbed his brow. What would Miss Ellena Trenton think if she knew how nervous her intended was? No doubt she had been raised to expect a match that was more pragmatic than sentimental. Goodness knew, he, too, had long ago given up any hope of finding love. And yet, if it were possible…

No, no, such thinking was foolishness. The best he could hope for was that she would accept him and honor him as her husband. Anything more was the stuff of fairy stories.

Lord Howell straightened to his full height. It was time to get on with more practical matters. He strode off to find his house-keeper. Miss Trenton might not be instantly charmed by her host, but Munro House would be putting its best foot forward for its new mistress.

ELLENA AND CHARLOTTE had been waiting in the solarium when James finally returned home. Charlotte was busy sewing, while Ellena read aloud to her. Clarence was playing on the floor under his mother's watchful eye. Within the scene of such domestic bliss, James sauntered in and kissed his wife on the cheek. She whirled around, pricking her finger on the needle.

"James, where have you been?" she demanded, sucking the injured finger. "We had to dine without you. And it was most appalling of you to desert us this morning." She stopped abruptly and pulled a face. "Whatever is that smell? Have you been drinking?"

"Don't fuss so, Charlotte. I may have had a few drinks. What of it?"

"'A few'?" She sniffed the air suspiciously. "I would say you've emptied an entire bottle of bad brandy. Whatever possessed you? It's the middle of the afternoon!"

James gripped his head with both hands. "Do be still, woman. Your buzzing is giving me a headache!"

"James Trenton, you tell me right now what is going on! Does this have to do with your appointment this morning? Have you had worrying news in business?"

"You could say so, m'dear." James gesticulated broadly. "I've been made to look a fool, haven't I? You try to help a man find luck in love, and this is how he thanks you."

"What on Earth are you talking about? What has happened? Ellena, have someone bring a cup of strong coffee for him."

Ellena rose at once and walked across the carpeted floor toward the bell pull.

"Do sit down, James," Charlotte insisted. "You look as though your legs may fail you at any moment."

"No, no, Ellena will want to hear all about her precious betrothed and how he threatened...*threatened*...her father." James smiled smugly, swaying slightly where he stood.

Ellena froze, midway across the room, but Charlotte was already continuing the interrogation.

"You saw Lord Howell? Why would he be at odds with your uncle?"

"Because he is a pompous prig who likes to throw his weight around and turn his nose up at it." James stopped and frowned. "I mean, he is a fat pig with a big nose." His eyes crossed with concentration. "What I mean is…"

Charlotte shook her head, ignoring his attempts at making any sense of his own insult. "I don't understand. Lord Howell has always been a most courteous and honorable man."

"Yes, yes." James waved a hand dismissively. "A pillar of society, our illustrious viscount, greatly esteemed among the distinguished nobility and toadying merchants. But not many have seen his dark side." He waggled a finger accusingly. "He may have fooled *you*, my dear, but I have challenged the dragon in his lair, and he does indeed breathe fire!"

"Oh, now you are just being dramatic," Charlotte declared, but her face was tinged with concern.

"Am I? You shall see for yourselves at dinner tonight." James wrinkled his nose in disgust. "He pretends to be so noble and upright, oozing with the pride of his ancient family name, when in fact he is nothing but a shrewd man of business who thinks himself above the rest of us. Just wait, he will reveal his true colors after the wedding contract is sealed."

Ellena finally found her voice. "If he has threatened Father…"

"Yes, James, Ellena has a point. Whatever has happened may affect her immediate future. This is all very upsetting. I think you should please explain the events from the beginning."

James seemed to consider this. The thought of reliving the details of his morning must have been instantly sobering, for he suddenly grew quite pale before sinking morosely into his chair. Charlotte and Ellena seated themselves on the sofa opposite him.

"Do not keep us waiting any longer, James," Charlotte urged. "Our imaginations will conjure up the most awful ideas."

"And well they may, my dear, well they may." James squirmed in his chair. "Aha… You see… Yes, well, ahem… I went to see our friend the viscount on a small matter of business. I had… In fact, I thought… It seemed reasonable… to, well, to enroll his assistance in procuring Ellena's wedding dress." He paused and shifted uncomfortably.

"Go on," said Charlotte impatiently. "Did he offer sound advice?"

"What?"

"On her dress. I assume you wanted his recommendation on a reputable dressmaker."

"Er, not exactly. It was more along the lines of finances."

Ellena gasped. It was more terrible a truth than anything she could have imagined. "But you had assured me that the funds my father sent were sufficient!"

"They were, they were. That is, they were adequate for the simple dress you had described. But I believed you needed something rather more splendid. After all, you are marrying our most prominent member of society. Your guest list constitutes all the finest Munro families. I felt certain—Lord Howell being such a *gentleman*, as everyone believes—that he would gladly assist us in acquiring a garment for his bride to match his public stature."

Ellena stared at him in abject horror.

"Er, well, it seems I misjudged him," James continued less certainly. "He was unwilling to help and would not even consider offering it as a wedding gift." He did not look his cousin in the eye.

Ellena was now trembling, her hands clenched tightly.

Then the dam wall burst.

"How *could* you? I am *mortified* at what he must think of us! It was never his duty to contribute toward my gown. He already carries the expense of the entire ceremony and festivities afterward. You had no right to approach him in this regard. If anything, you should have spoken to my father regarding additional funds. If you have compromised Father's position with Lord Howell, there will be no end to his fury. Not to mention the shame that I must carry into my first meeting with my intended!"

James answered sulkily, "There is no harm done. He assured me the matter was all but forgotten."

Ellena subsided a little. "We can all be grateful Lord Howell has been a gentleman to hold no grudge," she said through tight lips.

But James did not appear to share in her relief. "He is not such a gentleman as you all suppose." He smirked. "He looks after his own interests like any other man. You would not have thought him so chivalrous if you had heard his comments on your virtue."

Ellen stiffened. "What do you mean?"

"Surprised, are you?" James sneered. "Your affianced is not such a champion, after all. When he heard of your little incident with the brigands, he seemed far more concerned about your chastity than your general well-being."

Charlotte's soft voice broke in, heavy with disappointment. "James, this is vulgar and cruel. Do stop." She squeezed Ellena's hand. "I'm sure James is exaggerating. He is not himself this afternoon."

James scowled at his wife. "I believe Ellena has a right to

know what boorish manners her betrothed exhibited in this regard. If it were not for my intervention, he may even have called the wedding off."

"Surely not!" Charlotte's dismay was almost palpable.

He angled his head at Ellena. "You see, Cousin, my wife naively believes the best in people. But perhaps you understand men's weaknesses. Lord Howell will not tolerate a less-than-perfect bride. He cannot abide any threat to the hallowed reputation his name carries. If you are not the untouched trophy he expects, he will not hesitate to cancel the arrangements. He only cares for his own prosperity. Your feelings simply do not enter into it."

Ellena could find no words with which to respond. Her worst fears had been realized. James and his carelessness were as nothing compared to the terrible truth his actions had revealed about her betrothed. George Howell was every bit the thought-less, controlling despot she had prayed not to wed. Now, the marriage loomed ahead of her, a lifetime of captive misery.

James rose to leave, a little unsteady on his feet. "I think I'll lie down awhile. Charlotte, you may wake me when it is time to leave for his lordship."

His statement received no acknowledgement. Even Charlotte had no gentle repartee to lighten the mood. James waited a few moments, but his wife ignored him, her head turned to Ellena, her eyes moist with compassion. With a shrug, James carefully made his way from the room.

The two women remained together in stunned silence.

Ellena did not stir, but this belied the real turmoil within. Her feelings fluctuated between fury and humiliation. Lord Howell had already judged her and found her wanting. James's crude insinuations had left her in no doubt as to her future position with Lord Howell—she would be but a prize on display, her every aspect scrutinized to ensure she conformed to her husband's expectations. Her movements would be even more stringently ruled by her husband than they had been by her parents. He would choose her clothes, her friends, her interests—to ensure they were in keeping with what was expected of a perfect wife and viscountess.

Ellena's head swam with the cumulative tensions of the past four days. She was trapped in an ongoing cycle of misfortune. She wanted to push it all from her, to reclaim her sense of self, to rebel against all that sought to quell her spirit.

In this moment, she had to choose. If she submitted, she would be giving in to all that had been thrust upon her, accepting her circumstances as beyond her control. She would be crawling deeper inside herself to hide from the world and its impact upon her.

If, instead, she kicked blindly against her fate—just as she had thrown herself desperately into the river—she risked losing everything. A broken engagement was a humiliation from which one did not easily recover.

There was a third option.

It crept into her thoughts as if afraid to be seen, but she reached for it. It was a risk, but a calculated one. It would dare any man to challenge her dignity at his peril. She would fulfill her father's wishes, but on her terms. Lord Howell would find in her a little more than he had bargained for.

Ellena turned her steady gaze upon her companion, lifted her chin slightly and announced, "Charlotte, I will be paying extra attention to my appearance this evening. If you would be so kind, there is one small item in particular that I would like to borrow from you..."

CHAPTER NINE

Lord Howell paced the thickly carpeted floor of his bedroom in his best dinner clothes. The guests would be arriving any minute now, and he was sweating. The thought of hosting dinner triggered old insecurities. He had but one opportunity to make a good first impression on a lady, and he was always terrible at it. The fact that the person he had to impress would soon be his wife did nothing to settle his nerves.

As if this were not challenge enough, he had to include that insufferable James Trenton in his party. The fellow really was a horrible, little man. Having met him before, however, the events of this morning had not been altogether a surprise. It was some relief that his bride-to-be had been raised by the more somber Henry Trenton and was therefore unlikely to resemble her cousin in character.

Still, Miss Trenton was very young—only nineteen—without the weight of experience to toughen her heart. She would presumably have some romantic expectations. And he had no idea how to satisfy them. No doubt she would find married life a disappointment. It was all he could do to soften the blow a little.

He was better prepared than she for the challenges that lay ahead. Although he was but six years her senior, he had been trained in his duties as heir to the viscountcy since he'd been a mere boy. Miss Trenton might not yet understand the burden of her position. He would need to give her time, introducing her gradually to each facet of public life and, unfortunately, to all the self-absorbed women who formed a part of it. He prayed they would not corrupt her.

He checked the time on the wall clock. Would Miss Trenton want to be fashionably late? Or was she as eager to meet her betrothed as her cousin had implied? He snorted. He doubted James Trenton was a reliable source in such matters.

Lord Howell was thus pondering his bride-to-be's state of mind, when the crunch of wheels upon gravel alerted him to the arrival of her coach. He peered carefully around the edge of the first-floor bedroom curtain, hoping to catch a glimpse of his guest of honor. Below, all was quiet. The footman opened the carriage doors, but no one appeared from within the cabin. There were low voices. He identified one as belonging to James Trenton. It had a distinctive touch of urgency, being clipped, and pitched a little too high. Had Mr. Trenton had to persuade the shy young woman to approach her intended?

The viscount turned back to the center of the room, a little embarrassed for having spied on them. Let her take her time. He would wait until they were shown in before he descended the stairs to greet them. After all, he did not want to appear the eager puppy with his tail wagging hopefully.

It was some minutes before the great doors received their inquiring knock. As they swung open, large and noiseless on their well-oiled hinges, Lord Howell quashed a rising feeling of nervous expectation. He straightened his back and walked from the room across to the landing. At the top of the stairs, he hesitated—but only for a moment—before descending to the foyer to receive his guests.

ELLENA AND JAMES were both silent on their way to Munro

House. She was grateful her cousin did not attempt a pretense at civility when she was still angry with him. No doubt his head was aching, which was as much as he deserved. She had nothing kind to say to him at present and was happy to have Charlotte fill in the awkwardness with her friendly chatter. Charlotte must have taken their silence as a truce, for she spoke excitedly, as though they all shared a mutual joy at the prospect of meeting with the viscount.

They drew up to the main gates, and Ellena sucked in her breath. All animosity toward James was momentarily forgotten as she captured her first view of the magnificent building. The façade over the front entrance was intricately carved to reveal the Howell coat of arms. A filigreed network of interwoven leaves framed the design and extended to the pillars imbedded in the high wall. Above these delicate details rose the weathered features of several statues, exposed to the elements in their proud positions atop the soaring columns. The cumulative effect was an unmistakable declaration of wealth and heritage.

The grandeur of Munro House impressed her, even if its master might not. She had given little thought to the architecture of what was to be her new home. She had, until now, been consumed with crises of varying degrees. With the splendor of its design now apparent before her, a thrill of pleasure rushed through her. She would be mistress within these grand walls.

But first, she would need to conquer their master.

The carriage rolled to a halt and James, who had dozed off— no doubt still battling the effects of his earlier inebriation—woke with a start. Through the window, Ellena saw a footman approach to open the carriage door. She carefully unfolded a piece of deep-blue lace cloth that had lain upon her lap. James did not pay it any notice until she drew it delicately over her head.

"What's that for?" he demanded, forgetting that his right to demand anything was greatly diminished in Ellena's eyes.

"It's a veil," she answered calmly. "One uses it to cover one's head."

"Isn't it jolly?" cried Charlotte, clapping her hands. "Don't you see? Ellena is playing a little game with her beau—a sort of lover's intrigue." Her eyes sparkled with perceived fun. "I lent her my best lace. Doesn't she look just like the mysterious bride Lord Howell is expecting?"

James nearly choked at these words. "You can't be serious!" he spluttered. "Lord Howell is not a man for jokes. He will take your actions as an insult. This is no way to form a first impression!"

Ellena smiled a dangerous little smile within the sanctuary of her concealment. "I believe he has already formed his first impression, thanks to you. As a result of your interference, he has expressed concern that I may be somehow...lacking. As a sign of good faith, I will give him exactly what he wants—the perfect, untouched bride. I shall play the role he appears to demand. I shall not leave your home except in his company, so that he may be certain of my innocent actions. And...he will not see my face until he lifts my wedding veil next week. I would not give him cause to be tempted. I shall preserve my virtue in a manner fitting to assuage his most severe doubts."

James paled. "Please, Ellena, I beg you not to do this."

Ellena answered him with a stubborn silence.

"You can't... I must..." James floundered, then blurted out, "Your father would not wish it."

The tension in the cramped space thickened. Ellena leaned forward so that her face was inches from his.

"You were not so considerate of my father's wishes when you took it upon yourself to offend my betrothed this morning," Ellena hissed. "If I do not reclaim my dignity with this man in whose presence *you* have risked my reputation, I stand to be nothing more than a shadow as his wife. Since my honor is in question, I must stamp out all challenges to its just claim. I do not believe this contradicts my father's intentions."

James opened his mouth and closed it again. He rubbed his forehead.

Good, thought Ellena. *I hope I am giving him a headache.*

Charlotte looked from Ellena to him and back, biting her lip in evident dismay. Ellena had not revealed all to her until now. It had been a necessary omission to gain her assistance with the veil. Charlotte was too kind and agreeable to take such a stand as Ellena knew she must. She was sorry to have used her in this fashion, but if anyone should show remorse, it should be James.

Ellena rose stiffly and climbed from the carriage. She crossed the stony drive, stopping at the first of the entrance steps. "Are you coming, Charlotte?" she called, softening her voice a little. After all, none of this was her fault. Charlotte hurried to join her, a nervous smile hovering upon her mouth. The small party of three proceeded up to the heavy doors, where James reached for the thick, circular knocker without much enthusiasm. A neatly groomed butler greeted them and gestured for them to approach the foyer.

Charlotte touched Ellena's arm, her eyes gazing upward in apparent awe. "My dear, your foyer is grander than any reception hall in all of Munro's finest estates!"

Despite Ellena's apprehension at the imminent meeting, the assignment of the impressive room to her possession warmed her with a tingle of pride. It was truly magnificent. Marble floors shone in the candlelight. The ceiling was encrusted with frescoes. The two farthest corners boasted full-sized, bronze statues inspired by heroes of ancient Greece. Ellena knew, without having seen, that each room would be tastefully decorated with items that had been handed down through the generations, preserved faithfully, without need of frill or trinket to add further character.

The tapestries and paintings were sure to comprise an enviable collection. There would be suits of armor in a corridor somewhere, along with swords and shields once used by the Howell ancestors in the defense of their sovereigns. The grounds would be extensive, with manicured lawns and hedges, perhaps a greenhouse to facilitate the keeping of rare blooms, and most certainly a park with trees as old as the family crest. Ellena felt strangely at home.

Footfalls from the staircase situated between the sculptures pulled her focus in that direction. James all but ran forward to intercept his host.

"Your lordship," he announced, "I have the honor of presenting my cousin, Miss Ellena Trenton. Ellena, meet your betrothed, Lord George Howell."

CHAPTER TEN

THE NEWLY INTRODUCED couple stood frozen in a cameo of surprise. Slowly, George Howell turned his head to James, his gold-flecked eyes flashing beneath his dark forelock. "What is this?" he demanded, indicating Ellena's coverlet.

James could only stammer helplessly in response.

Ellena was equally stunned. Confusion hammered at her mind. "Lord Howell," was all she managed to utter aloud. She spoke these words carefully, for her lips had readied to form the gentler *Dominic*. Her pulse raced. Lord George Howell of Munro House and Dominic of the woodland cottage were one and the same. How could this be? There was no mistaking it. The two men were identical in appearance. And yet, not even their names were the same. Why, in a moment of shy forgetfulness, had the viscount introduced himself as Dominic?

More importantly, she could not believe that kind, thoughtful Dominic could ever utter such slander against a woman's character as George Howell had done earlier that day. Those were the actions of a haughty, unfeeling stranger. Yet here stood Dominic, her rescuer, *and* master of Munro House. And he had, indeed, questioned her chastity.

But Dominic would never have been so vulgar. Would he? Perhaps he had spoken in haste, a rude response to James's equally appalling attempt to gain funds to which he had not been entitled. Or was Lord George Howell truly a callous man? What did she really know about him? Could she trust him? Could she give Lord Howell the benefit of the doubt because he was also dear Dominic?

No, no, she must proceed with her original plan. Whatever she thought she knew about Dominic, it had been but a glimpse into his character. Perhaps he was only kind to helpless maidens whom he thought he would never see again. But of his wife—who would share his name and reputation—he might very well demand harsher terms.

Rebellion flared within her. She had had enough of being little more than a display of a man's wealth and power. She was a person. She had feelings. And she had been deeply wounded. Her honor had been called into question, the wedding proceedings threatened—all before she had even met her intended. Her offender must know that she would not stand for it. Respect must flow in both directions, or her entire marriage would be empty.

Ellena lifted her chin and declared in a voice that only shook a very little, "You will be pleased to know that I have taken note of your concern for my...*cardinal purity.*" She paused for him to grasp her meaning. The viscount's eyes widened. Good. He understood. "I, too, value a woman's innocence and integrity," she declared. "To this end, I pledge to remain within the confines of my cousin's home, save when you see fit to send for me. The veil merely prevents any lustful gaze from falling upon my person." Ellena gave a low curtsy, as if to add gravity and dignity to what she knew were hostile words. She held her ground and waited. Whatever his reaction was, it would show her the real man.

Lord Howell glared at James. "So, you told her, did you?"

James threw up his palms in protest, but the viscount ignored him. *Stupid, petty, little man!* James's foolish attempt at a bribe that morning had necessitated a strong response. But the spineless dog had not taken his punishment well. Instead, he had stirred animosity where delicate handling was most needed. Lord Howell imagined Miss Trenton's growing horror at the unfolding of the facts, and his heart sunk. Well, the damage was done.

He turned his gaze to his betrothed, who stood with quiet pride, challenging his unfortunate private comments with her best defense. He almost laughed out loud at the ridiculous retaliation to which she had felt driven. Perhaps he *did* deserve it to a degree. Miss Trenton could not have known the circumstances of his angry words. Her cousin would have spun the tale to his own advantage. Her actions were understandable if she believed her honor were at stake. He found himself almost admiring her. She was clearly intelligent, even spirited.

Aloud, he merely grunted a throaty *harrumph*. He would let her have her moment of triumph. Perhaps it would soothe her wounded pride sufficiently for them to commence a more regular course on the morrow. Yes…he would call for her and they would be able to talk in private. He would explain the circumstances of his hastily worded comment. He would even apologize. Miss Trenton would understand his intentions and rescind her dramatic decision. She would shyly remove her veil and they would look upon each other as man and woman. Yes, the situation was still salvageable.

A little voice called from a hidden corner of his heart: *It was all so much easier with Nancy. She liked you without reserve—you felt it, didn't you? She, too, was beautiful. Oh, yes, very beautiful. And her lack of dowry would not have mattered. Now you must endure the obstacle course of this courtship between strangers. But this is what you wanted—a girl of mystery who could not judge you—who had to accept you, as her father had willed it. What did you expect? That Miss Ellena Trenton would have no thoughts and feelings of her own? You will have to woo her like any other, even though she is already won.*

Lord Howell became aware of a petulant voice scratching for

his attention. James Trenton was wheedling like a hand-wringing debtor, piling assurances of goodwill upon pleas for his lordship to take no offense. All the while, Miss Trenton stood straight and still, disassociating herself from the embarrassing display. He had to hand it to her, she was viscountess material through and through: dignified, proud, self-controlled, calm under strain. He found he was smiling in spite of himself. He offered her his arm with a flourish of forced confidence. Whatever he did in these first moments, he must not regress to stammering.

"Your c-c…" He paused. Took a calming breath. *This didn't happen with Nancy.*

He shut the intrusive thought away and tried again.

"Your consideration toward my private concerns is duly noted, thank you." He breathed out relief, then cast a dismissive glance at James Trenton. "You may stop apologizing for your cousin. She has acted in good conscience, *haven't you*, Miss Trenton?" Lord Howell looked directly at his future bride, his gaze boring through the camouflage of delicate netting where his sight could not reach. She must not doubt his meaning—if her actions were less than noble, he would not tolerate them—no matter how much she terrified him. For now, he would assume they were well intended. But she would be unwise to risk such dramatic displays again.

Miss Trenton nodded almost imperceptibly. Then she took his arm.

For a moment, George Howell savored the first touch of his bride-to-be. She was wearing long gloves, but her lightly resting fingers were enough to send a tingle up his spine. He tried to block out the memory of another lady's hand, whose fingers touched his without the intervening propriety of a glove. Perhaps even now, those fingers were folded in prayer as their owner knelt beside her new sisters in faith.

To her, he had been Dominic. Caught off-guard in a moment of blind embarrassment, he had offered his second name, the one his friends used. And in that small cabin, he had been Dominic to her Nancy. No formality. No loathed first name. Just the intimacy of a friendship that could never be.

Lord Howell jolted from his treacherous thoughts. This certainly would not do! Shaking his mind free of all such imagery, he strained to resume his role as host. He cleared his throat.

"Shall we go in to dinner?" he asked, although he had already begun to lead the way. "Cook has been fussing all day. I do believe she was trying to impress her new mistress." He smiled in an attempt to bridge the divide between himself and Miss Trenton. But her veiled face revealed nothing.

THEY WALKED THROUGH to the dining room. As they entered, Charlotte resumed her habitual tide of commentary. Perhaps chatter was Charlotte's best coping mechanism, Ellena pondered. She was ashamed that she had created discomfort for her. She had been so determined to undo the harm wrought by these careless men, she had not fully considered the impact it would have on the gentle soul. She must do better. At least for Charlotte's sake.

"My dear Ellena!" Charlotte began with genuine enthusiasm. "What wonderful dinner parties you shall have here! I hope always to be invited. Lord Howell, you must know how much I have looked forward to visiting in your home. But since your sisters married and moved away, Munro House has not held one dance. I suppose you focus more on business meetings yourself. Men can be so dull in that regard. You will not prevent Ellena from entertaining, will you? Your home is well suited for laughter and lights. Do say you'll have a dance very soon. Ellena will be the absolute belle of the ball."

Charlotte's easy manner drew a warm response from their host.

"I should be pleased to have Munro House give its best for you, Mrs. Trenton. But you need not wait for a ball. There will be a grand enough gathering next Friday, after the ceremony. Perhaps that is why the rooms currently display so favorably—they have been given quite thorough attention in preparation for the wedding reception."

"I hazard to guess that they always exhibit impressively," Ellena commented. "Each item here is priceless in value. Your staff doubtless has strict instructions to give precise care to every detail."

Lord Howell—or was it Dominic?—tilted his head. "You have your father's eye for fine things, Miss Trenton."

Ellena blushed at his compliment. She was grateful to be able to observe her betrothed from the safe hiding place behind her veil. Seeing "Dominic" within his native environment made it very clear he was no mere sheriff, as she had assumed when she'd first met him in the cabin. She felt rather foolish for ever thinking of him in such simple terms. But how was she to have guessed the Viscount Howell would be sheltering from the rain in a spartan cottage?

He had been so shy and tongue-tied. Of course, that was a reasonable response to having a maiden wrapped in nothing but a blanket only a few feet away. Here and now, in the comfort of his home, he certainly did not lack eloquence.

The truth of it was, she had misjudged Dominic. And she had misjudged Lord Howell.

She gritted her teeth. The man had spoken harsh words. But it must have been a result of James's manipulation. Dominic was too gentle and George Howell too civilized in his response to her foolish veil for either persona to be prone to such wicked speech.

How absurd she felt, veiled in her betrothed's dining room. It had made far more sense in her head. But here and now, she felt ridiculous. She should just remove it. Such a gesture would show that she had made her point but was willing to build bridges—a far better beginning to her life with Dominic. Yes, Dominic. *Her* Dominic.

Her heart beat a little faster. She had hoped, over and over again, that her betrothed might be like the Dominic of the woods. Now she had her wish. Why let something petty stand in their way? Ellena allowed herself a little daydream in which she threw off her lace and declared herself. She imagined her betrothed's joy at discovering who she was.

Her dream evaporated abruptly. What if he should cry out, "Nancy!" in amazement? She could picture the confusion on the faces of James and Charlotte. How would she explain her previous encounter with their host? The last thing Ellena wanted was for James to know her secret. Even though Dominic was her betrothed, and their night together could therefore cause no lasting scandal, Ellena did not trust James one little bit. It was in his nature to tease her with insinuations. Or worse, he might blurt out her secret when he had been at the brandy again. No, it was too risky to reveal herself to Dominic in front of James. She would have to find another opportunity to do so in private.

Charlotte, meanwhile, had continued her admiring tour of the dining room. James was quiet and sullen. Having dropped his ingratiating act, he stood near the table, implying his readiness to start dinner. *A full stomach would do his curdled innards the world of good*, Ellena thought, and she touched Charlotte lightly at the elbow.

"Come, Charlotte, let us release his lordship from our furious zeal to exclaim at his every possession. Perhaps, if he pleases, we will receive a complete tour after dinner and you shall reward him with a charming song on his pianoforte."

"My singing cannot hope to repay such an honor," gushed Charlotte. "But perhaps a duet with his lovely lady would stir the gentleman's heart to consider your idea."

Ellena touched her draping lace self-consciously. "I'm afraid my contribution would be hampered by my present attire."

Dominic's eyes lit up with hope. "I understand your desire to…to epitomize all things virtuous. But would you not consider our circumstances here sufficiently modest? Perhaps enough to allow an easing of your constraints?" he coaxed gently.

Ellena wanted nothing more than to accommodate such a reasonable request. But the consequences were too risky. She stood, rooted in helplessness, an awkward silence rippling out into the room.

From his position by the table, James erupted like a popped cork from a very moody bottle. "Just take the silly thing off!" he all but shouted. "Can't you see how outrageous it is? His lordship demands it!"

Blood pounded though Ellena's body, and all clarity of thought deserted her. She blurted out an impulsive "No!", which caught even herself by surprise. Ellena wished fervently she had not sounded so stubborn. She would have liked to deal James a well-aimed kick, ladylike or not. If not for him, she would have given a more considered reply to the delicate request from Dominic.

Even Charlotte was taken aback. "But, Ellena, surely, you did not mean to continue with this game? Your poor beau has suffered enough being denied the joy of knowing your face. Shall we not put this cloth aside now?" She reached for its embroidered edge.

Ellena stepped back abruptly. Her heartbeat pulsed wildly. She was trapped in a situation that begged the one outcome she felt unable to provide. She dared not reveal her face so suddenly. She needed to prepare Dominic for the shock of whom he would discover when the masquerade ended.

Or maybe, her racing thoughts suggested, *maybe I should just throw caution to the wind and pray all will be well.* Perhaps that was best. Whatever the veil had once symbolized, its continued presence was only creating further harm.

Ellena reached her hand slowly up to her face at the same moment that James, wild with vexation, grabbed at the offending article. He would have wrenched it from her were it not for the iron grip of the viscount's hand upon his wrist, his knuckles flexed white with exertion.

"That is quite enough." Dominic spoke with the dangerous

calm of one whose patience was tested to breaking point. "This is still *my* home. Miss Trenton is my guest. She has chosen to wear this accessory tonight and—though we may find her choice unusual—it shall be honored. Is this clear?"

James whimpered under the tourniquet grasp. He nodded vehemently and was released.

Dominic's gesture stunned the desperate Ellena. It was the most noble use of power she had ever witnessed. And it had been done for *her* benefit—she who had dared to defy the man in his own home at their first official meeting.

She trembled as her heightened emotion subsided. "Th-Thank you," she almost sobbed. "I regret that I cannot repay you by granting what you all wish from me. I dare ask nothing, yet I beg your patience."

Dominic's expression softened. But a frown remained. To his credit, he did not question her stubbornness in retaining the veil. He must wonder what on Earth he had taken on when he'd chosen her as his bride. Still, she reminded herself, he only had himself to blame for the callous words he had uttered. If it had not been for his own foolishness, she would not have responded with a taste of her own.

He took a deep, cleansing breath. "We shall not speak of this further," he declared to everyone in the room. "Let us focus, instead, on enjoying an excellent menu from Cook and her able staff."

He walked to the corner of the table and indicated a chair to his right. "Will you not be seated, Miss Trenton?"

Ellena lowered herself into the proffered chair and began to tug at the tips of her gloves. She was uncomfortably aware of the ugly scratches on her arms that would now be revealed. Would Dominic notice how similar they were to Nancy's injuries?

Probably not. He had been so bashful around her in the woods. He had hardly even looked at her. Well, he would look at her now.

She thrilled at the thought of his gaze upon her. How confident he was in his own home! How she would blush if his eyes looked boldly into hers. But the veil prevented it.

Perhaps tomorrow he would do just that. He might cup her chin in his strong hand and trace the contour of her cheek with his thumb. She would lean into his touch. She would whisper his name. *Dominic.* Her very own, dear Dominic. She could forgive the awkward hero from the cottage almost anything. And if George Howell was no different, he would not let her down again.

Ellena laid her gloves upon her lap while the footmen settled the party in their seats and proceeded to bring helpings of steaming soup to the table. She noted the intricate painting on each bowl. The silverware gleamed with polish, each setting laid out immaculately. The smell of the aromatic herbs wafted up to her nose and tempted her toward the hot dish before her.

Her heart sank.

She could not put the spoon to her mouth.

After a few cooling breaths, the others sipped several spoonfuls before they noticed her predicament. There was an uncomfortable moment, then each resumed their discreet slurping, focusing with great concentration on their own square foot of table. No one was going to risk another incident. Ellena was on her own.

She sat for a while, stirring her soup hypnotically, as if waiting for it to spontaneously evaporate. Eventually, with a sigh, she slid her hand in under the lace and lifted its canopy away from her face to accommodate the movement of her spoon. She took care not to let the ornate trim dip into the contents of the bowl, bringing each mouthful into the seclusion of her drapery before consuming it. It was no doubt bizarre for the others to behold and no less so to perform. Ellena berated herself for this situation. She had imprisoned herself with her decision to remain veiled and had, just moments before, missed an opportunity to be released from it. She would have to bear it with some dignity. Oh, what stories the butler would share with the other servants about their strange new mistress!

Halfway through the next course, the strain eased somewhat and gentle conversation resumed. Charlotte provided for much of the lighter fare and James discussed matters of commerce, having mercifully steered clear of all drink bar one glass of wine, which he sipped slowly. Ellena, keen to know Dominic beyond these topics, turned the conversation to focus on him.

"Do you travel much, Lord Howell?"

"Some, yes, but mostly on business. I'm afraid there is little pleasure in holidaying alone. Besides, I am almost constantly called upon to tend to matters in the interests of the city."

"Your devotion is most admirable," replied Ellena. "So many gentlemen while away their time with activities of leisure. You, however, not only maintain your historical home and ensure a healthy income, but also further the cause of the common man under your care. It is small wonder you have not previously found time to marry."

"Why, Lord Howell," Charlotte remarked, "I do believe you are blushing! You shall have to become used to receiving compliments from your wife. A man of your stature is surely accustomed to hearing words of admiration."

Dominic shook his head solemnly. "Regrettably, Mrs. Trenton, I am seldom on the receiving end of such lofty praise—at least from a lady, that is. It will certainly be a novelty, but I shall endeavor to accept it graciously."

"Come now, sir, you cannot fool us," Charlotte insisted. "Young ladies throughout Munro must have swooned with disappointment when you announced your engagement to our Ellena here."

"Alas," said their host with a soft smile, "I am unaware of such fainting *en masse*. Perhaps it is just as well, as the multitude of their unconscious forms would have slowed traffic in the main shopping thoroughfare."

Charlotte clapped her hands in delight. "There! A sense of humor, to boot! Ellena, is your betrothed not the most eligible find? So much like my James when we first met."

So implausible was this comparison that Ellena, who had been delicately gnawing at a chicken leg, choked on a mouthful and coughed with great force to dislodge it. She waved away offers of assistance, taking several swallows of water to clear her throat. It wasn't long before she was settled again, with the added satisfaction of seeing Dominic suppress a smile behind his napkin.

As one course followed another, the mood became lighter, and James mercifully steered clear of the wine. When they had had their fill from the array of sugary dessert treats, Ellena felt emboldened to repeat her earlier request.

"Lord Howell, would now be an opportune time to see the rest of the ground floor? I know Charlotte would be delighted, and I would be grateful for a broader glance over your remarkable home."

He nodded. "Certainly, but only if Mrs. Trenton makes good on her promise to play for us. My pianoforte is greatly neglected. It would benefit from a woman's touch."

"Ellena sings and plays far better than I do," Charlotte declared. "Shall we not have her entertain us instead?"

Dominic looked at Ellena. She stared anxiously at her hands in her lap. "No," he answered, "I shall leave that pleasure to be savored at another opportunity. Tonight, Mrs. Trenton, if you will, we are your captive audience. Surely, you will not deny us that privilege?"

Charlotte's cheeks flushed. "Oh…well, if it must be so, I shall oblige, of course. But truly, it is best if I do not sing. My playing is pleasant enough, but my voice is barely passable. It is just as well there was no need to serenade my dear James. It would have been a disastrous courtship!"

"It would have been nothing of the kind," Ellena protested, "for my cousin is blessed to have you, Charlotte."

"Why, Ellena, what a sweet thing to say! I do believe I have never been as flattered as I have here tonight."

"A shame, don't you think, James?" Ellena asked, giving her

cousin a sidelong glance. "Surely, a married woman should experience at least as many compliments as her unmarried counterparts? If her husband does not pay her attention, she is certain to fall into ruin, like a once-cherished home that lacks paint and has patches of mold on the wallpaper."

James Trenton glared at his cousin. "Some women fall into ruin without the excuse of neglect. There are those who crave so much attention, they are not satisfied with that which only one man can offer. Soon, the master of *that* house finds his doormat quite worn-out with use!"

Ellena gasped in horror. "Oh, you are a wicked man, James—always considering things from the worst perspective. How did you ever win Charlotte's heart with such unromantic formulas?"

"Actually," Charlotte said, chiming in, "he was an exemplary suitor. You would be surprised, Ellena, to see your cousin so devoted in his adoration."

"I would indeed!"

"Not a day went by that I did not receive a thoughtful gift—a fistful of flowers he had picked himself, new thread for my embroidery, for he has always found my work quite clever, a velvet ribbon for my waist—so many that I cannot now recall them all. His attentions were kind and consistent. Are these not the hallmark of the perfect gentleman?"

They would be, Ellena thought, *if they were not associated with the manipulative bully I have known since childhood.* It was hard to reconcile James the husband with James the cousin who would pinch her arm when her father hadn't been looking.

"Truly," Ellena admitted, "I am forced to concede James a model among men if such was his manner of wooing. And does he continue his attentions with such vigor in his married life?"

"Not to the same degree." Charlotte shrugged. "But that is to be expected. I want for nothing, and James will spoil me with gifts at a whim. Indeed, I would not demand an infinite courtship. Being a wife and mother has shown me new joys that replace the superficial pleasures of being wooed."

"Ha!" James burst out triumphantly. "It appears you have underestimated the worth of quiet bliss, Cousin. Marriage is not the playground of flirtation. If a woman is to be likened to a house, as you suggested in your earlier analogy, then marriage is the climbing ivy that wraps about her and gives her a sense of home."

Ellena conceded defeat with a laugh.

"Dear me! I surrender! You have the victory, both in the argument and in your happy lives. Forgive me, James. I had no idea you were such an expert on matters of the heart. I wave the white flag and declare myself greatly enlightened."

James, however, remained serious.

"You tease and jest," he scolded, "but your own experience is sorely lacking. Still, you feel entitled to mock others because they do not reflect your unrealistic ideals."

Ellena wanted to take umbrage at his words. But there was too much truth in them for their sting to last. Instead, she answered meekly.

"You are right, James. I might complain that your comments are harsh, but they are accurate. It is convenient to laugh away one's error of judgment. And I have misjudged you in the arena of love. For this, I apologize. As for my inexperience, that is unavoidable. My naivety is the fault of circumstance. Blind hope and vague dreams are a stalwart against a fear of the unknown."

And with that, Ellena grew quiet within her thoughts. James was no angel. Yet he clearly doted on his wife. Would this be the case with Dominic also? Might he lapse into moments of sudden cruelty, only to regret them hours or even moments later? And would he ever show his callous side to her face? James somehow kept his true self fully separate from the person he was to his wife and children. Would Dominic manage that also? And would it be enough? She did not think she could bear having someone like James for a husband, even if his very best was reserved for her.

She wanted so very much to believe in Dominic. She *needed* to believe in him. As yet, however, there was too much she did not know. She raised her eyes uneasily to meet his own. But the veil prevented her from making any true connection.

DOMINIC SHIFTED UNCOMFORTABLY in his chair at Miss Trenton's left elbow. Her comments had caught him by surprise. Her fears were surprisingly similar to his. How alone and unprepared she must feel to take on the role of wife to a stranger!

He had no words of reassurance for her. Where should eloquence spring from when matters of the heart had always struck him dumb? Oh, he had presence enough where his money and title were respected. But where a glibness of tongue was required to win a fair lady, he was utterly helpless. It was easy to haggle with men of the trade. Their greed and hard terms were a challenge he quickly overcame, developing an intuitive sense of where the line was drawn between their interests and his and never backing down until they met him, toe to toe, at this line. However, the moment he found himself in the company of ladies, his mental mechanisms refused to function optimally. Even sweet Nancy, entirely dependent on his goodwill, had almost struck him mute. He had never stood a chance with the jaded women of Munro's elite.

Having grown up with his sisters' scornful looks, Dominic recognized it all too easily in the faces of the ladies of society. Their words were smooth with practiced deception, but their eyes contained private contempt. Any one of them would gladly have grabbed at the chance to be the Viscountess Howell, but it would not have been for the privilege of being his wife.

It should have been easier with someone like Miss Trenton, a woman who had not known decadence and snobbery. However, now that she was here, he found her far more complex than he had imagined she would be. Her integrity was without question. Her wit and intelligence demanded that he be ready for a challenge, but this was not entirely unpleasant. No, it was the finer points of interaction—the nuances between man and woman—that escaped him.

He did not know where to begin. Should he bring offerings of gifts, as Mrs. Trenton claimed her husband had done? The idea of imitating this man, even in a noble venture, was not inviting. Besides, what did Miss Trenton really want? He was positive she was not enticed by his wealth, as others had been, though she had a refined appreciation for things of value. One thing was certain: she had very definite romantic inclinations. Was this the way? It was not his one of his strengths. He would not know how to proceed, nor how to maintain such a path toward her heart. But perhaps…one grand gesture, something that said it all once and with such clarity that a stream of subsequent actions was not required.

Dominic replayed the events of the day with its myriad of new information, sifting for a clue to inspire him.

He found it in the unlikeliest of places and felt a surge of delighted triumph. He would have a little word with Mrs. Trenton when they were leaving. His bride-to-be would be receiving a gift after all.

CHAPTER ELEVEN

T HE ROOM HAD now fallen silent. Ellena and her companions looked expectantly at their host.

"Ah, yes, the promised tour," said Dominic, rising from his seat.

Ellena once again accepted his arm when it was offered, the newness of the action thrilling through her. She wrapped her fingers around the muscle that flexed beneath the sleeve of his evening jacket. He was strong, his nearness inviting. She wanted nothing more than to rest her head upon his shoulder. And yet, she did not yet know if it was safe to do so. If only she could be certain of his true nature. Besides, it would certainly confuse Dominic. Such a show of tenderness could not come from a woman who remained veiled in his company. Instead, she listened as Charlotte remarked on every detail, from the draperies to the clocks, while James barely concealed his boredom.

Their gradual winding in and out of rooms finally brought them to the one which housed the pianoforte. James threw himself into the comfortable arms of a decadently upholstered chair, while Charlotte took a seat self-consciously at the piano. She called softly to him.

"James, I am quite aquiver with nerves. Won't you stand by me and lend your voice to my playing? It will give me courage and perhaps even help to mask any false notes."

Her husband rose at once, crossed the floor, and positioned himself at her side. Charlotte beamed up at him and relaxed visibly.

"What shall we entertain them with?" James asked. "A bright ditty, or something to pluck at the emotions? Just not that awful new duet we learned at the Macraes' dinner party. The harmonizing was not properly set to the melody. It positively *gnawed* at the ears."

Ellena's mouth hung open. She shut it quickly, grateful for the secrecy she could maintain behind her veil. She had no idea her cousin sang well, or even enjoyed singing, for that matter. Each day, each hour, taught her so much that was entirely new. She looked sidelong at Dominic, curiosity twitching her mouth into a thoughtful pout. Had she already learned *his* deepest secrets?

Charlotte, meanwhile, had given the duet some thought. "It must be a song to woo by, slow and sincere, with a theme of requited love." She smiled warmly at Ellena. Then, quite suddenly, inspiration seemed to hit her. "Wait!" she cried, throwing her hands up as if to halt all further suggestions. "I know just the thing—my favorite by Burns!"

James knew it at once. "You mean, 'My love is like a…'"

"'…Red, red rose,'" Charlotte said, finishing the first line for him. "Yes, that's the one! I could play that without stumbling. I practice it so often at home. What do you think? It is perfectly suited to your voice."

A tender smile played upon her husband's lips. "Was it not the first song we sang together?" His eyes drifted to hers. "I remember. It was—until that moment—the dullest gathering I had ever had the misfortune of attending. The weather had turned the roads to mud. The ladies who arrived all complained they were ill-prepared for the chill in the air and that their new dresses were splashed by discourteous coachmen. Though many more had been invited, most stayed home to enjoy the comforts of their own fire and a warm rug."

"Mother had insisted I go," Charlotte recalled. "Father was complaining I was not getting good use from my new dress, which he had bought at great expense."

James nodded, his gaze imagining the scene as though it were before him. "I see it clearly, even now. It was the soft-pink one with the pale-green trim." He turned to Charlotte with a warmth that glowed on his lips and lashes that lowered with longing. "You appeared like a freshly picked bud amongst the faded blooms."

Charlotte flushed with evident pleasure at his endearing remembrance. "There were many other ladies present who were far lovelier than I."

James shook his head. "That may be so…in their eyes. But their vanity exceeded their appeal. You were, and are, blessed by your own modesty, my dear. Your childlike exuberance has always touched your cheek with the faint blush of breathless enthusiasm. It is most becoming."

The intimacy between husband and wife—both innocent and impassioned—caused Ellena to look away in an attempt to grant them privacy. Dominic, by contrast, was drinking it all in, staring at them intently, as though studying an exquisitely drawn sketch. His ears were quite red with felt emotion, but he did not draw his eyes from the scene before him.

Ellena cleared her throat to break the spell. "Ahem. I should very much like to hear the song that has stirred such happy memories. I am familiar with the poem of which you speak, but I have never heard it set to music."

Charlotte and James did not immediately withdraw their mutual gaze from one other. They positioned their bodies in readiness for music, but their eyes spoke of a deeper connection than mere song. When the first chords were played, and James gave voice to the lyrics, they were still truly alone in their own cocoon. His notes were rich and melodious, and the words poured out like a warm caress. Charlotte's fingers were steady and strong under its influence. The notes were slow and deliberate, each one granting room for the full, round tones of James's tenor. The heart with which he sang lent deeper vibrations to each chord.

Ellena was uncomfortably aware that Dominic was now looking at her. His eyes were filled with meaning. His mouth was soft and full.

A memory drifted up—of a man, this man, touching her hand at the end of her extended bare arm as if afraid he might break it; a man whose broad back had known the feel of her cheek as they'd journeyed on a shared horse; a man who had called her shyly by her given name.

No, she corrected herself, *that isn't true.* He had called her "Nancy." What would he think if he knew that Nancy sat right under his nose? Would he continue to look at her as he did now—with rapt attention and seemingly genuine interest?

The musical duo, evidently having warmed up to the idea of providing entertainment, continued with several more equally fine renderings of popular ballads and melodies. It did not matter that their audience neither applauded politely nor spoke with praise. Mr. and Mrs. Trenton were absorbed in their mutual indulgence and needed no external encouragement.

After a second song had followed, Dominic rose from his chair and approached Ellena where she sat perched upon a settee.

"May I join you? It seems we are not wanted." He indicated the couple at the piano.

She nodded and shifted aside to make room for him.

"They are quite talented," Dominic declared.

"I am as new to the enjoyment of their performance as you are," Ellena confessed. "Charlotte has always been reserved in her own praise, but it is remarkable that James's skill is not more widely known."

Dominic hesitated. "Er... Here in Munro, his willingness to take center stage is common knowledge." He tilted his head quizzically. "I gather you are not a regular visitor at Thorn Bush Hall?"

"Quite the opposite. Since our childhood, when we were often thrown together, I have encountered James only a handful of times at our own home, when Father has sent for him on matters of business. James did not sing then. There is no music of this nature in our home. Of course, I have been taught the more formal classics, but these lighter numbers are considered inappropriate. One does not attract the right sort of interest with frivolity and laughter."

"Interest? In what?"

Ellena hesitated. She had assumed he understood. "In… In…serious negotiations among…men of business." She tried to insinuate her father's mercenary approach to her prospects, realized Dominic did not comprehend, and gave up.

"I suppose your father feels it will distract them in their careful dance of numbers," Dominic answered, seemingly none the wiser.

"Do you not find it somber to live without music or society?" Ellena asked quickly, eager to change the subject. "I mean, especially now that your mother and married sisters are no longer sharing the household with you."

Dominic shrugged. "From what you have said before, I gather it is no different to the way you have lived at Trenton Grange."

"True, but you see, I *did* find it too somber."

"Ah! But you would have had tea with your neighbors, perhaps an afternoon of bridge? Music and parties are not the only means to lift one's spirits. I know your father limited your exposure to greater society, but I imagine you were a favorite guest among the few acquaintances you had in your hometown."

Ellena's gaze dropped. "Thank you," she answered rather more quietly. "Your assumption is flattering, but underserved. I do not wish to appear ungrateful for the well-intentioned efforts of my parents, but there have been many sacrifices expected of me. Mother limited my activities even in the neighborhood so that I might not come under the influence of poor character. I do have one very dear friend, but I doubt she would be granted access to the upper circles of Munro society."

Her voice cracked a little as she said this.

"Oh? What are her shortcomings that she should be denied such a dubious privilege?"

"She is limited by both birth and income, though her character is beyond reproach."

Dominic frowned. "If the latter is true, it sounds to me that society would be hard-pressed to match her qualifications. Her presence could only lend improvement to their company."

Ellena laughed at his obvious disgust with Munro's elite. "You do not have a favorable opinion of the members of the upper class," she observed. "Yet your position places you among them. How do you excuse yourself from sharing in the criticisms they must bear from you?"

A smile replaced Dominic's earlier scowl. "I do so by excusing myself as far and as often as possible from their company."

"Dear me!" Ellena feigned shock. "Shall I be left to fend for myself among these unfortunate individuals who share such stout disapproval from you?"

"I do not imagine they would be the slightest challenge for you." Dominic grinned. "You could send for your friend and offend their sensibilities by making her your first guest of honor. Ha! I shall want the front-row seat to that spectacle!"

Ellena was suddenly serious. "I would not use Jilly in that way. I know that you meant it in jest. It's just that she has been the best part of my childhood, and I could never suffer any harm to come to her."

Dominic's tone quickly sobered. "Yes, of course. I look forward to meeting the friend you hold in such high regard. But we shall not have her look a fool."

He tipped his head in thought.

"Would you like to have her visit with us awhile? Perhaps, when I need be away a distance on business, she could be sent for to keep you company. Would that please you?"

Ellena clutched her hands excitedly to her chest. "Very much!

Jillian would be beside herself with anticipation."

"Well!" His mouth widened into a grin, his eyes wrinkling, the gold flecks lighting up with mischief. "I hope she does not will me from my own home to facilitate her visit!"

"Indeed, she would not dream of it," came the earnest reply.

DOMINIC GLOWED WITH joy at the growing ease of conversation. He had just been himself. As he had been with Nancy. Did he imagine it, or were their voices very similar? Since he could not see her face, he had been listening keenly to her voice. And perhaps, because he had liked Nancy so very much, he wanted his betrothed to be just like her. It might be that they were from the same county, for there were certain expressions they both had used, and a lilt that suggested a common origin. Since Nancy was unavailable, he was grateful that there was something of her in Miss Ellena Trenton. In time, he hoped he might grow to care for his betrothed in her own right. He already felt a deepening connection between them.

He had even given her a moment of happiness. He felt certain he could do it again. Her happiness fed his own. And the possibility that this might be the start of a sound and blissful relationship drove him to act upon his next impulse.

"This Miss Jillian you speak of—she is clearly important to you. Let us make a plan at once. Why do we not have her remain for a few weeks after the wedding? Having someone familiar with whom to talk may help you adjust to married life."

He had not expected his suggestion to be followed by such a long pause. When Miss Trenton finally answered, it was with hunched shoulders and muted tone.

"It is a wonderful idea, and I thank you for suggesting it, but Jillian will not be attending the wedding."

Dominic was aghast. "How is that possible? How can your

closest friend not be present on such a day?"

Miss Trenton's voice was very small. "My parents are not willing to include her. You see, her father is our groundskeeper, and our friendship never carried my parents' blessing. I think they rather approve of the distance between us now."

His heart clenched at her words. He understood such loneliness all too well.

"Give me a moment," he said. "I want to show you something." He stood up and walked across to the mantelpiece, which was crowded with family portraits. He selected one and returned to their shared seat, tilting the frame so that Miss Trenton could see its contents. Displayed within was a group of three women, one seated and two others standing behind her. They were adorned with jewels and other finery. Not one was smiling, not even the shy, inward smile so often reserved for portraits.

"My mother and sisters," said Dominic, without sentiment. "My mother is from French aristocracy. It was from her family that Vivienne inherited her name, and I gained my second name, Dominic."

Miss Trenton's head lifted quite suddenly. "Dominic is your second name?" she asked.

"Yes, and I much prefer it."

"You do not like your first name, then? Is it not a family name?"

"It is true. Our father was also a George. My sister Georgina, who was born before me, was named after him, poor girl. Then, when he got the son he wanted, he promptly also passed his name to me, as if Georgina did not exist. It was very much the way Father did things, without much thought for others. It is therefore not a name I carry with any great enthusiasm."

"I see," Miss Trenton said quietly. "Dominic is a good name. I think it suits you well."

A peace settled upon him. "I am glad to hear it. It is yours to use freely when you and I are wed."

Miss Trenton lowered her head again, her fingers tracing the features of his mother's face as if to see him in them.

"A proud woman," said Dominic. "But one with a sad story. Father brought Mother back home with him after a business trip, as though she were part of the shipment he had acquired. Her continental beauty was the talk of Munro, and he loved to show her off at dinners like a new addition to his collection of assets. I'm afraid he was not a man of sensibilities. Money was his first love. Which is why he gladly bore the condescension of his peers for the sake of making more of it.

"My mother had no illusions. Her family had trained her to bear all for the sake of a good match, as it seems yours has, too. And these teachings became the foundation upon which she modeled her own parenting. In time, her beauty was dulled by a lack of laughter to soften the mouth. My sisters were spoiled by my father, who wished them silent and found that money ended their nagging."

Miss Trenton considered the portrait, then lifted her gaze to Dominic. "But you are not like them," she declared. "You are neither selfish nor miserable."

Her words stalled him. How could she know whether it was so? The wearing of her veil was proof that he had faults enough. Yet she spoke with confidence, as if experience had shown her what to believe. Her praise was so freely spoken, and yet he struggled to accept it. This was not how conversations with women usually went. It was a rare gift. One he'd thought would be limited to Nancy. To have such praise come from the lips of his intended was more than he could have hoped for at their first meeting. And he wanted a moment to savor it.

"Thank you," he said eventually. "But I did enjoy a different set of circumstances. I escaped the worst of my father's influence through my work, which occupied me from a very young age. I encountered many other young men who were apprenticed in their fathers' trades—clerks and accountants, merchants and bankers. Since we were young, we were not as sorely hampered by status then as we would be now. From them, I learned what comprised true character. It had nothing to do with wealth or titles. As a result, I have a handful of loyal friends, of whom perhaps only one would have met with my father's approval. We dine together as often as we can manage. If not for them, I would have pined away in my own company or, worse still, had to endure the false favor of those who would seek my friendship only to profit from it. So you see, I understand all too well. This Miss Jillian of whom you speak is a crucial part of your sanity and happiness. I will endeavor to convince your father she is an essential element of your wedding retinue, or at least an honored guest. Failing that, she shall be sent for at my personal invitation."

A long silence followed. Miss Trenton did not move, but her gaze held him with an intensity he felt rather than saw.

"This…" She faltered. "This is the nicest thing anyone has ever… I cannot find the words. You don't know what this means to me."

"Oh, but I do. That is why I insist. I am glad to be able to do this for you." Oh, she could scarce know how glad he was! All his adult life, he had struggled to make any real connection with a woman. He had always assumed he simply didn't have it in him. But he did! And this woman who was to be his wife had shown him it was possible!

Miss Trenton laid her hand lightly upon his. "Thank you. With all my heart."

Dominic looked at her hand as if it were a blossom, drifting down to rest. Its soft touch was both electrifying and soothing. He cherished the moment. It had been so easy! Such a simple gesture could make her so happy. He could do this. He just had to follow his instincts. His efforts would not be trampled upon. Miss Trenton would value them and think better of him. He could do this!

The hallway clock gonged sonorously. The duo at the piano stopped their light-hearted amusement abruptly. Dominic looked at his pocket watch. Midnight.

"Is it so late already?" marveled Mrs. Trenton. "How quickly the time has gone!"

"I'm afraid we must relieve you of our company, Lord Howell." James was suddenly serious and responsible again. "My wife needs her rest." His eyes fell upon her swollen belly.

"Midnight..." murmured Dominic.

Miss Trenton rose with her hand extended. "It has been a great privilege. I await our next meeting keenly."

Dominic took the proffered hand and brought it delicately to his lips. He hardly dared breathe for fear the moment would dissipate. The scent of her skin lingered in the air and he committed it to memory to savor at leisure. Then he released her.

Only a few hours hence, the sun would be up and he could awake with a light heart. He would call on her as early as etiquette allowed and there would be no further cause for her clandestine veil. He would be able to cherish her eyes and cheek and mouth, as he had the rest. He would find the right words to pay her compliments, and she would maybe touch his hand again, lingering a little longer, perhaps before withdrawing her warm fingers.

The party left the room in unison, led by Dominic. The guests collected their cloaks at the door, each thanking their host in turn for the charming evening. A footman helped James with his overcoat, then tended to Mrs. Trenton. When Miss Trenton stepped forward to receive her wrap, Dominic took it from the attendant and held it open to receive her.

"Miss Trenton, if I may?"

She stepped into the offered space while he drew the remainder of the cloth across her shoulders. Pulling the ribbon, she closed the neck and tied it deftly. Then she looked up into his face, the veil shifting as she did so, and said softly, "Please, call me 'Ellena.'"

He bowed in acceptance and replied, "And you must call me 'Dominic.'"

"Dominic..." She seemed to embrace his name with her lips. "Goodnight...Dominic." She turned to go.

James helped his wife down the steps and into the carriage, then turned to assist his cousin. The pleasures of the latter part of the evening had apparently purged him of his earlier disgrace and accompanying mood. He smiled slightly as he touched his hat to the viscount.

Dominic bid them safely home, then watched as their driver directed the carriage from the door of Munro House and down the lane. But never again out of reach. Never again would he need to long for a woman he could not have. He had found his Ellena. And the dream of Nancy could be put to rest.

He whistled a pleasant, aimless tune as he undressed for bed. He grinned happily at the thought of the gift he would present to his unsuspecting lady at their next meeting.

A flash of horror tightened his chest. He had forgotten to speak to Mrs. Trenton on the matter! He sat down in his robe and wrote a quick note, sealed it, and gave it to his valet.

"Fuller, I want you to send young Fred to Thorn Bush Hall with this letter first thing in the morning. It is for the lady of the house, Mrs. Trenton. Tell him to wait for an answer and that I am anxious for him to deliver it to me with all possible speed."

"Yes, sir. It shall be done exactly as you wish," Fuller replied. He was not the conversational sort, nor had he ever needed to be. Tonight, Dominic was especially thankful for it, as he wanted to be alone with his own thoughts.

"Thank you, Fuller. That is all."

"Goodnight, sir."

After his valet had left the room, Dominic retired to bed, a little less jubilant due to the brief crisis but happy nonetheless. He pictured Ellena in the carriage, making her way back to her cousin's home. He smiled dreamily at the thought of her and drifted off to sleep. The imagined carriage and its precious cargo pushed into the night with the slowed motion of dream thought.

All at once, the sound of new hoof beats filled the air, accompanied by shouts of "Whoa!" and "Hold!" Masked men drifted in from the surrounding darkness and drove the coach to a halt.

Mrs. Trenton's eyes were wide with fear. But not from the sight of the strange men. No, for it was James Trenton who drew a pistol from his waist and pointed it at his cousin. "I want your dowry. You shall give it to me or perish."

A bandit threw open the right door, distracting Trenton for but a second. The veiled woman grabbed this chance and threw herself from the door on the left, sprawling across the muddy road and rising again quickly in her haste to escape. With the violence of her movements, her covering was lost and her face was revealed.

It was Nancy.

The dream disintegrated and Dominic stirred in his slumber. In a moment, he was asleep again, this time more deeply, and no more strange images disturbed his imagination until the curtains glowed with the light of the morning sun.

CHAPTER TWELVE

A FTER A LATE breakfast alone, Ellena was just leaving the dining room when Charlotte met her in the doorway, and exclaimed, "Lucy told me you were up. Wait right here!"

She disappeared for a minute, while Ellena stood, obedient but perplexed.

When Charlotte returned, she was smiling broadly, her arms loaded with a large package.

"Look what has arrived for you!" she cried, her face bright with anticipation and a knowing twinkle. "I wonder what it can be?" Charlotte grinned, giving away her obvious knowledge of its contents and stirring curiosity within Ellena.

"There is a note with it." Charlotte thrust the folded paper forward so suddenly that Ellena barely had her hands open to receive it. She recognized the seal as belonging to the Howell estate and turned away to afford herself some semblance of privacy in opening it. It was but a single page, and she quickly perused its contents.

"He has a fine hand, does he not?" said Charlotte, peering around her shoulder. Ellena had noticed the same but was far more intrigued by the words themselves than the strokes of the pen. She passed the note for Charlotte's perusal and was rewarded with the receipt of the parcel, wrapped in fine paper tissue.

Charlotte read aloud.

My dear Ellena,

It is with profound regret that I must delay our next meeting. Several difficulties have arisen with a contract newly brokered, and I must tend to them to satisfy the parties involved. Please believe that it is only necessity that prevents me from calling.

To occupy you pleasantly in my absence, I have sent a gift for which you may find immediate use. I hope it shall prove satisfactory. If not, you may, of course, exchange it for something more suitable.

If it pleases you, I shall be glad of your company at church in the morning and shall take the opportunity to introduce you to the clergyman who leads our vows next week. Until then, I am indeed a sorrier man for the loss of your conversation.

Most sincerely,
Dominic

Charlotte's hand flew to her cheek. "Oh, my! Ellena, you have his heart in your palm! Such eloquent misery… You have slain the poor man with Cupid's arrow."

"He speaks with feeling." Ellena nodded. "It is easier in a letter, is it not? There is time to weigh each thought and choose each word without fear of interruption or disapproval at the first attempt."

No doubt he would have benefitted from such restraint when dealing with James. She had forgiven him now, but the sting of his barb was not quite worked out from under her skin. In time, it would smart less. And letters like these certainly helped put a balm on the wound.

"Nevertheless," she continued, "I did not expect him to sound quite so…eager."

Charlotte's laughter rang through the air.

"Goodness, Ellena! The man is completely smitten! And all without even laying eyes upon your lovely face. There shall be much more of the same—*eagerness*, did you call it?—before you are even bound in marriage. This letter is but a forerunner of many more such declarations. You may be sure of it. Now, open your present."

Charlotte followed Ellena into the drawing room and waited as she undid the string. She watched her cousin peel back the layers of paper and withdraw from its nest multiple folds of cream cloth. Ellena ran her fingertips over the leaf detail of the sheer, sprigged silk. Its design was embroidered with gold thread in an ornate stitch.

"It's perfect," she breathed, then she looked up at the beaming Charlotte. "But why?"

"Oh, don't be looking at me for answers. I simply replied to his note this morning."

"What note? When did it arrive?"

"With our earliest rising. Its plea was to know of your preference in fabric for the wedding gown. His lordship's servant made great haste to return my answer to Munro House. I am sure Lord Howell meant to bring this with him on a visit today. But I see he has sent it instead as an emissary. He also gave this card. It provides the name of a seamstress his family has used for years. Her needle is said to have created some quite enviable gowns for those ladies who can afford her."

Ellena's eyes returned to the costly cloth. "It is unlikely I fall into that category. Not with the remainder of the purse Father has sent."

"On the contrary." James spoke up from his chair behind them. He folded the morning paper and lay it across his knee. "If his lordship has provided the cloth, you have ample monies left to pay for the work upon it. I will even go so far as to say I will make up the difference in fees if it should come to that, though I doubt it will be necessary."

"Why would you do that?" Ellena was amazed.

"Because the viscount has made a noble gesture with this gift. Anyone can see it is an olive branch to us both. Though I imagine its message carries a little more than mere reconciliation in your case." He smiled knowingly. "As for me, I would be a fool to ignore its meaning. Perhaps…" He paused, looking down uncomfortably. "Perhaps I have been foolish before, reckless, even." He set his mouth grimly. "To regain the approval of an influential man, I am willing to make sacrifices."

Charlotte took his arm and kissed him on the cheek. "Well done, my love. You match his generosity with your own. It is so characteristic of you and a reflection of your good nature. I am pleased to have our cousin see you in this light."

Ellena, though surprised by James's confession, was not persuaded that he was now on par with Dominic. Her betrothed's letter and gift were intended to woo her, to bring her joy. As far as she could tell, however, her cousin's generous thoughts were ultimately self-serving. It wouldn't be long before his true colors showed again. As for Dominic, she must believe his one faux pas was an isolated incident, one he regretted deeply. Unlike James, her intended had done nothing else to show himself a villain. However, she kept her opinion to herself.

Charlotte's smile now radiated at Ellena. "Shall we send for the dressmaker straight away? You should have something to report to your betrothed at your next meeting. Besides which, we dare not risk the gown not being finished in time. There is scarcely a week remaining."

"Do as you will," said James. "Then I can finish reading my paper in peace." He shook the pages open again. With his body half-hidden behind them, he signaled his withdrawal from their society.

Ellena was glad of it. The day held far more promise without him in it. Charlotte at once dispatched a messenger to the dressmaker Lord Howell had recommended, and they awaited her arrival with great excitement.

Mrs. Pembridge—a short, stout woman with a thick bun and spectacles perched upon her nose—wasted no time in coming as soon as she'd been sent for. After all, the commission was for the bride of her favorite customer, she told the future viscountess.

She made short work of taking Ellena's measurements and then began the more detailed exercise of discussing the design.

"Really, something simple would suffice," Ellena insisted. "The material itself is so beautiful, it needs nothing more to enhance it. See for yourself." She indicated the parcel on the counter.

Mrs. Pembridge unrolled the mass of fabric and sucked in her breath. "I see his lordship has spared no expense. This must be a sample of his finest cloth. And we shall have no need to economize. There is enough even for a train, if you wish it."

"What do mean by *his cloth*?" Ellena asked. "Does he have a private collection of sorts?"

"Oh, no, my dear. Did you not know? The viscount is in the trade. Only the rarest and most beautiful materials, mind you— silk damask, purple velvet, Spanish lace. Much of the royal court is draped in his wares. You will know such luxury once you are his wife. This is but a beginning. Although it is a very fine beginning indeed."

Ellena felt embarrassed at her limited knowledge of her betrothed. She hoped to amend this in her next conversation with him. But she suspected it would take many such dialogues to learn all she wished to know of him.

"I do not think a train will be necessary," she pondered aloud, "although I shall ask Lord Howell if he wishes it."

"Of course." Mrs. Pembridge nodded, jotting this down in her little notebook. "And then there is the matter of the veil."

Ellena's breath hitched. How did Mrs. Pembridge know about the veil?

"The... The veil?" Ellena stammered, desperately thinking about how she could explain it away.

"Yes, not every bride chooses to wear one. Do you have a bonnet in mind? I could attach some of this silk to match your gown. Or do you prefer lace?"

Ellena exhaled her relief. "I think I will do without one, thank you."

If only that could be true today, Ellena lamented. She wished she could forget about this annoying complication. She would have to decide how best to manage it before appearing at church tomorrow, though she did not see how this would be possible without first meeting with Dominic. Bother! And things were coming along so nicely. If Dominic had visited with her today, as hoped, they might already have this disclosure behind them. Double bother! Now it lay between them once again, like a boulder in the road, threatening to upturn what had become a very promising start to their relationship.

"Well," said Mrs. Pembridge, snapping her little notebook shut, "I had best get straight to work. Even with the help of my assistants, it will be a difficult task to complete before Friday."

Ellena picked up the folds of fabric and touched the gold embroidery fondly before handing the parcel to the dressmaker. "I shall be sorry to see this fine cloth go, but you must take it with you, of course. I shall send you details of any further requirements once I have had the opportunity of consulting with his lordship." She smiled at Charlotte, whose hand rested lightly on her pregnant form. "I have one request, though. You must make a christening gown for Charlotte's baby from among the abundant lengths that remain."

"Oh, Ellena, how wonderful!" cried Charlotte, hugging her. "I shall gladly lend it to you when your first child is born. What celebration we shall share in its use!"

Ellena nodded happily. "Dominic will be pleased with the extent of the joy this gift has brought."

She smiled at the ease with which his name came to her lips. She wished she could speak his name in person. But that cursed veil would ruin the moment. If only she had some time alone with him. The longer she wore the veil, the more difficult it would be to justify it as part of her attire.

An idea formed in her mind. "Charlotte, do you think we might invite Dominic for a walk after the sermon tomorrow? I have heard Munro's great park offers a charming scenic stroll. I should relish the chance to stretch my legs awhile. Do you think it proper for me to extend the invitation, or shall we have James play the host?"

"Oh, I think it a splendid idea! And the invitation can only come from you. What a reward it will be for Lord Howell to receive such encouragement."

Ellena lowered her eyelashes shyly. "He hardly needs it. We are already engaged."

"That is of little consequence. The outcome of courtship is not simply to wed, but to win affection. No matter how dry the ink on the contract, my dear, love can only be sealed with a kiss."

"How poetic!" Ellena laughed. Charlotte's wisdom was simple but sound. "Then I shall send a message directly," she declared. "Mrs. Pembridge, if you will excuse me. Charlotte, I shall be in my room."

Ellena almost ran down the corridor in her enthusiasm. She decided to keep the letter short to avoid the troublesome rhetoric that would be needed in a longer draft. She would thank Dominic enough in person. She stated the invitation with polite cordiality, but signed it *Yours, Ellena*. That should indicate her feeling clearly enough. As long as he could forgive the embarrassment of her appearing veiled for the church service, not to mention walking about Munro Park like some Madonna from a painting.

Her heart pinched at the thought of his face turned away in pain and confusion. There was nothing else she could do. He would have to forgive her for this injury, as she had forgiven his.

She put these thoughts to one side, as she did with his letter. She wanted to write to Jillian, too, and save their errand boy the trouble of running out twice.

She sat awhile, staring at the blank pages before her. She didn't really know where to start. So much had transpired since her last letter, and much was best left out of the narration. Though she trusted her friend implicitly, she dared not risk revealing anything in case someone else read their correspondence. Best she focus on the positive.

Ah, she had it! She pulled a sheet toward her and began.

Dearest Jilly,

I have such excellent news! There will be no need to read the details of my wedding in a letter. My dear Dominic—Did you know he had a second name? I much prefer it to the stuffiness of "George"—is playing the hero and arranging for your attendance on the day! Father shall have to swallow his objections, as my betrothed is quite determined to please me in this regard. And that is but one aspect of his good character.

Oh, Jilly, I have been wrong to fear him. He is kindness itself. And his manners are impeccable.

Ellena paused in her writing. His manners *had* been impeccable whenever he was with her, whether in a cabin or in the grandness of Munro House. Then why could she not fully shake the memory of his hastily spoken words to James? It was petty of her, when he had done nothing but accommodate her needs. The latter was what she must focus on. It was unseemly to hold a grudge.

She dipped her pen in ink once more.

When Lord Howell (shall I stick to formalities?) discovered my sore want of friends on our guest list, he made it his first project to change these circumstances. I say "first" because, just this morning, I have been surprised with another pleasant scheme on his part. Can you imagine my feeling when not ten, but twenty yards of the sheerest silk were delivered to our door? It is the finest I have ever seen, embroidered with gold thread, no less! It is in lieu of the wedding dress lost with my trousseau. My original gown, though pretty enough, could never compare to the detail and workmanship that this new garment will display. And the seamstress has worked for their family for years. Already, I begin to feel like a true lady. There is a sense of belonging where, but yesterday, I was a stranger.

Truly, I am far happier than I could have dreamed possible, especially so soon after my arrival. Lord Howell has gone to great lengths to ensure my feelings are considered. Can it be, dear Jilly, that I should find joy where I expected only duty?

But let me not delay one more minute in telling you of our dinner last night. I cannot imagine anyone enjoying finer fare than was our privilege. And in such a house as would make a queen feel at home. In fact, I would be much surprised if, in its long history, Munro House has not been graced by the visit of a monarch. It is all grace and splendor. Not a single thing is out of place and nothing suffers from neglect. I have not yet had the opportunity to view the upstairs or gardens, but they surely exhibit just as splendidly. I fear no disappointment upon my discovery of them in due course.

Charlotte was all atwitter in her admiration, which spared me finding words in the uncomfortable novelty of our first hour there. She has been a stout support to me, though it cannot replace the loss of your company. Still, she is attentive to my needs as a guest in her home and amazingly wise in matters of the heart.

This makes me wonder what strange lapse of reason led such a sweet creature to accept James as her choice. She seems oblivious to all his faults. I fail to comprehend why Father felt it safe to leave the conclusion of my engagement in James's hands. He is exactly as I remembered him—self-absorbed and self-serving. He offers nothing that does not in some way benefit himself. He seems incapable of true generosity—the kind given solely for another's pleasure—but will sacrifice his dignity if he believes he can gain profit by it. And, all the while, Charlotte sees only good and praises him where a thrashing would have served just as well. Perhaps the less I dwell on that topic, the better.

Though I hate to admit it, James did touch on an uncomfortable truth last night. During one of our debates at the dinner table (I politely describe it as such, when really, it is always a sparring match), I was reminded that I am all naivety and inexperience, which ill prepares me for married life. They were unwelcome words, considering their source, but I cannot fault the observation. It makes me all the more grateful toward my intended, who traverses my awkwardness with his surefooted approach.

You may be pleased to find my mood so much lighter than it was when I left home only four days ago. I would not have you suffer concern where there is no longer a need. For this, we may thank dear Dominic, whose nobility, I am quite persuaded, extends to his character.

She did believe that, didn't she? One mistake, however abominable, did not necessarily indicate a deep-seated flaw in temperament. Dominic had shown himself a better man than that. She need not dwell on the past. Nor should she dread the future. Once the veil was discarded, all cause for deception would be removed. He would forgive her, as she had forgiven him. It was the right thing to do. And Dominic would do the right thing, wouldn't he? There was nothing to fear. She could proceed with courage.

As you once tried to assure me, dear Jilly, I feel confident that all will be well.

Meanwhile, prepare yourself for a journey to Munro and an elated reception from your friend who misses you and longs to tell you far more than one letter could hold.

Do not think this relinquishes you from your promise to write. I shall await your daily news as always, until the moment you may deliver it in person.

Please give my fondest regards to your family. Tell the Kinsey boys to be kind to their sister or I have a good mind to keep you with me here in Munro. Perhaps I should begin to inquire after the eligible young men who might be worthy of your hand. (What a delightful idea! To have you settled in the same neighborhood as myself would be the crowning joy of my new life.) For now, I will savor the good fortune of seeing you in a week.

Until then, my dearest friend and confidante, may you be well and happy, as am I.

Ellena

DOMINIC SAT ACROSS from two gentlemen in his lawyer's musty office. He was finding it very difficult to concentrate. Ellena must have received her little surprise by now. It was all he could think of.

He tried to imagine the expression on her face, but her features were unknown to him, and the picture in his mind remained incomplete. For a moment, he recalled Nancy instead. *Her* face was etched into his memory. Her bold gaze. Her perfect nose. Her soft lips.

They must fade into the past now. But it was hard when there was no vision of Ellena with which to replace them.

He couldn't wait to see his betrothed, free of her veil, so that he could dote on *her* features at last. Soon. Soon. But not soon enough. He wanted to picture her famously lovely face *now*. But he had to be patient. Instead, he remembered her hands, her soft skin. They would have touched the cloth, perhaps tentatively at first, then eagerly.

He wanted to do the same. He wanted to trace the outline of her face with the back of his fingers. Tenderly, until she melted into his touch. She would clutch his hand with her own and turn her mouth toward it, burying a kiss in his palm.

He shivered at the illusory feel of her lips. Heat gathered in his neck and drew into his cheeks. Fortunately, the two gentlemen were poring over the wording of the contract, and he had the opportunity to gather himself. Not that it helped. His thoughts strayed back to Ellena, to her bold honesty, her warm responsiveness when he'd given her the things she valued most. They were his values too. That made it easier.

For the first time, he believed he had found someone he could be genuinely happy with.

Well, for the second time.

He could safely release the memory of Nancy now, surely.

After all, what did he really know about her? Little more than he knew about his own future bride, if he were honest. But *that* would all change, and soon.

Tomorrow would be a fresh start for them. None of the awkwardness of a first meeting. No bizarre veil-wearing. Already, he felt the nervous apprehension of their brief courtship dissipating. There would be more of the open sharing of themselves. The thought of it brought such relief.

And something more. The stirring of feelings he had not dared explore before. He felt...safe. And a little giddy. Was this... Could this be...the beginnings of love?

He recoiled from the thought as if he had touched a burning torch. He dare not let such hope take root. It was too soon. He must keep a steady course. Women were complicated creatures. Tomorrow, she might just as easily reveal a less noble aspect of her character. No, he must ease into things. Keep his heart from rushing forward, lest it be broken.

And yet, despite his own council, and the meeting that demanded his attention, Dominic spent the better part of the afternoon daydreaming about Ellena, her exquisite hands, and how he would have a lifetime to hold them.

CHAPTER THIRTEEN

JUST BEFORE DINNER, Thorn Bush Hall once again received an unexpected arrival. However, it was not some*thing*, but some*one*, and the surprise was for Charlotte.

She bundled her new guest into the drawing room and declared breathlessly, "You'll never guess, James! Look who pays us the most wonderful visit! All the way from Steeples."

Her husband, who had paid little attention to her announcement, looked up at the mention of the town. His previous disinterest was replaced by a spreading smile as he rose rapidly to his feet.

"William! This *is* a welcome surprise. I am in dire need of a man's company. You have little notion of how much I endure as the only gentleman surrounded by talkative women." He clasped the man by the arm and pulled him into a brief embrace, clapping him on the back with the other hand.

"I do not pity you one jot, James," rallied the newcomer. "You are the only man I know who can complain of a lady's company. But if I may serve to relieve your misery by entertaining any such ladies for you, I am more than willing."

Ellena, who had been reading in a sunny corner, was able to observe without drawing attention to herself. She was not sure how she felt toward anyone so clearly liked by James, but she had learned from recent experiences not to jump to conclusions too soon. In a matter of days, she had assumed Dominic to be a sheriff of sorts, misjudged Lord Howell to be overbearing and soulless, and even failed to understand how much James loved Charlotte. There was definitely room for error in her thinking. She did not want to feel a fool again.

The gentleman was certainly handsome, despite being road-weary. His coat was a little dusty, but its deep-blue cloth was well tailored and brought out the color in his face, which would turn out nicely after a wash and shave. His hair was cropped quite short. His eyes were dark and penetrating. About his mouth there played a constant smile. It was a good face, and the rest matched equally well.

Her further private musings were prevented when Charlotte began introductions and revealed her hiding place.

"William, let me introduce you to James's cousin Miss Ellena Trenton. Ellena, this is my brother, William Cole."

The young man turned to find her, his face lighting up when he did so. He bowed civilly, though his demeanor was far from formal.

"A pleasure to make your acquaintance, Miss Trenton. My goodness, Charlotte, if I had known you had such a lovely visitor, I would have found my way here much sooner." His words were directed at his sister, but his eyes remained upon Ellena, her neck growing warm under his gaze.

Charlotte placed a hand upon her hip, the other hand wagging a finger in the air. "Be warned, Ellena, my brother is an incorrigible flirt. You had best keep your head about you, for he will fill it with pretty nonsense."

Mr. Cole shook his head sorrowfully. "If only it were so, Sister. But I dare say a woman of obvious beauty such as Miss Trenton must be sated with the attentions of eager men. My efforts are surely wasted among such stiff competition."

"Indeed, you have but one contender to fear, sir," replied Ellena. "It is Lord Howell, my intended. We are to be married next Friday."

"Ah, that is a formidable challenge." Mr. Cole touched his palm to his chest. "Truly, I am almost discouraged." He made a bow, raising his head with a wink. "Since time is of the essence, shall we dispense with the intricacies of vying for your affection? I might simply consider a duel—a far less cumbersome means of securing fair lady."

"Alas, Mr. Cole, I shall be faithful even in death. Perhaps this knowledge will spare you the trouble of pursuing what cannot be gained."

"On the contrary," said Mr. Cole, his eyes searing her skin while his mouth twitched playfully, "my charming but elusive Miss Trenton, your obvious attachment elsewhere merely guarantees that I may flatter you relentlessly without fear of being taken too seriously." His lips widened into a full smile. "I shall enjoy your company immensely, I think."

"There! What did I tell you?" Charlotte cried. "Is he not utterly without scruples? Ellena, I pray you not be offended by his forward manner. He is quite harmless."

"Now, Sister, how can you ruin a man's reputation thus? What gentleman wishes to be considered so impotent? Let her think the worst of me for paying too many compliments but never let it be said that I am only a kitten."

"I shall call you what I like, you roguish boy. Now come and get washed up. We cannot have you dine with us in this state, whether a kitten or a cad."

"I thank you, but hopefully, I will prove to be neither."

"Come now, William, a hot bath and shave will make you a new man." Charlotte pushed him toward the door. He caught her around the waist and planted a kiss upon her cheek.

"A kiss for your troubles." He grinned.

"Away with you now," Charlotte insisted, but her tone was softer, and her cheeks warmed with a gentle blush. She ushered him out of the room. James walked with him, chatting with an ease Ellena had never seen in him before. Certainly, Charlotte's brother was a breath of fresh air. Conversation at the table was sure to be far more pleasant than usual today.

Dinner was delayed by half an hour to allow their new guest time to make himself presentable. When Ellena arrived in the dining room, the others were already seated and chatting animatedly. Mr. Cole jumped up as she entered and held out her chair for her. She thanked him and slid into the seat.

"We have persuaded my brother to stay with us a few weeks," Charlotte announced happily.

"Persuasion was hardly required," Mr. Cole argued. "You dangled this perfect carrot before me the moment I entered your home."

Ellena made a pretense at indignation. "Am I to understand that I am akin to a vegetable and yourself likened to a donkey, Mr. Cole?"

"Why not? I shall not lie—I am as stubborn as any mule. Do you object, then, to being compared with something so utterly full of goodness?"

"No, I think I dare not, now that you have phrased it so cleverly." Ellena laughed in exasperation. "I think I will do well to heed your advice, Charlotte. Your brother has wit enough to confound reason."

"Ellena is not accustomed to being outdone," James interjected. "I caution you not to offend her sensibilities lest you lose her favor."

Mr. Cole raised an eyebrow. "I sense a little skirmish between you. How positively intriguing. Well, I shall have all the details soon enough, or torment you with my efforts. That is a little trick I learned from having a sister." He winked at Charlotte.

Ellena's lips were pressed thin with tension. "There is nothing to tell. James and I have different views on many things, but nothing particular that warrants further inquiry."

Mr. Cole leaned forward onto his elbows. "Such protest only heightens my curiosity. There is little point in delaying, you know. I shall wheedle it out of you all eventually."

Silence answered him.

"Come now, can it be so terrible that no one wishes to speak of it? Well, I *am* impressed. I have never known James to be so subdued on a matter. Congratulations, Miss Trenton, you have tamed him."

His well-aimed words had hit their target. James was instantly roiled. He puffed out his chest, his pale skin blotching into an angry pink, his freckles flaring like exclamation points.

"If anyone needs taming, then it is my cousin. She has not yet learned the art of discretion. She made a complete fool of us all by wearing a ridiculous veil to the dinner last night that Lord Howell had arranged for their first meeting. We were all humiliated in the process."

Ellena unclenched her teeth. "You are happy to forget your role in this outcome." Her eyes flashed angrily, but she resisted further comment.

Mr. Cole was astonished. "A veil? Like a mantilla? How does that offend?"

"No, dear," Charlotte explained, "it was over her face, like a bride. It was supposed to be a game, a sort of intrigue, but then it changed." She frowned.

"This is far more interesting than I could have hoped. What was the purpose of the game?"

"It was no game," snapped James. "Ellena wanted to prove a point about honor to his lordship."

"'Honor'? Surely, a viscount needs no lesson in this? How could he have acted dishonorably if they had not yet met?"

Charlotte tried to put the uncomfortable truth into words. "He made an unfortunate comment about Ellena's virtue, which James then related to us."

"And he threatened to cancel the wedding," James added smugly.

Ellena could stand it no longer. She rose abruptly and threw her napkin down, glaring at James. "I will not stand to listen to your abusive speech another minute. You are quick to repeat those narratives that do not stir your conscience. But you are far more guilty of dishonorable conduct than you would like to be reminded of. Your despicable actions then and now are an infinitely more damaging revelation of *your* character than can ever be true of Lord Howell. You will excuse me, Charlotte, but I've had enough of my cousin's hypocrisy."

She strode out of the room, seething from every pore. That vile, base, *contemptible* man! How *could* he speak of their private affairs so glibly? And with the clear intent to mislead Mr. Cole, too. She could not let him get away with it. If Charlotte's brother was shocked by her outburst, she would bear it willingly. She would apologize to Charlotte when she was calmer and could speak to her alone. As for James, it would be just as well to avoid him. Only a few days remained, and she would be rid of his insufferable presence. One thing was certain: James Trenton would not soon be receiving an invitation from the new mistress at Munro House.

CHAPTER FOURTEEN

AS IT TURNED out, William Cole was far from shocked. On the contrary, he was all concern when he found Ellena tucked away in the library. She had succeeded in avoiding her cousin all afternoon by frequenting those rooms he did not. She exchanged her sunny spot in the drawing room for a chilly-but-private corner in the library, where the necessity for a shawl was amply outweighed by the absence of James Trenton.

"May I intrude in your sanctuary?" Charlotte's brother inquired gently. His face was serious. All trace of mischief was gone. Instead, he had the appearance of a schoolboy who had broken his mother's favorite vase and was dismayed at seeing her loving face sour with displeasure.

Ellena shrugged. "The room is not for my use alone."

"But perhaps you wish it were," he ventured, remaining where he was in the doorway.

She hesitated. It was tempting to insist on her privacy. However, she had no quarrel with Mr. Cole. He could not have imagined what his playful digging would reveal, nor was he responsible for the spurious insults she had had to endure from his brother-in-law.

She tipped her open hand to him. "Enter at your leisure."

Despite her encouragement, Mr. Cole lingered where he was. "I regret being the cause of such unhappiness at luncheon," he finally managed to say.

Ellena lowered her book onto her lap. "You were not the cause," she answered firmly.

Mr. Cole remained unconvinced. "I suspect the animosity between yourself and James was re-ignited by my insistent prying. I only hope you believe that, had I known the nature of your disagreement, I would never have pushed for its revelation."

"I believe you."

"It is a great tragedy to have lost your favor before fully having had the chance to enjoy it."

Ellena laughed in exasperation. "You have lost nothing. Do stop looking so sad. I much preferred when you were gay and witty."

He looked at her hopefully. "Then we can still be friends?"

"Only friends?" Ellena arched an eyebrow, her mouth twisting with a suppressed smile. Mr. Cole's sorrow was so tragic, she felt compelled to shake him free of it, even if it meant she must use his own playfulness against him. "Was I not inspiration enough for a duel this morning? I seem to have fallen in your estimation more so than you have in mine."

At once, the old twinkle was back in his eye again. "Perhaps I was hasty to consider such drastic actions." He approached her with renewed enthusiasm. "I have come to deeper insights. I am convinced a woman of your caliber deserves to be wooed to the full extent of a man's capabilities. Perhaps I may start afresh by inviting you for a turn about the garden? The evening is unusually warm out. Far more so than in here, at least. I assure you, I have no wicked intent. Charlotte is sitting outside on a blanket, playing with Clarence. I shall be compelled to be on my best behavior."

"Have you no prior engagement with my cousin? He seemed very grateful for your company and is sure to loathe me benefiting from it instead."

Mr. Cole's smile vanished.

"I have befriended James as a brother-in-law. He is an attentive husband to Charlotte and pleasant enough in simple conversation. But I could never approve of his behavior today. Especially for the injury it caused you. For that, he shall have to make do without me awhile. Besides," he added, his mouth twitching coyly, "he is not nearly as attractive a companion as yourself. In that respect, he may find I have altogether forgotten about him."

Ellena hugged her book close and stuck out her chin with pretended obstinacy. "If I quit my reading now, then I shall not know what becomes of the heroine. Perhaps I will be less distracted another time."

Mr. Cole leaned toward her with casual ease, and Ellena felt a rush of implied intimacy. "I am also keenly interested in the heroine," he said, his warm breath upon her face. "I propose we decide the next twist in her narrative together. I do not think these pages contain the most desirable outcome."

Ellena's heart pounded at his closeness. It unsettled her, but she kept her bearings. She reminded herself firmly that he was merely teasing her and that there was no danger of indiscretion beyond this. Still, she would keep him gently at arm's length to be sure.

"I am certain the heroine marries her true love," she countered. "There can be no faulting such an ending. How can one suggest a better alternative?"

"If he is the only love she has ever known, then she has no standard for comparison and is sure to be satisfied." Mr. Cole held out his hand. "Shall we debate the wisdom of her decision as we walk?"

Ellena remained unmoving. "You make assumptions regarding the matter of choice, sir. Does this mean all women of your acquaintance are fortunate enough to choose their marriage partners? It may shock you, then, to know that this is not the case for everyone. Some ladies are merely grateful that the arrangement is not distasteful. The only decision involved is to purposefully rally against being miserable in circumstances beyond their control. Fortunately, *I* have been matched with a fine gentleman." The small, niggling doubt whispered in her ear once more, and she pushed it away from her with effort. This was not anyone's concern but her own.

William Cole straightened, then bowed. "Duly noted." He again offered his hand. "However, I believe where a walk in the garden is concerned, we may be assured of both free choice and a happy ending."

"You argue well and make fair comment," Ellena conceded. "Nevertheless, to keep the lines of battle clearly drawn, it is best I do not lean upon my opponent." She rose from her chair without his assistance.

Mr. Cole huffed out a short laugh. "How did I suddenly fall to the unenviable position of enemy?"

"Not enemy." She smiled. "Shall we say you are the revolutionary in the tidy governance of my thought?"

"I like the notion! It suits me well. Shall I stir up the masses, or attack with stealth?"

Ellena considered this. "I suspect you will do neither," she decided. "I do not see you as the type of man to boldly overthrow the ruling powers. I imagine you would rather use your charm to insinuate yourself into the favor of the court. From there, you would influence the sovereign behind the scenes without the added burden of taking over responsibility."

"A free agent with the ear of a princess. Hmm … You have painted me in a most desirable light. I shall endeavor not to disappoint your expectations."

With another solemn bow, Mr. Cole gestured for Ellena to lead the way out to the garden.

They left the dimness of the house behind and stepped into the balmy air of early evening. The scent of the season's last blooms lay upon the breeze. Hidden among the leafy boughs, birds warbled and twittered, fluttering invisibly overhead. The lawn lay in partial shadow, offering a measure of relief from the day's heat.

"I have thought upon the matter further," Mr. Cole said as they walked. "I think you shall do nicely in the role of a Spanish princess."

"Oh? Why Spanish?"

"Why, for the sake of your lace mantilla, of course." He grinned, saw her face cloud, and added quickly, "And because you have the pride and passion so distinctive of their nation."

"I am not sure whether you tease or flatter me. Either way, you are mistaken in labeling me a princess. I am but a merchant's daughter and grateful to be lacking in the airs and graces of aristocracy."

"Yet you were bold enough to challenge your betrothed at your first meeting. That is not the courage of a commoner."

Ellena turned her face away, embarrassed at the memory. "I prefer not to dwell on my unseemly behavior. I acted impulsively without giving my intended the opportunity to explain himself."

Mr. Cole cocked his head to the side.

"Will you not trust me with the truth of the events? I know there is much more than James cares to reveal. I am dismayed that Charlotte's husband could be guilty of something untoward in his dealings. It would reassure me if I knew to what extent he had shamed the household."

"I'm sorry," replied Ellena, shaking her head, "I am not comfortable in the role of informant. Let James give you honest answer, if he dares. I do not share his propensity for stirring ill will."

"That is very noble of you, Princess. But if your subjects are an embarrassment to themselves, their loss of favor cannot be blamed on your narration of the events. Besides, I cannot be sure that the truth I receive from his mouth will be the genuine article."

Ellena stopped and looked Mr. Cole squarely in the face. Perhaps he did not need to know, but she was grateful for the opportunity to defend Dominic. She took a deep breath for courage.

"These are the simple facts, and may it please you not to repeat them elsewhere."

"You have my word as a gentleman."

"Very well. To explain properly, I must take you back several days, prior to my arrival in Munro. Upon our journey here, we suffered the misfortune of being robbed by bandits. The coach was overturned in the melee and I fell into the river."

"Good heavens!" Mr. Cole's head drew back, his eyes wide, his brows arched. "What adventures you have had!"

Ellena frowned. "I suppose one might see it as such if reading a novel. Being in the thick of it is quite another matter."

"Of course. I did not mean anything by it. Please continue."

"Well, to put a point to it, necessity drove me to spend the night hiding alone in the forest with only the toppled carriage for shelter. Then, in the morning, I found help as I was slowly making my way onward to Munro."

She squirmed a little. Lying never sat well with her.

"Go on," her companion urged.

"The further details are of little importance. The essence of this chapter in the story is that my trousseau was lost, and my father sent money to replace my basic wardrobe and wedding attire. He put James in charge of the funds."

"I don't follow where the viscount enters the story."

"You will very shortly. You see, James had in mind to persuade Lord Howell to pay for my bridal dress. I suspect now that he intended pocketing the remainder of the money my father had provided, once these expenses had been charged to Lord Howell's account."

Ellena paused for Mr. Cole to express his shock at such behavior. She was a trifle disconcerted when he simply waited for her to continue.

"It may little surprise you that Lord Howell was angered by James's suggestion." Ellena looked pointedly at Mr. Cole, implying that he, too, should be angered by such appalling behavior. But she waited in vain. He merely looked for her to continue, his expression devoid of any indication that he shared her outrage.

Her expectations ruffled, she proceeded with somewhat diminished vigor.

"In his ire, Lord Howell spoke harshly. An action I am certain he now regrets," she added hastily, as much to convince herself as Mr. Cole. It was painful to be reminded of Dominic's careless words. Knowing her betrothed could bring himself to say such things, even if only when sorely provoked, troubled her. Would the continued wearing of her veil, though it be for just one more day, be enough to provoke him again? What, then, of their life together? Would she be forever treading on eggshells? How rare would his outbursts be?

"What did he say?" Mr. Cole asked when she remained lost in her own thoughts.

There was no getting around it. She would have to repeat the awful truth. But the words formed uneasily upon her tongue. "He indicated that the wedding might be called off, since there was no proof that I had not been...*compromised* when the bandits attacked." Ellena blushed at the mention of these details.

At last, William Cole was moved to make comment. "What? Did he really make such a statement? This is most irregular behavior for a well-bred gentleman."

Ellena's head drooped. "I cannot say what manner of speech my cousin used for his lordship to consider such an aggressive response. I only know that James insists upon repeating the viscount's comments to hurt me yet fawns like a groveling cur in the presence of the very man he slanders."

Mr. Cole pondered these words. He seemed to be struggling with the truth of it. "I beg you forgive my impertinent question," he said eventually, "but is it not possible James was well-intentioned in his actions on your behalf and puts on a servile act to protect you from further injurious comments by your betrothed?"

Ellena shook her head. "I understand that you seek good in

one who is married to your sister. However, let me assure you, James's intentions are entirely self-serving. It was his greed that led to the confrontation with my intended. If Lord Howell were truly an unreasonable man, he would have responded with equal rage at our dinner meeting. Instead, he showed restraint and compassion when I threw my challenge at him."

"Are you referring to your wearing of the veil?" Mr. Cole asked gently.

"I acted impulsively. It was a mistake. Dominic does not deserve such treatment." She spoke quietly, almost to herself.

"May I ask what impulse drove you to wear your face covered? It sounds an odd punishment, if you will pardon my saying so."

Ellena sighed. "There is no doubt I would do things differently, given the chance. At the time, I was infused with the indignity of my honor being called into question. My cousin's words convinced me that Lord Howell was tyrannical in his expectations and I was afraid to be absorbed into such a relationship. I was desperate to make a stand against this perceived future. I hoped that, if I challenged his attack on my reputation, I could re-establish myself as someone worthy of respect—his respect. So I covered my face and promised to cloister myself here, at Thorn Bush Hall, to emphasize my innocent virtue."

Mr. Cole's expression remained unchanging and did little to reassure her. She felt acute embarrassment, all too aware that her words made her appear petty and desperate.

"Oh, I know it sounds ridiculous," she protested to his unspoken rebuke, "but you cannot know the fear I carried in my heart. I was to marry him, no matter what his nature. I could not have known that he was so different from the way James had portrayed him. I felt doomed to a life as my husband's shadow, never daring to speak against him while he ruled my every movement. I thought that if I challenged his unfortunate comments, he would know I could not be trampled underfoot."

Was that all it had taken? Had her bold action set the tone?

Did Dominic understand that his crude speech had no place in their marriage? If so, the wearing of the veil for one more day would do no lasting harm. And when her true identity was revealed, he would agree that the deception had been necessary. She would know tomorrow. But not knowing *now* left her depending on trust rather than certainty. Why was tomorrow so very far away?

"Do not fear my judgment, Miss Trenton." William Cole's words were soft with sincerity. "You have but proved yourself worthy of my admiration. I could not possibly waste my flattery on a little mouse who does not think herself deserving."

His voice rose now, with a sense of drama. "You, dear *Infanta* of Spain, have the fire of a warm-blooded people in your spirit. You have flung down your gauntlet and not lost the ensuing battle. Instead, I imagine the poor viscount was quite defeated by your eloquence and fine features, which"—and here he angled his head playfully—"are not restricted to your face."

Ellena blushed deeply. She had not expected Mr. Cole to turn her confession into a compliment. She was relieved that he viewed her veiled theatrics in such a generous light. She had expected him to chide her, tell her there had been a better way to handle her offence. Instead, he had taken her side. His bold admiration was not entirely unwelcome. Still, she stayed her course. She was determined to pursue her original intention of reclaiming Dominic's good name.

"I thank you for your kind words, sir. However, you have the benefit of hearing my explanation for the veil. You did not experience the shock of first meeting me in my clandestine dress. It is proof of my intended's good character that he did not enjoy your advantage yet behaved as if he had. He mercifully paid little attention to my odd attire and accepted my explanation with amazingly good grace."

Mr. Cole clicked his heels and nodded his head stiffly in a formal acknowledgement. "Then I concede he is a fine man to recognize your worth."

Just as suddenly, he relaxed again, and the old twinkle returned to his eye. "I do not thank him for it, though, as his honorable bearing makes it much more difficult for a usurper to win the ear of the princess."

Ellena's mouth drew into a broad smile. "Quite impossible, it is true. I shall not encourage you with a lie. Though I am surprised that a talented flatterer like yourself has not already found a lady with whom to pursue a more lasting mutual admiration."

Mr. Cole threw himself onto a nearby bench with an exaggerated sigh.

"Alas, it has been my pleasure and my burden to seek that very thing throughout the last several months. My mother sent me to Steeples for the summer with orders to find a suitable bride. As you know, Steeples is to the North what Bath is to the South—a fashionable place for unmarried souls to gather in the hopes of curing that ghastly social ailment: spinsterhood. Those who fail at this during the winter season in Bath, fly north like migratory birds to find succor in the summer delights of Steeples.

"However, despite the promising sound of such an assignment, I was dismayed to find that all the best ladies had already been claimed in the spring! Of course, there is one who seems to have been hiding at my sister's house…"

"Hardly hiding"—Ellena laughed—"though my self-imposed seclusion here might suggest otherwise. Also, I am engaged, so your theory still holds true that all prospects are taken. That is, if I am to be counted among the 'best ladies.'"

"My dear Miss Trenton, had I met you before, Steeples would not have seen my face at all."

Ellena ignored this claim out of hand, having now become quite used to his manner, which could not possibly be taken seriously. Instead, she lowered herself primly onto the bench beside him and asked, "Will you be waiting for the promising new buds of next spring, or have you simply moved your search to Munro?"

"For now, I am grateful to visit with my sister. I had planned to resume my quest once I had tarried here a week or so. But the good fortune of your company has added to the pleasure of my sojourn."

"Indeed, your timing is impeccable. One week earlier and I would still have been residing with my parents. One week more and you would have found me already settled at Munro House."

Mr. Cole leaned in towards her, his hands laced behind his back. "Truly, I sense a measure of fate interceding on my behalf."

Ellena brushed the comment aside. "And what sort of woman does your mother see you fated to wed?"

"At this juncture, I am sure she would be satisfied just to see me settled at all. I am fortunate in that our elder brother is married, has produced a string of children, and resides near our parents in Fernbridge, where he also assists Father at the bank. There has, as a result, been little pressure upon me to perform similar acts of respectability until now."

"What has brought about the recent change?"

"Father has decided my life is in need of direction. In fact, he has clear ideas on how this may be achieved. It is his desire that I should enter the clergy. He has even managed to find a position for me not far from home, where the resident vicar is about to retire and no suitable replacement has yet been found."

Ellena's eyebrows arched in astonishment. "I confess I cannot imagine you in the role of a clergyman, preaching sermons and administering sacraments. It seems a very solemn profession for someone who has such a wicked wit."

"Oh, I wholeheartedly agree with you. I would far rather be holding a young lady's hand than sealing it in marriage to another. Besides"—Mr. Cole grinned—"how am I to sleep through the homily—as usual—if I were presenting it?"

"You really do paint a most obdurate picture of yourself!"

"Alas, my father knows all too well the impiety of my nature and sees the call to service to the community as my chance for moral salvation."

Ellena's eyes widened. "A banker with a taste for principles. That is refreshing."

"Ah, more's the pity," Mr. Cole complained. "If he were but a lover of money, he would have no quarrel with me except to find a wealthy wife. But he is consummate in his goodness, a trait you will have observed in my sister—and in my brother, if you had met him. He and our father constantly seek ways to further the cause of the common man. As for me, it would appear there was little virtue left to be distributed, my siblings having absorbed so much of it already. It is a great mystery to my parents how I have come to be so utterly decadent despite their careful example."

"I am sure, sir," Ellena retorted, pursing her lips, "that you exaggerate in the hope of an exclamation of protest from me in your defense. You should not risk so base a portrayal of yourself for fear I accept your testimony at its word and protest not in the slightest."

"Ha! You have found me out! It is well I did not add more dire descriptions, since you are unwilling to defend me."

"I do not know you well enough to offer too full an opinion. My silence must not be seen as a condemnation when it is merely the result of caution."

"I should well like my reputation to be upheld as passionately as you have done for Lord Howell. He is a fortunate man to have won such loyalty so soon."

"It is true I have known him but a few days longer than yourself. And our start has not been a smooth one. But we have rallied well. After all, it takes two to overcome difficulties with any real success. His willingness to do so speaks well of his character. The kindness and thoughtfulness he has shown since allows a rapid development of admiration on my part."

"Ah, well, there he clearly trumps me. Fortunately, what I lack in noble deed I make up for with enviable good looks. It is a great consolation."

"You are too much!" Ellena laughed and rose from her seat. "I am quite convinced you need no favor from my lips since you recommend yourself so highly. What a shock it must be when a lady does not respond as you expect. Or have all creatures of my sex always swooned in your presence?"

William Cole stood to join her. "Not at all," he replied, as they resumed their garden meander, "but then a lady's weakness of sight or a hardness of hearing easily explains her indifference to my handsome features and eloquent speech."

"And will you be using your smooth words to persuade your father you are not meant for the clergy?"

"I fear the persuasion is all one-sided and originates with my parents. My mother hopes marriage will settle me into respectability and bring about a greater soberness in my character. My father remains obstinate that I will find no useful purpose except in the church. Currently, with neither of their expectations fulfilled, I can be sure of no peace under their roof. It is best, then, that I do not return home without the promise of an engagement, so that at least one of my parents may be happy and the second challenge deferred a while."

"Poor Mr. Cole. Is there not another career you may pursue that might equally please your father? A military commission, perhaps?"

"I have considered this. If nothing else, I would cut a fine figure in uniform." He struck a pose, his chin up, his hand across his chest. "It might even be advantageous in obtaining the attentions of the lady I desire." He tilted his head toward Ellena. "Are you partial to a military man, Miss Trenton?"

"I should imagine you need please your father before you concern yourself with *my* approval, Mr. Cole."

"It is true I would not be serving my fellow man in the manner my father has in mind. But there is the element of discipline and possible sacrifice that lends a certain appeal to this alternative."

"I see there is no reason to mourn your situation. You have it well in hand."

"Perhaps, after all, marriage is the harder challenge of the two. Finding a fit partner is fraught with danger."

"How so?" asked Ellena, though her own thoughts cast back at once to her night in the cabin with Dominic. She felt a brush creep into her cheeks at the memory of her near nakedness with a man she had come to desire.

Mr. Cole, unaware that her mind had turned to such carnal contemplations, sighed woefully. "The moment a woman has been deemed wholly unsuitable by any and all standards, she is sure to attach herself to me with uninvited ardor. She will giggle and flutter her eyelashes and stick to my side like a burr. She will intimate to her friends that the wedding date is all but decided and the announcement a mere formality. All the ladies of any character then immediately distance themselves from me in polite deference to my newly-betrothed status. Any assurance on my part that the engagement is a misunderstanding is seen in extremely bad taste toward the feelings of my 'poor betrothed'! By the time the truth of my assertions is revealed, the same ladies are then too embarrassed to speak to me, having not trusted my protestations to be real. It is all very frustrating."

"How vexing for you!" Ellena tutted. "It is well you have arrived in Munro. Here, at least, you are under your sister's protection. She will know which ladies to keep you from and will provide you safe passage to the very core of good society." *Or,* thought Ellena, *I might have in mind the very person that would suit you, Mr. Cole.* But she kept further thoughts of Jilly to herself. For now, at least.

"Certainly," answered the unwitting gentleman. "She has already afforded me an introduction to yourself. That is already a marked improvement—one I am sure to have difficulty bettering."

"You are too kind."

Although Ellena enjoyed the light repartee with Mr. Cole, their circuit around the flowerbeds set her thinking of her planned walk with Dominic in Munro Park. Soon her current companion faded from her thoughts as her focus shifted to her own dear gentleman. And the more she dwelled on the promise of their next meeting, the more she thrilled at the anticipation of it. Her whole body tingled as she imagined how closely they would walk together. She would, at last, be able to lean against him, feel his strength as she had done on horseback. Perhaps he would wrap one of her hands in his own, the warmth of his touch spreading up her arm into her heart.

Her excitement was marred by one vexing factor: the issue of the veil was yet to be resolved. She hoped it would be but a brief obstacle, quickly overcome. She was no longer a complete stranger to him. The beginnings of affection were clear in his letter and his desire to spend time with her. Might he not then be willing to forgive the necessary delay in removing the troublesome shroud? She had yet to see any indication that he was a man James Trenton could drive to foul speech. Yet was it wise to assume such behavior was as rare as it had been vulgar?

She considered writing to him, explaining all before their next meeting. It would be a relief to cast aside any disguise and proceed without its encumbrance. But this day was full of distractions for Dominic. There was the risk that he would be busy in town until very late. When he returned home, he might have no energy left to give any attention to his correspondence. What if her letter lay upon the tray until morning? Even then, Dominic might hasten to church without gleaning its contents. If she could be sure that he would read it, a letter was the easiest solution. But it left too much to chance. No, it seemed the veil would have one final encore before she discarded it at Munro Park.

Ellena had the semblance of an idea for what to wear at the church service. She did not wish to make a fool of either Dominic or herself. Her covering would have to be more subtle than the cloth of lace borrowed from Charlotte. She had something simple and tasteful in mind. After this walk, she would get down to the business of the needlework required.

The evening cooled. Ellena and her strolling companion

returned to the house and retired to their rooms for an hour or two until the whole family gathered again for a light supper and coffee. James behaved as if nothing untoward had transpired between them earlier. Ellena guessed he was eager to maintain Mr. Cole's friendship and that it had little to do with her feelings. Charlotte, who seemed always happy when given any opportunity to avoid *un*happiness, continued as attentive hostess, doting sister, and tolerant wife. Mr. Cole steered clear of any further ticklish subjects. And Ellena successfully restrained her tongue when James lauded the excellent prospects rich, young widows made in the marriage mart.

It was still early when Ellena excused herself and returned to the solitude of her room. She wanted to write Jillian of the new guest and did not wish to wait another day. Her next letter the following afternoon would be dedicated solely to news of Dominic.

She dipped her pen in ink and began without delay.

Dear Jilly,

A second letter today! You must be curious as to the events that have prompted such prolific writing. I shall not keep you in suspense.

There is a new guest at Thorn Bush Hall. His name is William Cole. He is Charlotte's younger brother—only a year older than myself. He seeks refuge here from the exhausting process of finding a wife, an activity that has occupied him fruitlessly these past three months in Steeples.

I am much surprised that he has had no success, as his manners are charming, to say the least. He has a very easy manner and seems to be a friend to all he meets. It is a relief to have some distraction from James and his abominable attitudes.

Truly, I think I may have found a match for you, one whose arrangement would also suit me well! Mr. Cole shares your lively ways and sensitive heart. Of equal importance, his family resides in Fernbridge, which, though nearly two hours' ride from here, is still a good distance closer than the four hours to Trenton Grange. Of course, he may not choose to remain there, as he considers a commission in the military. But this makes the prospect even brighter, since he may well be stationed here in Munro, which would place him near his sister, and you near me—a thought so glorious, I scarcely dare consider it!

Now, already I can imagine your protestations. Let me dismiss each one in turn.

First, he has little need for a good dowry, as his parents are more eager to see him settled than in possession of such funds. His father is determined that he should enter the clergy, but, if you knew Mr. Cole, you would laugh at the idea. Do not be alarmed—it is no reflection upon his moral character. When you meet him, you shall agree he is simply more suited to a uniform than a collar.

Second, his lack of success in finding a suitable partner for marriage does not indicate any fault in his person. On the contrary, I believe his nature so amenable to the fairer sex that he is flustered with the variety of willing ladies from whom to choose. However, if I were to direct his thoughts, he may find he is able to rest his focus on one lady who comes so highly recommended by myself.

Third, the fact that he is still a stranger to you should be no discouragement. See what good fortune I have had in this matter!

Ellena's quill stilled a moment. Was it *all* good fortune? She shook herself. No, no, no! She would not spiral into doubts again! Dominic was a good man. Time would show her faith was well-placed.

She forced her attention back to the letter. She would focus on matters she was sure of, like Mr. Cole's charm and what a good match he was for her friend. Yes, that was best. Jilly deserved such happiness.

We shall not speak of engagements until you have met him and won him instantly with your gentle affability and lovely eyes.

To recommend him further, I shall mention that he is, without a doubt, very handsome. Shall I mention his dark eyes or his ready smile? Certainly, he has an excellent tailor, for his tailcoat does his fine frame justice. Also, he loves his sister. The last trait will, I am sure, be a stout endorsement to yourself, perhaps even more so than the others I have mentioned.

There it is, then—my motivation for burning a candle into the night. Should such an exciting discovery not be shared at once? I have in mind to pour honey in his ear with the mention of your name. And we shall see if he does not then earnestly seek your arrival, as I do.

Until then, I remain ever your friend,
Ellena

CHAPTER FIFTEEN

O N SUNDAY MORNING, the Trentons' driver brought the carriage round to the front of Thorn Bush Hall to take the family to church. Little Clarence stood just inside the main entrance, one pudgy little paw tucked into the hand of his nurse, the other clutching a favorite blanket. He was waiting to wave before going outdoors to play.

Ellena was last to emerge from the house, dressed in her role of veiled mystery and fervently hoping that it would be the last time she had to do so. For the most part, her attire followed the dictates of fashion, modesty, and occasion. Her gown—being of palest-blue muslin—echoed her youthfulness, but it closed stiffly at the throat with a high, stand-up collar, the long sleeves buttoned at the wrist, suitably modest for church. The soft fabric gathered in a high-waisted Empire line and was utterly void of adornment, being a morning dress. Only the bonnet sported a wide, sash ribbon of matching, cloudlike blue.

Here all predictability ended, for the rim of the bonnet had been altered with the addition of a short, stiff veil that gathered at Ellena's chin, to be rolled up and back if she chose to uncover her face. This was, of course, her serious intention to do as soon as she had a chance to set matters right with Dominic.

Charlotte thought it was very tasteful and entirely appropriate for church, and she said so. James declined comment. His disapproval was so obvious as to have no need for expression, though the word "mockery" may have been mumbled under his breath. Mr. Cole, on the other hand, was barely able to contain his intrigue.

"I was under the impression you wished to abandon this chastisement of your betrothed, Miss Trenton, especially in lieu of his chivalrous behavior, which you described so eloquently yesterday."

Ellena blushed. Her unusual headdress made her self-conscious, and she was all too well aware how she would draw attention to herself at church. But what could she do? If Nancy Fallon stepped from the Trenton carriage, Dominic would be stunned and flustered. It was neither the time nor place for revelations of this nature. To that end, their private stroll at Munro Park could not come soon enough. Meanwhile, some sort of explanation was necessary to satisfy Mr. Cole.

"You are right, of course," she said, nodding. "I now regret my promise to remain covered thus, and very much wish it unsaid. But a formal declaration of intent, such as I made upon meeting Lord Howell, can only be undone with an equally formal statement of retraction. Else my oath, though perhaps too hastily given, will not be regarded as honorable. Today, I hope to put this petty business behind me. It cannot be too soon for my liking."

"Oh, Ellena," Charlotte said warmly, "I am so pleased to hear you speak with such wisdom."

James snorted, cast a quick glance at Mr. Cole, and withheld further opinion.

Ellena marveled at the stabilizing effect of Mr. Cole's presence on James's otherwise outspoken ways. She was very grateful they were all riding together. Her cousin was sure to resist making snide remarks while his brother-in-law remained present.

It was only a short ride, and they approached their destination after barely ten minutes had passed. The tower and steeple of Munro's well-frequented Anglican church was visible from some distance, though an avenue of tall trees prevented its low stonework walls from being seen until one was almost upon them.

Lord Howell's carriage already stood outside when Ellena arrived. She recognized the coat of arms on the door. He must have been keeping an eye on the road, for the moment she descended from the compartment of her cousin's carriage, Dominic was there to receive her hand.

He looked up with happy expectation, but his smile faltered when she emerged from the gloom of the carriage interior and he saw her covered face. He rallied commendably, but Ellena regretted causing him such pain. He was not angry, or, if he was, he hid it well. There were no harsh words, no outbursts. It boded well, though a trickle of nervous tension slid through her veins. She could hardly wait until their walk a few hours hence, when she could relieve them both of this burden.

To put his heart at ease, she held his hand a moment longer than required for her feet to safely reach the ground. "Dear Dominic," she said with pronounced tenderness, since he could not see the sincerity upon her face. "You remain ever chivalrous. And your gift yesterday showed a thoughtfulness to match. I have been anxious to thank you for it in person." Ellena dipped her chin shyly. "Truly, your absence has been sorely felt," she murmured.

His smile grew deeper. "It has been a test of patience to delay our visit until today," he confessed. "Your invitation to a walk made the wait easier to bear, knowing such a pleasant outing was in store. Thank you for suggesting it."

"Oh!" Ellena cried, lifting her head once more. "It is but a small gesture when compared with the grandness of your own! I am comforted that you shall not only hear my repeated thanks but may see my joy in wearing your beautiful cloth in just a few days. It really is the finest silk I have ever seen! Your taste is exquisite."

Dominic beamed. "You are too kind."

"Indeed, I am not," Ellena insisted. "In fact, I shall elaborate further on your fine qualities while we walk in Munro Park." And she would mean every word of it. For here she was, replete in offensive garb, and yet he smiled and welcomed her. He had missed her! He would forgive her. All would be well. Her heart swelled with joyful anticipation.

Dominic solemnly bowed his head. "The time with you will be ample reward. I do not need flattery to encourage me."

Ellena's answer was overruled by the church bells sounding their call to worship. She looked around for Charlotte, but the rest of the party had already entered the building. Since Ellena would be sitting in the Howell pew, it mattered little, but she had hoped to introduce Dominic to Mr. Cole. She was sure they would like each other instantly. But, as seemed to be the case with many things, this, too, would have to wait.

She entered the building on Dominic's arm. A small thrill ran along her spine at the thought of walking up the same aisle in just a few days, her lovely gold-trimmed cloth folded about her, and Dominic awaiting her with a bright smile. She was acutely aware of the eyes of the congregation following her now as she passed each row. She felt their curiosity attempt to penetrate the depths of her discreet veil. Soon, she reminded herself, this would no longer be necessary. Then they could behold her outright and satisfy their interest.

She slid into the pew that displayed the Howell family crest, musing at the fact that it would be hers also in a very short time. Dominic seated himself beside her, leaving sufficient space between them to indicate to anyone watching that he knew the boundaries of propriety. And many were watching. Of course, none would be so bold as to stare outright. But for the sharp-eyed Ellena, it was easy to spot the head inclined in pretended conversation with a neighbor, or the cough followed by a furtive glance in their direction.

As soon as the Reverend Keith entered, the congregation settled. With a brief nod in Dominic's direction, he at once began his rigorous sermon. He exhorted the congregation to look to their neighbors as their brothers, to serve the poor with compassion, and remember that God watched over all their thoughts and deeds. He was quite passionate in his speech, though Ellena wondered how many people were taking his words to heart. How many of them listened and nodded but secretly thought ill of both neighbor and brother? She knew that James, for one, viewed the poor as an untidy closet in society, the door of which was best left shut. At least Dominic—Ellena noticed with some satisfaction—was leaning slightly forward, as if eager not to miss a word.

She took it as a good sign that such a man as Reverend Keith would lead their vows. It was a sacrament she did not take lightly. She therefore listened closely to his words and took to heart the teachings he offered. And when the last blessing had been followed by the last *amen*, Ellena was grateful for the opportunity to meet the good reverend.

The worshippers filed from the building to their various carriages. The vicar greeted each person in turn, despite his congregation numbering in the hundreds. His lean face readily creased into a smile, his greying hair bouncing lightly as he nodded his head in conversation.

Dominic approached, leading Ellena lightly by her fingertips. "Reverend Keith, may I introduce my intended, Miss Ellena Trenton?"

"A pleasure to make your acquaintance, Miss Trenton," began the friendly vicar, turning to address Ellena. "Ah, Lord Howell, how delightful to see a young woman practicing such modesty," he exclaimed, indicating Ellena's altered bonnet. "You are blessed indeed to have found this rarest of qualities in your future wife. Tell me, Miss Trenton, do all maidens wear a veiled head covering to Sunday services in your hometown, or are you a rarity there, too?"

Ellena frowned slightly. "I am afraid I would be considered more of an oddity in their eyes, but I thank you for your kind perspective." She hastily changed the topic. "May I say how much I was moved by your words this morning? Your message was so encouraging. I am sure our wedding service will be equally inspiring and prompt us to strive for a deeper purpose in our married life."

"You are very kind," said the reverend, who then turned to Lord Howell. "Your lordship has made a fortunate match indeed in one as generous-spirited as Miss Trenton. I look forward to giving your union my official blessing next week. Now, however, I must give my attention to the rest of my flock. If you will both excuse me…"

Lord Howell tipped his hat. "Of course. Until Friday, then."

The vicar was already turning to the next congregant as he answered. "Yes, till Friday. Good day, Lord Howell, Miss Trenton. Ah, good morning, Mrs. Trenton," he called to Charlotte as she approached.

"Good morning, Reverend," Charlotte replied, stopping as she reached Ellena's side. "Good morning, Lord Howell. I apologize for not speaking with you earlier, but we arrived with so little time to spare before the service. I trust you are well."

"*Very* well, madam," Dominic answered, "especially since we have been blessed with such fine weather for our walk. I was thinking to take Ellena along the broad path beside the stream, toward the Italian gardens. Do you not agree it the best choice for a first taste of Munro Park?"

"It is certainly one of my favorites," Charlotte agreed. "Actually, I have come to ask if Ellena might ride on ahead with you. I know it is not the done thing, even though you are engaged. But you are due to wed in less than a week. Perhaps we might make an exception this once? It is, as you have said, such a lovely day. The air is unexpectedly warm and windless. I was hoping to fetch Clarence from his nurse and bring him to the park directly, that he might play there a little while you walk. He does so love an outing, and there will not be many such fine days remaining this year."

Dominic bowed solemnly, but Ellena could see the edge of a very happy smile upon his lips. "It will be a pleasure to accompany Ellena myself," he assured Charlotte, "especially after being denied the privilege yesterday. Shall we meet you at the fountain near the entrance, then? Or will you make your way to us at the terraced gardens?"

"Oh! Please do not delay your walk on account of us. We will find you once Clarence has had his fill of chasing the ducks. Thank you for accommodating us."

"Not at all. Till later, then."

At once, Dominic shifted his attention to Ellena.

"Shall we go?" He offered her his arm. Together, they approached the waiting carriage.

Ellena's heart beat a little faster as they settled in the compartment, alone with each other for the first time since he had known her as Nancy. Dominic was so close and the space so confined that she could smell his cologne. There was a woody undertone with notes of citrus and something else she couldn't quite place. Or perhaps it was his natural scent. Whichever it was, it had a heady effect upon her faculties and robbed her tongue of intelligent speech for most of their journey to Munro Park.

She wondered if Dominic experienced the same difficulty, for he said little of consequence. Did he ask himself why her fragrance seemed so familiar? No, that could not be. Upon their first encounter in the woods, Ellena had been soaked and muddy, her damp, earthy smell not at all similar to the delicate, floral cloud that settled upon her now. There could be no unexpected reminder of Nancy within Dominic. As yet, he seemed unaware of the dual identity hidden behind Ellena's persistent veil.

The lull in conversation was not entirely unwelcome. Unfamiliar with the neighborhood, Ellena did not know how long the ride would take from the church to the park, and she was unwilling to begin a discussion in case it should be interrupted by their sudden arrival at their destination.

When the magnificent lawns finally came into view, all other thought was briefly forgotten. The gardens and small patch of woodland stretched on a great distance, becoming lost to sight as it curved over a rise. A large, open area spread before them, with a rectangular, manmade lake and an enormous fountain central to the scene. Several couples strolled around its axis, branching off and away on a preferred path that would take them up the slope and onto their eventual destination. Some gentlemen carried small picnic baskets, while others strode fashionably with a cane. Chaperones trailed after a few of the younger couples. Ellena was grateful an exception had been made for her. It would make her revelation to Dominic more private.

"Would you like to stay a moment and admire the architecture of the fountain?" Dominic asked politely. "It is a recent commission and speaks to more modern tastes. You will find no baroque sculpture, only clean lines and symmetry. I am told that is now the fashion."

Ellena smiled to herself. She imagined that someone with such a long and rich family history would greatly prefer designs that reflected the character of the past. She cast her gaze upon the marble structure, its high plume of spray feathering into the sky. It was spectacular. But she had more urgent matters on her mind.

"Thank you, I have seen enough. I would rather stretch my legs a little. I believe you mentioned the Italian gardens? That might be a more worthwhile place to stop and consider the intricacies of design. Besides, it is so crowded here, and I feel my attire draws rather more attention than I would like. In fact, I was hoping to speak with you about the matter and would prefer not to have a passing party eavesdrop."

Dominic needed no further encouragement.

"Of course," he answered. "I, too, would be grateful for an opportunity to clear the air." He began at once to guide them along the path that led in the desired direction.

Ellena, now confronted with the moment of truth, felt suddenly awkward. What would Dominic say when she revealed that she was Nancy? She could not simply blurt it out. Where to start?

"I suppose I should begin by saying that I bear no grudge for the comments you made to James about me." It was true. She had chosen to forgive him. It was easier now that she was more confident of it having been an isolated occurrence.

Dominic opened his mouth to interrupt, but Ellena spoke quickly.

"I understand now, all too well, the circumstances in which you uttered those regrettable words. James has, but yesterday, led me to a similar display of frustration where I, too, spoke less elegantly than I would have liked."

Dominic was the picture of contrition. Tall as the man was, towering over her, his shoulders now softened and his eyes sought the floor. "It was, as you say, deeply regrettable," he admitted. "I am thankful that you have allowed me the benefit of the doubt."

His humility further convinced her that his better nature was his true form. "Let us dwell on it no more, then," Ellena said, pleased that they could put the first of their obstacles behind them.

"Forgive me," Dominic continued tentatively, "but if you bear no further resentment for my folly, why do you remain shrouded? I understood you chose to do this as a reaction to my careless speech to James. If all is resolved, can we not dispense with the covering?"

"There is more," explained Ellena, and she halted in her speech. This was it. She felt the drama of the moment build. When she lifted the veil, it would be as if meeting Dominic all over again for the first time. She wanted to do so now, to stand proudly and bravely before him—fully Ellena, truly *his* Ellena.

The sensation subsided, a wave retreating from the shore. The moment of revelation was not there yet. First, she would have to explain.

"Um..." she began somewhat ineloquently, "I have a rather startling secret I need to confide in you."

Dominic pulled up short.

"No, no," Ellena protested. "Let us continue with our walk. And do not stare at me in such alarm. We will draw attention to ourselves."

Dominic hesitated, then complied. They resumed their walk, but Ellena could feel the tension in his arm. She needed to find the words quickly, before any more of their time together was spoiled. Already, they had reached a long, grassy section that led onward through a copse of trees. Presumably, the Italian gardens were just beyond the small woodland, where the chattering and chirping of martins rose and fell. The gardens would be a popular gathering point for picnickers. She must speak now, while they were still some distance from other Sunday strollers.

"Dominic." She said the name softly, tenderly, calling up the intimacy she had felt when he'd first offered his name to her. "Do you recall where you were on Tuesday night?"

He jolted at her words.

"You do not need to answer," Ellena continued briskly. "I know where you were. I know about Nancy Fallon."

Dominic stopped in mid-stride and swung around to face her, his cheeks blanched and eyes wide.

"It… It's not what you think," he stammered, all poise and dignity abandoned.

"I know exactly what to think," Ellena insisted. "It is your knowledge of this other woman that forced me to retain my veil."

Dominic's face drew tight with distress. "I assure you, the c-circumstances were quite innocent! You have n-no need to doubt my actions!"

Ellena waved her hand to dismiss his concerns. "I am well aware of this. Do not fret about my opinion of the young lady or your encounter with her. In truth, I am very well acquainted with Miss Nancy Fallon." She reached for the tip of her veil. "I know her as well as anyone can, for she and I are…"

"There you are!" called a familiar, cheerful voice. William Cole came striding down the grassy slope toward them. "I see the princess is with her noble knight," he noted with a good-natured grin.

Dominic turned to face the newcomer squarely.

"And who are you, sir?" he inquired with a scowl.

Ellena was equally agitated by the interruption. What terrible timing! Mr. Cole could not have chosen a worse moment to make his appearance. But here he was, with his open smile and bright eyes. And that charming wit that had so perked up her mood in the garden yesterday. Ellena felt her annoyance melt away. Remembering her manners, she made a hasty introduction.

"Dominic, this is Charlotte's younger brother, Mr. William Cole. He is staying at Thorn Bush Hall—recovering from his failed attempt to secure a bride in Steeples this summer," she added with a playful jab. Then, as if remembering herself, she concluded more formally. "Mr. Cole, may I introduce you to Lord Howell, my intended?"

"Lord Howell." Mr. Cole bowed politely, touching his fingers to his hat. "What an honor to meet the man who has captured the heart of the princess. You must know what a narrow escape she has had." He grinned. "Had I known of her existence before your betrothal, she would have been wooed exhaustively until she agreed to marry me. Alas, I can now only sulk from a distance at losing the opportunity. You are indeed the most fortunate of men."

Dominic's expression clouded. He did not even so much as nod to acknowledge the newcomer. The sudden change was obvious, and Ellena noticed at once.

"Dominic, what is it? Is something wrong?"

"No, of course not." His answer was a little gruff and caught Ellena by surprise. In contrast with the brightness of Mr. Cole, Dominic suddenly seemed rough and surly.

A warning shot up her spine. She tried to soften the mood with the light banter that worked so well with Mr. Cole. "Oh, dear, it seems my dear Dominic is lost for words." She followed this with an attempt at laughter, but it sounded awkward and false.

"We are not all great wits and chatterboxes," Dominic grumbled. "Some men prefer a quiet dignity over a superficial camaraderie."

Ellena was shocked at the change in his tone. She stared at him in disbelief, hardly knowing what to say. Was this the side of him that James had seen? But how had Mr. Cole triggered it? He had hardly said a word, and that which he had said could not be compared to the offense James had given.

Mr. Cole raised an eyebrow but continued to smile.

"I daresay you have a point, Lord Howell," he addressed the bristling man. "I myself am a great supporter of quiet dignity, especially where speech would have revealed something of a less excellent nature." He watched as color crept into his opponent's cheeks. "Then again, there is much to be said for idle chatter as a buffer in awkward conversations."

Before the recipient of his remarks could erupt with indignant rage, Mr. Cole turned to Ellena and added quickly, "I apologize for interrupting your walk. Charlotte has asked me to deliver a message. Little Clarence was sleeping very soundly, and she felt it unwise to disturb him and force an outing upon him. She has therefore remained at the house. She asks that I wait for you by the fountain and deliver you home in time for an early dinner once your walk is done. I have brought the phaeton, so that we may travel in the open with propriety. I trust this is acceptable?"

Lord Howell, meanwhile, had found his tongue. "I will take Miss Trenton home myself, thank you," he announced stiffly. "There is no need for you to waste the rest of your morning on such an errand."

Mr. Cole was not deterred in the least. "I assure you, sir, there is nothing that requires my attention elsewhere. It would be the high point in my otherwise dull day to accompany my sister's cousin home."

"I thank you," the viscount managed with barely concealed irritation, "but it is not our business to provide your entertainment. You may oblige us by letting Mrs. Trenton know Ellena already has a ride—with her betrothed. If you will be so good as to excuse us…" He emphasized the finality of the conversation by turning his back to Mr. Cole and reaching for Ellena's arm.

Ellena had witnessed the rise in tension and had not fully understood its cause. After all, Mr. Cole could not be taken seriously. She sensed no harm in his words, no reason for Dominic to take umbrage at them. She was sorely disappointed that her betrothed should speak with such clear distaste toward Mr. Cole, who, after all, had only been trying to help. She made an attempt to placate the irate viscount. "Dominic, I can't think that…"

"It's all right," Mr. Cole reassured her. "I will take my leave." He looked grimly at her simmering partner. "Miss Trenton is expected no later than two o' clock."

"She will be home with time to spare," came the curt reply.

"Very well. Good day to you, Lord Howell. Miss Trenton, I bid you an enjoyable resumption of your courtship." Then he turned and retraced his route, shrinking from sight as he topped the rise and descended.

Ellena stared at Dominic, who had calmed a little since the perceived menace had been removed.

"What on Earth was that about?" she demanded. "What cause have you to treat Mr. Cole so poorly?"

"I don't know what you mean." Dominic sniffed. "I merely answered the man as he deserved."

"How can you say such a thing? Mr. Cole was all benevolence and good humor. What must he make of your comments? And to think I defended your actions to him but yesterday. Yet you treat him with disdain for no reason."

Dominic's forehead puckered in a frown. "You speak of me with him? You gossip about me to another man? And does he like to spoon the treacle of his charm into your ear while you do so?"

Ellena stared at him with her mouth open, his surly question ringing in her ears. "What can you mean to be saying such things?" she asked, her equilibrium quite shaken.

"You need to ask me this?" Dominic's agitation was stirred by a new thought. "Tell me, do you wear your veil with him?"

"What?" His question set off an alarm in Ellena's mind.

"When you talk so freely about personal matters, does he also look freely upon your face?"

"I… We… It's not the same," Ellena answered miserably.

"Isn't it?" Dominic straightened his back. "I see."

"Dominic," she tried to explain, "we are both guests under the same roof. I can hardly spend the entire day in this garb." She indicated the veil that still remained between them.

"Yes," Dominic mulled, "you are under the same roof. You show him your face, which you deny me, your intended. You confide your innermost thoughts to him. There is much opportunity for such intimacy *under the same roof.*"

Ellena took a step backward. "What can you mean?"

"I think you understand me perfectly. I cannot help but wonder at the ease between you and a man you have just met. How does it happen that he feels entitled to speak so casually, unless you have encouraged him? How much have you encouraged him? How much has he felt the right to claim?"

He stopped abruptly, his breath heavy, his jaw tight.

Ellena trembled as his words sank in. Tears stung her eyes, though she knew he could not see them. Her voice, when she spoke, was thick with restrained feeling.

"You think very little of me to say such things."

Silence followed. Dominic's face was unreadable. Ellena's tears fell now, slipping across her cheeks. Her sight blurred as more tears formed, and she reached a hand in under her veil to wipe them away. Her action caused a break in the wall of Dominic's stony expression. Instant regret flooded his features. His mouth softened. His scowl vanished. He lowered his eyes in shame.

But it was too late.

Anger built within her. She did not know this man. He had

revealed such steady character when he had been Dominic in the woods. But he had smeared her good name to James at the smallest provocation. Then he had shown understanding and sensitivity at dinner. But now he accused her of...of...terrible things! How dare he! She had given him the benefit of the doubt, had been about to reveal her identity as Nancy, eager to move on with their relationship. And he had thrown her trust back in her face. How could he think such base thoughts about her? What reason had she given him to believe her capable of such shameful behavior?

No, the fault lay with him!

Fury radiated from her in waves. Her shoulders grew stiff, her hands balled into fists.

Dominic, by contrast, slumped into a pose of self-defeat.

"Ellena, I...I'm so sorry. I don't know what came over me. There is no excuse..."

He reached out his hand in appeal, but she backed away rapidly, almost stumbling in her haste. All the while, she kept her eyes firmly upon him, as if she feared his final transformation into the monstrous brute he had hidden so well until now.

Dominic was not as she had hoped or believed. Despite his shameful comment to James, Ellena had convinced herself that he was a gentleman of the highest caliber, someone with whom she could be vulnerable and still safe. She had tried her best to shut out all doubt. But now she was confronted with the awful reality: he was, after all, a petty and callous creature, and she wished herself far away from him.

She looked about her, searching for an escape. She recalled the retreating form of Mr. Cole, and turned, at once, to follow. With renewed purpose, her pace quickened, and she all but fled the scene that still anchored Dominic. She hurried up the slope, the force of her emotions driving her on until she topped the rise. In the distance, the great fountain, so splendid to her optimistic gaze but a short while ago, now seemed to rage powerfully, echoing her own tumbling, overwhelming thoughts.

After a few moments, she heard hasty footsteps behind her. Dominic drew level with her, caught her by the arm and turned her toward him.

"Ellena, p-please wait. L-Let me explain."

She tore her arm from his grasp and cried out, "There is nothing further I want to hear from you!"

"But you m-must know I d-did not mean any of it. You c-cannot think I would really…"

"I don't know what to think anymore! You have fooled me with your chivalry and your … your pretense at integrity. Think what you like of me in your prurient imagination. You have shown yourself capable of a baseness I would not have believed possible if a man like James had declared it so. But from your own lips, you condemn yourself as everything he described."

Dominic hung his head. His speech slowed as he fought to control his stutter. "You are right to despise my actions just now. Your rebuke is no less than I deserve. But it is the foolishness of a moment and does not reflect my true opinion of you. I reacted poorly to the way Mr. Cole has ingratiated himself to you. I should not have implied you were at fault. I allowed myself to be goaded by his honeyed words and presumptuous intimacy toward you."

"Mr. *Cole* is not to blame for your appalling assumptions. He has never, could never, make such vile suggestions about my person as you have managed to do without provocation. And Mr. Cole, unlike yourself, would not have the gall to question my innocence while carrying the secret of a rendezvous with Miss Nancy Fallon. Perhaps you question in me what you know yourself to be guilty of. Shall I ponder what feelings you have for your little rescued maiden?"

Dominic was silenced.

Good! Let him writhe in guilt! Let him drown in it! Who was he to judge when she had seen how sorely he'd been parted from "Nancy" at the convent gates? She had forgiven him once before. This time, she would not make it easy for him.

"Nothing to say?" she asked, expecting no answer. "I think that says enough in and of itself. You will do me the kindness of saying nothing further to me at all. I shall find Mr. Cole and have him escort me home. Good day, sir."

Ellena gathered her skirts and hastened away toward the road. She saw the phaeton from a distance. Mr. Cole was climbing up the step but turned at her call and stopped in apparent surprise. She waved for him to wait, and he strode toward her. When he reached her, he found her trembling. Ellena clasped her arms to herself to try to stop from shaking. Mr. Cole looked up and past her, but Dominic was nowhere near.

Ellena was fighting for self-control. She could scarce think what to say. "I want to go home," was all she managed.

Mercifully, Mr. Cole asked no questions. He merely helped Ellena atop the high vehicle, where she sank into a miserable silence. He grabbed the reins and clicked his tongue to signal the horses. The phaeton lurched forward, and the suddenness of the action forced a sob from Ellena's throat.

The carriage rolled on. And the distance between Ellena and Dominic grew.

CHAPTER SIXTEEN

DOMINIC SAGGED ONTO the seat of a bench a few feet away. He had to admit, William Cole could not be blamed for this mess, but he loathed him nevertheless. The man had looked at Ellena with a most perturbing intensity—and a knowledge of her lovely face that Dominic had not yet been allowed to share. And that smug smile! Not to mention the impudence of seeing himself as a suitor if Dominic had not claimed her first. It was enough to make his blood boil.

The fact that Ellena appeared to delight in the fellow's jokes still chafed at him. The easy manner that Mr. Cole enjoyed epitomized him as the very opposite of Dominic, who had never been comfortable making light conversation with a woman. But William Cole had skipped easily into Ellena's favor in just one day. Dominic felt a ridiculous urge to growl and bare his teeth at the charming young man.

Thanks to the presence of that accursed veil, Dominic could not tell if Ellena had smiled prettily in response to Mr. Cole's comments, or whether her eyes had rested upon the young man as his had upon her. Her bearing had certainly lacked any reserve.

Old, deep-seated insecurities had resurfaced within the hidden chamber of his mind. If only he had pushed them back. But he had released them. He had said such ugly things, things that utterly shamed him now. Oh, he had gone too far, much too far.

The momentum of his own fears had carried him over into the abyss.

If he was worried about the influence Mr. Cole had over Ellena, his own behavior had not helped him in this regard. He bitterly regretted the advantage he had so stupidly provided his opponent. And much, much worse: he had once again insulted the woman who was to be his wife. He had shown himself a petty, insecure fool. He had so desperately wanted to like her, to be liked by her. Now she could only despise him.

But that was not all. Her parting challenge was one he could not easily dismiss. What *did* he feel for Nancy Fallon? He had become attached to Nancy in their short time together. He could not deny it. But he had set these fledgling feelings aside. He had committed himself to a life with Ellena. Still, he acknowledged a fondness, an easy connection, with the stranger in the forest. He knew he must not entertain such sentiments, yet they lingered at the periphery of his thoughts.

A haunting echo of Nancy's smile filtered through his mind. Thinking of her made him further ashamed of his outburst. He had said harsh things that Nancy would have found just as despicable as Ellena had. The expression he had been unable to see on Ellena's face was all too easily imagined in the eyes of Nancy. It tore at his heart.

A sudden thought struck him. Ellena had declared herself well acquainted with Miss Fallon. Was it possible they would talk of this ghastly incident? Would they now unite in their revulsion of him? If so, it was doubly hard to bear.

Dominic contemplated his marital future with Ellena. It was a struggle to blaze a path to each other's hearts over the obstacles of misinformation and the awkwardness of being strangers. And he had just given their progress a terrible setback. Where would they begin to pick up the thread of their unraveling connection? He groaned. He did not have the answers, but he was in desperate need of them. He berated himself for the unnecessary crisis that now needed to be overcome. As if this courtship had not already been enough of a challenge.

He heaved himself up from the bench with a sigh. He could think of nothing but to give Ellena a little time to overcome the worst of her injured feelings. He did not think a further apology would help at the moment. She had rejected his repeated attempts outright. He would give her a day, though they could scarcely afford it. But she deserved a little more time to resent his actions before he asked her once more to forgive them.

Meanwhile, he had other responsibilities. Besides his usual duties, he still had to make final arrangements for the wedding. In five days, they would be man and wife, for better or worse.

Dominic flinched. Why, oh, why, did the "worse" have to happen so soon?

ELLENA SAT IN utter silence across from Charlotte's brother in the jostling carriage. She bit her lip as Dominic's terrible words repeated themselves in her mind, until the physical pain of it broke into her thoughts and released her briefly from their taunt.

Her disappointment in her betrothed was deep and bitter.

But what had she expected? To know a man but a few days was no knowledge at all.

Dominic had never before seen her in conversation with an eligible stranger. There had been no opportunity to test his nature in this. Was he a jealous man, then? Was this even his greatest fault? Or was this the beginning of a string of unpleasant discoveries? How unreasonable would he be if he felt truly threatened?

Ellena tried to calm her racing thoughts. Perhaps this was his first taste of jealousy. Having experienced its appalling effects, he might now be utterly purged with shame. Even then, how could she forgive this second insult to her person? He had turned on her. All because he disapproved of Mr. Cole.

She looked up at her companion. Poor Mr. Cole. Such ill treatment simply for having a genial nature. There was no threat there. After all, was she not already bound to Dominic? And did she not behave with absolute loyalty to him at all times?

A trickle of guilt slipped from her conscience. She had kept the truth of her identity from him. It had been done to protect them both, but it was a secret wall between them nevertheless. The veil had created distance where there should have been connection. And it remained between them still. Anger flared again. The veil had not caused this! It had been Dominic's own dark assumptions about her friendship with Mr. Cole. He simply did not trust her. And if Dominic did not trust her, he would treat her with little respect, now, and always.

Ellena thought of her own parents, whose marriage turned on her father's axis. She did not want to be reduced to an obedient shadow, fearful to displease. She couldn't live like that. She couldn't!

But she would have no choice. A distrustful husband would not give her the loving gentleness she so desperately hoped for. Yet, as much as she longed for affection, she would not beg for it.

In spite of her determination not to, she began to cry once more. The sobs she had bit back now broke free from her heart. In an instant, Mr. Cole had pulled up the reins and produced a handkerchief from his pocket. He grasped the veil and folded it back.

"Do not hide your tears from a friend, Miss Trenton. There is no shame in having such deep feeling. Rather, I wish you would confide the cause of your sadness to me, that I might render some sort of useful service for once in my life." He offered a lopsided smile. "Think how proud my father would be if he knew I had counseled a young lady in distress as my first act of selfless responsibility."

Ellena sniffed and wiped her nose. "Thank you. But I am not your responsibility, Mr. Cole."

"As there is no one else, I will gladly see to your well-being.

That includes wiping away tears and lending an interested ear. You will not deny me my first venture into selflessness, will you?"

Ellena waved her hand in exasperation. "Oh, I hardly wish to be accused of such a thing, when I have already been accused of sufficient guilt in worse matters."

Mr. Cole's brow drew into a puzzled frown. "Not by your noble viscount? How can this be?"

"Believe me, I am tortured by the very same confusion. He has revealed a most disturbing side to his character this morning."

"I hate to admit it, but he did not seem the man you had portrayed in our discussion yesterday."

"Oh! Do not remind me of it. You must think me the most infatuated fool to have so staunchly defended him, only to be exposed to that same error in his nature the very next day."

Mr. Cole set his jaw firmly. "I cannot possibly think ill of you. But I must greatly despise Lord Howell if he is the cause of such distress. I cannot think what grievance he may possibly have against you."

Ellena stared at her hands in her lap, the soggy handkerchief clutched in her fingers. "His claim is certainly unfounded upon fact. I am embarrassed to say it aloud."

Mr. Cole's expression was grim. "I have a suspicion I am mentioned in his complaint."

"Yes!" cried the miserable Ellena. "I groan at the very idea, but it is true. How did you guess?"

"It was not a great feat of deduction. He clearly disliked me from the moment we met. And you left the park mere minutes after I did. It seems logical that the argument stemmed from his feelings toward me."

"Logical, perhaps, but not reasonable." Ellena wrung her hands. "Oh, Mr. Cole, I am bitterly sorry that you are in any way implicated in this pitiful jealousy. I cannot tell you how it mortifies me."

"On the contrary." Mr. Cole smiled, a hint of his playful charm just below the surface. "I am hugely flattered! To think a man as powerful and influential as Lord Howell might feel threatened by a nobody like myself... Why, it's positively uplifting to the ego."

"But you're *not* a nobody! You are a kind and decent man. I would have thought Dominic could recognize that as I have."

"My dear Miss Trenton, your pity for my reputation is very touching but quite unnecessary. I am sure that, whatever his lordship has said, he now desperately wishes unsaid. What man could hurt you and not immediately despise himself? He will make amends, I am sure."

Ellena clamped her lips together. "That may be so, but it will not be a simple task. He has not only maligned your character but suggested I was a willing participant in a clandestine entanglement."

"With *me?*" Mr. Cole barked a sharp laugh. "If it were not so outrageous and offensive in its untruthfulness, I would be grateful for the compliment." His wry smile slid from his face. "What could possibly have prompted such an extreme allegation?"

Ellena was quiet. She could not tell Mr. Cole about her pending confession to Dominic, and how the problem of the veil would have fueled Lord Howell's imagination.

The uncomfortable silence prompted Mr. Cole to withdraw his question. "I am sorry. This conversation is only adding to your distress. We shall not dwell on the details. I am sure you will find your betrothed greatly humbled at your next meeting. A favorable outcome may yet be achieved."

Ellena did not share his optimism. "I have little choice in that," she remarked soberly. "I am bound by the wishes of my father and the whim of my betrothed. If he is not motivated to act with common decency, there is little I can do to improve the situation."

She was quite miserable. Embarrassed by the inclusion of Mr. Cole in the scandalous outburst from her betrothed, Ellena could not bring herself to even look at her companion. And Mr. Cole, unable to provide solace, sat mutely next to her for the remainder of their journey to Thorn Bush Hall.

Upon their arrival at her cousin's home, Ellena slipped from the carriage with muttered thanks and fled to her room. She discarded her bonnet and threw herself onto her bed. Releasing the despair she had suppressed in Mr. Cole's company, she sobbed into her pillow. She abandoned herself to its soft, down-filled depths, raging against all that was unfair and unkind in the tightly-spun web of her life. Finally, the pent-up emotion depleted, Ellena sank into a stone-like sleep.

An hour later, she was awakened by the light knocking of a servant at her door.

"Please, miss, I was told to say dinner is ready to be served."

"Thank you, Lucy. Tell Mrs. Trenton I'll be there shortly."

When she was alone again, Ellena washed her face in the porcelain basin near the window and tidied her hair as best she could by adding a few pins. Then she proceeded down the hall to the smaller dining room, apprehensive of the reception she might expect from her cousin and Charlotte.

But she had feared their comments needlessly. James was involved in deep discussion with Mr. Cole. Charlotte smiled knowingly at her and merely said, "I trust your walk exceeded all expectations if you spend so much time writing letters in your room. Your parents no doubt gain much solace from their daughter's happiness."

They did not know? Ellena looked at Mr. Cole, who returned her gaze with his usual warmth before giving his attention once again to James. He hadn't told them! A flood of relief replaced her trepidation. She felt enormous gratitude toward Mr. Cole for sparing her the further pain of interrogations and explanations, especially at the hands of her cousin. For now, at least, she had a little space to recover and think. Not that there was much she could do. Whether or not she forgave Lord Howell was immate-rial. Their wedding would still take place, and they would have to declare a truce for the sake of marital peace.

Of course, she had yet to remove her veil and declare herself.

The thought made her shudder. Until now, she had believed he would understand her reason for remaining shrouded. Once the lace was discarded, they would resume a more normal courtship and a promising marriage.

But he had been triggered into hasty and lurid speech by such a trivial conversation surrounding Mr. Cole. How could she possibly know what would set him off next? If he believed that her lingering lie was a sign she was untrustworthy, he might very well turn against her once more.

She chewed slowly, barely tasting the roast mutton, and spoke hardly at all. It mattered little, for James and Charlotte led the conversation in turns. Occasionally, Mr. Cole would give her a reassuring smile, but for the most part, Ellena was grateful to be left alone.

After the meal, she returned to her room, claiming a touch of fatigue from the walk and unusual heat. Charlotte sent a pot of tea after her but otherwise left her to herself to rest.

In her room, Ellena sat dejected at the window. She plunged through the range of emotions that had tortured her since the confrontation in the park. Rage, confusion, shock, dismay and humiliation battled for supremacy, until, to her surprise, she tired of them and reached a pool of calm beyond. She wondered what Dominic was doing right now. Was he thinking of her? Did he agonize as she did? Did he search his mental resources for a solution to the thorny situation he had created? Or had he recovered himself, even justifying his behavior?

Somehow, despite the misgivings she now experienced, she could not picture him as anything but wretched under the circumstances. She remembered his face and drooping shoulders before she had walked away. A tiny spark of pity surfaced, and she did not extinguish it. Perhaps it would yet guide her to reconciliation. If they could but surmount the problem of the veil.

She put aside her musings before they regressed again into negative thoughts. Unwilling to re-enter into the society of the household so soon, she cast her eyes about the room for distraction. She had no desire to read or sew. Perhaps she could write to Jillian a little earlier today. It would certainly be difficult to harbor angry thoughts while picturing her friend. She settled herself at the writing desk and dipped the pen in readiness.

Dear Jilly,

I have not yet received your letter today, as I am writing a little earlier than usual and have come to expect your replies only in the late afternoon post. As a result, I do not know what you think of my project to marry you to Charlotte's brother. I can only say that recent events have proved my suggestion to be a most favorable one.

She paused here. She fully intended avoiding all references to Dominic, for fear her emotions might surge again, drawing her into the vicious spiral of anger and depression. Besides, it would only upset her friend to know she was unhappy. Instead, she would give her attention to a little matchmaking.

Mr. Cole is a man of great character. He is entertaining in conversation and sensitive in matters requiring delicate handling. A fine blend, do you not agree? I think you would match both his wit and heart with certain ease. And I am convinced his parents would be grateful for such a worthy daughter-in-law. True, you do not play the piano or enjoy painting, but you have abundant common sense and generosity—traits that I understand are much prized by Mr. and Mrs. Cole.

They are a sound family, Jilly, and one that would be blessed with the addition of such a daughter. The only drawback is that you would have James for a brother-in-law! For that, I cannot offer any solace, except to say that Mr. William Cole is fine compensation indeed.

I have been kept from furthering your cause with him this morning, as I attended church, followed by an outing to Munro Park. But I am committed to a fresh start tomorrow. Mr. Cole shall find me a faithful friend for mentioning your name and encouraging your alliance.

Shall I test his mettle by speaking immediately of your three rambunctious brothers? Perhaps it will tempt him with the thought of many sons of his own. And if, instead, he is discouraged, then it is well we know of what poor stuff he is made to have so small a matter deter him.

I cannot wait for you to meet him. Has Father spoken of you accompanying him and my mother to the wedding? You must alert me to any reticence on his part, as I shall hold Lord Howell to his promise to intervene on your behalf.

If all goes smoothly, I shall see you within a few days. I shall remove myself from all other society upon your arrival and steal you away to confide all my secrets. You may be surprised how much ink has been spared in leaving these out of my letters. Of course, I will have to pause in my flood of narration to introduce you to Mr. Cole. I wonder if even the juiciest of tales will then be able to lure you away from him. We shall see how well I have judged your mutual compatibility.

Until then, I wait eagerly for more of your written news. It is a precious surrogate for the loss of your company. Please do not neglect writing a letter for even one day until you are with me in Munro.

Your friend forever,
Ellena

CHAPTER SEVENTEEN

THE FOLLOWING MORNING brought no news from Dominic. Ellena could not guess whether he had once again been held up with business, or if he chose silence in the absence of a clear plan of action.

Maybe the space between them was exactly what they needed. She was not yet ready to forgive him outright. He had regretted his actions and apologized, but the offense still smarted. Perhaps Dominic waited for her to extend the hand of reconciliation. She considered this, then pushed the idea aside. No, he must take the lead.

The truth was, Ellena knew she had overreacted by marching off like that. Enough time had passed for some clarity to settle upon her thoughts. Yes, Dominic had crossed the line and said a most despicable thing, but he had quickly returned to his senses. He deserved to be reprimanded sharply, but they would never solve their problems if she ran from them.

What was clear, however, was that her betrothed was a man easily made jealous. The knowledge was both flattering and worrying. For this reason, he must make the first move. It would reveal his state of mind. Would he still be humble today? Or had his thoughts once again taken a wrong turn? If he were genuinely contrite, he would do his best to make amends.

Ellena allowed herself a few more minutes of self-pity, then grew tired of her own company. She had spent most of the previous afternoon in a state of self-imposed exile from the family. Now a distraction was needed to keep her mind from harboring subversive thoughts.

James was away at the office—a small mercy. But Charlotte, too, was occupied. Little Clarence had developed a light cold and fretted whenever his mother left him for even a moment. Unwilling to linger in solitude any longer, Ellena sought out William Cole. A little constructive matchmaking was just what she needed to perk herself up. She cared little for propriety at this juncture. There was no one to observe and judge their behavior, one way or the other. And if they *were* watched, they would merely be seen in conversation. She would take care not to stand too close to the gentleman, just in case.

She discovered her subject under a sprawling ash tree in the garden. He was deeply engrossed in a letter and sat almost motionless upon the shady bench. Ellena halted her approach, not wishing to intrude upon his privacy. She watched his expression shift from surprise to concern as he chewed his lip absently in contemplation of the letter's contents. When he was done, he folded it neatly and inserted it into his coat pocket. He rose to return to the house and spied Ellena standing at the foot of the path. Immediately, his face broke into a bright smile.

"Miss Trenton! You appear as an angel in my darkest hour of need."

Ellena blushed and stepped forward. "I cannot imagine what use I may possibly be. But I will serve in whatever capacity I am able. Have you had bad news?"

Mr. Cole shrugged. "That depends upon how you look at it, I suppose. Father is out of patience with me. He is convinced I make no real effort to find a suitable match. He believes I only pretend to do so to avoid committing myself to a purposeful career. I am to produce a wife in the next six months or accept the offer at the vicarage—which, I now hear, includes the tantalizing incentive of marrying the retiring vicar's youngest daughter. However, I know the girl, and she is a sad little thing. All doom and gloom—a most distressing quality in one so young. I do not believe she will find any of my jokes funny, and this would be a severe punishment for my sensitive ego."

He sat down quite suddenly, as if the thought was too much for him.

The sight of such a mirthless Mr. Cole filled Ellena's heart with pity. He was not one for somber moods, and his current state did not suit him at all. Fortunately, Ellena believed she had a cure for his condition.

"May I join you?" she asked, indicating the bench that he occupied.

When Mr. Cole nodded, she sat at once, settled her skirt smoothly, and tilted her head up at him. "It just so happens I am an expert judge of human character and recognize instantly what you seek in a wife."

A warm smile spread across Mr. Cole's face. "I have no doubt you are amply qualified. For who better to know this than one so perfect for the role herself?"

His words, though said in jest, twisted like a knife in Ellena's heart. Mr. Cole did not doubt her as Dominic did. He only saw good in her, while her intended, the man to whom she was bound, readily sank in his opinion of her.

"Ah, yes," she replied, bitterness shallow upon her tongue. "But as I am previously engaged, we shall have to rule me out. It is most unfortunate, but there you have it."

"As you say, most unfortunate," replied Mr. Cole, his familiar twinkle rapidly returning. "I have a good mind to reconsider my offer of a duel."

"Mr. Cole," Ellena scolded, "you know as well as I do, you are far too much of a gentleman to assault a man without provocation. Besides, I am convinced that, once I were available to you, the allure of the forbidden fruit would vanish, and I would no longer seem worth the winning."

"Oh, but you are wrong on both counts. I have been sorely

provoked by your viscount. Not only has he audaciously claimed the one lady I consider worthy of my admiration, but he has succumbed to a contemptible attitude in the treatment of same lady. Both actions are worthy of severe consequences. As for your assumption about forbidden fruit, you fail to recognize the pleasure exacted by a hunter who wins his trophy."

"Am I your prey, then?" Ellena asked, the thought shivering through her in a way that both thrilled and alarmed her.

"Certainly. But do not fear, for my only weapon is Cupid's arrow. And, based on my experience in Steeples, I am clearly a poor shot!"

Ellena relaxed as her companion's tone returned to its earlier lightness. "Poor Mr. Cole. Perhaps you have not chosen your targets carefully. To begin with, it is always best to choose a lady who is available—one who is neither engaged nor married—and who has a willing heart."

"Hmph, such maids there were aplenty in Steeples. But, as you say, this is merely a starting point. There seems to be a constant supply of unmarried women. However, one often discovers the reason for their unwed status once one gets to know them a little."

"I can see you are a discerning customer." Ellena nodded sagely. "That is why I am willing to help you. You will be able to recognize a priceless artifact when it is offered to you."

"And what will be the qualities of this treasure that I should consider her worthy of investing my heart?"

"Well, firstly beauty, of course. There can be no denying the importance of a pretty face. No woman is so naïve as to think a man does not care for such things."

Mr. Cole scratched his chin. "I would like to defend my sex and say it is not true, but you have me at a disadvantage, since it is a bald fact. Does this disgrace the male gender with its superficiality?"

"No more so than it implicates women." Ellena shrugged. "We are as fond of a handsome appearance as you are. However, we tend toward a willingness to put practical needs over aesthetic preferences. It is in our best interests to be married, and wealth adds appeal in the absence of physical attraction. Does this, then, make us mercenary?"

Mr. Cole's tone grew solemn. "It is a woman's burden and privilege to be cared for by a man. In such a dependent position, it can only be seen as wisdom to choose a partner who can provide a stable and reasonable income. Very few who choose love over all else find their empty stomachs agreeing with their decision."

"A sad truth," Ellena agreed. "But love has a way of following where breadcrumbs are laid. If the woman has a pleasing look that stirs her husband's heart, and he gives her every reason to trust in a secure future, there are few obstacles to affection. Love in marriage is not lessened when it follows rather than leads."

"Hmm, a secure future, you say," Mr. Cole mused. "So, we have established that there are certain parameters that must be met by myself also. Income is clearly ranked at the top."

"We shall give consideration to your qualifications in due course. But let me complete my inventory of those qualities you may expect in the bride I select for you."

"You have my undivided attention."

"After beauty, there can be no question as to what characteristic should be next on the list. Can you guess?"

"Now you are cheating, Miss Trenton," Mr. Cole scolded. "It is *you* who are estimating my perfect needs. You cannot consult with me for information."

Ellena laughed. "Your answer confirms what I already suspected. The woman you seek must have the joint qualities of intelligence and good humor—the first to match your bright wit, and the second to take no offense from it."

"Ah, already, she is a rare find, indeed. I cannot abide a tedious partner in conversation. It has been my unpleasant experience that many young ladies find their own chatter quite entertaining, oblivious of the agonies they impose upon their weary listeners. Whatever else I may be obliged to endure, this would be the least bearable. I should sooner marry an ugly bride than a dull one, for it is easier to close one's eyes than one's ears."

"You, sir, are incorrigible! But I assure you, the wife you seek is not as unattainable as you fear."

"Well!" Mr. Cole leaned back and folded his arms across his chest. "This *is* good news! Dare I ask what other hidden talents this prospective bride boasts of?"

"By all means, allow me to elucidate her many charming attributes. Her family will, by twist of good luck, live a fair distance from your own, guaranteeing a minimum of interference from your in-laws. At the same time, she is the kind of daughter and sister who has a strong family feeling, teaching her the principles of loyalty, sacrifice, generosity, patience, and forgiveness. You must agree that these are worthwhile traits in a life partner."

"I cannot disagree. But I suspect that you are describing a lady perfect in so many aspects that none such can exist."

"You doubt me needlessly. Your disappointing experiences up till now have marred your faith in the fairer sex. But towns less frequented than Steeples often hide the most precious gems. Of course, you may have to compromise on more trivial matters. She might, for instance, carry only the humblest of dowries. Perhaps she does not sing as well as you, or she has little skill on the piano. She may lack your sister's gift for needlepoint. But I suspect none of these shortcomings would be critical in your consideration."

"No, I am not moved to reject a lady for any of these faults. Certainly, a large dowry would be welcome, but its absence is not so grave a loss as would be a lack of wit or beauty."

"Then it is settled. I shall review my memory and my circle of acquaintances for the ideal match. Do not be surprised if she is presented to you within the week."

"A week! That will be well-managed, indeed. And I will be sorely in need of suitable company to replace yours when you become Lady Howell. Well, Miss Trenton, I am satisfied with your efforts."

Ellena waggled a teasing finger under his nose. "You celebrate too soon, Mr. Cole. We shall now consider what *you* have to offer, since my perfect protégée cannot be aligned with poor stock."

"Ha! I am not afraid of your scrutiny," he replied, shaking a finger back at her. "I know that I already satisfy the first and most important two requirements: wealth and fine features." The back of his fingers traced his lapel. With a tilt of his head and eyebrows arched, he demanded, "In light of these, what further expectations can be of equal weight?"

Ellena was unimpressed. "Your handsome looks cannot be denied. However, the wealth you offer as surety in your cause belongs to your family, in which you are not the firstborn. As such, you neither own nor stand to inherit any sizable fortune and must rely on an allowance and your own income, which is currently non-existent."

Mr. Cole grew quiet. "You are a cruel bargainer, Miss Trenton. I can see your family's reputation in this arena must be extended to include your own prowess."

Ellena pursed her lips. "You cannot avoid the facts by offering me scraps of flattery. I will not recommend you to any friend of mine if you do not have the means to care for her in a fitting manner. I do not expect you to pursue your father's dream that you follow a life in the church. But do you intend to make a determined effort in a military career?"

"I can see that it shall need to be investigated sooner rather than later if I am to enjoy your support. I have an uncle who might sponsor a commission in the infantry. I shall write to him and see whether he may be persuaded. Will this suffice as a first step?"

Ellena nodded. "It will do nicely."

Mr. Cole brightened. "Well, then, let us assume I make a favorable impression in my new uniform. Dare I ask what other failings I shall need to overcome?"

"Ah, Mr. Cole, you are blessed in having such a dear friend in me that I can find no other shortcomings. You are protective of your sister: the sign of a devoted family man. You are lavish in your attentions—though occasionally they may be misplaced. Your humor is refreshing, your compassion endearing, and your desire to respect your parents' wishes admirable. In short, you are excellent material with which to entice a young lady into marriage."

"I am relieved to hear it." Mr. Cole's eyes, free of their usual twinkle, gazed earnestly at Ellena. "Your opinion matters a great deal. I would not like to gain another's approval before I had won yours."

"Then you may put all such concerns to rest, for my approval has been secured."

"I thank you for that." William Cole bowed his head.

Ellena was aware of a strange emotion stirring in her heart. The more she considered Mr. Cole as a suitor for Jillian Kinsey, the more she observed the qualities that commended him. As she studied him more keenly, she appreciated more deeply his good nature and neat frame, his dancing eyes and mischievous smile.

Prior to Dominic's reprehensible slander on her moral conduct, she had been content with her future. She had believed him to be a kind and generous soul, one who did not abuse his power and who considered her feelings. Yes, he had erred grievously, but she had still thought him a promising match, one in which love could tread surefootedly.

But it occurred to her now that Mr. Cole could boast of similar claims. He showed her consideration and respect. In addition, he was gallant and so very likeable. And, although she would never tell him this for fear his ego would become inflated, he really was devastatingly handsome. She found herself envying Jillian for the match she would make, especially now that Dominic had fallen somewhat lower in her esteem. Mr. Cole's enchanting qualities shone even more brightly as Dominic's star dimmed.

In the midst of her rambling thoughts, Ellena spotted Lucy at the top of the steps to the garden. The shy maidservant made her way toward them, a slender figure in her starched uniform. "Excuse me, miss, but there are two ladies of Munro here to see you. They are waiting in the drawing room."

"To see me? Oh! Very well. I will join them in a moment. Thank you, Lucy."

Ellena frowned a little at this unexpected visit, but Mr. Cole positively beamed.

"You said you would deliver ladies for my consideration, but this suggests a foresight I can hardly fathom!"

Ellena shook her head. "I cannot take the credit for their arrival. I am as much in the dark as you are. Shall we investigate together?"

Mr. Cole stood up at once. "That, Miss Trenton, is an offer I cannot refuse."

CHAPTER EIGHTEEN

ELLENA AND MR. Cole made their way back to the house and through to the bright and airy drawing room. Because Charlotte was still with Clarence in the nursery, making sure his cold had not become a fever, no one had been tending to the two visitors who waited in the sunny spot by the window. They were both dressed very fashionably in wide skirts and tall bonnets with decadent frills. The two ladies were clearly close friends, if one were to judge from the way they stood and spoke, their bodies framed in a private circle. Ellena did not recognize them, and a nervous apprehension took hold of her. Mr. Cole, on the other hand, entered the room smoothly and confidently, assuming the role of host in his sister's absence.

"Good morning, ladies. We apologize that you have been kept waiting. Unfortunately, Mrs. Trenton cannot join us. She is currently absorbed with maternal duties. With your permission, I shall stand in for her. I am William Cole, Mrs. Trenton's brother. And this is Miss Ellena Trenton, her cousin, whom I believe you have come to see. May I introduce you?"

"Miss Irene Sangford," the taller woman announced in a languid drawl, dropping her hand at the wrist to shake Mr. Cole's limply. "And this is my friend, Miss Olivia Bathurst."

"Pleased to meet you." Ellena nodded, though she was as yet undecided whether she was truly pleased or not.

Miss Sangford acknowledged the statement with a slow blink. "We hope you do not mind us dropping in on you without an appointment. We did leave our cards before. And Mrs. Trenton is a known acquaintance." She spoke with the sort of regal composure that suggested nothing she did could be frowned upon. She continued without waiting for approval or reassurance.

"We were visiting my aunt and uncle, who live on the same lane, and thought it a perfect opportunity to welcome you to Munro, Miss Trenton. You must know that your engagement is the talk of the town, and it vexes the ladies of society that Lord Howell has not held a dance to celebrate your arrival or brought you to the theater, where we might have the pleasure of admiring the bride he has selected."

"I see," Ellena answered, her tone sober and reserved after the easy conversation with Mr. Cole. "Well, you have found me. Shall I ring for tea?"

"That would be very kind. Do you see, Olivia? I told you she would not feel it an imposition."

Olivia Bathurst was a particularly pretty young woman—almost girlish—with soft skin, a clear complexion, and bright-golden ringlets. She stood in stark contrast to the dark, narrow features of Miss Sangford. Miss Bathurst was exactly the sort to attract a gentleman's eye. Ellena hoped she was already spoken for, else she posed a potential threat to Jillian's chances with Mr. Cole.

However, as soon as the lovely young lady spoke, Ellena knew that Jilly's prospects were safe. Miss Bathurst had a voice that could cut glass. Shrill and piercing, it made one want to complete sentences for her in the hopes of terminating her speech.

"Miss Trenton is very gracious, to be sure," Miss Bathurst trilled.

Hearing her for the first time, Ellena winced a little. She was determined to keep a stony countenance but dreaded any future utterance from Miss Bathurst's mouth.

"Won't you be seated?" Ellena proffered the chairs with their leaf-green, slipper-satin upholstery. She felt oddly relieved at the quality of their workmanship, as if her family had something to prove to these visitors. Well, they would find no fault here, she assured herself. From the damask wallpaper to the hand-embroidered sofa cushions, the attention to detail was commendable. She allowed herself a little smile of pride.

The foursome distributed themselves evenly about the room. Silence followed.

Ellena felt an explanation was demanded of her. "I can assure you," she began earnestly, "Lord Howell had no intention of slighting the good people of his hometown. In truth, I only arrived late last Thursday and have had little time to meet with his lordship myself, let alone attend any social events. And, of course, there is to be a large gathering after the ceremony on Friday, to which all of Munro's gentry is invited."

"Yes, we will be attending with our respective families," Miss Sangford answered a heartbeat before Miss Bathurst could speak. Ellena stopped herself from grinning at the comedy in their actions. Their friendship obviously did not prevent Miss Sangford from taking precautions lest Miss Bathurst speak too frequently.

But Miss Bathurst persisted. "We had hoped to invite you to tea," she began.

"Yes," Miss Sangford continued hastily, "Olivia and I had first intended to arrange our very own welcoming committee. But a strange rumor exists that you have resolved to remain in your cousin's house until your wedding day. That is, of course, other than to attend church. We thought this rather odd and ignored the report, naturally. Still, we thought it wise to bring our good wishes to your door, so to speak, just in case there was some truth to the story."

She spoke with a calculated smoothness, but her eyes burned with unspoken curiosity.

Ellena wondered how such a rumor had spread, but it was not difficult to imagine a source in either her household or

Dominic's, since James could be as indiscreet as any of Lord Howell's servants may have been. The footman who opened the door at Munro House would have heard her bold declaration to his master when she had first arrived—veiled—for dinner. Such a juicy bit of information could easily have been passed on within the household and beyond, through huddled conversations at the market or whispered confidences with the housekeeping staff of other homes. Ellena cursed herself for allowing their conflict to become public knowledge.

Miss Sangford continued. "We could not guess at what might persuade a young lady to avoid the many attractions Munro has to offer, especially when it is her first experience of our fine city. The only conclusion, then, is that his lordship demanded his betrothed's seclusion prior to the wedding, though the thought has a rather medieval ring to it, don't you think?"

Ellena felt her hackles rise. "I can assure you, Lord Howell has not insisted upon any restrictions in my movements. Any rumor to that effect has no factual basis."

"Oh, indeed?" Miss Sangford sat back, deflated. She exchanged a look with her friend that suggested they had wasted their time.

But Miss Bathurst had her own contribution to add. "You know, Miss Trenton, there is no need to defend the viscount to us." She leaned closer, as if sharing a secret. "We know your acquaintance with him is brief. We, however, have known him all our lives and are no strangers to his odd behavior." She sat back, nodding knowingly.

"Is that so?" Ellena inquired with mock interest.

"Oh, yes." Miss Sangford's carefully maintained illusion slipped a little in her eagerness to divulge a damning tidbit of information. "A mutual friend of ours was introduced to him at a charity dinner. He barely nodded—and said not two words to her. It was a terrible slight. But when another gentleman approached, he completely ignored her and entered into earnest conversation with the newcomer." She sniffed her disapproval.

"We do hope he will be more attentive to *you*, Miss Trenton."

"Mother says he is too proud for his own good," Miss Bathurst said, able at last to contribute to the conversation. "He does not speak to anyone if he does not wish to, and he makes no apology for it."

Miss Sangford quickly added, "I once heard his sister ask him whom he would choose from among the ladies of Munro for his bride one day. Do you know what he said?" The answer clearly irked her. "He said, 'I would sooner remain a bachelor.' Can you believe such an insult to us all? It seems he was in earnest, too, for here you are, Miss Trenton."

Ellena smiled sweetly. "I hope you will not despise me for my good fortune."

"Goodness, no!" cried Miss Sangford, her envy masked with little success. "For who would have him after such an unkind cut? Begging your pardon, but his wealth and position could never entice *me* to consider his proposal."

"Then it is well he did not make one." Ellena maintained her smile, though it had taken on a rather humorless quality.

"Er… Yes, of course…" Miss Sangford floundered a little.

Ellena gazed into her empty hands, as if they held the answers. "It seems," she continued coolly, "I shall have to console myself in my unhappy situation by making the most of his fortune and my newly acquired status. I realize a lady of your fine position cares little for such things, but I am grateful for the opportunity. Already, he spoils me. He has provided the most exquisite silk for my wedding dress—an unnecessary expense, but then I suppose he does not feel it."

Irene Sangford went quite pink with restrained emotion. Ellena fully expected her to hiss as the pent-up pressure of her jealousy escaped her, but Miss Sangford recovered herself and tried a new angle of attack.

"We saw you at church on Sunday, from a distance. But we had no opportunity to be introduced. However, we did notice your quaint, little veil. Is this the custom in your local community?"

Ellena tensed. "It is not typical, but I am not one to be led by conformity. I am sure you are no stranger to modesty, Miss Sangford. I believe Reverend Keith encourages the ladies to pay more attention to his sermons than to seek compliments through their appearances."

"Yet you continued to wear your face covered while walking in Munro Park. Is this also part of your spiritual regimen?"

"I did not realize I was being watched so closely. Do you observe all strangers with such vigor?"

"My brother took his wife for a picnic," Miss Bathurst interjected. "He recognized the viscount and assumed the lady behind the veil must be his intended. He spied no chaperone, but then modern couples do flaunt the rules, don't they?" She waited for Ellena to respond.

When no reply was forthcoming, she cleared her throat and continued. "Well, I suppose you did say you were not one for conformity. Anyway, the whole town has been buzzing with excitement since your arrival, and my brother knew we would want to hear that he had seen you. He was disappointed not to have seen your face, though."

"My style of dress may have been a little severe," Ellena agreed. "But, as you see, it is not part of my daily attire."

Irene Sangford tilted her head to her friend. "We suppose ourselves privileged, then, to meet you face to face, if you will pardon the play on words, since no one else seems to have had the good fortune."

"On the contrary, Miss Sangford," Ellena replied, "it is merely a case of opportunity. Since I have had little time to explore Munro, its inhabitants will have had little means to observe me. I did visit your main thoroughfare on Friday morning, but perhaps the outing was too short for news of my presence to spread to interested parties. I am sorry to have kept you in suspense until now. I hope the reality does justice to your expectations of me."

Irene Sangford took so long to piece together a polite reply that Miss Bathurst was able to answer.

"Indeed, Miss Trenton, you are quite as lovely as one might hope. Isn't she, Irene?"

"Yes. Lovely." A heavy pause followed.

"I would have thought," Mr. Cole suddenly declared, "that Miss Trenton easily exceeded anyone's imaginings."

The visitors' mouths fell open at his bold statement. They exchanged a meaningful glance. Miss Sangford drew in her breath to pass comment, and Ellena steeled herself for what might follow. It was with no small relief that she spied the maid arriving with the tea.

Miss Sangford held her pose while Mr. Cole helped himself at once to the dainty cakes that accompanied the hot beverage. Ellena poured for each person in turn and offered the little cakes to her guests, frowning at Mr. Cole when he reached to take more. He only grinned and disclaimed how much she was like Charlotte.

Amid the clinking of cups, spoons, and saucers, the three ladies composed themselves. But as the tea cooled and the cakes became crumbs, the women continued their delicate warfare.

Irene Sangford fired the first volley. "We are much surprised that a lady like yourself, whose qualities seem to draw broad admiration"—she cast a sideways glance at Mr. Cole—"would settle for so droll a choice as Lord Howell. Can his title really be so attractive that you would choose it over the attentions of a more charming gentleman such as, say, Mr. Cole here?"

"Ah, Miss Sangford." Mr. Cole sighed dramatically. "This is the very question I have been asking myself since the moment I arrived at my sister's house and discovered the hidden treasure that is Miss Trenton. But no amount of gentle persuasion will make her change her mind, you know. She displays a most arduous loyalty to her betrothed. I imagine she has left many frustrated suitors in her wake."

"How fortunate for the viscount to have found such dedication in an unpredictable situation," Miss Sangford continued coyly. "After all, I understand you have but recently met."

Ellena's frustration mounted. She wished Charlotte would come and relieve her of the company of these guests. Even James would do at this point.

"You seem well-informed in all matters pertaining to my engagement," she conceded. "I hardly need answer, as any information I may add is no doubt already in your possession. Lord Howell must be very grateful to know such friends as yourselves look out for his best interests."

Miss Sangford nodded sagely, as if this were her very sincere concern. "Then you may understand the general feeling, Miss Trenton, when the most prominent member of Munro society has selected a bride who is not from among his peers."

Ellena had had enough. "I confess you have me greatly confused. Who is to be pitied, exactly? Shall it be myself, for the inglorious privilege of marrying a gentleman whose offensive pride and lack of social graces leave the fairer sex indignant with neglect? Or are we to commiserate with the viscount, who must be truly feeble-minded to ignore his background and responsibilities in choosing a bride so far beneath his stature that it alarms those protecting his interests?"

Miss Sangford twisted her head to the side as if warding off an attack. Her mouth opened, then closed again with a "tch" of the tongue. "My dear Miss Trenton, there is no need to adopt so violent a defense! We are merely asking what is on everyone's mind."

"Then I strongly suggest that Munro's townsfolk find more meaningful subjects with which to occupy their thoughts."

Miss Sangford responded with cool detachment. "You might wish to remember, Miss Trenton, that you are a stranger, not only to your intended, but to the people of this great city. You would benefit greatly from any kindness offered to you. Misplaced pride may cause you to alienate those members of society whose support you will later seek. You are unlikely to win back favor once it is lost. Consider your delicate position. Is it not wiser to grasp the hand of friendship when it is offered?"

"To be sure," Ellena replied briskly, "the moment I receive kindness and something resembling true friendship, I shall embrace it heartily. But I am not so desperate in my situation that I will consider idle curiosity and coarse judgments a substitute for these."

Irene Sangford's voice grew thick with warning. "You tread very roughly on unstable ground, Miss Trenton. You treat with disdain a privileged connection you have barely earned."

Ellena placed her saucer on the table with a rattle of fine china. She lifted her chin defiantly.

"Is it a privilege to serve as target for your condescension and scorn, simply because my family is not part of the gentry? I'll have you know my father is as much a gentleman as any title-bearing lord. I can only hope that this is not the typical welcome one can come to expect from well-bred ladies in Munro's upper echelons. Fortunately, I suspect not all will be driven by envy and malice, though this would easily explain Lord Howell's desire to seek a wife elsewhere."

"Well!" Irene Sangford rose like the sails of a galleon. "I think it is time we took our leave, Olivia. Miss Trenton has chosen vulgar insults as her thanks for our well-intentioned advice."

Ellena did not even bother with the niceties of etiquette, staying firmly in her seat. "I shall not beg you to stay," she declared bluntly. "Mr. Cole, will you be so kind as to see our guests out?"

Miss Sangford seethed with the insult of it. "Come, Olivia." She sniffed. "We shan't stay to endure any further displays of Miss Trenton's country manners."

"But I haven't finished my cake," complained her friend. Irene Sangford delivered a withering glare that caused Miss Bathurst to rise quickly and wipe the crumbs from her lips. She followed the tall frame of Miss Sangford from the room as Mr. Cole—looking very grim—led them down the short passage to the foyer.

When their carriage had left, he returned to the drawing room. Ellena was standing at the window, her hands clasped tightly behind her back. The anger she had struggled to restrain now bubbled out in his familiar company.

"The nerve of that woman! She's no more a duchess than I am, but she struts with all the airs and graces of a high-born lady. How *dare* she speak to me with such conceit? And then to expect my gratitude for it!"

"She can be in no doubt as to what a poor impression she has made," Mr. Cole assured her. "It is most likely the first time anyone has stood up to her. You have no need to fear the sequel to such a visit. She will not torment you again."

"Oh, but she will!" Ellena groaned, sinking into a chair as the gravity of what had transpired struck her. "News of our heated exchange will be distributed with great speed and, of course, her special brand of prejudice. She will have her revenge by the bucket load, and I am powerless to prevent it. Can matters get any worse?"

Of course they could!

In less than a week, she had fallen prey to highwaymen, been betrayed by her cousin, slandered twice by her betrothed, and wrapped herself up in a lie she was struggling to rid herself of. Offending two gossiping harpies, who would make haste to spread word of her verbal thrashing to all and sundry, seemed paltry in comparison.

Why should it stop there? Why should it not all fall apart? Perhaps Dominic would again give in to a reckless outburst, making it ever harder to forgive him. Perhaps she would throw off the ridiculous veil, but it would be too late. Having been lied to and manipulated by her might destroy any basis for trust that he had.

What a mess! Ellena had no idea if any of it could be salvaged.

She sank deeper into the chair, wishing it would swallow her up entirely. Right now, it seemed the best solution for a hopeless situation.

CHAPTER NINETEEN

ELLENA WAS THE picture of misery. She sat, silent and gloomy, in a chair by the window. The tea had grown cold. The uneaten cakes remained untouched.

Mr. Cole, quite devoid of his usual humor, paced the room.

"Do sit down, Mr. Cole," she urged. "Your agitation does not lessen my own."

But Mr. Cole did not sit down. Instead, he flung out an arm and exclaimed, "You should not have to endure this! You have had nothing but ill treatment—from James, from Lord Howell, and now from ladies who can scarcely be called such. Your engagement to the viscount has brought you nothing but sorrow. Your father has done you a great disservice to bind you to this man."

But Ellena's thoughts were elsewhere. She gazed out across the garden. She wished she could have stayed there all morning and never come inside to be abused by false hospitality. Dominic had told her about such ladies, and his words had not been warm. She could see all too easily how regular interaction with this sort of conceit and venom would make a gentle man despair and withdraw.

All at once, she missed him. She recalled his shyness in the cabin, when she had been Nancy to him. She remembered how moved he had been—after their dinner together—by the tender intimacy he had beheld between James and Charlotte. And she could not forget how lost he had looked before she had strode away down the long, low hill at Munro Park. Despite his great wealth and position, he had a simple heart that hoped to find acceptance and affection as much as hers did.

She loathed the way Misses Sangford and Bathurst had spoken about him, like some curiosity. They enjoyed the implied prestige of a connection between their families and his yet behaved without the accompanying loyalty and respect. She did not doubt for a minute that Irene Sangford had felt slighted when she had not been considered for the role of Viscountess Howell. Ellena tingled a little at the thought of trumping the insufferable pretender.

But was she really any more deserving?

Dominic's own contribution to the disastrous visit in the park notwithstanding—she had stormed off with childish indignation, unwilling to hear any apology or consider the consequences of the veil that remained. This was hardly the behavior of a serene wife, one who would need to forgive many faults, as he must hers.

Granted, circumstances were unusual, to say the least. They were, after all, little more than strangers to each other. And their progress was further complicated by their unwittingly-shared secret and the embarrassment of the veil.

But, in the end, they were allowing their engagement to become a mockery. The visit from the two outspoken ladies had taught her this. If nothing else, at least their mean honesty had served to open her eyes.

She and Dominic would have to make a concerted effort to overcome the tangled start to their future together. And she had to do her share. This meant sorting out the confusion once and for all.

She was due to have a fitting for her dress tomorrow. This would be a good opportunity to slip away and visit with Dominic without any interference, even the well-intentioned kind created by Mr. Cole. They desperately needed to talk things through, without the added burden of masquerade and secrecy.

Ellena felt much better for this conclusion. Laying down her anger was surprisingly liberating. She would hold Dominic accountable for his actions. But she would also hold open the door to reconciliation.

She looked up at Mr. Cole to indicate her improved mood and was surprised to see him staring at her with some intensity.

"I fear you trouble yourself too much on my behalf," she said with concern.

His eyes blinked as if he were surfacing from a trance. "Sorry? Did you say something?"

"Yes, I said you take my problems too much to heart. I value your friendship, but I do not wish to become a burden to you."

"Miss Trenton," he answered with great earnestness, "you could never be a burden. If it were in my power to relieve you of your unnecessary suffering, I assure you, I would act."

"Thank you, but I must make my own way. I think I know what I must do to smooth the path forward." She stood to add finality to her words. "If you will excuse me now, I will look in on little Clarence. Perhaps I might even prove useful, for once, and gift Charlotte a reprieve from her duties."

Mr. Cole nodded, but his focus remained elsewhere. Ellena wondered at the degree to which he was disturbed by her troubles. It was, she felt, an indication of the loyalty he showed as a friend. Although she wished he would not take so much upon himself, she was nevertheless grateful that he cared.

Ellena made her way to the nursery. There she spent the rest of the morning reading to her little nephew, who, though not well enough to run about, was also not ill enough to sleep soundly. Once or twice, he napped briefly, during which time his attentive aunt could rest her own eyes a little.

Tomorrow would be a critical day for her, a chance to bid a final farewell to the myth of Nancy. The veil could be discarded. No more would Dominic fall prey to petty jealousies, for he would be confident in her affection for him. He would be able to see it clearly in her eyes.

There was some nervous apprehension that accompanied her plan. But a semblance of peace prevailed within Ellena, knowing all entanglements would soon be removed. Hope permeated her thoughts. The worst was now behind her.

With nothing further to worry her, Ellena closed her eyes a while. Any minute now, Clarence would be awake and demanding another book. *Little boys*, she thought, as she drifted off, *can be surprisingly tiring.*

DOMINIC LISTENED TO Mrs. Anders with half an ear. His aged housekeeper was a very capable woman who had been with the family for as long as he could remember. Really, any instruction he gave her was a mere formality. But every day she reported the state of the household to him, as if he knew anything about it. That had always been his mother's domain. And, after a lifetime under her influence, Mrs. Anders functioned as if his mother still watched over her every move.

Right now, she was reassuring him that all went according to schedule with preparations for Friday's reception. But his head wasn't in it.

"I feel confident, your lordship, that the new Lady Howell will find no fault with the proceedings. The staff will not let you down."

Ha! If only the new Lady Howell could feel the same about him! He had certainly let *her* down. More than once. Everything that had gone wrong for them had been his fault. He had rushed the engagement without giving them a chance to meet—or, for that matter, giving her a choice at all. He had spoken carelessly with her cousin, a man renowned for his lack of discretion. Certainly, the veil-wearing fiasco had been her doing. But it had been brought on by his own reckless words.

And then there was the disastrous walk in Munro Park. He cringed every time he thought of it. That such speech could have come from his own lips! That he should even have spawned such foul thoughts! If he was capable of such vulgarity, how could he be certain he would never hurt her again?

"If that will be all, my lord, I will return to my duties." Mrs. Anders stood with her wrinkled hands neatly folded into each other.

"Yes. Yes, thank you, Mrs. Anders. I am happy to leave things in your capable hands."

"Thank you, your lordship." The housekeeper turned on her heel and left the room with her usual purposeful step.

How he envied her! To be so sure of what the next step should be that one could take it with confidence. Her duty was clear. Perhaps that clarity was her true north, guiding her forward with certainty.

His duties were rather more complex. Not only was the entire estate his responsibility, but the continuance of the Howell name too. There was no getting away from it. It had to be done.

But he had another responsibility—to Ellena. She had been dragged into his world without any say. And how had he thanked her? Perhaps, after all, she would be better off with someone like the charming Mr. Cole.

Or perhaps not. The mere memory of that man made his skin crawl—the way he had fawned over Ellena! Still, his own actions had hardly been exemplary. And now they were not even speaking to each other. He was willing to apologize again, but then she would be required to forgive him. And why should she? He had no excuse. What could he offer other than regret?

Maybe—and his heart sank like a lead weight at the thought—maybe it was time to do what was right for Ellena. Maybe it was time to let her go. She should be free to love someone more worthy of her. He wasn't convinced that Mr. Cole qualified for the role, but it should not be up to him to decide.

Dominic drew a sheet of blank paper toward him and stared helplessly at it. It was the right thing to do. But it was not easy giving up on the dream of what could have been. He gripped the quill with resolve, dipped it in ink, and began to write.

To Mr. Henry Trenton of Trenton Grange,

Sir, it is with a heavy heart that I send this letter. While I am, by nature, a cautious man, I have acted hastily in brokering a contract for your daughter's hand in marriage.

Dominic's thoughts ground to a halt. This wasn't going to work. How could he ask for an end to the contract without insinuating that Ellena was to blame? Henry Trenton would never believe he had simply changed his mind or that he thought himself a sorry match for Ellena. He would assume his daughter had been at fault and that Dominic was merely being tactful about it. After all, why would a viscount risk the embarrassment of a failed engagement if she weren't the cause of it? And for a gentleman to break an engagement... Well, the Trentons were likely to sue. *Especially* the Trentons. Henry Trenton would not see his financial advantage snatched away.

Now that he thought on it further, what would Ellena's prospects be if he ended their arrangement? What sort of match could she make if she had been discarded for no good reason?

He snatched at the barely-written letter and crushed it in his fist. There was no easy escape. He and Ellena were bound by the expectations of his own foolishly brokered deal. There was nothing for it but to forge ahead, regardless of how challenging that would be.

A knock on the door of his study made him look up.

"Sir," said Branson, "your one o' clock appointment is here."

Was that the time already?

"Show him in."

"Yes, sir."

The butler disappeared and Dominic stepped around his desk

toward the center of the room in anticipation of his visitor. At least it wasn't Simmons. He was only expected at two. But he always took Simmons more seriously than the others, and he wasn't mentally ready for him yet.

It was time to get back to work. He looked at the crumpled paper in his hand. The situation with Ellena would have to wait. He tossed the discarded letter into the fire and watched it sizzle, glow, and disintegrate. He sighed. If only all his problems could be dealt with as easily.

CHAPTER TWENTY

DIRECTLY AFTER DINNER, Ellena sat down to write her daily letter to Jilly. She pulled a sheet of paper from her writing desk and carefully opened the small pot of ink. However, upon taking up her quill, she found the nib to be blunt and in need of a trim. She was about to pull the bell ribbon to call Lucy and request that a knife be brought to her, when she bethought herself. The servants would be having their meal now, and it seemed unnecessary to disturb them for such an unimportant errand. She would simply go fetch a knife from the kitchen herself.

She passed no one on the stairs. James was in his study; Charlotte was sitting with Clarence again; and Mr. Cole had taken the curricle into town on some errand. Most of the staff would have been assembled in the kitchen, enjoying their afternoon meal before resuming their duties. Ellena proceeded down one of the narrower passageways that connected the main house to the downstairs. She heard the sound of conversation and laughter and knew she was headed in the right direction.

Nearing the entrance to the large kitchen, Ellena could make out the sound of Lucy's voice. It was surprisingly light and confident, so different to the shy girl who always drew Ellena's curtain and made her bed. She was about to enter discreetly when she heard Lucy say, "Did you hear the latest talk about Miss

Trenton?"

Ellena froze in mid-step.

"Who's that, then?" came a nasal voice Ellena did not recognize.

"It's the lady visitor, Dirk," explained Lucy, "the one engaged to Lord Howell."

"From what I hear," rasped the intruding voice of Jonathan Pikes, "that is a sorry match, indeed."

Ellena's curiosity turned to dismay. Jonathan Pikes was the head groomsman, a man with a sharp tongue, and prone to bouts of temper. During her short stay, Ellena had heard him reprimand the stableboy harshly for the slightest mistakes. And now his disagreeable thoughts were turning to her.

Mercifully, they were followed by the more reasonable tones of Ned, the coachman.

"I don't know where you heard such nonsense, Mr. Pikes. I have had the privilege of taking Miss Trenton about several times, and she seems perfectly suitable for his lordship. After all, did he not choose her above so many others? He is a man of great discernment. He would consider carefully before making such a choice."

"That may be so," countered Lucy, "but perhaps the gentleman was not fully informed as to her character."

Shock hit Ellena squarely in the gut. Was this really what quiet, little Lucy thought of her? Ellena was very grateful when Ned came to her defense once again.

"No, Lucy, that cannot be. Lord Howell has his finger on the pulse of the entire city. I've heard he has a small army of informants. He knows every thought freshly uttered by every man in Munro. He does not seem the type to be easily misled."

"Ha! Women are a crafty bunch," jeered Mr. Pikes. "Never underestimate their wily nature. They will wink and smile to get what they want, and you'll discover too late you've been played for a fool."

"And you should know, Jonathan Pikes," the cook, Mrs.

Lategan, quipped. "You've been a fool more often than most!"

Laughter erupted at the crowded table. Ellena could imagine the simmering figure of Mr. Pikes hunched over his plate.

"I'll have you know, Mrs. Lategan," he growled, "that I would never be led by the nose by some skinny lass just because she made eyes at me."

The nasal tones of Dirk interrupted with a snicker. "'Course not. That's 'cause no young girl would waste 'er time on yer sorry self."

"Now just look here, I…"

"Hang on a minute," Ned called out. "Lucy had something she wanted to tell us. Give her a chance, will you?"

"Oh, do stop grumbling under your breath like that, Mr. Pikes," complained Mrs. Lategan. "I can't hear the girl speak."

Ellena had been thinking the same thing and now leaned forward to hear better.

"Right," said Lucy. "Well, I suppose you know Miss Trenton is staying here until the wedding, come Friday."

Mr. Pikes cut in again. "They say she never leaves the house but for church on Sunday on account of some oath she swore to the viscount."

"That's right," said Dirk, "and she wears a veil all the time, like them Eastern wimmen wot has rings in their noses and wotnot. Do you think she has a nose-ring then, like a bull?"

"No, no, of course not," Lucy snapped irritably. "The veil is apparently part of some oath of chastity or something."

"I don't see how a veil can protect someone's chastity," grumbled Dirk. "Don't you need some kind of armor or summint?"

"You mean a chastity belt," Mrs. Lategan explained calmly. "And the veil is only a symbol of her purity, not a means of guaranteeing it."

"Am I going to get my story told today, then?" Lucy's voice bristled with frustration.

"Sorry, lass," said Mrs. Lategan. "We won't interrupt again."

Ellena, rooted to the spot just outside the door, found that hard to believe.

"Right. As I was saying, Miss Trenton is staying here at Thorn Bush Hall. But so is Mrs. Trenton's younger brother, Mr. William Cole. He is very handsome and without any attachment at present."

"What of it?" asked Ned. "Having one's brother to stay is no crime, be he handsome and single, or neither."

"Yes, but I know Miss Trenton does not wear her face covered in his presence. Where's her pretty oath when he's around, then?"

"That's no mystery," Ned answered. "She can't be expected to prance around the house all day in a headdress, can she? It's not practical. Anyway, it's silly to wear the jolly thing in the first place, I say. This isn't the Dark Ages, you know."

"Oh, Ned!" Lucy retorted. "It's only for a week, not her entire wedded life."

Mr. Pikes snorted. "Wouldn't be much of a wedded life if her husband couldn't even get a proper look at her."

"Jonathan Pikes!" Mrs. Lategan cried, evidently outraged. "There'll be none of that sort of talk at my table, thank you very much."

"I'm not saying anything this lot don't already know. Anyway, it stands to reason, doesn't it? Why do you think his lordship chose a girl without a title? She would have to be a real beauty to have gotten his attention. And now he isn't even offered a peek at the wares."

"I'm sure," Mrs. Lategan replied primly, "that Lord Howell is a man of infinitely nobler character than yourself, Mr. Pikes. It will not be a burden for a gentleman of integrity to wait but a week to satisfy his curiosity."

"I heard he is to receive a sizeable dowry from the young lady's father," Lucy added. "That is sure to hold his attention while he waits for his bride to be revealed."

"And a good thing too," agreed Mrs. Lategan. "It's an expensive business keeping a fine house. And Munro House is the finest of all. I am on friendly terms with their housekeeper, Mrs. Anders. *She* said that the lady dowager told the servants the house should be prepared at all times for a visit by the king. When she left to stay with her elder daughter, she handed a book of instructions to Mrs. Anders so they would not slack off in her absence."

"That's the wealthy for you," Lucy complained. "All day, while they embroider and eat their biscuits delicately, they expect the staff to move mountains, yet they offer such poor wages, we can barely care for our families."

"That's right," agreed Mrs. Lategan. "Our own master once docked me a week's pay because the meals were late. But that was when Becky was sick in bed with influenza and I had to do all the work alone." She paused before adding, "Now, Lord Howell, on the other hand, he's a fine man and a gracious employer. Mrs. Anders told me he pays his staff extra at Christmas time so they can treat themselves a little. I've never heard her say a cross word about him. I wonder if they'll feel the same toward his bride?"

"Not if she's flirting with other young men," chirped Lucy.

"Who says she's flirting?" Dirk wanted to know. "I thought you said she never goes out?"

"Shh! Let Lucy speak."

Ellena was sure she did *not* want to hear what Lucy had to say. But she was transfixed by the conversation. She listened in mounting horror as the servants discussed and judged her private affairs.

Lucy continued. "This morning, Miss Sangford and Miss Bathurst called on Miss Trenton. I lingered in the passage and overheard some of what they said. At first, all three ladies spoke softly, but later they were fairly at each other's throats. I heard Miss Sangford say that Miss Trenton would not accept their offer of friendship. And Miss Trenton rudely shamed them with the fact that his lordship had selected her over a lady from his hometown. The two visitors left in quite a huff."

"Typical!" cried Dirk. "These foreign wimmen are nothing but trouble with their strange customs and wotnot."

"She's not foreign, Dirk," explained Mrs. Lategan. "She's from the country, only a few hours away. A Northerner, just like us."

"It doesn't matter where she's from," insisted Lucy. "What gives her the right to look down on us?"

Mr. Pikes snorted. "That will be the money talking. Now that she's marrying up, she thinks she's above everyone else. That sort is even worse than them who's born into it. These self-made families haven't the same class."

"Quite," said Lucy. "One would think the young lady could appreciate the privilege she is marrying into. But it seems she has her eyes on a lighter prize, one perhaps more suited to her status."

"Who? Not Mr. Cole, surely?" Mrs. Lategan cried.

"The very same," replied Lucy. "The gentleman fairly drooled over her, even going so far as to say he wished he could marry her instead."

"How shocking!" declared Mrs. Lategan. "To play the coquette and dandy! Are they not ashamed?"

"Apparently not," said Lucy. "And they are guests under the same roof. The opportunities for indiscretion are plentiful."

Dirk snorted. "No wonder she never leaves the house…"

The echo of Dominic's accusation through the mouths of the Trenton staff struck Ellena like a dagger to the heart. It was appalling that they, too, should have such lewd thoughts. Worse yet, it meant Miss Sangford and her friend would likely think the same. Was all of Munro gossiping about her? Is this what had set Dominic off? After all, hadn't Ned mentioned that the viscount had eyes and ears everywhere? Ellena felt quite sick at the humiliation of it.

"That is not all," Lucy continued. "Miss Trenton went on to speak most critically of her betrothed, calling him proud and wasteful and"—she searched for the word—"feeble-minded. Yes, that's it. Feeble-minded! I ask you: is that the way to talk about your intended?"

That was not what she had said! Lucy really was a very unreliable eavesdropper. How had she managed to catch Ellena's words but not their meaning? Ellena had to fight the urge to march into the kitchen and set them straight.

"I'm sorry to say it," Mrs. Lategan tutted, "but the good gentleman seems to have made a terrible mistake. Does he not suspect anything?"

"You heard what Ned said. His informants are everywhere. It will not be long before she and her affair are found out. Then there will be a right to-do."

"She deserves nothing less," said Mr. Pikes. "Throw her out on her ear, I say. Send her back to her little country town, if they'll have her. Munro is a decent place. We don't need our finest family shamed by its connection with the likes of her."

"Hear, hear!" chorused several voices, equally passionate in the defense of their great city.

Ellena had heard enough. She fled back up the stairs, the knife for her quill completely forgotten. She fairly ran to her room and threw herself onto her bed. In a moment, she was up again, crossing the room to lock the door. She did not feel safe anywhere anymore.

She knew servants talked. But the malice of their gossip was astounding. Even shy Lucy and the steady Mrs. Lategan were willing to entertain the most false, despicable thoughts about her.

She would never be able to look at Lucy in the same way again. As for Mrs. Lategan, every time Ellena ate anything in this house, she would remember the hands that had prepared the meal and the mouth that had slandered her. She was absolutely humiliated.

At least Ned had stood up for truth and reason. And he had mentioned an interesting detail—Lord Howell had informants, people who would ferret out the truth for him. Well, good! They would discover nothing that could shame her. Not if they were after the truth.

Ha! She wondered if any of them would discover their employer's little secret. Or was the fact of Nancy Fallon so well hidden that even a trained eye or ear could not discover its existence? After all, she was sure Dominic would have been as careful to suppress the events at the cabin as she had been.

Ellena shifted to the bay window seat and looked down into the garden. Outside, the sun shone through a lacework of leaves, leaving complicated patterns on the lawn. She opened the latch and let some of the cooler afternoon air freshen her stuffy room. She would rather have been walking than sitting cooped up in here, but she was not yet ready to leave the sanctuary of her room. Or she could have been writing to Jilly. But, alas, there was the matter of her quill needing a knife.

The feeling of being caged was frustratingly familiar. Ellena had hoped to put such sensations behind her when she'd left her father's house. At least there she had had Jilly to confide in. Charlotte was sweet enough but likely to share her stories with James. Mr. Cole was sincerity itself, but she was wary now to be alone with him, lest the servants find new fodder for their gossip. As for Dominic, well, time would tell.

She sat a while longer, savoring the scent of the roses that wafted up from the flowerbeds below. The lively chirping of birds, however, made her envious of their freedom. What could she do to reclaim some small measure of her own?

It was the lies that really affected her. And that others had been so willing to believe them.

The thought stuck.

Willing to believe anything they were told.

A tingle of inspiration ran up her spine.

At once, she was upright. She crossed the floor and tugged the bell ribbon. Then she unlocked the door and pulled it open. She took her seat, this time by the writing desk, where she prepared her ink and paper to resume writing.

"You rang, miss?" Lucy's voice was once again subdued, her

tone humble, her manner willing to serve. Or, at least, there was the appearance of these characteristics.

Ellena turned to the door where Lucy stood. "Yes, I am needing a knife to trim my quill. Will you fetch one for me? I am eager to write to my family. It has been such a busy morning, I have neglected my correspondence. It is just as well Lord Howell did not attend me today. For when he is with me, *I can think of nothing and no one else.*" She sighed theatrically.

"Yes, miss." Lucy nodded. "If you don't mind me saying, we are glad his lordship has finally found a bride that pleases him. There was talk he might remain a bachelor."

"Was there? Talk, indeed... Well, the less said about such frivolous chatter, the better, hmm?"

"Yes, miss."

"After all, should someone like his lordship not choose especially carefully? He holds such an important position in society. He cannot afford to be unwise in selecting one whom he will trust with his name and reputation. He cannot be compared to other, *more ordinary men,* such as my own cousin, or Mr. Cole, for example. For, though both are men of some dignity, they cannot hold a candle to the viscount. I am indeed fortunate to be regarded so well by him. I should never like to disappoint him."

"Yes, miss." Lucy nodded obediently. Then clarity dawned and her eyes widened. She added hastily, "I mean, *no,* miss!"

"Well, now, Lucy, I have kept you long enough. Go ahead and fetch me that knife now."

"Yes, miss."

"Oh, and Lucy?"

"Yes, miss?"

"Won't you ask Mrs. Lategan for a pot of tea? And tell her I am so sorry that Becky had the influenza. I hope she is fully recovered now."

Lucy faltered a moment.

"M-Miss Trenton, Becky has not worked here for some months now. She left to take care of her brother when he was injured at the sawmill."

"Did she? How strange. I was certain I had heard something... Ah, no matter. Who knows where I picked up such an odd bit of information. Never mind."

Lucy hesitated. Ellena, who had turned back to her desk, now looked up again.

"Run along now, Lucy. My letters are waiting. And don't forget the tea."

Lucy gathered herself and bobbed an awkward curtsey. Then she disappeared down the long corridor toward the kitchen.

Ellena leaned back in her chair, satisfied. Lucy had new information to glibly share with the rest of the servants—details to counter their slander and give them pause. It was a small victory, but it was enough to lift her spirits. Later, she might even take that walk in the garden.

But not with Mr. Cole. No, she would be more careful now. There was too much at stake.

CHAPTER TWENTY-ONE

THE VISCOUNT DID, indeed, have a number of informants, though not perhaps as many as some might suppose. He tended to assign individuals to problematic areas where he suspected the occurrence of corruption or mismanagement. In so doing, he often learned more than he intended to discover, which created the impression that he knew all.

Today, however, the rumor mill was at work. This always created difficulties for his little band of listeners and watchers. They were not an unkind sort. Just good at what they did. But rumors were tricky. It was difficult to separate fact from fiction as the tide of talk carried the flotsam of anecdotes and opinions generated from hearsay. Today, in particular, Dominic watched his news-bringers flounder, for the rumors were connected to him personally. The topic of discussion: Miss Trenton and her visitors.

He sat patiently as, one after the other, his informants stood sheepishly before him, each twisting his hat in his hand and mumbling a brief summary of the debate among the townsfolk. He listened with a most unnerving calm and scarcely a twitch of his hand to dismiss them. This continued for the better part of an hour, until the arrival of Mr. Simmons.

If the rest of his informants could be likened to rats, scurrying through town in search of morsels of news, generally despised by anyone who bothered to notice them, then Mr. Simmons should rather be described as a mole. He seemed to burrow deeper than any of the others, waiting patiently for a change in the air around him that suggested something out of the ordinary, sensing the tremor of excitement and finding the smell of a new truth. Secrets trickled along invisible currents to his receptive ears. He was the viscount's most valuable listener.

Because his reports were always the most detailed and accurate, Dominic valued them most. Simmons was therefore received with a sense of relief by his employer, who stood up from his chair the moment Branson ushered the man into the viscount's study.

"Mr. Simmons! At last! I have been hoping to receive word from you today. What do you make of all the buzzing in town? Is it as bad as it sounds?"

Simmons cleared his throat.

"Milord, I do not know what you have already heard. I can only make my own report. Whether it is unhappy news, only you can know."

Dominic sighed. "Proceed, Mr. Simmons."

The short, dark man stood with his feet planted apart, his one hand wrapped around the other wrist, his gaze focused on an invisible point, as if reading his statement from the floor some distance ahead of him.

"At three o' clock this morning, the night watchman at your warehouse was asleep on duty again."

"Had he been drinking?"

"Solidly since he came on duty, sir."

"Hmm, he has been warned before. He shall be given no more chances. I shall have to find an immediate replacement."

Dominic sat down and scribbled a note to himself while Simmons waited. As soon as the informant was given the signal, he continued down the list of his briefing.

"At a quarter past nine this morning, Mr. Fortescue of the bank accepted a bribe from…"

"Oh, you can skip that. I've followed it up already."

"As you wish, sir. Then, a little after eleven this morning, a Miss Bathurst and Miss Sangford called upon Miss Trenton at Thorn Bush Hall. It was a short visit, as they had a falling out with the lady they'd come to see. At twenty minutes to one, Miss Sangford visited one of the local haberdasheries, the one in the town square. There, several ladies heard her speak with disapproval of Miss Trenton. The general tenet of her complaint was that Miss Trenton had been offensive to her guests and too attentive to Mr. William Cole, who, it seems, made his admiration for Miss Trenton bluntly known. That is all that can be considered factual, milord."

William Cole. Why did he keep turning up in the conversation whenever Ellena was mentioned? So, she had been "too attentive." What had she done? Laughed at his banter? Looked at him too frequently? Lowered her lashes at him? Or had she merely turned to him for support, adrift in the mire of Munro "hospitality"? How could he really know? His informants could only glean so much.

Simmons paused and cleared his throat uncomfortably. "Erm… In my experience, sir, people do like to talk. They seldom pay attention to the truth of what they talk about."

"Yes, no doubt, Simmons. But as you will know, they are happy to treat their subject as though it *were* all truth. In time, it does not matter who said what to whom. The saying makes it so."

Dominic sighed deeply. He knew the ladies in question, of course. They were part of the endless parade of possible matches his mother had invited to her bride-finding balls. Miss Bathurst had been harmless enough, easily distracted by the buffet of eats. But Irene Sangford had been more determined. Her family was rumored to be distantly related to Queen Charlotte, but they carried no title. Yet they clung steadfastly to their claim of royal connection in the hope of gleaning some advantage from it. It certainly gave Miss Sangford an inflated sense of importance.

She had done little to hide her true feelings, clearly considering him a bit of a buffoon. He assumed it was because he did not take her as seriously as she felt she deserved. And yet she had been very attentive to him. Her motives had not been particularly subtle.

When his mother had given up on finding him a suitable match and left to stay with his sister, Georgina, Miss Sangford had mercifully considered him a lost cause and stopped pursuing him. She, like so many of Munro's ladies, had never shown any real interest in him, only in his money and title. Which was why he had cast his net wider. And Ellena had entered the scene.

Dominic had not expected this decision to be received with joy by the women of Munro. However, he knew equally well that they would never dare utter such opinions in his company. He had trusted they would extend the same courtesy to his intended. He was greatly disappointed that Misses Sangford and Bathurst had shown so little discretion in their visit to Ellena. Miss Sangford—he imagined quite easily—had stepped out of line. And Ellena—he knew from personal experience—would not have let her get away with it.

He felt a brief moment of pride, even glee, at the thought of Ellena putting her envious guest in her place.

Then the gravity of the situation bore down on him once more. This was more than idle gossip. There was a hint of truth in the report. Ellena was sure to have "been offensive" in the eyes of the haughty Miss Sangford. And Mr. Cole, he considered grimly, could quite likely have defended her with overdone bouquets of praise. Was it possible that the rest was true also? Did Ellena, in turn, pay undue attention to her hero of the moment?

He hesitated. He had accused her hastily once before. She might well have been goaded into defending Mr. Cole by some clever ploy from Miss Sangford. Ellena was a loyal friend—that much he knew for certain.

He drummed his fingers on the table, then came to a decision.

"Mr. Simmons, I would like you to pay special attention to anything new on this topic—anything that is above mere talk, that is. And report to me immediately. Do you understand?"

"Perfectly, milord. Will that be all?"

"For now. Thank you."

"Good evening, sir."

"Good evening, Mr. Simmons. Please see yourself out, if you will."

Within a few steps, the little man had blended into the shadows beyond the study doorway. Shortly thereafter, the front door closed with a soft click. But Dominic was not paying attention. His thoughts were filled with new doubts. Was it possible that Ellena had defended William Cole for reasons that extended beyond friendship? In the park, had she fled in supposed outrage because he had stumbled upon the truth? How little of Miss Sangford's malicious commentary was exaggerated?

He dared not risk any action at this time. He could not confront Ellena to demand the facts, and he was reticent to approach her with a renewed apology, since he was sure of neither her guilt nor her innocence.

The wedding was but four days away, and it was maddening that he could not converse adequately with his intended. He allowed himself a few moments to sulk.

This would not have happened if he had been engaged to Nancy.

She had become to him a symbol of all that was pure and perfect in a woman. She did not play silly games or battle for self-control. Her manners were gentle and reserved, drawing him from his private cocoon into easy conversation. She was a dutiful daughter, placing sacrifice over self-interest. He felt sure that, for Nancy, parting from him had been another such sacrifice. In this, she had shown wisdom and maturity, and he greatly esteemed her for it.

Instead, he was bound to Ellena, whose outspoken ways were both refreshing and disturbing. She seemed willing to meet him halfway each time that he extended the olive branch, but when would she simply come to stand by his side? If her heart was with another, the answer must be "never."

He rubbed his temples and eyes to clear his mind of such distressing thoughts. Tomorrow, he had a fitting for his wedding clothes at Mrs. Pembridge's. Events had a momentum of their own. He hoped to find peace before he was carried over the cliff of regret like a rushing waterfall. He would wait one more day. If there was something hidden between William Cole and Ellena, Mr. Simmons would ferret it out. Just one more day, and he would act decisively, either way.

CHAPTER TWENTY-TWO

THE NEXT MORNING, Ellena was ready for her talk with Dominic and optimistic about the hoped-for outcome. But she wanted no audience for the event. Before breakfast, she stopped Charlotte in the passage and approached her with her plans, though she was careful not to share the full details with her.

"I was hoping, dear Cousin, that you would permit me to borrow the coach. I have an appointment with Mrs. Pembridge in town. She wishes to make the necessary adjustments to ensure a smooth fit. Would it be an inconvenience?"

"Not in the least! I am delighted you should escape the limitations of our home. It has been a great concern to me that you have seen so little of our beautiful city, choosing rather to be cooped up in the confines of Thorn Bush Hall. Give me but a half hour, and I shall be ready to accompany you."

"No indeed, I must ask you to take no offense, but I would rather go on my own."

"Oh?" Charlotte's head tipped askew in surprise. "I am not sure that James would approve of you going unchaperoned. May I ask why you will not have me?"

Ellena looked at her feet, genuinely flustered.

"I had hoped to surprise Dominic with a visit."

Charlotte's whole face lit up at these words.

"Well! That is a very good reason, indeed! I must say, Ellena, you amaze me. I would never have had the courage to act on my own when James and I were courting. But then, perhaps I am just a little old-fashioned. There is certainly no reason why you should not treat his lordship with the pleasure of your company. And as for your seeing him alone, there can be little fault, as you are to be married in a mere three days. However, I do think it best that James at least accompanies you into town. He will be wanting to go in to the office after breakfast."

"Thank you," Ellena replied. "Er… Would you mind not telling James about my plans? We do not see eye to eye on most matters regarding my engagement. I would prefer not to hear his opinion on my newest decision."

"Really, Ellena, I don't think…"

"Please? This whole experience has been difficult, to say the least. Just once, I would like to do something good without James spoiling it."

Charlotte hesitated. "Would you not at least consider taking Lucy with you? She would hardly be noticed."

"I would rather not be spied upon while I make amends for the veil. Dominic and I must speak alone."

"I hardly think 'spying' is the word I would use…"

Ellena bit her tongue. Lucy's recent actions had shown her that the word was very apt indeed.

"Nevertheless, I would prefer dealing with this in private."

Charlotte appeared to give it some thought, and yet the frown on her face suggested she remained unconvinced.

Ellena regretted putting her in this position, but she had to insist.

"I'm not asking you to lie. Just don't say anything if he doesn't ask. *Please.*"

Charlotte breathed out heavily. "Very well. But if James wants to know your plans, I will not keep them from him."

"Of course. That is all I ask."

It would be enough, Ellena told herself. James showed very

little interest in her, except where it directly affected his pocket-book or his standing with the viscount. Since her visit to Mrs. Pembridge hurt neither, he would not inquire further. Or so she hoped.

Charlotte and Ellena entered the breakfast room together.

James had already eaten and was hidden behind the morning paper. As far as Ellena was concerned, this was perfect. He would scarcely hear a word anyone said.

"James," began Charlotte, "you won't miss the carriage once you're at the office, will you? Ellena needs to have a fitting with Mrs. Pembridge. Our coachman could bring her back afterward. Ned is a solid character."

A grunt of agreement came from James, who scarcely bothered to lower the newspaper.

"If the carriage is being prepared, may I tag along?" asked Mr. Cole. "I am a little restless about the house and have in mind to attend a show." He leaned back in his chair. "I trust you could recommend several shows to amuse your idle brother, Charlotte."

"Indeed." His sister nodded. "There is one production in particular that is much talked about, but I fear it is too solemn for your tastes."

"Ah, but I am soon to be a military man. I shall have to become accustomed to more severe topics if I am to be considered stout enough for patriotic service. Military life is a marriage of sorts, isn't it? I mean, a sort of 'until death do us part' arrangement, really."

A dry voice quipped from behind the newspaper, "With the advantage that you need not have her family 'round to dinner, nor labor to supply her tastes in clothes."

"James!" Charlotte threw a hand upon her hip. "Do not encourage my incorrigible brother!"

Charlotte turned and wagged a serious finger at her brother. "As for you, you wicked boy, Father will not consider this a suitable substitute for a bride of flesh and blood. Jest if you must, but do not forget the gravity of your position. You know I do not mean to cause offense, but Father's patience will run out eventually."

"Why, Charlotte! That is the closest you have ever come to actually scolding me." Mr. Cole laughed. "You shall have to do far worse to put a dent in my stubborn armor, though." Charlotte opened her mouth to retort, but her brother interrupted. "Now, now, don't fret. I know you mean well. I assure you, I take the matter of finding a wife most seriously. In fact, Miss Trenton is dedicated in assisting me. How can I fail when I am led by her?"

A dubious *"hmph"* emanated from behind the newspaper, but nothing more was said.

Ellena blushed. She had not meant for her delicate promotion of the as-yet-unrevealed Jillian Kinsey to be publicly proclaimed. Fortunately, no one could suspect that Ellena's true motives in finding his match were to find one also for her friend. In a few days, Jillian would be among them, and her sparkling presence would be irresistible. Ellena hugged herself with pleasure at the thought of their discovery of each other. It was a sure blend of excellent natures.

As for her own prosperity, she was boldly reclaiming her right to it today. After the dressmaker's, she would stop at Munro House and lay all her cards on the table. If she could not forge a truce with Dominic today, then it would not be for want of trying.

The journey into town proved unexpectedly quiet. James was absorbed with a contract, which he held almost up to his nose to read in the dark cubicle. He finished scrutinizing its wording before alighting from the coach for his first meeting of the day. Mr. Cole, too, was a little distant. He seemed to be working through the logistics of a problem, for he frowned occasionally as if analyzing the difficulties before grimly setting his mouth with a determined solution. Ellena guessed his thoughts lay with his sister's stern warning at breakfast. Charlotte did not normally touch upon his affairs. Her decision to speak up was an indication of how dire his situation would be if his parents were not satisfied with his progress.

Pity welled up within Ellena. It seemed she was not the only one with challenges to overcome. She pulled her shawl a little more tightly around her shoulders. The autumn chill was setting in, the carriage filling with its cool breath as Mr. Cole descended from the warm compartment onto the main street of the theater district.

"Shall I have Ned bring the carriage round for you this afternoon?" Ellena asked.

"That will not be necessary, thank you," Mr. Cole answered. "I have not yet decided which production shall enjoy my patronage today. I cannot give you a time to indicate the conclusion of my business here. I shall make my way home when I have tired of my own company."

"Then I wish you a pleasant morning."

"And to you."

Mr. Cole tipped his hat to her as the coachman clicked his tongue and lightly slapped a rein to motion the horses on.

Outside the dressmaker's shop, Ned waited as Ellena stepped onto the cobbled sidewalk, then steered the coach a hundred feet farther down the street, where the road was wider and he could wait without congesting the traffic of the busy morning.

Ellena hastened toward the entrance. A proud sign hung above it, indicating—in gold letters—the establishment of Mrs. Pembridge, Dressmaker. Ellena smiled up at the vanity of that costly gold leaf, remembering the sense of self-importance the fussing, little woman had revealed at their first meeting, especially due to her connection with the Howell family. It seemed a great many people desired any such connection.

Ellena set her jaw grimly as she considered Dominic's unenviable position: to be fervently desired as an icon and stepping stone of success, but never to be claimed just for himself. She was still pondering this idea when the door below the thought-provoking sign opened and a tall figure emerged, donning his hat and nearly colliding with her.

"I do beg your pardon," said a very familiar voice.

It belonged to none other than Lord Dominic Howell. He lowered his hat by way of apology, then raised both hat and eyes to the person into whom he had almost propelled.

"Nancy?" he ventured, looking closer as if to make sure it was her. Then he looked about him at the crowds of busy pedestrians, straightened up, cleared his throat, and added, "Ahem, I mean, *Miss Fallon*." He frowned. "It *is* you. But why are you here? And your clothes..." He stopped abruptly.

Ellena, too, was at a complete loss for words. She had decided against her veil, since it was only Dominic who knew her other identity, and she had only expected to see him later, in private circumstances, where his surprise and confusion could be resolved without the interference of onlookers. This sudden meeting caught her totally off-guard, and she fumbled for the right response to his reasonable questions.

Thankfully, Dominic had found his tongue again. "Forgive me," he urged, "I do not mean to make such blunt inquiries. It's just that, well, I had not expected to see you again. Certainly not in town, anyway. And you are not dressed like one of the sisters. Are no you longer at the convent? Has something changed? I'm sorry, I do not mean to pry. I'm just..."

Happy to see me? Ellena finished his sentence in her mind. Her feelings were a complete jumble. Dominic did indeed seem pleased to see her. But he thought she was Nancy. *Did he just sigh? Did he sigh for Nancy?* Ellena was thrilled, because she *was* Nancy. But he did not know that. Why was he pining after someone who was not his betrothed? Well, she was, but... *Oh, bother!*

"Dominic." She uttered his name, and the rush of intimacy returned. Ellena tried to find words as her flustered thoughts struggled to settle. "It is a strange coincidence that I should find you here," she admitted. "This very day I had planned to seek you out and speak with you. Much has happened since our parting but a few days ago. There have been...complications. I have not taken sisterly vows. But this is not the place to talk. I need to tend to another matter at this moment. Would it be possible for me to see you at your home in, say, an hour?"

Dominic, whose eyebrows had been dancing through a range of emotions, now relaxed them and radiated a smile instead. "I would be more than happy if you would call on me. Shall I send a carriage for you?"

"No, that won't be necessary. I will manage on my own. Please forgive my brisk manner, but I am expected at an appointment very soon and must save all pleasantries of conversation for our later meeting."

"Very well. Er... There is no ill news, I hope?"

"No. But I shall explain everything shortly. Now, if you will excuse me..."

"Of course. Let me release you to your other commitments."

Ellena bobbed her head hurriedly and rushed down the street, turning the first corner she came to. She waited several minutes down the side street. To avoid uncomfortable glances, she feigned interest in the display behind the glass, which belonged to a jeweler. All the while, she watched, from the corner of her eye, to see whether Dominic had passed by. When his distinctive figure was not forthcoming, she assumed he had tended to business in a different direction. She quickly left her post to return to Mrs. Pembridge's.

"Ah, Miss Trenton," Mrs. Pembridge hailed her from behind a counter strewn with pins, ribbons, and oddments of lace. "I had begun to wonder if I should see you this morning, after all."

"I do apologize for my tardiness. Though I am certain the dress is well worth the wait."

"Your gentleman was just here. You must have missed him by mere minutes. He looks most handsome in his wedding suit, if I may make so bold a statement. And, I dare say, once we have completed work on your attire, the two of you shall outshine even the most fashionable guests at your wedding."

Ellena smiled at the dressmaker's lavish praise, knowing it

was aimed more at her own handiwork than the living mannequins who would wear it.

The woman led Ellena to the privacy of a back room to fit on this garment that would earn her such public admiration. It was indeed a work of art. The material had been gathered at the midriff and shoulders in such a way as to swirl with the leaves in the embroidery. It lay upon her figure smoothly, with the subtle, golden glow of the embellishment complementing her creamy skin.

Mrs. Pembridge beamed with professional pride, fully aware of the masterpiece her team of seamstresses had created. Hardly a pin was needed. It was as good as ready.

"I'll finish the last touches and send it to your address tomorrow."

"Thank you for your quick work. I cannot imagine how you managed such fine stitching in so short a time."

"Ah, these old hands have many years of experience, my dear, and my staff is comprised of the best among their peers. Of course, it helps when one has such inspiring materials to work with. But thank you for the compliment. It is very satisfying to have yet another happy customer."

Ellena smiled. "To be sure, Mrs. Pembridge, you will have to turn customers away once the ladies of Munro realize you are the magic behind my appearance on Friday."

The little shop owner didn't even blush at the excessive compliment. Instead, a happy glaze came over her eyes. Ellena half-imagined the ambitious sign outside being replaced with one of solid gold, so meaningfully did Mrs. Pembridge stare ahead of her as though endless streams of affluent customers filled her giddy mind.

Ellena left the dressmaker in her blissful state and took herself off to find Ned and the carriage. Within minutes, she was on her way to Munro House, her heart pounding with nerves and excitement. Thank goodness Ned was the driver. He had been the sole voice of reason among the gossiping servants. She could trust him to be discreet. She doubted he would speak of her clandestine visit to the viscount. Then again, trust, she had discovered, was a fragile thing.

As the grand building once again came into view, Ellena allowed herself a moment to drink in its inspiring architecture. Soon it would be her home. She would do everything in her power to make sure it was a happy one.

At the top of the wide steps, she lifted the knocker and released it. Footfalls followed. The heavy door swung inward. The footman who had opened it stood to one side, and Branson appeared in the frame as a footman finished pulling on the door.

"It's Miss Fallon, is it?"

Ellena nodded. How confused the man would be on Friday when she was introduced to the staff as their new mistress!

Dominic rushed toward her from the foyer. His earlier smile was now rather more tentative, faltering and reappearing with a quirk of his lips. It was a worried smile, which spoke at once to Ellena's heart.

Well, she thought with some satisfaction, *the time has finally come to put an end to all that.*

CHAPTER TWENTY-THREE

DOMINIC COULD HARDLY believe Nancy was right here, in his home. It was as if the last week had been completely erased and he stood alone with her again, her sincere eyes looking directly upon him without flinching or judgment. Yet there was something more guarded in her manner than he had previously known. He wondered what had happened for her circumstances to appear so changed.

The footman offered to take her shawl, but she declined.

"No, thank you. I think I will keep it with me, for the rooms are large and there may be a draught."

"I think you will find the library a sunny place," said Dominic, gesturing in that general direction.

It felt right to have this meeting in his favorite room. The library was not only sunny, but just the sort of space where Dominic felt most comfortable. It was filled with hundreds of impressive leatherbound volumes, a writing desk, a small table upon which now rested a tray with exquisite, tiny cakes, and finally, plush chairs in which to sit back and release one's cares.

Nancy draped her wrap across the back of a chair, a movement echoing her actions on that first, rain-soaked night. Dominic felt suddenly shy and exposed, as if, once again, all that separated her from him was a thick blanket and not the stylish attire of a well-bred lady.

The platter of miniature sweets echoed memories of a plate of cold meats and bread, and the delicate hands that had offered them to him for breakfast.

But Nancy did not appear to be distracted by these things. She came straight to the point.

"I imagine you must feel some confusion by my presence here today," she began.

"Honestly, yes," Dominic confessed.

"I hope you will not think my unexpected re-appearance inappropriate, but there is a matter of some importance that I must discuss with you."

Dominic's heart skipped a beat. Ellena knew Nancy. She had said as much in Munro Park. Was their falling-out the reason for Nancy's urgent need to talk to him? He tried to stay calm, but his pulse was racing.

"I shall endeavor to be of help where I can," he said, praying that his speech would not regress once again to a stutter.

Nancy leaned forward, a sudden eagerness in her bearing. "No, Dominic," she insisted, "it is *I* who intend to help *you*. There is something I must tell you regarding your intended, Miss Ellena Trenton."

Dominic groaned inwardly. He remembered their ruined outing in the park, his dismal comments, and Ellena's fiery reaction. Had she written to Nancy and told her everything? Perhaps they had even spoken in person. Exactly how well-informed was Nancy? How close was their connection? Dominic needed answers.

"How is it you know Ellena?" he asked.

"Ellena and I share more in common than you might think," Nancy answered with a smile. "Our adventures in the forest, our time at the convent, our..."

"Of course!" Dominic cried, as understanding dawned. "I should have made the connection! Ellena spent the night at the convent before proceeding to Thorn Bush Hall. Simmons mentioned as much in one of his reports. *That* is where she came to know you."

But Nancy shook her head. "In truth," she said, "Ellena has known me, to some degree, all her life—though Nancy Fallon was then but the stuff of stories."

"I'm afraid I don't follow."

An insistent tapping at the door made them turn around abruptly. Branson stood quietly, no doubt aware that his intrusion was unwelcome.

"I'm sorry, my lord, but you did say to let you know the moment Mr. Simmons arrived."

Dominic became suddenly somber. He looked at his pocket watch.

"Simmons is unusually early," he muttered. "I wonder what he has uncovered?"

"I'm sorry?" Nancy asked, confused.

Dominic looked from his watch to Nancy. He could not ignore Simmons. The man only had one subject to investigate, and that was Ellena. If he had rushed over to report something, it had to have been important.

He rose to indicate his intention to leave, but his resolve softened when he looked upon Nancy.

"This is most inconvenient," he apologized, "but I shall have to delay our conversation awhile. Are you able to wait, or shall I arrange for a postponement?"

Nancy shook her head. "No other issues challenge the importance of my visit here. I cannot leave until matters are resolved and I am at peace that the truth has triumphed over confusion. Conclude your other meeting at your leisure. I will be here."

Dominic's eyes darted to the door and back. "I shall make every effort to return within the half hour. I am grateful for your patience."

He fairly rushed from the room, not because he was eager to leave, but to expedite his return. He found the waiting figure of Mr. Simmons in his study and stopped abruptly in his stride.

Something was wrong. Mr. Simmons had his hands shoved deep into his trouser pockets, his weight shuffling from one foot to the other. His eyes darted more than once to the door and back, as if he were marking the exit for a quick escape. The natural ease of the little man, which enabled him to blend so successfully with his surroundings, was completely off-kilter. He was clearly in unchartered territory emotionally, which did not bode well at all. Dominic resigned himself to the likelihood of terrible news.

"Out with it, Simmons. Whatever it is, just be done with it."

"Milord…" Simmons faltered.

"Do your job, man. Don't keep me waiting." The viscount growled. The unusual gruffness of his tone jolted the stalled Simmons into speech.

"My lord, I followed Mr. Cole today as he entered the theater district. I had hoped to learn more of his character, or at least catch any references to Miss Trenton that he might make in an unguarded moment."

"I see. And what did you discover?"

"He entered the premises of a production that had no performance scheduled for the day. Since this was rather odd, I waited outside, assuming he would not linger there. Within twenty minutes, he had emerged again, this time with a young lady on his arm. Er… She was wearing a veil."

Lord Howell straightened up at these words. Why would Ellena meet Mr. Cole in such a clandestine manner? He felt the slow trickle of ice in his veins at the obvious answer.

Mr. Simmons confirmed what Dominic dared not imagine. "He… That is… Mr. Cole… He-He looked about to see if anyone was watching. They never saw me, of course. He lifted her veil and… he… er… kissed the young lady." Mr. Simons swallowed. "They laughed and walked down the street. I followed briefly, but it was just, well, more of the same, milord. I'm so terribly sorry."

"What did she look like?"

"Milord?"

"The young lady. Was she beautiful?"

"Yes, my lord. Slender, with auburn hair. And, of course, a deep-blue veil."

"Yes, I know the one. Thank you, Simmons. You may return to your normal duties."

"Er, one more thing…"

"Yes?"

"I noticed the Trenton carriage on the drive."

"What? *Now?*"

"Yes, milord. I wonder if it's been here long. Because I only just left the theater district, and Miss Trenton was still there."

"Miss Trenton is not my visitor."

"Ah, I see. That explains it, sir." Simmons said nothing more.

"Does it?" Dominic was not sure it did. Why would Nancy have come in the Trenton carriage? Was she staying with them as Ellena's guest? It was something he would have to ask her.

"I may have something else for you to look into," he mumbled absently to Simmons.

"As you wish, milord."

"For now, I know enough. Do see yourself out."

"Yes, milord. Thank you, milord."

The diminutive form of Mr. Simmons retreated from the room, leaving Dominic alone in the shadow of his news, though a midday sun brightened the rest of the world outside. He thought bitterly of Simmons seeing the face of Ellena when *he* had resolutely been denied the privilege. He thought of the hands of William Cole upon the willing Ellena, his lips against hers. Her mouth—that so vehemently had protested any indiscretion, shaming Dominic into submission—had curved into a laugh as she'd enjoyed the *amour* of a man she had defended as a mere friend. And he, Dominic, had apologized to her, *begging* for forgiveness. But his instincts had been right all along. And she had played him so easily. He seethed with rage at the torment he had endured at the hand of this duplicitous hussy—the lengths to which he had gone to accommodate her seeming insecurities and so-called wounded honor. He had wooed her and humbled himself before her, even thinking they'd shared the same fears and concerns. *Fool! Fool!*

And she had almost gotten away with it.

A sudden, terrible thought struck him. Had she sent Nancy here to speak for her? Was Nancy a decoy while Ellena lavished her affection on another beau?

Dominic struggled to reconcile such an image with Nancy. If she was involved as an accomplice, it must surely be unintentionally. The thought of dear, sweet Nancy being caught up in this sordid business made him balk.

A fury gripped him. No more would he be the dupe in Miss Trenton's little game. He would denounce her before all the world. Her bold words and clever charms were no longer enough. He had found her out. And not a moment too soon. This very day, their engagement would end, and she would be exposed for the shameless fraud she was.

He strode down the corridor to the library, ready to strike the first blow against Ellena. He would sever this friendship she enjoyed with Nancy. He relished the first taste of revenge.

But, upon reaching the doorway, he caught sight of Nancy ensconced in her chair, a book open upon her lap, her knees drawn in closely as she sat, engrossed in the narrative before her. He could remember so well how she had sat in a similar chair not too long ago, a blanket gripped with equal vigor, and then the emergence of a creamy, slender arm as they had exchanged introductions.

The momentum of his anger was all but spent as he stood transfixed by the presence of Nancy. No, he would not be raging against her. He could never speak to her in tones that only Ellena deserved. Instead, he cleared his throat very gently, almost inaudibly, so as not to frighten her from her pages.

She looked up at once and, seeing him returned, immediately cast the book aside. "I hope all is well?" she asked. When he did not answer, her forehead furrowed and her smile slid from her lips. She rose and moved toward him. "What is the matter? You look troubled."

Her sincerity drew him to her. He wished he could take her smooth, milky hand and pull it to his cheek. What a comfort she would be! He fought the urge and turned away slightly, his eyes upon the rows of book-laden shelves.

"I'm afraid I shall have to end our meeting rather abruptly. A grievous matter has come to my attention and I must act without delay."

"Something, I hope, that can be resolved?"

"Oh, it has but one outcome, decided for me. But I must see it carried out."

Nancy smiled encouragingly. "I admire your dedication to your duties. It must at times be a burdensome responsibility."

"It is especially so when it forces me to end our visit. But this cannot be avoided."

Nancy's smiled dissolved. "But what of Ellena? There is an important revelation you need to hear. It will remove many of your concerns. Can we not meet again a little later, when this other matter has been tended to?"

Dominic's expression was grim. "I think I know all I need to about my betrothed. There can be little you have to add that can influence me at this point."

His tone had a testy edge, but her sense of urgency prevailed.

"But, *Dominic!*" she cried. "You need to know. It's *me...* I'm..."

Dominic held up a hand to halt her speech.

"I know who you are. And I cannot believe Miss Trenton would stoop so low as to involve you. I'm afraid I have no interest in your further defense of your friend. Her own actions are quite revealing and your contradiction of them will only aggravate me. I do not wish to enter into such a distasteful discussion with someone I so heartily respect."

Nancy's face blanched. "But I thought you wanted to reconcile with Ellena? That you desired but the confirmation of her willingness to do so?"

Dominic could bear it no longer. His towering figure glowered as he spat out his words. "Your *friend* is not worth defending. You would do well to mix in better company. I will no longer entertain any discussion on this topic."

Nancy stared, her mouth slightly open, as Dominic fought for self-control.

"You will have to excuse me," he finally managed. "Please consider our meeting postponed for the present."

He turned and left the room quite suddenly, not daring to speak, for fear of offending his cherished guest any further.

ELLENA STOOD, CONFUSED and alarmed at this development. Whatever had caused this change in Dominic had taken place while he had been called away. With whom had he met? How could one meeting so prejudice him when, but minutes ago, they had been making such progress?

There was little point in speculating about the unknown while standing in the middle of the library, her welcome overstayed. Ellena collected her shawl and withdrew from the room. In the passage, she passed Branson and then a maidservant. They looked at her briefly before going about their business. Ellena felt flushed at her solitary presence in their master's house. She hastened to the front door and saw herself out, grateful to find the friendly face of Ned, who was patiently waiting outside with the carriage.

"Where to, miss?" he asked as the footman held open the carriage door and helped her up the step.

Ellena did not know the answer. She was feeling more than just a little lost. Her good intentions this morning had come to naught. Dominic seemed angrier than ever, even struggling to maintain his composure in front of whom he assumed was

Nancy. She had been unable to achieve her purpose with this visit. The truth remained shrouded, the outcome dangerously ominous. She had failed. Not only today, but in all she had attempted since leaving home but a short week ago. The assumption of a fake identity had been the beginning of a long string of errors in judgment that had led her ever further from her purpose. She had failed herself, and somehow she had failed Dominic, though she knew not how.

There seemed little point in trying to explain the veil, or anything else to him now. If he could not restrain his fury with "Nancy," he would have no patience at all if she tried to reconcile with him as Ellena. Would she have to appear veiled at their ceremony on Friday? Such a public place was hardly the right venue for revelations and confused discussion.

It felt as if her heart was weighted with stone. No outcome looked hopeful. Their marriage would begin with acrimony and regret. And the years ahead? Could they survive a relationship founded on manipulation, mistrust, and temper?

It was with a very miserable and despondent spirit that she sat in the cubicle of the carriage while Ned waited expectantly for instructions.

In the distance, at the edge of her hearing, the convent bells began to chime the noon hour. At first, she barely noticed them, engrossed as she was in her own misfortune. However, their clarity penetrated her consciousness and called out their insistent advice. Ellena felt relief as she understood their message. Time spent in quiet meditation would bring her muddled thoughts to order. Her cousin's home could not offer that sanctuary, and Dominic's own church had a vicar who, in his thoughtfulness, might ask too many questions. No, it was the convent, with its private chapel, that would serve her needs best.

"Miss Trenton? Should I make for Thorn Bush Hall?"

"No, Ned, thank you. Not yet, anyway. I have one more stop to make. Could you please direct the horses to the abbey? I am much obliged."

CHAPTER TWENTY-FOUR

WHEN ELLENA RETURNED to her cousin's home, she felt greatly refreshed. An hour of solitude in the chapel of the convent had worked a miracle upon her weary spirit. She had drawn comfort from her time in prayer, releasing control of her situation and gaining calm instead.

Charlotte greeted her at the door, quite flustered, a mixture of concern and excitement dancing across her features.

"Ellena! Where have you been? We were expecting you back ages ago. And look, a letter is waiting for you from his lordship. I must say, the messenger seemed eager to part with it. I hope it is not news of a discouraging nature. Did your visit go well? But the letter will speak for itself."

Charlotte quickly pressed the object of her intrigue into the hands of Ellena, then stood expectantly as she stared down at the sealed document.

"Well, aren't you going to open it?"

Ellena's most recent memory of Dominic hardly served to encourage her prospects in opening the letter. But it could not be avoided. Her fingers released the seal and unfolded the single sheet.

The familiar hand that had marked the page had been brief in its communication. The cool and blunt salute boded ill, and Ellena read on silently in trepidation.

Miss Trenton,

I shall be brief.

Despite my original ardor in establishing a connection between your family and my own, your recent indiscretions have filled me with a violent opposition to it.

Put quite simply, your reckless liaison with another demands the immediate severance of our engagement.

Your father has been alerted to my decision.

I will enter into no discussion on the matter, either with your father or yourself, having had my fill of the Trenton tactics of persuasion.

Since you deemed it fit to flaunt your affair in public, you will feel no shame when the reason for my actions becomes general knowledge. Despite the sordid nature of such a revelation, I feel the truth is required to protect my family from being accused of unfairly breaking contract. You will have to bear the consequences of your faithlessness alone. My only pity lies with your family, whose reputation must surely be tarnished by the stain upon yours.

Having no desire to waste another moment on this topic, I bid you a speedy departure from Munro. Your presence here will not serve to soften my resolve.

I remain,
Howell

"Oh!" Ellena gasped as she sank into a chair. "How can he believe that I…?"

She re-read the bitter words, searching for an explanation that made sense. He seemed so convinced of his facts. Certainly, he would never risk a scandal without some sort of proof. But how could evidence exist of an action that had never taken place?

Her thoughts cast back to the interruption of her meeting with him earlier this day. With whom had he consulted? Could it have been Miss Sangford, come to pour poison in his ear? But he would not have deserted Nancy to receive someone like Miss Sangford. Besides, she seemed to remember the butler referring to a Mr. Simmons, someone Dominic appeared to have been expecting. Who was this Mr. Simmons, and why would Dominic trust his word? She knew the viscount to have a string of informants who could confirm or refute any gossip from the streets. A lie about her character or behavior would be easily discovered. Why, then, had a lie convinced him? It made no sense.

Charlotte, meanwhile, had gently drawn the paper from her cousin's unresisting fingers. Ellena's face felt cold with shock, and, as Charlotte read the page, she, too, blanched at the news.

"But, Ellena! What can he mean? You have never left the house alone until this morning…"

Her words trailed off.

"You did go straight to Munro House from Mrs. Pembridge's, didn't you?"

"Of course! How can you doubt me? How is it everyone is so willing to think the worst of me?"

Charlotte looked at her hands. "It's just… Well, some of your choices have been a little…unusual, dear. And you can be a bit…*secretive* at times."

Ellena stared at Charlotte. She was right, of course. But that didn't make Ellena guilty of wrongdoing. Oh, this was such a mess! What could she do? There must be *something* she could do!

Ellena stood up abruptly, her body restless with agitation.

"I must write to him, Charlotte. He must be convinced of my innocence. Oh, what will Father say when he receives such shocking news? My reputation is in tatters! It is so unfair! How can Dominic be so thoroughly deceived?"

Charlotte's expression was grim. "I'm sorry. I know this is hard to hear, but I do not think he will receive a letter from any of us at this time. Perhaps if we leave him be awhile, he might entertain some discussion of a reasonable nature."

"No, it will be too late! Already, he has sent a false report to my family at Trenton Grange. Soon, he will announce to all in Munro the official breaking of our engagement, along with his reasons for doing so. His accusations must be grave indeed if he is to take such an unprecedented step. Father will have his head for breaking the contract!" She shuddered. "I cannot wait, Charlotte. Don't you see?"

"I understand. But I'm afraid any attempt at explanation or reconciliation will be ignored. Still, if it will make you feel better, we will try."

Ellena thought for a moment. She still had one card left to play. If Dominic would not listen to Ellena, perhaps he would receive a note from Nancy. She would tell him everything. He would have to understand how impossible it was for Ellena to betray him when she bore the heart of Nancy. It was worth trying. She had everything to lose if this failed.

She seated herself at the writing desk in the solarium and began to write briskly.

Dear Dominic,

It is with a great sense of urgency that I write to you. The interruption of our earlier conversation could not have been more disastrous. There are things you must know, and any further delay could bring ruin to an innocent family.

I will come straight to the point, as there is little use for eloquent ramblings under the circumstances.

When you met a woman at the door of your cabin that pivotal night and helped a stranger in distress, you rescued not Nancy Fallon, but Ellena Trenton.

I know such a statement can only come as a great surprise, seemingly unbelievable. However, perhaps my explanation will clarify matters.

When I—that is, Ellena—found myself outside your cabin that night, I did not know what to expect from the stranger within. I could not have known that he would be a man of honor and generosity, least of all that he was my very own betrothed!

To protect my family—since I was in a compromising situation with an unknown gentleman—I assumed a false name and thought myself very clever for the deception. What a ghastly mistake it was!

When I met you in your full capacity as viscount and future husband last Friday evening, I was grateful for the veil, as it prevented an embarrassing reunion between yourself and a fictitious character.

But this, too, only complicated matters further. I desperately sought an opportunity to reveal myself to you. I was, in truth, filled with gratitude and joy in the knowledge that the kind, gentle Dominic of the forest was to be my husband. I confess I had been more than a little envious of the easy friendship I could share with you as Nancy—so much better than the awkward dance of etiquette and entanglement I experienced as Ellena. Doubtless, this was your experience also.

You may remember I was attempting to tell you the secret of my double identity at the park. Our interruption by Mr. Cole was most untimely and regrettable in its effect upon you. But this is a small matter compared to the terrible situation in which we now find ourselves.

This morning's efforts at reconciliation were no more successful than the last. This time, however, I cannot hazard any guesses as to what may have triggered your belief in a disloyal Ellena. I can only hope fervently that, if you could trust Nancy, then you will have faith in your Ellena, who is one and the same.

Without understanding the source of your doubts, I earnestly ask that you confide them to me and grant me the opportunity to defend myself.

There remains little I can add, except this: I have admired you from the moment I met you. The difficulties we have encountered notwithstanding, I would still heartily be your bride, if you will have me.

I hope with all my heart that you can accept my explanation and reassurances, and that you may cherish your Ellena as you did when she was but a simple girl called Nancy.

Warmly and sincerely,
Yours in faith,
Ellena

She quickly re-read the letter, satisfied that it contained every essential element. She sealed and addressed it, then handed it to Charlotte, who left to seek out the messenger boy.

Ellena sat quietly with her hands in her lap. There was little she could do now but wait. She had to trust that her prayers would be heard. It was out of her hands and would follow its destined course. Whatever happened, she was no longer in control. She was mildly surprised to discover that this actually offered some relief. Which was just as well, for it would take great calm and courage to exercise the necessary patience in waiting for Viscount Howell's response.

DOMINIC WAS ALL too aware that his surliness was affecting the servants. He could imagine how joylessly Branson now knocked at the entrance to his study, but he was in no mood to be charitable. Dominic uttered a gruff, "What is it?" and waited impatiently for the butler to enter.

"My lord," said Branson, "there's a letter come for you from Thorn Bush Hall."

"Did I not give clear instructions I wished to have no contact with that family? Why are my wishes not being respected?"

Branson was unperturbed. He had worked at Munro House when the late viscount had been lord of the manor. Dominic's surly mood would have no effect on him at all. "Well, my lord, it's just that this letter is from Miss Nancy Fallon, so I wasn't sure what to make of it."

"Why would she…? Never mind, just give it to me."

The butler handed over the offending article without ceremony and received permission to leave.

Alone once again, Dominic turned the item over in his hand. There was something familiar about the handwriting, but he couldn't for the moment put his finger on it. As for the contents, he supposed Nancy wished to address their foiled meeting. But why was the letter sent from Thorn Bush Hall? Had she stopped by to call on her disgraced friend? Perhaps she'd even hoped to warn Ellena that his mood was dangerous.

Ellena must by now have received his letter in which he denounced her actions and broke off the engagement. Had she put Nancy up to writing on her behalf? He felt sure she must have. Ellena would be desperate, her deceit and betrayal unraveling suddenly in the face of its discovery. Sweet Nancy would be only too willing to help mend the rift. Ellena could have twisted the facts to gain the pity of her kindhearted friend.

Dominic stared at the letter once more. He was in no mood for Ellena's machinations. He cast the letter aside, unopened.

He sat down with a grimace. Tomorrow, he would have to make some sort of public announcement. Reverend Keith had to be notified, and the guests made aware that the wedding was off. He did not relish the thought of a scandal. Even though the shame would not be upon the Howell name, he knew all too well the type of reaction to expect from the Miss Sangfords of the world.

His stomach knotted. Was that it, then? Did he have to settle for a lady of Munro after all? Was someone from the *ton* more likely to be faithful? No, he did not think so. If anything, such a lady would merely be more subtle in her betrayal. Perhaps that was why Ellena had been so easily found out. She lacked the worldly experience to sustain a subterfuge.

The worst of it was that he had actually liked Ellena. She could have been enough.

But he wasn't enough for her.

He had failed once again. Even when he could choose from any woman in society, he had chosen poorly. Oh, how his sisters would gorge themselves on his misery!

Dominic drummed his fingers on his desk. Really, the only advantage in all of this was that he had been spared the humiliation of discovering the infidelity during their marriage. But it was very small consolation indeed. It did little to lift his dark mood, and he sat in broody silence for a long while as the shadows lengthened across the floor of his study.

SOME DISTANCE ACROSS town, Ellena sat with equal gravity, awaiting a letter that did not come.

CHAPTER TWENTY-FIVE

ELLENA REMAINED SUBDUED for the rest of the afternoon. She was grateful for Charlotte, who kept anyone from disturbing her. Despite her self-imposed solitude, Ellena heard Mr. Cole arrive back at the house and protest loudly at the extreme prejudice shown by the viscount. James was less vocal, but his reaction was easy to imagine. He would feel no pity for either Ellena or the Howells but would immediately calculate the damage to his own fortune by association with such scandal.

Ellena felt horribly out of place in this house, in this city. But she was unwilling to leave, lest a letter should arrive from Dominic. Besides, she felt certain her father would have a strong opinion as to what was to be done, and she dared not risk angering him any further. So she waited meekly until well into the following morning, when a messenger finally arrived.

A solemn Charlotte appeared at the door to Ellena's room, carrying a note. Ellena could tell at once the letter had not come from Lord Howell. She recognized her father's hand. Her own shook slightly as she unfolded the paper.

"Does he offer advice or instruction?" Charlotte inquired hopefully. She hid her concern well, but Ellena knew that her own misfortune had placed a heavy burden upon this household and its reputation.

"I am to expect his arrival Thursday morning. He has a business matter to attend to today but leaves by coach at dawn tomorrow. I'm afraid his mood is unforgiving. This delay will only aggravate him further. I cannot count on his sympathy. This is a blow to his name and expectations. It will be a difficult task to convince him of my innocence when I myself do not fully understand what it is I am guilty of. And, I'm afraid, if I *do* succeed in proving myself free of fault, Father's fury will turn instead upon the Howell family for their treatment of me. Neither scenario could have a satisfactory outcome."

"Poor Ellena," soothed Charlotte. "Perhaps tomorrow will offer its own answer. There is still time."

Ellena knew the likelihood of a last-minute miracle to be small but said nothing, not wishing to undo Charlotte's efforts. Instead, she smiled bravely and squeezed Charlotte's hand as a mutual encouragement.

"Maybe you are right. We cannot give up. Not yet, anyway."

She gained little comfort from her own words. Her prayers had not been answered. Dominic remained stubbornly silent. Soon, shame would wash over her entire family, and she was powerless to stop it.

After Charlotte had returned to her domestic duties, Ellena remained secluded in her room. She had not written to Jilly today and, for the first time, felt no inclination to do so. Would Jilly be aware of the grievous news? What would she make of it? Surely, she, of all people, would not believe the slander?

Ellena dwelled upon the furious reaction of her father, pictured her mother's disappointment, and imagined the frenzied conversations among the servants. But she found it impossible to include Jillian in any of these scenarios. Her friend would likely be amazed and confused, but Jillian knew Ellena too well to believe that there was any truth in these accusations.

The comfort in knowing there remained at least one person who still believed in her was enough to coax Ellena from the self-imposed exile of her room. She slipped downstairs and out into the garden, where the chilly day required her to wrap up in her cashmere shawl.

The air was crisp and snapped at the soft, unprotected skin on Ellena's face and hands. She walked briskly to fire her internal furnace and drive off the pinching cold, as well as to vent a measure of her frustration and helplessness.

She did not want company and was briefly annoyed when she heard herself being hailed from beyond the yew hedge.

She turned to see Mr. Cole approach. He walked quickly and purposefully in her direction. For a moment, she entertained the possibility that a letter had arrived from Dominic. However, as Mr. Cole neared, she saw his hands carried no such message of hope.

His lips were tight and his gaze firmly focused—unusual for such a light-hearted gentleman.

Ellena, anticipating nothing beyond his usual geniality, waited where she stood for his rapid stride to deliver him into her company.

⇥⟫⟩⟨⟪⇤

DOMINIC HAD SLEPT very poorly and awoke with a lingering sense of unease. The origin of his misery was not Ellena. Instead, he was haunted by the rift that the events of the previous day had created between himself and Nancy.

He regretted his curt behavior at their parting. Her surprise reappearance in his life had been such a welcome event. He had been especially thrilled to find that she was exactly as he had remembered her. His tortuous courtship had often led him to compare his betrothed with Nancy, and he had considered in his deepest, most honest heart whether he might not perhaps be idealizing Nancy in his memory. Her conduct yesterday had banished all doubts. She was still the same selfless, genteel spirit he had first met.

Dominic pondered what might have been if he had met Nancy under different circumstances. One thing he knew for certain: he would have been more persistent in discovering her situation, had he not already committed himself to engagement with another. If her family were indeed of good standing—be their fortune limited or not—he would have pursued the question of her future with Mr. Fallon, her father. He remembered well her filial obedience in joining the sisterhood, though her dispassion for the choice rendered her was clear. He would have made polite but insistent inquiries in the hopes of proving himself a worthy substitute to a life in the convent. Dominic liked to think Nancy might even have welcomed such an alternative. Surely, he did not imagine the tenderness she had shown him?

Instead, he and Nancy had ignored the feelings that had awoken gently at their meeting in the forest cabin. They had done the honorable thing, following the paths that had been laid before them. For this, his only thanks had been to wrangle with his betrothed from the first and ultimately discover her deceit. He would have looked the pretty fool, indeed, if he had not found her out when he had. Marrying a dishonorable woman would have meant a lifetime of regret for him and disgrace upon the family name. He was most indebted to Mr. Simmons for his timely salvation.

As for Nancy, were her circumstances also changed? There had been no time to touch on her situation during their brief meeting yesterday. He had had no answer to the burning question as to why she had not been wearing a wimple, but instead had been dressed like a lady of some means. Had her father rethought his plans for his daughter? Was it possible? If there was even the remotest chance…

He scarcely dared to think it. The removal of Ellena from his future by her own reckless actions left him free to consider other, more promising options. For the first time, he could allow himself to dwell, without guilt, on the possibility of a deeper acquaintance with Miss Nancy Fallon. He would, of course, have to proceed with caution and delicacy, especially once the circumstance of his broken engagement came to light. He would need to take great care not to add any unnecessary risk to his reputation, which would surely be under scrutiny along with Ellena's. But he could take the initial step. He could confess his hopes to Nancy—the one who called him by his name boldly but without presumption.

He imagined Nancy's surprise at such tender words from him, and her zealous attempts to soothe the tensions between him and Ellena. But he would soon put such protest to rest. Nancy would see Miss Trenton for the minx she was and abandon any further defense of her friend. She would be freed of any misplaced loyalties and could accept his humble declaration of affection without the burden of guilt. His biggest obstacle with Nancy would be her deep sense of propriety. It was a hurdle he would willingly tackle, cherishing its very presence as an indication of the quality of person upon whom he was now investing his efforts.

With his thoughts diverted onto this new, quite delightful track, Dominic dressed for a late breakfast. He hummed a tuneless but happy song as he descended the stairs and proceeded to the dining room. He settled into his chair while a footman poured his coffee. Cup in hand, Dominic leaned back— contentedly munching on his buttered toast—and cheerfully contemplated his prospects with the lovely Miss Nancy Fallon.

CHAPTER TWENTY-SIX

WILLIAM COLE MAINTAINED his grim-lipped expression as he drew alongside Ellena at the far end of the lawned garden.

"May I join you?" His inquiry was gentle, unassuming.

"I'm not very good company at the moment," she warned.

Mr. Cole nodded his head sympathetically. "That is perfectly understandable. You have been made to endure so much in the past few days. You have borne it all admirably. But your suffering has not escaped the notice of those who care for you and are concerned for your happiness."

Ellena found little encouragement in his words. "There are very few supporters who remain." She bit her lip. "I fear they might regret their association with me in the weeks to come."

"I hope you count me among your loyal friends."

"Thank you, but I hardly think you would want to volunteer for so fruitless an exercise."

Mr. Cole's passion was stirred at once.

"Wherein lies the difficulty?" he demanded. "You are one of the most steadfast, virtuous, and deserving young women I have ever known. I cannot understand how this is not obvious to all who meet you, especially someone with such a reputation for discernment as your betrothed."

"We are no longer engaged."

"Yes, of course," said Mr. Cole, his enthusiasm instantly curbed. "I'm sorry. I did not mean to be insensitive." His arms that had, but a moment ago, flailed wildly, now hung by his side.

Ellena's eyes stayed upon the tips of her shoes as they paced the soft lawn. "I shall have to bear much more than such idle references, Mr. Cole. In the immediate future, I may expect severe chastisement from my family and the mocking jeers of the entire Munro community, who—let us be honest—never wanted me here to begin with."

"The more fools, they. It is a small matter to lose the favor of a city filled with self-aggrandizing braggarts and wagging tongues."

"Even if I could shut out their voices from my mind, the repercussions do not end there. This does not impact myself alone. It will damage my father's standing among his peers, my mother's ability to show her face in society. Even James will not escape the whip of its tail. And though I feel little pity for him, there is his growing family to consider."

Mr. Cole shook his head slowly. "I marvel at your selflessness. Even now, under duress, you think only of others and pay little heed to your own losses."

Ellena stopped and turned, her woeful eyes upon Mr. Cole. "How can I think only of myself? My disgrace comes at a great price to others. I cannot wallow in self-pity when there are others who share the cost of my downfall."

"But you are completely innocent! Are you not enraged by the injustice of it?"

Ellena threw up her arms in exasperation. "Of course I am! I do not even have clarity on the charge, except that it incriminates me with another! I do not know whom. The *when* and *where* are also mysteries, and ones I am unlikely to solve since the viscount will not speak of it. It is this inability to defend myself that most frustrates me."

There was a brief silence. Ellena had halted her speech before her emotions could overwhelm her. She would not speak of her deepest loss. It was true, her courtship with Dominic had been fraught with difficulties, but it had promised much: stability, position, even love. In an instant, all had now been torn from her grasp. Even when she had walked angrily from Dominic at the park, it had been with the knowledge that she had been angry with her *betrothed*. Now she had nothing, not even the hope of a new connection. For who would unite with a young woman of tattered repute? It would surely be the most desperate of matches when the lady was in such a disgraced position. She was in the prime of her youth, yet all that stretched before her now were endless, empty years.

"Pardon me for saying," Mr. Cole persisted, "but I find Lord Howell's behavior rather suspect. Why will he not speak plainly and provide whatever evidence he believes he has? Forgive me, but do you not think it possible the viscount may have created this story to free himself from his contract with your father? Perhaps his accusations are a reflection of his own guilt."

Ellena shook her head solemnly. "Why would he take such extreme action? It was his free will to seek me for his bride. His dowry demands were met on reasonable terms. Why would he bring the association of scandal with his name when our engagement was the fulfillment of his own wishes?"

Mr. Cole's next words were spoken carefully, as if he knew the injury they might cause. "Perhaps—and I say this with the greatest respect to your person—perhaps you were not exactly what he expected. Could it be he had hoped for someone of a more docile, less challenging nature? Maybe he assumed a young lady from the country would be less sophisticated, more easily charmed by his awkward manners, and grateful for the hand of a nobleman. I do not mean to imply that you are somehow lacking. Far from it. In truth, I wholeheartedly believe you were too much a woman for him, if you will excuse such forward speech. He seemed ill prepared for a relationship with someone as intelligent and spirited as yourself."

Ellena pondered this. "There is a hint of truth in your observations. I do think perhaps my nature was more demanding than he had expected. Especially when I arrived veiled at his doorstep for our first dinner. But he made great efforts to accommodate the one who challenged him so."

"There you go again!" exclaimed Mr. Cole, his voice rising. "Why do you insist upon defending him, even now? He has been grossly unjust in his treatment of you. You and your family face unnecessary difficulties because of his false accusations. Yet you persist in pointing out his virtues, which, frankly, I suspect, are quite limited."

"I am merely speaking the truth. As much as his latest actions have bewildered me, I cannot deny the elements of goodness of his character outside of these events. He has amazed me as much with his better qualities as he has with his flaws. I certainly do not believe he would perpetuate a lie simply to rid himself of me—if, in fact, he desired my departure. No, someone has whispered this falsehood to him, someone whom he trusts implicitly. There is no other explanation for his radical behavior."

Mr. Cole walked on in silence, his frustration quite evident. His arms were rigid at his sides and the muscle in his jaw flexed irritably. His mood did not lighten, and Ellena felt tension radiate from him to match her own.

Perhaps he realized that he was only adding to her discomfort, for, when he spoke again, his words were softer, though the essence of his speech was the same.

"Very well," he conceded, though he seemed to do so grudgingly, "let us assume the good viscount carries no blame in the lie other than to foolishly accept it as fact and then thoroughly denounce you. Is that not enough? Does this not call into question your regard for him?"

Ellena's lips pressed tightly upon each other, then opened so she might say sternly, "You seem determined for me to show disfavor toward the viscount. You appear to think I am not sufficiently distressed by his actions and attitudes." Her voice pitched higher. "Do you not see that I am afraid to step toward the edge of that cliff? I cannot contemplate such an excessive reaction to his folly. What if he should come to his senses? If I am to forgive him, I cannot have dark rage and scorn in my heart."

"*Forgive* him?" Mr. Cole spluttered the words. "Why would you want to forgive him after his despicable behavior? Did he not accuse you of liaisons with me even before this? He seems to me to have a consistently jealous heart. You are fortunate to have escaped him, Ellena."

At the sound of her name—uttered so passionately by a man so earnest in his defense of her—Ellena stopped and turned to him. Mr. Cole's face was tortured with emotion. To use her name was a liberty she had not granted. *Could* not grant. And yet a measure of gratitude rose within her. His ardor in championing her cause was a refreshing relief after her recent lonely hours.

"I was wrong about you too, it seems," she began.

At her words, Mr. Cole froze. "What do you mean?" he asked, his mouth pinched, his eyes darting to the side.

"When I first met you, and you called me a Spanish princess, do you remember what I said?"

Mr. Cole released a tense breath. "I don't recall exactly," he answered.

"I called you a revolutionary, and predicted you would attempt to overthrow my orderly thoughts. I remember you rather enjoyed the image. But now I see instead you are the most loyal of friends, a man whose only interest is to uphold the dignity of your sovereign. And for that, you have our thanks."

She bowed her head regally and managed a little smile. William Cole had once again managed to lift her spirits and, for the first time since her fall from grace, she felt a smattering of relief.

CHAPTER TWENTY-SEVEN

IT WAS A beautiful day, despite the icy fingers that infiltrated the snug interior of the Howell family carriage. The proud crest stood out brightly on the doors, the sun pouring its light into the crisp, clear morning air. The viscount was enjoying the luxury of surveying his surroundings as they paraded past his window. His mind was normally occupied with some matter requiring his attention—whether a delicate negotiation, a tiresome committee meeting, or a dreaded social event. Today, he had freed himself of all other commitments and was delighted to rediscover the pleasures of idle observation.

The avenue of trees that lined the lane upon his estate was ablaze with the spicy colors of autumn. The horses' hooves and carriage wheels kicked up a flurry of fallen leaves that were joined by the downward drift of more leaves from the stately boughs above.

Through his carriage window, Dominic spied two leather boots atop a ladder. He angled his head upward and saw the figure of a gardener whose well-practiced arms manipulated large shears across the surface of a hedge. Several chimneys of Munro House, as well as those of a great many smaller dwellings beyond its landscape, smoked gentle plumes of domestic activity.

Dominic sighed with satisfaction. Despite the turmoil of the previous day, he felt at peace in the knowledge that *this* day promised a new beginning. There was a degree of nervous apprehension, but it was not the usual, tortuous discomfort he experienced when faced with the prospect of approaching a young lady. Nancy simply did not conjure up the same dread. Her straightforward speech, the earnest focus in her eyes, the absence of malice and, most comfortingly, the unmistakable admiration she carried for her friend Dominic—all these tied into a package so perfect, so enticing, it left no room for fear or doubt.

He was pleased that the route took him along the outskirts of town rather than through its bustling center. Not only could he savor the magnificence of nature's spectacle, he would also be untouched by the decadent flavor that was at Munro's heart. Today, he desired freshness, newness, a cleansing of sorts. Circumventing Munro's core kept him from the distraction of its sensual materialism.

Soon, the horizon was pierced by the steepled tower that crowned the church among the abbey's clustered buildings. It was a bittersweet reminder of his first parting from Nancy, seven discardable days ago. His heart began to pound a little harder as the carriage wended its way toward the secluded commune. His conveyance bore him the full length of the drive, beyond the point where he had been forced to leave Nancy a week ago. At its apex, the driver halted, and Dominic descended from the cozy interior of the carriage into the vigorous cold of the shaded courtyard.

Footfalls approached as a middle-aged nun responded to what had to have been the unusual sound of carriage wheels on a weekday morning. She seemed to immediately recognize the crest and the man and hurried forward to greet their unexpected visitor.

"Your lordship, is there some way we may be of service?"

"Yes, I believe so. Thank you, sister. Could you direct me to the abbess? I have a matter I hope she can help me with."

"Certainly, milord. She is currently at meditations, but you could wait in her study, if you wish. She won't be much longer."

"That is very accommodating of you. I am most grateful."

Dominic followed her squat, black-clad shape through an archway and down a corridor. He waited outside a simple wooden door as the short, stocky figure extended a hand from the recesses of her layered garment and knocked. Receiving no answer, she led him into the room and gestured to a chair. Dominic noted that the furnishings were simple and the attention to order was meticulous. Shelves with books had been polished to a shine and devoid of the familiar, dusty smell he typically expected from such large volumes. The desk was clear of all but the essentials, which, surprisingly, included a humble clay vase and a single bloom, most likely from their immaculate garden.

"She will be ten, at most twenty, minutes," said the nun. "Shall I bring in some tea?"

"No, that won't be necessary. I am content to simply wait."

"Very well. A blessed day to you, then."

"And to you, sister."

Despite the calm of the room and the warmth afforded by the uncommon luxury of it being carpeted, Dominic was grateful when its regular occupant returned a mere five minutes later. Waiting gave too much opportunity for his thoughts to wander. He could not afford self-doubt now. He had committed himself to this avenue of investigation and must see it through.

The Mother Superior, like her study, appeared neat and functional. Dominic rose when she entered and promptly sat down again as she waved her hand dismissively at his chivalry.

"I am intrigued to know what brings our town's most illustrious citizen within these humble walls," she mused aloud.

"Well," Dominic began, then he stopped. Suddenly, he was not at all sure how to proceed. After all, it was hardly standard procedure to enter a convent and request to see a novice privately. Then again, what else was there for it but to blunder ahead and hope for the best?

"I know it is unorthodox, but I was hoping to speak with one of your postulants."

Her serene face filled with surprise. "May I ask what purpose such an interview could possibly serve?"

"It is hard to explain. You see, a week ago I assisted her in reaching your abbey after she had encountered some difficulties on her journey here."

"So it is a particular young lady with whom you wish to speak?"

"Yes. I'm sorry. I did not make that clear."

"I don't recall any novices entering our sisterhood as recently as that, nor one who had any problems prior to her arrival."

"She may have neglected to speak of me, being embarrassed at receiving assistance from a stranger at the time. I am also under the impression she has not yet taken her vows. This is ultimately why I have come to speak with her. You see"—he squirmed a little as he continued along the uncomfortable topic—"she entered the convent life solely to respect her father's wishes, and I believe her true happiness may lie elsewhere."

By now, he was blushing quite deeply and the Mother Superior, who seemed to understand him better than he had hoped, took pity on him.

"It is not the way of the Church to make brides of Christ from those who would rather be, shall we say, more traditional brides. That is one of the reasons why there is at least a year of study and reflection before any vows are considered. However, this is a private journey, and any questions that arise regarding her choices should originate with her. I'm afraid your interests would interfere with what should be a personal decision on her part."

"But she has already been influenced! By her father, that is. She believes that this future is his intention for her. Does she not deserve to know there are other possibilities, ones that she may already have hoped for but perhaps dared not believe possible?"

"You speak very passionately about a young girl you have met but once, even though the circumstances may have been romanticized by the element of rescue."

"She… Well…I do not wish to make trouble for her…"

"I think it best if you declare everything honestly. If you truly want what's right, the truth cannot be avoided."

Dominic sighed. "Very well. She came to see me at my home yesterday."

A sharply-raised eyebrow indicated combined disapproval and amazement at his revelation.

"This is quite serious. Our novices are sequestered here. It would be difficult for her to have left unnoticed, let alone to have made her way to your home."

"We-ell, she also had an appointment in town, I believe, because I ran into her, quite literally, when I was having my wedding suit fitted."

"Lord Howell…" The abbess now spoke quite sternly. "Your explanations paint a most disturbing picture, not the least of which is to remind me that you are already engaged! What possible purpose could it serve to raise the hopes of an innocent young woman, content to obey her father? Do you not feel your actions are somewhat lacking in propriety? Even if I had patience with a young woman's infatuation, I could not possibly be party to any unscrupulous behavior involving one of our postulates— no matter how willing the foolish child was to involve herself in your affairs."

Dominic, now committed to his path of action, persisted.

"You are right, of course. Let me hasten to clarify. Firstly, I can officially announce the end of my engagement to Miss Ellena Trenton. The reasons will become apparent soon enough, but the decision is final."

"Oh, I am sorry to hear that," the nun said with a sorrowful shake of the head. "Sorry, indeed. Miss Trenton spent a little time here upon her arrival in Munro. Forgive the boldness of my opinion, but she seemed a fine person—generous, responsible, godly."

Dominic's face darkened. "You knew her but a short while, by your own admission. She had other, less flattering qualities that had little to do with morality. Let us leave it at that."

"Of course. I did not mean to interfere. However, under the circumstances, I proceed with caution, you understand."

"Certainly. This leads me to offer further reassurance. When Miss Fallon came to see me yesterday, it was with no motive other than to help a friend. She risked much, I know, leaving the confines of these grounds without the proper authority, but she had such earnest desire to assist in what, alas, turned out to be a wasted cause."

The abbess spread her fingers on the table and leaned back. "I'm afraid I am now quite lost. This clarifies little, if anything." She raised her palms. "And who is Miss Fallon?"

"Miss Nancy Fallon. That is the young woman with whom I seek to speak."

"Alas, I am now thoroughly confused. Did you not say you were desiring a conference with one of our novices?"

"Yes. I have come to respectfully request that you allow me a private conversation with Miss Nancy Fallon, the young woman whom I delivered here last Wednesday morning. Her carriage had been attacked by brigands and the coachman had disappeared, so I shared my horse with her. She asked to be brought here, as her father intended for her to join the sisterhood in Munro."

The abbess folded her hands upon the desk. "It seems there is some misunderstanding. The only soul to arrive here on Wednesday last was Miss Ellena Trenton. She also spoke of being robbed on the forest road. She looked rather the worse for wear, having had to, I believe, spend the night alone in the rain with only the wrecked carriage for shelter, poor child. We took her in until she could contact her family."

She thought a little more. "Let's see ... Who else? Oh, of course, Father Montrose stopped by to consult with me, as is his habit on a Wednesday. But there were no new novices, rescued or otherwise. Of that, I am certain."

Dominic was more than a little perplexed at her stubborn refusal to admit that Nancy was there. Could she simply be mistaken?

"Perhaps another nun admitted her?" he ventured. "I am sure you have a multitude of responsibilities…"

"Which include an interview with all new arrivals," the abbess concluded patiently. "I am sorry, Lord Howell, but if such a young lady had been brought to our abbey, it would not have been long before I had welcomed her and addressed her on the basic rules of our life here. Even an unexpected guest like Miss Trenton was brought to me immediately. No, I am afraid you have been misled somehow."

Dominic was now utterly deflated. "I do not understand," he said, mostly to himself. "Ellena knew Nancy, knew of her misadventure en route to Munro. They spoke of me with the closeness of friends. Nancy said they had met here." He frowned. "No, no, that's not right. She said she had known Ellena all her life, but I assumed they had been reunited here due to the uncanny fact of their similar harrowing experiences at the hands of…"

His voice trailed off. Somewhere in his mind, a lever slipped into place and slotted the cogs of two very important gears that began to turn with slow and devastating precision.

His head swiveled up to focus on the abbess.

"Could you describe her?" His voice sounded thick and mechanical in his ears. A terrible rush of information was delivered by the unforgiving and unstoppable process that pounded through his brain.

"Pardon?"

"Ellena Trenton. Could you tell me what she looked like?"

There was a pause. The nun's face puckered in confusion. "You want me to describe your betrothed? Is this some kind of joke?"

"Oh no, no, no. Believe me, this is far from being a laughing matter."

"But surely, you must already know…"

"Please, just humor me. Tell me in as much detail as you can what you remember about Miss Ellena Trenton."

"Very well, though I do not see how this can help. She is tall enough, and slender. A comely lass, if that's relevant. Her hair is brown. No, chestnut, I think. I seem to remember her eyes are a mixture of brown and green. I only noticed because she has a most striking manner of looking one directly in the eye when speaking, and one senses it is due to an unflinching honesty rather than a lack of humility. She was kind and respectful at all times and made no attempt to disrupt our routine for her own convenience. Actually, she was exemplary in her devotions, and it is entirely possible, though Miss Trenton is not Catholic, that our younger sisters may have benefited from her presence here. I do not think there is much more I can tell you."

"That is ample, thank you." Dominic's voice was husky with contained emotion.

"Is that an accurate description of Miss Trenton?"

"I do not know. But it *is* a true rendering of Miss Nancy Fallon."

⁂

THE LITTLE CHAPEL was empty, thankfully, when Dominic entered its sanctuary. He needed time to think. His reality had been shattered. He needed to piece the fragments together again.

Dominic had left the abbess without much explanation. What could he say when everything was unraveling in his mind? She had not pressed him for answers, which was a mercy, as he would have been unable to provide them in his current state. When she had recommended the solitude of their chapel, he had gratefully exited her company.

He perched on a pew near the door, his elbows on his knees. He struggled to reconcile the characters of Nancy and Ellena, who were now, miraculously, one. How had such confusion come about? And how had the truth remained obscured for so long? Step by step, he reviewed the events since that rainy night in the forest.

So, it had been Ellena, and Ellena only, whose carriage had been attacked. Ellena who had fought the fear and the river's cold current to arrive at his door. It had been his own betrothed. And when he'd bumbled the introductions, she had not known he had been her very own Viscount Howell, and not to be feared. He did not question Ellena's need to hide her real name. He understood all too well what reservations she must have felt at confiding in an unknown man in an isolated place.

But Ellena was so different from Nancy!

Wasn't she?

And yet Nancy's face belonged to Ellena. And Nancy's gentle heart. He felt the thrilling prickle of excitement. He had seen her, known her, from the first! The woman whose veil had so baffled and frustrated him had stood before him wrapped only in a blanket and blind trust; had greeted him with her naked arm extended in faith and friendship; had slept her warmth into the newly-starched shirt he had loaned her; had ridden at his back and gently rested her cheek against his receptive frame. All the intimacy he had associated with Nancy and desired possible with his betrothed, had, all along, been a memory he'd carried of Ellena. He trembled slightly at the blessing of it. The feelings he had never dared hope to evoke in the heart of a woman had been offered to him by the very woman from whom he had desired it most.

He had believed his one chance at happiness had been lost after their parting at the convent gates. She had retained the identity of Nancy until the last. Of course she would have done so. She would have wanted to protect her family—as he also had—never speaking to anyone of the night they had met. The innocence of their time together was easy to understand firsthand but difficult to explain to others. Neither of them could risk the implications of impropriety.

If, on that first night, he had given his full name and title, introducing himself properly instead of his casually-mumbled attempt, all mystery would have been dissolved. Instead, she had been left to draw her own conclusions about him.

And then he had insulted her to the unscrupulous James Trenton, who had cultivated fear and indignity in the unsuspecting Ellena. Her fierce pride had been warranted. The trepidation she had felt about him at the dinner had been real. Yet despite their clumsy progress as a result of the veil, they had nevertheless connected that very night.

Of course, by then, Ellena had known exactly who he was. She had seen that Viscount Howell and the stranger of the woods had been the same man. But it would have been impossible to reveal as much in the company of her cousin for fear of the implications. How could they explain their compromised situation, having been alone with each other in a woodland cabin? She knew better than to trust James with discretion. Mrs. Charlotte Trenton, bless her heart, most likely would have found the whole predicament thoroughly romantic. But it was a risk Ellena had wisely not taken.

Instead, he and Ellena had strived to overcome the obstacles of their official introductions at Munro House. They had confided their loneliness to each other. And he had been able to please her greatly with his offer of her friend's presence at their wedding. Such were the simple pleasures Nancy would have treasured. And, he admitted to himself guiltily, he had thought of Nancy a great deal, even during the course of dinner with his betrothed at his side.

Now that he knew Nancy and Ellena were one and the same, he could truly celebrate that Nancy *was* his. And Ellena had tried to explain as much during their next meeting in the park.

Munro Park.

Ellena had wished for there to be honesty between them. She must have been on the verge of identifying herself as Nancy. That is, until the interruption by Mr. Cole. How that man had stirred the bile in his blood! But that was no excuse. His reaction to Mr.

Cole's familiarity toward Ellena had been extreme, abhorrent, and instantly regretted. His apologies had been hopelessly insignificant in comparison.

He recalled with shame how—despite his deplorable behavior toward Ellena—he had continued to fret over Nancy and what *she* would have thought of him. He had entertained private feelings for someone he had believed was not his intended. The fact that the object of his affection had been his to admire all along did not diminish his guilt, since he had sought a prize he had, at the time, believed himself unentitled to.

He must now confess how readily he had accepted Ellena's guilt as a necessary requirement to free himself in pursuit of Nancy. How horribly, bitterly ironic! Ellena, meanwhile, had cast aside all reservations, all self-seeking resentments, and, in her guise as Nancy, had labored to achieve a reconciliation.

Each tender thought Dominic had of Nancy rightly belonged to Ellena. Each quality he'd savored in the former, the latter possessed. And when he had suspected the worst, she had resiliently pursued the path that was best. Even when Mr. Simmons had brought his devastating news, she had not deserted.

A chilling paralysis struck him: Simmons had rushed to bring his report straight from the scene that had supposedly incriminated Ellena with Mr. Cole. Yet Ellena, in the role of Nancy, had arrived before Simmons. It was physically impossible for her to have been seen with Mr. Cole at the time Simmons had observed them.

His heart clenched into a fist. Could Simmons have been mistaken? His best informant had never failed him before. Simmons had even described Ellena down to the characteristic veil she wore. But if Ellena had been on her way to Munro House at the time, how could she also …

"Lord Howell?" The even tones of the abbess were tinged with concern.

Dominic broke from his thoughts with a start.

"I'm sorry to disturb," she said, "but I thought it may be of use to share what little can be confirmed as fact."

He stared up at her with dumb incomprehension.

"I have spoken with Sister Mary Bernadette. She is in charge of receiving all novices and also keeps a detailed record of guests and donors. She is gifted in administration."

Dominic remained unable to formulate a sensible answer.

"The point is, she has no record whatsoever of a Nancy Fallon, or any other Nancy for that matter. However, she can confirm the arrival of Miss Ellena Trenton and the brief duration of her stay, as well as the kind donation she made upon her departure. I do not suppose this solves your mystery, but perhaps having the facts makes it easier to rule out possibilities."

She paused and received little by way of response other than his subdued, "Thank you for your trouble."

"There is one more thing, though it seems of little consequence. Sister Mary Bernadette mentioned that she had been pleasantly surprised to see Miss Trenton here in this very chapel just yesterday. She had not disturbed her, as the young lady was earnestly at prayer, but remembered feeling gratified that our humble sanctuary was a meaningful refuge to a friend of the abbey. I do not know what value such information carries but felt that it was best to share it with you in the hopes that, somehow, it may assist you in finding the answers you seek."

"Did the sister say what time Miss Trenton visited the chapel?"

"It must have been just after midday prayers, because she always does her rounds then. Does this help at all?"

Dominic sat back, defeated. "I don't know. Possibly it merely confirms what a fool I have been." His troubled thoughts remained on Simmons, and he added, "There is another source I intend to consult who may hold a vital clue to the mystery that remains."

"I pray you find what you are seeking."

"I pray it is not already too late."

The abbess hesitated. "If I may offer a word of advice?"

"Certainly. Any wisdom is welcome."

"It would appear that this young lady, Miss Fallon, does not wish to be found. It may be best to leave matters at that."

Dominic breathed a sigh.

"You are right, of course. However, her destiny has become unexpectedly tied to that of Miss Trenton. If my suspicions are confirmed, then I have misjudged my betrothed most unfairly and she deserves to be vindicated. You will concede that is an avenue that must be explored."

"I would never discourage you where your motives are well-placed. I admit a degree of relief at my comparatively routine existence. The world beyond these walls offers little I could covet if your current predicament is any indication. You will forgive my bluntness. I suspect that, at present, you feel much the same."

He lifted his gaze to the abbess. "You are an astute observer. Perhaps I will yet recover a modicum of the peace I once knew. To that end, it is best I take my leave at once." He stood to do just that. "Thank you once again for your kind assistance."

"I only wish there were more I could do. I wish you success. Go with God, your lordship."

Dominic stepped out into the thin sunshine with renewed purpose. Mr. Simmons would be summoned at once and properly debriefed. Dominic would then investigate the matter himself. Nothing less could satisfy him now. He must trust only his own eyes, his own ears. The past he had clung to, the dream of Nancy, had evaporated. The future was unclear but ready to be written. He would make sure, this time, that the mark he left on it could endure scrutiny.

As if to confirm Dominic's resolution, the convent bells chimed the melodious hour. Each sounding toll struck the present into the past with unflinching finality. The wheels of the Howell carriage, in turn, obediently drew Dominic into the next act of the drama. This time, however, he would be no puppet.

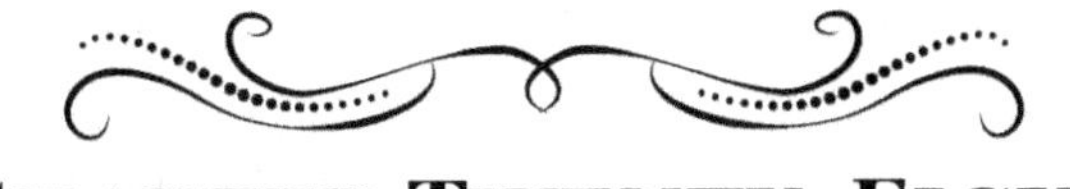

CHAPTER TWENTY-EIGHT

IN THE GARDEN at Thorn Bush Hall, William Cole remained uncharacteristically serious.

"May I play the devil's advocate for a moment?" he asked.

At his somber tones, Ellena reined in her briefly improved mood.

"If you must." She frowned. "Though I cannot understand why you would wish to linger on such painful topics."

He bowed his head. "Forgive me. Causing you further misery is the last thing I want to do. I would not have you endure another moment of this melancholy when it is in my power to cure it. What if I could offer some tangible hope for your situation? Would that coax you into humoring me awhile?"

"I trust you not to promise falsely," replied Ellena, fastening him with her gaze.

"Of course," he answered. "You can trust me."

"Very well. You have my attention."

"Thank you. To begin, I must touch briefly upon the unfortunate facts of your current situation. Shall we assume, for the moment, that the viscount will remain resolute in his decision? There is no question, of course, that such an attitude would be unreasonable, even foolhardy. But let us assume his irrational behavior is not temporary. Or we may question whether your father, having discovered the ridiculous nature of the accusations against you, would allow his lordship the leniency of a reconciliation—assuming the stubborn gentleman even sought it. What, then, does the future hold for Miss Ellena Trenton? Once all the ripples of the broken engagement have subsided, and the families have resumed a semblance of normality, what will become of my dear friend, the Spanish princess?"

Ellena was slow in answering. She had not really considered what lay beyond her current situation. Although her hopes of some concord being reached were failing fast, she had not entirely given up. But there were her father's wishes to consider. He might, as Mr. Cole pointed out, be far too outraged to contemplate anything other than justice for his family. Would he still desire an association with the Howell name after its ambassador had heaped shame upon their heads? She could not say, and waited with trepidation for the arrival of her father. Her most urgent mission was to convince him of her innocence, a matter she was quite at a loss to attempt. These being very real and immediate crises, she had spared little energy to consider what shape her life would take when all the tumult of Munro was behind her.

"I have not given it much thought," she replied honestly. "It feels premature, to say the least, to ponder matters beyond the present. Besides, I have relinquished control over my fate. All my independent actions to date have led me no nearer to happiness than when my destiny was dictated by others. Let my father have his say. Let the viscount follow the bent of his thinking. Their decisions cannot draw me farther from peace than I have meandered by my own misdirection. My future will be what it will be."

Mr. Cole waved his hand in evident frustration. "This is the talk of one who has given up in the absence of perceived alternatives. You see your future in terms of your father's arrangement with Dominic Howell. Should these two gentlemen declare a truce, you are once again a bride to his lordship. Failing that, you return to the seclusion of your father's home. But what of *your* happiness? Does this not enter into the bargain?"

The corner of Ellena's mouth lifted in a bitter smile. "I did not presume the luxury of happiness before arriving in Munro," she answered wryly. "Why should my current circumstances improve upon this? I have been educated to assist my family as a bargaining tool. That is my lot. What other purpose can a daughter serve?"

Mr. Cole appeared genuinely stricken by her words. His features twisted into an echo of that pain. When he spoke, his voice was tight with sorrow.

"It grieves me to hear you speak this way. Why should your personal feelings matter so little? And to have you disparage your own worth—it is unbearable. You are an intelligent, vital being. You deserve a life with someone who values you."

"In fairness, Mr. Cole, I do not believe my father would so ruthlessly pursue advancement that he would choose a husband of obvious poor character. As such, I can say he considers at least a portion of my happiness."

The effect of these words on the gentleman was immediate. He perked up at once and asked with some eagerness, "Then you think it possible, even likely, that he will seek another match for you?"

She shrugged. "I suppose I can hope for little else." A short, mirthless laugh escaped her lips. "Of course, Father may not feel I am half the winning asset that I once might have been."

"Perhaps therein lies a blessing for you," Mr. Cole urged. "He may consider a lesser prize than the viscount to be well won. A humbler man, who is not filled with self-importance, may more fully appreciate the gift that is you. Your irresistible charm, your unwavering loyalty—these qualities will surely be treasured by someone not made arrogant by power and position. I warrant Lord Howell did not feel his status and ambitions would be elevated by your union. A simpler man would not harbor such concerns and could treasure you as a woman, instead of counting your worth as investment."

Ellena marveled that her companion could hold such romantic ideals about marriage. She had not been raised to consider these a necessity for contentment. A man of decency who offered her security had been uppermost in her expectations. Anything more would be welcome but not required. Could Mr. Cole's upbringing truly have allowed him such free rein that he believed anything possible, that any match he preferred might be favorable to his parents? If that were true, he was blessed indeed. But this was not her reality.

"It appears you would almost have me celebrate the loss of his lordship's favor," she admonished him. "You paint a picture of domestic bliss with a doting husband. This is not necessarily my destiny. A lesser match could mean a lesser man, one who knows me to be a tarnished acquisition. He may count on my humiliating rejection here in Munro to guarantee the upper hand in the dowry barter with my father, as well as throughout our wedded life. I could become little more than an easily-won trophy, an item over which to gloat at the bargain of it."

Mr. Cole stopped and stared at her, his lips slack with amazement. "I little wonder at your willingness to seek reconciliation with Lord Howell if such is your gloomy prediction of the alternative! Your sheltered existence has done you a great disservice if it has taught you only to expect the worst and resign yourself to its miserable conclusion. Have your scant experiences promised only disillusionment? Have you met none who could point to a more comforting end? Has nothing inspired you to believe in a happy outcome?"

"I don't know," Ellena answered miserably. "It seems so unlikely, especially under my current circumstances."

"Bother these circumstances! They are done, history, an unsalvageable mess that you are well free of, soon enough. Apply your mind, instead, to this better task. Picture yourself with an undemanding man, one who understands you and you, him. There would be no awkward dance of suspicion and betrayal. Imagine, as you had me do, that a perfect match exists, perhaps even waits for you this moment to recognize his presence where he stands in the wings. What if he were ready to step up and claim you with all his heart, if only you would acknowledge the possibility?"

Ellena reached into to her imagination, her gaze lost in the distance. But in her mind's eye, she found nothing which she could cling to. She looked down, her fingers intertwined protectively within each other.

"It seems a pointless exercise to play a child's game of naïve fantasies," she murmured.

"No! It is not pointless!" Mr. Cole all but shouted.

The intensity of his response caught Ellena by surprise. His attempt at cheering her spirits had become something more, something that was personal and passionate.

Mr. Cole remained animated with emotion, his hands gesturing wildly in step with his feverish words.

"You think it is a fantasy. But I tell you, you will find such a man with the greatest of ease! He will care little for dowries and rumors. Your father will find him the easiest partner in negotiation. Such a man will have but one demand: a short engagement. Lord Howell will be nothing but a distant, distasteful memory. Instead, you will find fulfillment with your true mate."

Ellena sighed. "Such a sketch is prettily painted. It would be a rare joy to find such a man."

She turned away as the pain of its unlikely occurrence stabbed at her heart.

All at once, Mr. Cole's hand was at her arm, reaching across to turn her to him. He held her gently but firmly, the fingers of his other hand tracing the curve of her chin to lift her face to him.

Her eyes widened with surprise. He looked directly at her, and once again, she noted the determined set to his jaw that had characterized his expression all morning. In contrast, his voice was warm with emotion when he spoke.

"Ellena, do not despair. *I* would be that man."

LORD HOWELL STOOD outside the entrance to one of Munro's smaller theaters, a nervous Simmons at his elbow. The viscount was not sure whether the little man feared his report would be found somehow lacking, or whether he was simply uncomfortable in such an exposed position. Simmons looked longingly at the enticing shadows within the alcove of a doorway. He squinted unhappily in the bright light of early afternoon. But Lord Howell was not in a sympathetic mood.

"Is this the place?" he asked curtly.

"Yes, milord," came the voice from his elbow.

"Right," said his lordship, who promptly stepped forward into the empty foyer of the venue.

They made their way through the dim interior toward the depths of the theater. Simmons visibly relaxed in the gloom, his shoulders losing their tension as he blended spontaneously with the murkiness of the unlit hallway.

Lord Howell tried one of the doors and, finding it unlocked, stepped into the cavernous space that housed the patrons' seating. Upon the stage below, a rehearsal was in progress. Satisfied with his discovery, he beckoned his informant closer.

"Do you see her?" He indicated the actors.

Mr. Simmons, now once again in his element, peered expertly at the figures enacting their various roles.

"There." He pointed confidently at a lovely brunette, almost hidden among the small crowd of lesser characters portraying the village folk.

She was pretty enough, though she lacked the poise of a lady of society. She bore a very vague resemblance to Nancy—or Ellena. Of course, the young woman would not have needed to be an exact replica of his betrothed, only to have been of comparable build and with similar features for the subterfuge to work.

The viscount strode smartly down toward the tableau of characters, who stirred from their roles at his approach. The producer of the drama swung around, agitated at the interruption.

"This is a closed rehearsal. No members of the public allowed."

The impressive figure of Lord Howell stepped forth into the illumination afforded by the footlights.

"I'm sorry to disturb you." His voice rang out in the silence. "But I would like a word with the lady who appears to be selling apples at the market."

The producer's mouth hung open a second as he recognized his visitor. Then he shut it quickly and sprang into action.

"Yes, of course, your lordship. Maggie, come down here a minute. We are very honored, your lordship, that our humble production should attract the interest of someone of your obvious good taste. It is a great encouragement to our players when their hard work and talent are recognized by a worthy patron."

"Yes, yes, certainly. Could I please borrow this young lady for a few minutes? I promise to return her shortly."

"Fine, fine. We can proceed as easily without her."

Maggie, who had likely been all aflutter at being singled out by their city's most affluent citizen, glared at the producer's words. But she soon regained her composure and followed the viscount from the busy arena to the comparative privacy of the foyer.

"Simmons, you are certain this is the woman?"

Young Maggie jumped a little as a short figure emerged from the hovering shadows.

"Yes, milord. She was dressed rather more finely and her hair was done up differently, but there is no question that it is the same lady I observed yesterday."

The object of their attention now became decidedly nervous, as her person and movements became the center of their scrutiny.

"Excuse me," she protested, making as if to leave, "but I should be getting back to rehearsal. My part is coming up soon."

The viscount put out an arm to stay her. "Do not be alarmed, my dear. I have a few questions for you. That is all. No harm will come to you."

She shifted uncomfortably and glanced back at the door to confirm her escape route. Lord Howell was unmoved by her fears and proceeded with his questioning.

"Were you approached yesterday morning by a young man offering to reward you for an hour's easy employment?"

The bluntness of his question seemed to shock her, and she stammered in response.

"Y-Yes. But it was nothing unsavory. He merely wished to win a bet with some friends. They had wagered he could not get a handsome woman to step out with him." She hugged her cheek to her shoulder shyly. "He told me he was afraid of losing the bet." Her eyelids flew open. "But he was so very charming and extremely handsome. I thought it strange he should not already have a lovely lady upon his arm." She shrugged. "Anyway, he asked me to pretend to be his partner for an hour so that they might see us together. I have younger siblings to support and could use the money, so I agreed."

"Did he ask you to wear a veil?"

"He did." She nodded briskly, then faltered. "That is not a crime, is it? He said it was very fashionable in Spain."

"Did you wear it over your face at any point? And did he lift it and kiss you?"

"Yes." She blushed. "How do you know all this? Was someone spying on us? Why is this important?" She paused, her mouth forming an "o" of horror. "Is he married?" Her hand flew to her mouth. "Is he … Is he *dangerous*?"

"Oh, yes, my dear, he is extremely dangerous. He has risked the wrath of a very powerful enemy and laid waste the reputation of an innocent woman who trusted him."

Maggie was now quite crestfallen. "Am I in some kind of trouble?" Her lip began to tremble. "He seemed such a kind gentleman."

"My dear, gullible as you were to join him in his trickery, you are not at risk. But another has been damaged needlessly by your supposedly harmless exercise. Perhaps you may think more carefully before swooning again before false charms."

"I did not mean any harm." Poor Maggie was almost in tears by now. "What is going to happen to me?"

Lord Howell straightened to his full height. "*You*, my dear, are going to sell apples on stage. As for your mystery friend, he is about to receive his just desserts."

CHAPTER TWENTY-NINE

ELLENA STARED IN mute astonishment at William Cole. In all the uproar of recent days, she'd thought nothing could surprise her anymore. But his extraordinary declaration of feeling had done just that.

"I realize this is not something you would previously have considered," he admitted. "Your loyalty to Lord Howell, however misplaced, is commendable. In fact, it only adds to the many reasons why I love you. Do you not see? We are a perfect match. Our temperaments are well suited. You would make me try harder at everything I do. And I would make you happy. That is all I have wanted since I met you."

He stepped in more closely toward her and wrapped her hands within his.

"Ellena… How I have longed to say that name! I know I could make you happy. Would you let me try?"

Ellena drew her fingers quickly from his grasp. She looked upon Mr. Cole in dismay.

"You are right when you say I could never have conceived of such an arrangement. I cannot fathom why you think it is now appropriate for me to do so."

Mr. Cole offered one quick nod of the head, then continued with the same enthusiasm as before. "Certainly, there is a period of adjustment to be expected. We must allow the dust to settle and the formalities to be dealt with. But dearest Ellena..." He reached for her hand again. "You can be adored in a way the viscount and his stuffy family honor could never afford you."

Ellena stepped back hurriedly to create distance between them. Mr. Cole's hands remained extended a moment longer, then clasped each other as if a contract had been sealed. "I will speak to your father as soon as the sting of this crisis is less sorely felt. I know my own father would be delighted at my choice. And Henry Trenton would surely value the connection to a banking family of good repute."

Ellena threw up her own hands as if to stop the flow of words. "You rush ahead into a future that is shaky, to say the least."

"And I will wait. Ellena, can you not grasp the depth of my feelings for you? You will make me the man my parents have always wished me to be. And I will cherish you as you deserve. No small-minded 'ladies' will be allowed to brush you aside without my intervention. No high-minded 'gentlemen' will be granted the opportunity to sully your reputation. I will protect you and love you. Is that not what you want?"

Ellena could not look at him at all. The zeal with which he spoke shone from his face. His feelings were as a lantern he had kept covered, but which now glowed brightly and with abandon. She could not bear to see it. It should not direct its beacon so wholeheartedly at her.

"You have thought about this a great deal, I see," Ellena considered grimly.

Mr. Cole radiated warmth from his eyes, his mouth, his very soul. "From our first meeting, you touched a place in my heart." His voice was thick with feeling.

"And I believed we were good friends," said Ellena, her gaze remaining downcast.

"We were. We are!"

Ellena finally lifted her eyes to him, as if seeing him for the first time.

"But I confided in you as I would a friend. I interpreted your actions as those of a friend, and nothing more. Yet there were these feelings, hidden beneath the surface."

Mr. Cole thrust out an agitated hand. "What would you have had me do? I respected your engagement. It is the viscount, not I, who trod upon your trust."

"Yes, but perhaps he could sense something about you that I was blind to. Maybe there was within him an unconscious awareness of your deeper interest. Maybe that is what fueled his suspicions that there was something between us."

"We did nothing to warrant his ending your engagement."

There was a sullenness to his answer. Or a wariness. Ellena could not tell which.

"No," she conceded, "but I allowed a freer intercourse between us than would have been possible if I had guessed your feelings. I trusted that all was done in good humor. I believed Charlote when she called you harmless. Our banter was a release at a time when I most needed it. But I see now all too clearly it was not as innocent as it should have been. I blame myself for such foolishness. And I fault my family for giving me no opportunity to learn wisdom in these matters."

The weight of realization bore down on her. All those moments of teasing and laughter had led to far more pain than they had delivered her from. She had made a fine mess of things. "My actions," she confessed, "though I meant them only in the lightest vein, have not been construed thus by witnesses." Ellena winced as she recalled the gossip among the staff in the kitchen. "Whoever sought my downfall, and the ruin of my engagement, relied on my naivety and indiscretion. If I had been more vigilant, Dominic would have had no cause to doubt my loyalty."

Mr. Cole's forehead creased into a frown. "Your mysterious enemy is simply Lord Howell's own mistrust and insecurity. As such, it is perhaps not an enemy, after all, since it revealed the weak nature of a man to whom you narrowly escaped being married. Who could possibly have lied so convincingly that it caused him to break your engagement, if his own faults had not fanned those whispers into flames of jealousy?"

"I don't know," Ellena countered miserably. "I only know he would never perform so public an action as calling off the wedding if he did not believe himself justly motivated."

"No, no, no!" Mr. Cole cried as he paced to and fro. His hands waved in agitation, then clutched at his hair. "You will *not* start that again. You will not stand there and defend that…that…that *toad* to me again! I offer you a life with the prince of a fairy tale and yet you worry about the frog!"

Ellena's mouth grew firm. "That is the problem, though, is it not? This picture you paint is but a fairy tale. Tomorrow, my father arrives and may insist that I go through with the wedding. Where, then, is your dream?"

Mr. Cole's forehead puckered. "But surely, you would refuse? You could explain that we are in love and…"

"But we are not."

"I'm sorry?" He shook his head, as if trying to dislodge what he had heard.

"My dear Mr. Cole, only yesterday I was trying my utmost to find a path back to Dominic. Even this morning, I hoped you were carrying a letter of reconciliation from him. You have assumed my failure in this is permanent and have proceeded most hastily with your hoped-for courtship while I yet desire an amendment of Dominic's decision. You speak with me of love and romance at a time when I pray these very things are still possible with my intended. If you cannot see the inappropriateness of your amorous declaration, then your thinking is even more misguided than Dominic's."

"No! You cannot compare me to him! I have loved you unswervingly. I have risked…" He caught himself, as if stepping suddenly away from danger. "What I mean is… I have made sacrifices, while Lord Howell has made wicked assumptions. I will not believe you still prefer him as a match for you."

Ellena crossed her arms tightly. "What you believe is your

own affair. I can only tell you that you have greatly altered my opinion of your sound judgment. Where before I beheld in you a kind and thoughtful friend, I now see a man whose motive is *his* happiness, not mine. Oh, protest if you wish, but you have interpreted circumstance to favor your interests and neglected to consider what is important to me. If my happiness were truly your chief consideration, you would be helping me solve the dilemma of proving my innocence to Dominic. It matters little whether you approve of my continued desire to be the bride to Lord Howell. A true friend would support my venture and not add to my burden with self-serving delusions of romance."

William Cole stood absolutely still. All his passionate declarations and protestations had been knocked out of him. His hands hung limply by his sides. His breath was shallow, his lips moving silently, as if any words would now prove hopeless.

Eventually, he drew a deep breath and straightened. His voice, when he spoke, was robbed of its earlier vigor.

"I see I have made a grave mistake in speaking too soon. Perhaps if I had waited. But in my enthusiasm to declare…"

Ellena held up her hand.

"Please, do not think that your timing is the sole reason for your lack of success. I am sad that one whom I have trusted so well with my confidences should now show so poor a measure of insight. You fail to understand me or what is truly important to me. The absence of this vital component makes for a poor match, indeed. As such, you could never make me happy. I am only sorry that, while you have lost what you hoped would be a wife, I have lost what I believed could be a dear friend."

With the finality of these words still ringing in the air, Ellena turned and walked away so that Mr. William Cole might not see the tears stinging at her eyes. For the first time in her often-lonely life, she felt truly, utterly alone.

THE ATMOSPHERE AT Thorn Bush Hall had become strained, to say the least. What conversation survived served but a minimal function—the request for the passing of the sugar at tea, the muttered pardon as two bodies approached the same doorway, the tentative inquiry after a mislaid book.

So when a delivery was made to the residence, the distraction drew a surprising amount of interest from the aimlessly-occupied inhabitants.

When it was determined that the recipient was to be Mr. Cole, Ellena felt a deep pang of disappointment. She still clung doggedly to the hope of a last-minute reprieve from Dominic, though she was forced to concede the likelihood of this was fast diminishing.

Mr. Cole looked curiously at the basket of shiny, juicy apples, his lack of response offering no clues as to who may have sent it. The messenger had come from town and was not associated with any families they knew. Mr. Cole withdrew a sealed letter from among the fruit and opened it reluctantly before his little crowd of onlookers. It contained a note and a pamphlet that, at a glance, appeared to advertise an unfamiliar theater production.

Ellena noted a spark of recognition in the eyes of Mr. Cole as he stared at the object in his hands. But what startled her even more was something at the top of the page—the Howell family crest!

She fought back the urge to grab the letter from him. Why would Dominic have sent such a curious collection of items to a man he had previously despised?

Mr. Cole, meanwhile, had read the contents of the letter. Ellena fervently hoped he would share the message with the rest of them. Instead, he turned a ghastly, pale shade as his eyes darted across the words. He looked quite ill, and Charlotte began to move toward him as it seemed he would sway from his feet. He shrugged off her concerns, thrust the letter deep into his pocket and, muttering an incoherent excuse, disappeared from the room.

"Well! What do you think all that was about?" Charlotte

began as her brother's retreating form vanished from view.

"Perhaps your father has grown impatient that your brother has not found a suitable match and has sent for him," James ventured.

"Then why would he send apples and a recommendation to see a show? It makes absolutely no sense at all."

"Whatever was in that letter has shaken him up, that's for certain. But do not make yourself overly anxious, my dear. I'm sure he will confide in his sister when he is ready."

Ellena kept her thoughts to herself. Informing the others that the viscount had apparently arranged the delivery would not explain much of anything. It would only be another incident where Dominic had caused an unpleasant stir in their lives. Mercifully, Mr. Cole's failed proposal remained a secret. The less said about that, the better. Charlotte did not need further upset, especially in her condition.

Meanwhile, Ellena's imagination was free to speculate upon the contents of the letter. It was obvious that its sentiment was not as generous as the accompanying items might have suggested. Even the gifts contained great mystery. Was Dominic inviting Mr. Cole to join him at the theater? And why had he included a basket of fruit—in particular, apples? These seemed innocent enough. But Mr. Cole's response had been so severe, the letter could only contain news of a most disturbing nature. And why would the viscount waste his time distressing one as insignificant to his existence as Charlotte's brother? Any dislike Dominic may have felt toward Mr. Cole was surely now of no consequence. Without an engagement, there could be no jealousy.

Ellena allowed her mind to turn over each morsel of information for a further clue until she was satisfied that she had investigated what could be understood, which was very little. Eventually, she resigned herself to waiting for final clarity.

More waiting! She thought the hours in this day would stretch to an infinity of agitated inactivity.

She considered writing to Jillian but was numbed by the

prospect of where to begin her miserable story. Besides, chances were good she would be sent home in the next day or two. Then she would have all the time in the world to pour out her broken heart to Jilly.

She felt embarrassed at having given her friend such hope of a good match in Mr. Cole. Though she trusted in Jillian's forgiveness and understanding, this did little to combat the humiliation of it all. And when her father arrived tomorrow, he would be sure to remind her of how utterly she had failed.

CHAPTER THIRTY

DOMINIC WAS MORE than just a little satisfied with his handling of Mr. Cole. He sat back in his chair, twirling his bone letter-knife between his fingers. His little gift should have been delivered by now. It would render Mr. Cole few options. Whatever path he pursued would be an act of desperation. It would most certainly bring his just reward. And Dominic could simply sit back and observe the outcome.

Ellena, on the other hand, was a topic requiring much deeper thought. But even here, Dominic no longer felt helpless frustration. He was once again in a position to *do* something.

He had barely begun the weighty consideration of how to proceed with the circumstances of his ruined engagement, when the noise of heightened activity at the great doors drew him from his study.

A small assembly of familiar faces was gathered in the entrance, as cloaks and wraps were discarded after a chilly journey. Beatrice Howell, his mother, was looking quietly about her, taking in the details of her old home, while her daughters and their husbands all talked simultaneously. Two small boys chased each other about the statuary of their uncle's foyer. Their infant brother lay sleeping in the arms of a nursemaid.

The invasion of the Howell clan caught the master of the house completely off guard. In all the confusion of the past two days, he had failed to notify them of the canceled wedding. To be honest, he had failed to notify anyone except Ellena and her father. In fact, currently, his greatest distress was caused by a lack of clarity on how to proceed with this very matter. There was now no proof of any indiscretion on Ellena's part.

If he entertained thoughts of a reconciliation, would her father even allow it after he had unfairly accused his daughter?

He had very little time left to think. The wedding was still officially taking place in two days. He had little time to rebuild burnt bridges. And he could do nothing without first speaking to Ellena's father. With all these thoughts consuming him, the arrival of his family for an uncertain wedding was vexing, to say the least.

Already, his sisters were arguing over to which rooms the footmen should take their luggage, their old accommodations not being suitable for married ladies. And the Dowager Viscountess Howell was conspicuously taking stock of how the household had been run in her absence. Dominic knew his mother. She would be restraining the urge to draw a gloved finger across the nearest surface.

He took a deep breath and stepped forward to greet them.

The finely arrayed heads turned toward him and, at once, Dominic felt the old glance of scrutiny from his sisters. He pulled himself to his full, impressive height and withstood the predictable survey of disapproval that would sweep over him. He was master of this house. They were his guests. Their petty judgments were insignificant in comparison to the confusion and turmoil of the past week. He would give them no opportunity to derail his fragile equilibrium.

"Mother," he greeted the dowager viscountess, planting a gentle kiss upon her cheek, "how well you look. The life of a grandmother must agree with you."

"It is certainly less demanding zan motherhood," she replied in her lingering French accent, then immediately followed up with, "How is Munro House? Are all standards of ze household being met? If not, I could talk to Mrs. Anders for you."

Dominic suppressed a smile. Lady Howell was a merciless taskmaster, it was true, but he had also learned that her fussing was an expression of love, one of the few she had been able to sustain in a loveless marriage.

He gestured about him. "Feel free to examine the evidence before you. If you are not satisfied, I shall leave it to you to remedy what is necessary." He received a brisk nod in reply and turned his attention to the rest of his guests.

"Are these my nephews?" He took their small hands one after the other. "You have done well, Georgina. They are fine fellows and shake hands firmly."

Their father, tall and slender and just beginning to bald, took the hand that was offered him. Beaming proudly, he ruffled his boys' hair, causing them both to reach up and pat the disturbed strands into place once more.

The Duke of Eyresborough laughed. "It seems they are afraid to lose their locks as I have." He looked about him. "It has been too many months since we have visited. Thank you for the invitation."

Dominic addressed him warmly. "Sir, you are most welcome. I do not know if our climate is as mild as that to which you are accustomed in Eyresborough, so I have arranged for you and your family to stay in the east corridor. The rooms receive sun throughout the day, and there is a door leading straight onto the gardens for the boys to romp if they wish."

He turned to his other brother-in-law, who had been looking upon his nephews with what Dominic assumed was a degree of envy. Vivienne had produced a long list of demands, the latest of which, Dominic believed, was for a dovecote she just *had* to have. But she had produced no sons. No children at all. Chesterley, who was from a large family, never complained or expressed resentment, but his face had grown sad as the years had passed. Lines had settled about his mouth where children may have lifted them.

"I shall enjoy some time with my nephews," he said, looking up at the duke. "Do they enjoy a spot of cricket?"

"I am not certain they are able yet to wield a bat, but a game of ninepins would not go amiss," their father answered.

"Excellent!" replied Chesterley, his mouth creasing into a rare smile. "How are you, Howell?" he asked, reaching to take Dominic's hand.

"Well enough, thank you. Let's get you settled so that you may enjoy a game with the boys before sunset. The south corner rooms will be made available for you. Vivienne may be surprised that I remember her doting on the main bedroom there for most of her childhood, but Mother always reserved it only for honored guests. I believe you now qualify." He pivoted to face her. "Mother, I thought you would be most comfortable in the familiar surroundings of your old apartments. I trust everyone can find contentment with these arrangements?"

Indeed, everyone could. Footmen transported the luggage to the various lodgings. One of the rooms in the east corridor became an instant nursery. The younger ladies freshened up while their husbands retired to the sunny recesses of the library for an hour's peace. Only the dowager viscountess remained in the company of her son as the rest dispatched themselves to preferred locations.

"Dominic," began the lady in her usual, forthright manner, "forgive me for seeming to doubt your capabilities. When I left to stay with your sister, I swore never to interfere with ze running of Munro House. I must, however, inquire whether you feel all proceeds according to schedule for Friday's festivities. I had expected far more bustle about ze house. Ze servants have not slacked in my absence, I hope?"

"Not at all, Mother. Preparations have merely been suspended for the moment."

She wrinkled her nose. "At zis late stage? It seems impractical, to say ze least."

"I'm afraid there have been some unforeseen developments.

A most awkward set of circumstances has occurred."

"With ze staff? Is there a problem?" She straightened her shoulders. "Perhaps I can assist you in zese matters. Zis is, after all, where much of my experience lies."

"If only it were that simple." Dominic sighed. "I suppose it is best if you know the whole story. I could use a woman's perspective."

He gestured her to the privacy of his study, where she perched upon the least-comfortable chair as if to indicate her expectation of a brief conversation. Surprisingly, Dominic found solace in her habitual impatience. It was predictable and businesslike at a time when he had been all but consumed with instability. He pulled a chair around to face her and seated himself in preparation for a lengthy explanation.

"It's hard to know where to start. I suppose I shall begin with the worst and explain in reverse." He took a steadying breath. "My engagement with Miss Trenton is currently broken."

She arched an eyebrow. "'Currently'?"

How like his mother to note the more subtle facts!

"Well, yes. I'm afraid it may not be temporary. I have made rather a fool of myself, Mother."

Lady Howell was unmoved by his confession. Instead, she settled more deeply into her chair and pinned her gaze upon him to indicate her undivided attention.

"Tell me everything," she said.

A WEARY HOUR later, the flow of information was exhausted. Dominic had declared everything, even the original encounter with Nancy. His mother was a woman of unquestionable discretion, and relief poured forth as his story unfolded in the safety of her private hearing. He felt no shame in revealing his weaknesses and mistakes to a woman who knew them already.

She sat quietly for a minute or two, assessing all he had said and thinking upon the awkward position her son had created for himself.

At last she spoke.

"You say zis Mr. Cole is no longer a threat?"

"He has been dealt with."

"I assume you have chosen a means by which to do zis that does not add to our current disgrace."

He flinched a little but knew her question was fair. "I have been most discreet."

"Good. Then it seems your faculties have returned to you. Ze rest is quite simple. You will have to apologize to the lady and her family and resume your engagement. No one else knows of your humiliating error. At least public shame has been spared us."

Dominic knew his mother was merely being blunt in her assessment, but he squirmed as she spoke.

"I do not know whether your recommendation is so simple, Mother. She may want nothing to do with me."

"She will do as her father expects. I know Mr. Trenton. He is a formidable character."

"For that matter, *he* may want nothing to do with me."

His mother pursed her lips. "Nonsense! He will swallow the insult for the resumption of the connection with our name. With him, it is always careful calculation. Perhaps we can reduce the dowry as a compensation for his hurt pride. He will take the bait. You will see. It is a mercy you did not publicly declare zis engagement broken. There is still much room for negotiation. But you must act quickly."

A spark of rebellion fired in his heart. "What of *my* feelings? Miss Trenton has not been entirely honest with me in her dealings. And she has made an open mockery of me with her veil-wearing, as though I had medieval notions of maidenhood."

"Dominic," his mother said sternly, crossing her arms, "are you sulking?" She freed an arm to point an upward palm at him. "I was under ze impression you understood there to be no moral reproach upon Miss Trenton, after all. Why would you now cling to petty grievances when you confess your own actions have not been blameless?" Both hands now waved along with the rhythm of her obvious frustration. "Come now, my son, the time for juvenile moods is gone. You are in every way the picture of a proper viscount. Now it is time to be truly a man."

Dominic hung his head miserably. He knew his mother spoke true, but the emotions evoked were still close to the surface. He did not want to act again in the heat of the moment. Goodness knew, he had done enough of that already. No, he needed to think with icy clarity if his decisions were to be respected. He rose to indicate the discussion was at an end.

"Henry Trenton arrives at Thorn Bush Hall on the morrow. It is pointless addressing reparations with Ellena without his approval. I will send for them both, and we will see what can be done to mend the situation. If you wish, I will consult with you again before proceeding. Now you must please excuse me."

He removed himself speedily from the room before she could add anything further.

But he was not yet safe.

Georgina and Vivienne had recovered sufficiently from their tiring journey to resume the amusing pastime of tormenting their brother. Dinner provided the perfect opportunity to practice their old habits.

"Georgie," Vivienne began, knowing he hated when she called him that, "will you be taking your new bride on a tour of the Continent?"

It was an innocent enough question on the surface of it, making Dominic immediately suspicious.

"I'm afraid my duties here prevent me from traveling much," he answered. "You will remember it was the same with Father when he was viscount. And then there is our business to attend to, also."

Vivienne sniffed. "Really, is it quite necessary to carry on like a tradesman when you have a title? I cannot *possibly* imagine my dear Chesterley doing anything as common as all that."

Their mother's voice cut in sharply. "I do not think the earl minded that your dowry was greatly enhanced by ze profits we made. Nor does the Princess of Wales hide her face in shame at the mention of the Howell family, when it is our cloth that dresses her."

Georgina snorted in disgust. "No, Mama, it is certainly not *our cloth* that makes her hide her face in shame…"

"Georgina! We will not discuss ze private affairs of our regent's wife, nor will we judge those whose sad lives are so very different from our own. As for your brother, he has been able to maintain the estate without debts, a rare feat, indeed, in our current economy."

"But, Mama," Vivienne persisted, "his life is so *dull*. Poor Miss Trenton will be stranded at home with nothing to do while he works. It is most ungentlemanly to have so little leisure."

"I have ample opportunities for leisure, Vivienne," Dominic countered. "I enjoy everything Munro has to offer. It is a beautiful city for walking or riding. And I regularly attend the theater and lectures offered by our societies. Why, just last week…"

"Oh, that!" Georgina waved her hand dismissively. "I suppose Miss Trenton might enjoy these little excursions, seeing as she comes from the country. I, too, thought much of Munro when I was a child. But the duke and I now find ourselves quite often in London, and there really is no equal. It is too terrible, Georgie, that you should be denied the pleasure of more elegant society. By comparison, Munro is thoroughly unsophisticated."

"I don't think…" Her husband the duke tried to correct her, only to be interrupted by his sister-in-law.

"It is exactly as you say, Georgina," Vivienne agreed. "How little we knew the shortcomings of Munro until our husbands rescued us from it. How ever do you bear it, Georgie?"

Dominic focused on the piece of pheasant he had balanced on his fork. "I assure you both, I am quite at peace with the awful truth." Then he thrust the fork past his lips and chewed in silence.

He knew better than to argue or become defensive. The best he could do was keep the conversation short.

He noticed that Eyresborough and Chesterley had learned to do the same, as they said little to nothing that might encourage their wives. Nor, however, did they do much to *discourage* them. No doubt the duke had learned to trust Lady Howell to take her daughter in hand, since the matriarch lived with them. As for Vivienne, Dominic assumed Chesterley's drooping countenance had as much to do with his wife's tongue as it did the absence of a bigger family. The best the two husbands could do was to steer the conversation toward safer subjects whenever an opportunity arose.

But Dominic's sisters were not so easily discouraged.

"One can only hope your bride is as easily satisfied," Vivienne goaded. "I am told she is a great beauty. You must be sure to keep her entertained, lest she find other distractions to amuse her. Such a lovely creature would have no difficulty acquiring new…shall we say…*hobbies?*"

She managed to keep her expression neutral, but her sister's smirk escaped unguarded.

Their mother put down her fork and sat back in her chair, her fingertips resting on the table. "Truly," she said sternly, "I do not know which is worse: that I have raised such addlebrained daughters, or that such fine gentlemen are now mute with embarrassment at your crude speech."

"Oh, Mama," Vivienne said, "you are too easily…"

"Enough!" Dominic rose like a furious specter. "In short succession, you have insulted my business, my city, and my betrothed. You have forgotten that you are guests in *my* house. You do not even show our mother the proper respect. But I will tell you this: you will learn to show respect, and quickly, or you will not be welcome here. If I *ever* detect even a hint of such nuance aimed at Miss Trenton ever again, it will be the last time you speak in my presence."

And with that, he pushed back his chair and strode from the

room. His exit was followed by a stunned silence.

Dominic marched to his study. By the time he'd reached its door, much of his bluster had left him. He threw himself into his chair and stared ahead into the murk of the night. The fire was low, and its embers gave little light. He got up and touched a wooden splint to the dying coals, then transferred the tiny, new flame to the Argand lamp on his desk. The optimistic glow that surged into existence did not reflect his mood.

He was not looking forward to the day that lay ahead. He wished he could undo all the harm and chaos of the past week. His sisters' behavior was the least of it. If anything, they had reminded him whose side he ought to be on.

Despite the way in which he and Ellena had stumbled through their brief courtship, she was truly everything he could have hoped for. But she would probably never forgive his callous mistreatment of her. All the regret in the world could not lessen the impact of his actions. Even if his mother were right, and Henry Trenton could be reasoned with, was it fair to expect Ellena merely to fall in line with a decision once again made for her? If only he had some way of knowing he still had the remotest chance to win her favor. It would make the dreaded confrontation tomorrow less daunting.

Dominic sat for a while in the almost-darkness supplied by the single lamp in the large room. He rested his face in the cup of his hands and savored the undemanding solitude.

Before long, however, he became aware of a shadow that had come to stand quietly at his elbow. A clear, firm, loving voice pervaded his troubled being.

"My son, hear me now. Do not allow the mistakes of ze past to form ze regrets of ze future. There is no perfect woman, just as you can be no perfect man. In the end, zis pain will matter little in comparison to the agony of losing her. You love her. Go to her. All will be well."

A soft kiss on his forehead, then the quiet figure left the room. Dominic looked up with gratitude. A calmness had descended upon him, and he felt that if he retired, he might manage to sleep now. He reached for the lamp, his hand brushing against a pile of papers that slid sideways, separating into a muddled pool of documentation across his desk. An unopened letter stood out against the backdrop of loose pages, and he reached for it instinctively. With trembling fingers, he unfolded the page. He scarcely breathed as he read the precious contents.

When he was done, he carefully folded the words back into their cocoon and held them to his heart. All the answers he had needed had been right there, under his nose. All the fear and doubts were quite suddenly removed. She still wanted him! After all his abominable behavior, she would open her heart for him!

Years of insecurity were met with one single certainty: this woman loved him. She was committed to their future. No stupidity on his part, no flattering words from Mr. Cole, no misunderstandings wrought by the universe would tear them apart. She was here to stay.

He wished he could write back straight away, declare himself equally devoted, put her troubled thoughts to rest. Should he saddle his horse and ride to Thorn Bush Hall, calling up to her window like the lover she deserved?

No. There had been enough impropriety, both real and imagined. From now on he would be her champion. He would cherish her and defend her with his last breath. Let other men desire to take his place. He would not be shaken ever again. Ellena had forgiven him all. He would strive to be worthy of such a gift.

Oh…

His delirious thoughts skidded to a halt.

Mr. Henry Trenton was on his way. He would be furious. And well he should be. But, oh, if Ellena could only be strong in the face of her father's anger. If she would stand with her intended when the time came. Surely, Mr. Trenton would rather avoid public embarrassment? And if he saw that they were a good match after all…

Be brave, Dominic. There is hope.

Trembling with anticipation for all that must still be resolved, Dominic took himself off to bed. He did not know if he would manage to sleep, but he must try and rest. Much was at stake. Tomorrow would be a very busy day, indeed.

CHAPTER THIRTY-ONE

WHEN MR. COLE did not join them for breakfast, Ellena was relieved. They had not spoken since his unwelcome declaration in the garden yesterday. Under the circumstances, it was impossible to salvage their friendship. Without it, William Cole was best avoided.

However, Charlotte's explanation for his absence set the house on edge anew. Her brother had, after much thought, decided that they had enough on their hands without the presence of an idle guest. It was time he took stock of his own life. He was returning home to give his father the excellent news that he would accept the offer of the vicarage, and the vicar's daughter.

This last comment made Charlotte smile, in spite of the shock at his sudden departure. "At least I shall soon gain a new sister. I have always liked Miss Verity Lockhart."

But Ellena was grim. She was not at all sure he had made this decision for the right reasons.

"This is really most unsporting of him," declared James, "to up and leave us without even a proper goodbye."

"Poor James," commiserated Charlotte. "I do believe you shall miss him even more than I. Still, I am quite certain we shall receive an invitation to visit him at the vicarage. I think it is good that his life should have some direction. It will greatly benefit him to settle into a responsible position."

Charlotte spoke confidently, although a little faster than usual, as if she were hurrying to hide her disappointment at her brother's impulsive behavior. Did she suspect a connection between his hasty departure and the odd gift that he had received? It was certainly on Ellena's mind. She knew Dominic had played a role in Mr. Cole's sudden taste for a career in the clergy. There could be no doubt that his letter had sought the immediate departure of Charlotte's brother. But what had been the motive? Was it petty revenge from a failed suitor? Or did the two men share a secret that deepened their mutual dislike of each other?

She pondered these thoughts for the better part of the morning. It kept her from thinking of the looming confrontation with her father.

Henry Trenton arrived a few hours later, just as the day was warming up nicely and Ellena was considering an escape into the garden. He barely contained his thunderous outrage long enough to greet James and Charlotte before demanding to see Ellena in the privacy of the library. As soon as the door had closed behind her, her father had ample to say.

"How could you have let this happen?" he began as he paced to and fro. Ellena stood, hands clasped together tightly, head bowed, as she waited for his anger to take its course.

"Is this the thanks you show to your mother and me? You have never wanted for anything, least of all a suitable match in marriage. Your future was one any young woman would envy. Yet you have been selfish and ungrateful, choosing instead to satisfy a common schoolgirl's flirtatious desires. We did not teach you such disgraceful mores."

He stopped to catch his breath. Then a new thought struck him. "I will tell you where this seed was cast. This is the influence of that unbridled Kinsey girl and her wild brothers. We should have cut off all contact between you. Now look where our leniency has gotten us!"

Ellena looked up in horror, her eyes wide with shock. "No, Father! Jillian cannot be blamed for any of this. I am accountable for my own actions."

"Then you acknowledge your guilt and shame? I must say, I am surprised you should speak so glibly under the circumstances."

"You misunderstand me, Father. I merely wish to clear Jillian of any part in this. I do not, by these words, confess any wickedness."

It had not been wicked to engage in witty conversation with Mr. Cole, had it? She admitted to a degree of foolishness, yes. And a weakness for the flattery of the exchange. But she had meant no harm. And she had learned her lesson, hard and fully. But to say she had been wicked…

"It is true I have been willful and thought myself clever. But I can swear honestly I have done nothing immoral. Nor have I stooped to hurt our family simply to enjoy some private pleasure. This you must believe."

"Must I? You are gone from our home scarcely a week. Yet despite the protection of your cousin and the sound education from your parents, you have attached to yourself the title of *coquette*! It is my understanding that most of Munro finds you at least in part an amusing sort of clown show, while others denounce you outright as some sort of hussy. James has explained the situation to me at some length, and the details are enough to curdle the stoutest blood."

"James?" Ellena balled her fists. Her throat tightened. "You trust the word of James over your own daughter? Has he bothered to include that chapter of the saga where he so greatly offended the viscount that the engagement was nearly broken before it began?"

Her father shrugged. "He has confessed that an error in judgment made him speak out of turn. But it was clearly a minor misunderstanding, since your introductions proceeded that very evening."

"I see. It is easy to pardon James because the effects of his actions were resolved. But this was possible only thanks to Dominic's generous nature."

Mr. Trenton stopped his furious pacing and looked at his daughter with a quizzical expression. "Who is Dominic?"

"Lord Howell," Ellena explained. "It is his second name, one he reserves for his close friends. And me."

Her father's brows dropped into a frown. "You speak of your betrothed by name and use terms of admiration, yet you betray him with another. Perhaps, because he is a man of honor, you expect to be pardoned as easily as James was. But a small slip in judgment cannot be compared to outright betrayal. Truly, Daughter, I cannot grasp your flippant attitude. You seem to feel no remorse."

Ellena drew her eyes to meet her father's. "I wish I could persuade you of my innocence. I *have* made foolish mistakes, yet none are as grievous as that of which I stand accused."

"How, then, do you explain the serious charges against you? It is hard to believe such terrible allegations would be made by Lord Howell unless they were founded upon fact."

Ellena hung her head. "I cannot explain the circumstances that caused Dominic to turn so vehemently against our engagement. I can only say he is sadly mistaken in his assumptions."

"You suggest that he is willing to risk my displeasure and his public humiliation on a whim?" He snorted. "That does not seem likely."

"I do not know what misinformation motivates him to such rash action. I only ask, Father, that *you* believe in me. You are right to say you have taught me well. I could never willfully do anything to jeopardize our good name. If anything, the extent of my error has been to protect the honor of myself and my family with excessive measures. I have tried to explain this very iniquity to Dominic but have been obstructed in my attempts at every turn."

"What are you talking about? What, exactly, has been going

on? Is this about the veil you wore? I do not consider that offense enough to call off a wedding. Besides, James said Lord Howell was most gracious in the face of your insult. Really, Ellena, what else have you done to offend your betrothed?"

"Nothing intentionally. But there have been incidents that created…*misunderstanding* between us."

Henry Trenton opened his mouth to object to her vague reply but was silenced momentarily by a knock at the door. It was Charlotte.

"I am so very sorry to interrupt, Uncle, but I thought you would wish to open this immediately. It was delivered by messenger from Munro House."

"The Howell estate?" Mr. Trenton's eyebrows lifted. "Hmm, it seems his lordship has something further to say on this matter."

He opened the letter with somewhat less reserve than that to which he was prone, while Ellena stood frozen, her heart pounding in her ears. It seemed an eternity passed as he read the few lines. Then he turned toward her and declared, "Lord Howell requests the immediate attendance of ourselves upon his person. I must say, his tone lacks the bitterness of his previous communication. That is something, I suppose."

He folded the page with a degree of restored calm. "Well, Ellena, it would appear you shall have a chance to redeem yourself. That is, unless you wish to confess your misdeeds now before a confrontation with your accuser."

Ellena, under the sway of delirium, barely heard a word. Hope and dread fought for supremacy within her heart. She did not know what might have prompted this summons. Could it have been connected with the equally mysterious letter to William Cole? Whatever his reasons, Dominic seemed to be carrying out a deliberate plan. She wondered what role he had in mind for her.

CHAPTER THIRTY-TWO

THE CARRIAGE RIDE to Munro House was dominated by silence. Mr. Trenton had nothing further to say to his daughter at present. As for Ellena, the condition of her nerves did not allow for conversation.

Approaching Dominic's home, without wearing a veil or being under the guise of Nancy, she felt strangely exposed. What would be his reaction when he looked upon her for the first time as her true self? Had he read her letter? Did he know that she and Nancy were one and the same? If he had refused her letter and not yet discovered her secret, he would certainly be startled when Nancy Fallon arrived with Ellena's father. If he had been so thoroughly convinced of guilt she did not bear, how outraged would he be when her deception was uncovered? She could not bear another outburst. She still winced when she thought of the last.

She felt her chest tighten as the carriage slowed and then halted on the gravel drive. A footman opened the door, and she descended from the protection of the cubicle. The great doors of Munro House swung open, as if their arrival had been watched for. Branson led father and daughter solemnly to Dominic's private study.

Its door stood open, revealing two figures in deep conversation within the recesses of the room. At the servant's gentle knocking, both heads looked up, and the taller figure, belonging to Lord Howell, rapidly approached his guests. He dismissed the butler, then beckoned his two visitors to join him.

"Mother, may I introduce Miss Ellena Trenton? Her father, I believe you know. Mr. Trenton, Miss Trenton, Lady Beatrice Howell."

"I know of Mr. Trenton by reputation only." The woman, whose elegance and bearing left Ellena feeling thoroughly uncivilized by comparison, smiled. The dowager reached out a graceful hand to Ellena's father, who tipped his forehead to it in a remarkably debonair way. His reaction astonished Ellena. After all, his dry manner was legendary.

Equally intriguing, however, was the fact that Dominic had introduced her quite calmly to his mother, with neither a hint of confusion as to her identity, nor the condescension of a man who felt wronged. He now stood in poses that alternated between polite courtesy and an awkwardness reminiscent of their first encounter in the forest cabin.

"So," continued the elder woman in a tone both friendly and encouraging, "shall we attend to ze matter at hand? I am sure any delays for ze sake of idle conversation would be deemed wholly inappropriate at zis juncture. If you don't mind, I should like to be present during ze proceedings. I trust zis is not an intrusion?"

Henry Trenton nodded. He seemed incapable of proper speech when addressed by Lady Howell. Nevertheless, Ellena felt certain he would find his tongue soon enough when accusations were made toward his family.

The dowager viscountess gestured the guests toward a plush sofa and joined them on an adjacent seat. With his audience established, Dominic began a somewhat hesitant speech. In contrast to his mother, whose manner was easy and confident, Dominic found it hard to look at his guests, though an embarrassed glance or two were cast toward Ellena.

"I must begin by apologizing for the circumstances that necessitated this meeting." He swallowed a few times. "I...I realize these seem strange words from one who has taken brash action of late." He halted. The floor held his gaze.

Ellena's heart flared with hope. An apology! Even a confession of sorts. Had he changed his mind? She searched his face for clues. Poor man, he looked just as lost as when she had first met him.

Dominic turned helplessly to his mother, who nodded almost imperceptibly to coax him onward. He took a deep breath and sighed it out. Dominic looked at his hands, then up at Mr. Trenton.

"I am afraid the only way to proceed with any success is to embark on a retelling of events. I hope you will bear with me, sir, and be generous with your understanding as certain details are disclosed."

Henry Trenton set his mouth grimly and waited. The silence in the room was now quite deafening.

"As you are all aware," Dominic began, "Miss Trenton left her parents' home last Tuesday on her way to Munro. Her carriage was attacked by highwaymen and she escaped by allowing the river to carry her a great distance downstream from the brigands."

He paused uncomfortably. The next details were rather embarrassing, and Ellena did not envy him having to recount them. She could only imagine what her father's reaction would be when he heard about their overnight interlude. It had been her hope that this chapter of their story could have remained untold.

"As it happened," Dominic continued, his fingers tugging absentmindedly at his cravat, "I was also in the vicinity that afternoon. Having been caught in the rain upon my way home from a business matter in Chisholme, I found shelter in a huntsman's cabin that my late father had used on many occasions."

Ellena sensed the beginnings of a faint blush upon her cheek. The imminent revelation was even more awkward in front of someone as thoroughly unsentimental as her father.

"Miss Trenton discovered the cabin a short distance from the river and took the risk of throwing herself upon the mercy of its occupant—me."

Henry Trenton shifted slightly in his seat at this remarkable coincidence, but kept silent no doubt awaiting full disclosure. Dominic cleared his throat.

"*Ahem*, yes, well, as the weather was not conducive to safe travel, we realized we would be obliged to spend the night together in the cabin." The heat of color spread across Dominic's face.

Mr. Trenton's features clouded, and he made to interrupt, but Dominic hastily resumed the narration.

"Not having met before, we had no knowledge of each other's identity. Caught off-guard, I did not introduce myself properly. Miss Trenton, in turn, must have been deeply concerned that her reputation would come to ruin, despite the innocence of the encounter, for she chose to use a false name. So it was that I met a charming young woman whom I believed to be Miss Nancy Fallon and whom I understood was on her way to take vows at the convent in Munro."

Henry Trenton's barely restrained indignation now burst forth. "You passed the night together, *alone*? Do you realize how this sounds?"

"Certainly, I do, sir. And I believe it was exactly a reaction such as yours that made your daughter assume a false identity with me. We were both painfully aware of the possible slander if our unchaperoned encounter became public knowledge."

Ellena did not know where to look. She remembered all too well how *very* unchaperoned they had been. It had been but a blanket that protected her maidenhood. That, and Dominic's chivalry.

Dominic seemed to be struggling with the same recollection, for his cravat appeared to be growing ever tighter, if his desperate finger at his collar was any indication. "I hasten to assure you," he said after some throat-clearing, "that, though we necessarily shared accommodation, I slept in a chair with my back turned to the bed upon which Miss Trenton rested. Propriety was observed as far as practically possible."

This did little to settle the ruffled feathers of Mr. Trenton, who opened his mouth, no doubt to say so.

But Lady Howell spoke first. "*I* believe all blame to rest on circumstance and find no reason to question their motives or behavior. Our children have been taught to exercise discretion and maintain the sanctity of their person. We have raised them well. Do you not feel ze same, Mr. Trenton?"

The quiet assertiveness of the dowager left little room for a rebuttal, and Mr. Trenton did not argue further. "I see no point in harping on the details of that night," he agreed. "I can appreciate the efforts in keeping the encounter a secret. But this brings me no nearer to understanding how we arrived at our current situation."

"I am afraid the story is but at its beginning," explained Dominic. "Much confusion and misdirection was to follow."

Ellena groaned inwardly. She was grateful that the secret burden of Nancy Fallon was finally released. But matters were far from settled. How much more of their muddled courtship would her father have to hear? She willed Dominic to hasten his speech, though she could not be sure she was urging him to a happy outcome. Her fingers laced and unlaced each other, and she chewed her lip until it hurt.

Mercifully, Dominic seemed just as eager to plough through the necessary clarifications, and he gathered speed as he explained.

"The following morning, the storm having passed, we pressed on to Munro, where I left the lady I knew as Miss Fallon at the convent. She resumed her true identity at once and proceeded with the betrothal, as expected of her."

Dominic straightened to his full height. "Sir, your daughter's behavior, from start to finish, was everything you might rightly expect of her. However, the same cannot be said of your nephew,

Mr. James Trenton. He did your family no service when he visited me on Friday morning and implied that the wedding might be delayed if I did not cover the expenses of the new wedding dress."

"What?!" Ellena's father roared with indignation. "He had no such commission from me!"

"I realize that," Dominic replied calmly. "Unfortunately, his insidious efforts to gain funds caused me to speak harshly about the character of Miss Trenton and question her fitness to marry. In short, I insulted Miss Trenton when it was her cousin who had stoked my fury. At the time, I felt justified, little imagining the man base enough to repeat my words to Ellena. Obviously, she found such statements on my part offensive and humiliating. Since I had insulted her virtue quite unfairly, she arrived for dinner at Munro House with a veiled face and a declaration of piety. It was done to defend her honor. An extreme action, to be sure, but one to which she felt driven by my own lack of restraint. So, you see, for this I cannot fault her."

Relief trickled into Ellena's chest. Dominic was building bridges. Was he trying to make his way back to her? Her heart grew tight once more. There was much yet to undo.

Mr. Trenton shook his head. "I do not understand. You defend my daughter, yet you drive her name into the ground and break off the engagement. I think you should explain yourself at once, for my patience is at an end."

The pacifying tones of Lady Howell cut through the tension. "I'm afraid there is rather a lot more to be said. I have heard ze entire story and can say zat, muddled as it is, only a thorough examination of all ze facts will offer a satisfying conclusion."

Henry Trenton grunted impatiently but said nothing further. He nodded curtly at Dominic, who resumed his tale.

"Despite the initial introductions having been so poorly managed, I discovered that my betrothed was indeed a young woman of quality. Dinner ended well, and"—he looked warmly in Ellena's direction—"I believed we both looked forward to our next meeting."

Ellena's heart skipped a beat as his eyes rested on her. There was no mistaking it—he still cared for her. Her pulse raced at the realization. So it wasn't too late! *Oh, do be quick, Dominic,* she urged him with her thoughts. *Finish this wordy tale and tell me all is well!*

But even as Ellena's whole being was flooded with hope, Dominic now faltered in his narration.

"Well, go on," Mr. Trenton urged gruffly.

Dominic took a steadying breath.

"Your daughter," he continued at last, "I believe made several attempts to explain that she was, in fact, the lady I had met at the cabin. She had not yet discarded the veil, and I had not yet seen her face or identified her as both Miss Fallon and Ellena."

"If you ask me," grumbled Ellena's father, "the whole thing has been handled poorly from the start. All this subterfuge and tiptoeing around issues… What a song and dance!"

"You are right, of course," came the even tones of the Lady Howell. "However, ze children have persevered in their muddled, little way and might wish to see zis through to a simpler end. Shall we put up with their youthful foolishness a little longer?"

"Very well," he acceded, "but do get to the point."

Dominic's attention was still focused on Ellena. Though he addressed her father, it was her face he studied. She knew he was coming to the crux of the matter. He would be looking to see how she responded. She fidgeted with the cloth of her skirt, anxious for the worst to be over, praying that whatever he said could allow her to forgive him. She so desperately wanted to forgive him. Especially when he looked at her like that with his whole heart upon his sleeve.

"There was one further complication," Dominic declared. "Mrs. Charlotte Trenton's brother arrived at Thorn Bush Hall at exactly this time. He became immediately devoted in his attentions to Ellena. For her, no doubt, it was flattering and meant nothing more. However, for Mr. Cole, it was more than an idle interest. The extent of his obsession was soon to become evident."

Dominic spoke briskly now, and Ellena clutched a fistful of her skirt as she braced herself for the hard truth that must surely follow.

"On Tuesday morning, Mr. Cole enlisted the services of a local actress to perform a little public scene for my special attention. The lady's figure and features are very similar to those of Miss Trenton, for which very purpose she was chosen. Knowing my informants are constantly on duty, he was confident that I would hear of my intended parading on the arm of another man. And, to ensure my total outrage, he lifted the veil of the imposter and kissed her several times."

Ellena was white with shock. She could never have guessed Mr. Cole to be capable—let alone guilty—of such underhanded dealings. What abhorrence Dominic must have felt! It was little wonder he had discarded her so suddenly and utterly. What agony of betrayal! Even now, she could see the pain of her own feelings reflected in Dominic's eyes.

"So this was the cause of the broken engagement," Henry Trenton said quietly.

Dominic nodded. "Unfortunately, I discovered only the following day and quite by chance that the damning event had been a cruel sham. By then, I knew you had already received my letter, breaking the engagement. To be honest, I was not at all certain whether either you or your daughter would consider my retraction and deep remorse to be sufficient grounds for the engagement to continue."

Ellena's heart thundered.

Dominic took a deep breath and released it with great feeling. "So, there it is. I cannot apologize enough for the emotional upheaval this has caused. I can only offer my sincere regrets and assure you that my actions were motivated by what I believed was just cause. This being proven otherwise, I can offer little consolation, except to say I wish I could undo my rash decision. You see…" His voice caught a little. "The only uncomplicated fact in this entire saga is that I love Ellena. Everything else is peripheral."

Ellena felt suddenly that the room was too small to hold her heart. It soared from her breast on wings of relief and gratitude. She smiled at Dominic with unreserved affection, pouring out the feelings that from the first had been suppressed and fettered by the clumsy chain of their tortuous courtship. She wished to fly from her chair and encircle Dominic with her arms.

But her father had more to say, and his words anchored her for the moment.

"So you wish to honor our agreement and continue with the wedding proceedings?"

Dominic shook his head vehemently. "Oh, no, sir, I wish to do far more than that. I hope to spend a lifetime with a woman whom I probably don't deserve. I want to look into those eyes whose beauty was denied me until now. And I pray that tomorrow might be the beginning of something new and, dare I say, joyful for both of us."

"Hmph," Henry Trenton grunted, clearly unimpressed by the flow of so much sentimental nonsense. "There is the matter of public scandal that cannot be blithely swept under the mat or buried under romantic effusion."

"As I understand it," came the voice of bland reason from Lady Howell, "ze only people of consequence who know of ze unfortunate turn of events are currently in zis room. Mr. Cole has, I believe, much to lose by speaking out. As for your family, ze only unreliable character is your nephew Mr. James Trenton. However, I have every confidence you will know precisely how to deal with him."

She smiled knowingly and was rewarded by a grim look from Henry Trenton. Yes, James would be no challenge at all.

Lady Howell continued. "Of course, we admit a measure of inconvenience and discomfort has been thrust upon you. We hope you will see fit to adjust ze dowry to your satisfaction, without in ze process delivering an insult to our family. Perhaps we can discuss these details, and then our children can refresh their acquaintance?"

"Just a moment, Mother." Dominic had not taken his eyes from Ellena since he had made his declaration. "Before we proceed, there is one more person with whom I must consult."

"What do you mean?" Ellena's father demanded impatiently.

"I mean," said Dominic, his gaze still fixed upon Ellena, "that Miss Trenton must give her permission."

"That is not necessary," her father said.

"Oh, but it is. I cannot in good conscience demand what is not offered freely."

"*I* have offered it." Ellena's father replied tetchily.

Dominic ignored him. Sinking slowly to one knee, he bowed his head and asked quietly, "Miss Ellena Trenton, will you have me? I am not all I wish to be. But I believe you are the one who will help me become that man."

Ellena brought her hands to her mouth. Tears pricked her eyes. She swallowed hard, trying to stop herself from crying with joy.

When she did not answer, Dominic lifted his head, his face strained with anticipation.

"Yes," she said at last, allowing a sob of happiness to escape with that one word. She took a deep, shuddering breath. "Yes, my dear Dominic, I will have you."

"Well!" said Mr. Trenton as Dominic swept Ellena up into his arms. "It seems we may proceed after all."

Dominic cupped Ellena's fingers to his lips and pressed a kiss upon them. "Wait right here," he said.

As if she would go anywhere! As if her world had not at once become anchored to his, her heart tethered to his own for eternity.

For the next hour, she waited, her emotions rising and falling as she dreamed of their future together and felt it could not come soon enough. Ecstasy and nervous excitement battled for supremacy. And relief. Oh, so much relief!

She could scarce believe when her father reappeared with—not quite a smile—but a quirk of satisfaction about the mouth.

"All is well?" she asked him.

"Indeed. I have secured a most pleasing reduction in the dowry obligations and have drafted a letter to Trenton Grange, sending for Mama at once." He cleared his throat. "And Miss Kinsey."

Ellena looked past her father's shoulder at Dominic, who stood smiling like the cat who had gotten the cream.

"You remembered!" she cried.

"It was important to you," he replied.

Lady Howell stepped forward and gestured to Ellena's father. "I think we can safely leave them to themselves, don't you think? There is to be a wedding tomorrow, after all. I don't know about you, Mr. Trenton, but I have far too much to do than watch over two people who have already broken every rule in ze book. Let them be wed and be done with it."

Ellena's father merely said *harrumph* and then added sternly, "See that you are home before dark, Daughter." He made a stiff bow to his hostess. "If you will excuse me, I will be returning to Thorn Bush Hall. I need to have a few words with my nephew," he added grimly.

Ellena—though sorry not to witness that delicious conversation—was happy to remain with Dominic, and to have him all to herself at last.

The house became busy with renewed preparations over which the widow Howell took control as smoothly as if she were demurely sipping tea. Meanwhile, Dominic led Ellena into the garden, where they settled into the cozy curve of a sculpted bench.

The chaos of the preceding days was finally behind them. To Ellena, it felt as though she had shrugged off a heavy coat and was able, at last, to feel the sun upon her skin again. She sat so close to

Dominic that his breath fell upon her exposed neck as he spoke, and sent thrills of delight up and down her spine.

"I owe you a profound apology," he said. "It seems to happen far too often. But I have every intention of making this the last."

"I have wronged you too," she replied, her eyes cast down. "The whole fiasco with the veil. I did not mean to deceive you. But the lie took on a life of its on. I lost the means to control it. And," she added, her neck drooping further, "I misjudged Mr. Cole quite utterly. I shall never allow such a thing to happen again. I have learned my lesson. All such flattering speech shall be reserved for you alone."

"I should have done better," said Dominic. "I allowed my infatuation with the mysterious Nancy to aid the clouding of my judgment. I may not have been disloyal in my actions, but my heart was divided. That was unfair to you, to have you compete with a ghost."

Ellena looked up at him though her lashes. "Did I win?"

"You had won from the start," he replied. "I just didn't know it yet."

"Then all is well." Ellena leaned contentedly against his powerful arm.

"You forgive me, then?" He smiled, the answer already evident in the delicate hand that rested in his.

"With all my heart," came the reply.

She felt a little shudder of joy trill through his broad frame. Ellena tilted her head against his warm shoulder. He drew his arm around her and pulled her even closer. She smiled up at him and found his lips waiting.

He pressed his mouth gently to hers and a tide of heat flooded her body. His mouth was so soft and the hand that encircled her was so strong. She gasped a little as he released her, his fingers tracing the curve of her arm.

"Dominic," she whispered.

"Yes, my Ellena?" he murmured, his lips caressing her hair.

"Kiss me again."

His mouth slid down her cheek and met her parted lips. Dominic's arm, wrapped around her, grew tighter, and she pressed up against him, breathing in his scent. They lingered in this intimate embrace, then parted breathlessly.

Nothing further was said. And peace enveloped them.

CHAPTER THIRTY-THREE

OUTSIDE THE CHURCH, the wedding guests milled about, waiting for the bride and groom to emerge. Their carriage gleamed in polished anticipation. Lady Beatrice Howell had already made her way to Munro House to ensure all was ready and to her satisfaction. The rest were eager to be on their way. The dowager's festivities were legendary.

Jillian Kinsey preceded the couple as they stepped into the sunlight. From a basket at her elbow, she drew flower petals to adorn the path for the newly married couple, who were instantly surrounded by well-wishers.

Henry Trenton shook the groom's hand. Then, tentatively—and not a little awkwardly—he took Ellena by the shoulders and kissed her lightly on the cheek. "Daughter," he said, with a nod of acknowledgement. And then, seemingly satisfied that he had done what was required of him, he stepped back.

In a moment, her mother had moved into the vacated space, her face wreathed in smiles, her eyes wet with tears. She pulled Ellena softly into her arms and whispered, "I am so proud of you—today, and always. May you both know happiness." She glanced up at Dominic, whose face shone upon his new wife. Looking back at her daughter, she rested her hand tenderly upon her cheek. "Yes, I think you will."

Ellena's eyes stayed upon her mother until she felt the warm embrace of Charlotte around her. "Sorry!" Charlotte laughed as she patted her own belly, "I did not mean to jostle the bride. Nor would I want to crush your dress. It truly is a masterpiece."

"Thank you," replied Ellena. "It won't be long before you have your own sample of Mrs. Pembridge's workmanship, and a beautiful baby to wrap in it."

"What's that about babies?" came the cheerful tones of Jillian. "Does someone need me to mind a baby? I am very good with children."

"Jillian has had ample practice with her brothers," Ellena added, throwing her friend a knowing look.

"Perhaps it is time she thought to have children of her own." Charlotte smiled encouragingly. "And her association with our esteemed Howell family should ensure her an excellent match."

Jillian's eyes lit up. "I believe Ellena already has someone very particular in mind for me. Didn't you say he was…?"

"No longer available," Ellena said, cutting in quickly. "Sadly, all the best are taken so quickly, are they not?" She slipped her arm through Dominic's, careful to avoid her friend's look of disappointment. There would be time enough to explain later. Jillian would understand what a narrow escape she had had. But today was not one for dwelling on Mr. Cole.

Her husband looked out over the sea of bonnets. "I'm afraid we shall have to reserve this conversation for another time, ladies. We are holding up the crowd. And I am certain the guests are eager to be done with the formalities. They must surely prefer the comforts of Munro House over the stone steps of the church."

"Oh, yes!" cried Charlotte, who was keen to find a plush chair sooner rather than later. "But you can ride with us, Miss Kinsey. Can't she, James? I can point out the sights along the way, and you will be far better company than my James, who has never enjoyed a wedding other than our own."

"Waste of money," grumbled James.

"You will not mind?" Jillian inquired of Ellena. "I can wait until you are ready to leave, in case you need anything."

Ellena smiled up at Dominic. "Thank you, Jilly, but I think we will be satisfied with our own company for a few minutes in the carriage. We still have many people to greet here, and then I shall have to play hostess as soon as we arrive at the house."

"I think you will find," Dominic chimed in warmly, "that my mother will have everything well in hand. Today you are the guest of honor. There will be time enough to acclimatize to the running of the household." His arm slid protectively around her waist. "Now, let us see to our well-wishers before they lose all patience with us."

Ellena nodded and turned her attention to the crowd that waited to greet the new Lady Howell. Other than her family, she knew very few faces. However, she instantly recognized the features of Miss Irene Sangford, who boldly stepped forward, inserting herself ahead of Dominic's sisters.

"Congratulations, your lordship," drawled Miss Sangford. "The prize is indeed yours. Now that the curious veil has been removed, we can all appreciate how Miss Trenton's beauty has captured you."

Ellena stiffened, but Dominic answered coolly, "Indeed, the *viscountess* is a true vision. You will be pleased to know that I have found no equal to my wife. Long before her face was revealed, she was the most beautiful woman I had ever known. As such, you may wish to step aside now, that others may enjoy her presence."

A pale arm belonging to Miss Olivia Bathurst drew the gaping Miss Sangford from the spot where she stood rooted. Dominic's sisters shook their heads and tutted as she withdrew into obscurity.

Georgina was the first to find her tongue. "Well! It will be a cold day in July before we see *her* kind accepted into the inner circle at Eyresborough. It is hard to believe, Brother, that such deplorable manners can be tolerated in our dear old hometown. What has happened to the *standards?*"

Dominic rolled his eyes.

Ellena interceded hastily. "We appreciate your loyalty, dear Sister. In fact, we rely on your visiting us frequently to sift unsuitable elements from our company. Of course, you may then run the risk of estranging yourself, by your regular absence, from the fine people of Eyresborough, but I am sure you will find this a small sacrifice."

Dominic coughed into the back of his hand. Ellena innocently inquired whether all was well, but he could only manage a vigorous nod.

He tucked her arm into his and they surveyed the remainder of the waiting onlookers. Life no longer felt such a burden. They would never again need to endure anything alone. Ellena smiled up at Dominic and knew that nothing would ever again be too hard to bear.

As if in agreement, the church bells announced their celebration to all who would hear. For a few brief moments, it drowned out the din of the congregated crowd and enveloped the couple in its noisy, happy cocoon. Yet when its final echoes had faded once more, the magical bond held and sustained them as their shared journey began.

Author's Notes
Catholics during the Regency and why I have taken liberties

When we read a book of Regency fiction, we are often drawn to the romantic elements—grand balls with elegant dresses, gloved hands that long to touch, a secret rendezvous in the library, or lovers eloping to escape from unyielding guardians. These are but a few of the dreamy scenes we reach for when our imaginations enter the Regency world.

Less-magical themes—such as war, poverty, and politics—might offer a backdrop to the plot but are never the focus. What we truly care about is how our couple deal with these challenges and whether their bond can survive such troubles.

Now, enter religious persecution, stage left. Throughout several centuries and a succession of monarchs, the British people had been forced to adopt either Catholicism or Protestantism in fluctuating order. Prior to the Regency period, it was the turn of Catholicism to be outlawed.

Sadly, the Regency era itself (1811-1820) was no stranger to such matters. While the Catholic faith was legalized again in 1791, and its practice tolerated, open acceptance did not exist. Catholics were denied military commissions and seats in Parliament, although many other positions were open to them.

Moreover, certain basic rights were still forbidden. For example, Catholics could not even marry each other without first being married in a Church of England (Anglican) ceremony. Marriages of mixed faith could occur but were discouraged by both sides.

This state of affairs should affect the plot of *Ellena's Secret*. It would have been highly unlikely for a viscount in good standing to choose a Catholic wife—not banned as such but certainly not recommended. For Viscount Howell to seek out Miss Nancy Fallon as a potential bride, he would have expected her to renounce her faith—an unlikely scenario if her father had been devout enough to send her to a convent to become a nun.

Could love triumph over parents and church and government? Well, of course! But to make religion a subplot would be to spend time having our sweethearts argue about issues best left to scholars or philosophers, and not romance authors. Besides, it would be offensive to Catholic readers for the hero to assume the heroine would just throw away her beliefs for a man she barely knew.

Maybe you read *Ellena's Secret*, unbothered by the way the author skipped over these facts of the day. In which case, no harm done. However, for those who balked at the author's apparent ignorance of such facts, I feel I owe this author's note.

The crux of my novel was for the lovers to overcome a myriad of challenges, almost entirely caused by themselves. To include messy religious issues would have detracted from what was fundamentally at stake. And yes, I could have at least mentioned, for the sake of realism, that Lord Howell's desire to marry Nancy would have been controversial in terms of their conflicting faiths. But I urge the reader to enjoy the story for what it is—fiction.

Apologies to those who frown upon my artistic liberties. I trust the adventures of Ellena and Dominic are exciting enough to overcome such reservations.

Long live the struggles and victories of lovers throughout history. Huzzah!

Acknowledgements

Ellena's Secret (originally called *First Impressions*) was the first romance manuscript I was brave enough to enter into writing contests, even before it was published. The confidence I found to do this was thanks in no small part to the valuable input I received while the work was still unpolished. Thank you, from my heart, Suzanne Smith, Bex Drate, Carolyn Kuhn, Mary Lautzenhiser Bellon, and Brenda Fullick Wise, all of whom contributed to a much richer version of my manuscript. I have grown so much as an author thanks to you.

Brenda Liebenberg, Teresa Raposo, Gill Groll, and Cassie Lewellen—my beta readers—thank you for your time and enthusiasm in the early days when I first let strangers judge my work. You were willing to take a chance on an unknown author and gave me hope to keep at it. And here we are!

To the team at Dragonblade Publishing, thank you for believing in me and mentoring me as I traverse the tricky terrain from keyboard to print to shelves (whether real or digital).

And to you, my wonderful, loyal readers, thank you for bringing these pages into your life. What a privilege to have spent these hours with you. Let's do it again soon.

About the Author

Elizabeth Donne writes sweet Regency romance, a natural outpouring of a lifelong love affair with English literature.

She has spent most of her life in Cape Town, South Africa. In 2015, she moved to Iowa with her husband, their two children, two cats, and their African bush dog. When she's not writing, or discovering the secret wonders of the Midwest, she is enthusiastically introducing her visitors to the joys of drinking *rooibos* tea. With a biscuit, of course.